Cat's Tale

T.S. Mos

ISBN: 978-1-7336587-0-6

Contents

Prologue

My name is Catherine Alexander-Blair. Though I have written this book as a work of fiction, it is, for those who once knew me, much more. For those friends and acquaintances who endured the agony of not knowing what happened to me, who went through countless hours of searching, praying, and pestering the local authorities to continue the search after my disappearance, this is an answer. I do not expect many to believe my story. Hey, I live it and I'm still having a hard time believing it! The truth is that there are creatures out there and among us that we have relegated to the pages of fiction, though they are not always content to remain there. Some, perhaps many, insinuate themselves into our lives in one manner or another and that is perhaps how these myths remain alive and very vivid. Anyone who knew me may be thinking, while reading this, that I must surely have been safely secured in the local asylum when I wrote it, or I'm just an opportunistic author jumping to make a buck and a name for myself off the past notoriety of this tragedy. This is not the case, I assure you. For those who knew me best, my bandmates in Hunter's Moon, Kurt, Kevin, Bob, Brian, and Sean, and my neighbors on Enterprise Boulevard, this is an accurate account of what happened to me and what has become of me. Yeah, guys, it's really me, Cat, after all this time. You were my friends, my buddies, my adopted stepchildren, and I have missed you with every day that has passed since last we met. Some of you will not believe a word of what you are about to read. You will see lunacy, deception, possibly a grifter's scheme and that's all right. Whatever helps you sleep through the night. Those, however, whom I loved and who I thought loved me, I beg you, read on please. Those who would know the truth, if you still even care, read on and believe!

Chapter 1

The sound of squealing metal in the distance followed by a crashing boom woke me with a start and, gasping, I lurched to sit upright. Shock and confusion hit me when I was jerked back down by the restraints encircling my wrists and ankles. The sudden impact cracked the back of my head and I moaned, nearly laughing, at what I'd done to myself. The room in which I'd awakened was so very dark that I could make out no details. The startling sounds that had roused me brought images of prison cells with clanging steel bar doors to mind, but I had no memory of being incarcerated. Panic clutched my throat, leaving me unable to scream or even call out for help.

Swallowing hard, forcing myself to be calm, I concentrated on figuring out where I was and how I came to this. The pain was like a living thing, distracting me and making clear thought all but impossible. The muscles in my legs, back, and neck were screaming in spasm and stiffness. My spine felt like it had been replaced with an iron bar. My hands and feet were numb due to the restraint straps, which had been carelessly or intentionally fastened too tightly. My breathing was ragged and shallow, my breath stale and sour. So many questions swirled in my mind, with "where am I," and "how do I get out of here," struggling for top billing. Over the course of my life I had awakened in some surprising and unusual places, but never had I experienced anything like this.

"Help me, somebody," I whispered, for some reason not daring to cry out. "Help me, please."

Silence.

Then from a distance, "As you wish, Little One," a liquid, melodious voice intoned.

"Little One?" I thought aloud, "No one has ever called me that. I am not little."

Darkness claimed me as a fiery stab of pain shot through my left arm and I was gone, unconscious or asleep.

When I awoke, the room was still dark, but I could discern planes and angles in the shadows. The thought struck me like a revelation, "It's daylight out there," I whispered. Then the enormity of how far I was from "out there" hit me. It occurred to me that I might never see the daylight again or feel the sun's warmth on my face. Tears trickled down my cheeks and tickled the edges of my ears. I pulled at my wrist restraints and tried to lift my head. My hands could move no more than an inch or so and I was too weak to lift my head to clear the pillow. "Oh, Cat, Cat, what have you gotten yourself into now?" I whined softly as the absurdity of that question, perhaps tinged with a little hysteria, set in.

The air was neither warm nor cold, but was heavy with the odor of age and pungent with the smell of warm soil and rich groundwater. I could detect no sound save my own heart beating and my own breathing. Though the shadows around me were varying shades from black to silver-gray, I had the impression that the room, perhaps not much larger than a closet, was made of stone. There was something about the way my whispers died that suddenly made me think my surroundings were not those of a prison cell but a mausoleum.

I whimpered," Oh, my God, I'm in a mausoleum."

A moment ticked by. Silence deafened me. I drew a deep but unsteady breath.

"No, why in Heaven's name would I even think such a thing!" The voice of reason reasserted itself, "I know, too much Poe all those years ago! I've picked up his fear of premature interment! Waking up in a mausoleum is just the scariest thing I can think of. Stop being such a drama queen and think, Cat! There must be an explanation." My words echoed off the nearby walls then fell quickly silent.

Pain gripped my muscles again and I cried and tried to move about. Sweat broke out all over my body followed by chills so severe I was afraid my teeth would crack from the intensity of the chattering. After what felt like hours of sobbing and whimpering, I must have cried myself to sleep.

My eyes snapped open. I knew somehow that I was no longer alone. The air felt different, heavy, charged. I waited as silently as I could. Suddenly my pulse quickened, my heart started pounding in my chest, and my ears began to ring. Though my mouth had gone dry, I was determined to address the situation.

"Alright," I croaked with a voice dry and raspy," I know someone is there. Please talk to me. Please tell me what is happening."

Silence answered.

"Please, please, please," I begged, "talk to me. I can't stand this silence."

Nothing.

The noise of my own body resumed. I thought I might be insane.

"Maybe this is what it feels like to be insane… so crazy you can't hear anything over the beating of your own heart or the blood roaring in your ears," I mused at a whisper.

"No, Catherine," a very masculine voice answered my thoughts, "You are not insane. You are, however, mine now. As it was always meant to be. You are mine."

"I don't know who you are, but I belong to no man," my voice cracked as I fumed with false bravado. "And I'm Cat, not Catherine."

"Interesting," my unseen captor insisted, "and an ironically correct statement, Cat. Yet you are indeed mine."

I swore I could hear the smile on his face.

"What is this, some kind of kidnapping thing? Because my family has lots of money and they'll pay anything to have me back," I lied to the darkness.

"Nice try, Kitty Cat," the voice chuckled sardonically, "you have no family left and they had no money to speak of for generations. Though you are comfortable financially you are by no means rich."

"Okay, so you know me, you know I'm not wealthy. Then why abduct me like this? What are you? Some kind of sex pervert or serial killer psychopath?" I challenged. "You might as well kill me now because I'll never go along with you or do what you want, you sicko."

Silence spun out around me. I wasn't sure if I had insulted my captor or if I had hit too close to home in figuring out my situation. Perhaps, even now, he was busy silently sharpening a blade to slit my throat. More to keep the dialogue going and keep the silence at bay I called out, "Please, let me see you. Who are you? Why am I here?" Suddenly self-pity and frustration gripped me and I sobbed.

Flames abruptly sputtered and leapt from sconces on the walls; I was right they were stone. I squinted and momentarily closed my eyes, partially blinded by the light after the prolonged darkness.

"I don't think we're in Kansas anymore, Toto," I wondered softly, as I took in my dismal surroundings.

3

"Kansas?" the incredibly masculine voice rose.

"You know, Dorothy, The Wizard of Oz?" I called out to no one, "The movie?"

"Indeed?" the voice purred, then the silence resumed.

Time seemed to stop, as did my breathing. Apparently my attempt at levity and reference to the classic film had fallen flat or was unappreciated.

"You may call me Sin," a voice seemed to resonate and reverberate around the room.

"Is this some kind of joke?" I cried, half-laughing, "I'm being held prisoner by Sin? Okay guys, where is the camera? Brian, Kevin, if this is some of you guys' sick shenanigans, I will so pay you back. I admit it, you got me. You really had me going, but that's too much. It's ridiculous! Sin?" I laughed, "You should have come up with a more realistic name like Gemini Killer or Charles Manson or something. And, hey, what did you shoot me up with? What was in the hypodermic?"

"Just a little something to keep you calm," the silken voice answered.

Silence.

"Come on, whoever you are," I called, "the joke's over. Come let me up! Sean, Bob, come on guys this is enough. "

I frantically searched as much of the room as I could see from my position. I was alone and yet the voice continued.

"I have been known by many names throughout my long years and I have found, in the beginning, it's best to keep things simple. Think of me as "old as sin" or "dark as sin.""

"You're serious?" I retorted. The humor suddenly fled my mind and concern for my future returned. There was no reply.

"When can I see you? Why do you hide from me?" I cried, then moaned as the pain resurfaced, "I hurt. Why do I feel like this?"

"I know you hurt, Cat, be calm and I will explain the situation to you," the voice became stronger as I heard footsteps, no, bootheels, approach to my left. The flames from the torches on that side of the room seemed to dim as Sin stepped into my line of sight. My breath caught in my throat at the sight of my captor and I realized just how critical my situation had become. This was no joke.

He was very tall, at least 6'5", and glided forward with the grace of a dancer. His hair was sparkling silver, straight and thick and fell·

4

just below his shoulders. His face, rather longish, was well chiseled and gracefully shaped with a wide brow, high cheekbones, and aquiline nose. His skin was alabaster porcelain in its perfection. His eyes were piercing pools of ink and, as he stepped forward, they sparked with electric-blue flashes, like static. From my position, all I could see of his wardrobe was a silk or fine-spun white shirt. It set off his features perfectly. "Sin" was exquisite and his beauty made me all the more fearful. Suddenly I understood why he had called me "little one"; for compared to him I was indeed little.

Pain suddenly wracked my body and I fought to hold on to consciousness. "What have you done to me?" I gasped. "Why do I hurt like this?"

"To answer your first question," he smiled, "I have fed from you. That is why you are so weak. As to your second question, by my feeding I have "infected" you, if you will, with a little bit of myself. Your body is now trying to fight off the infection, though it will be unable to do so. You now feel my hunger and my needs, though magnified in your weakened state," he answered calmly as if he were reciting a grocery list and not telling me the most outrageously bizarre thing I had ever heard.

"You fed off of me, like, drank my blood?" I yelled. "What are you crazy?"

"Please, calm down. It will not help your physical state to get excited," he smiled as he bent over the bed and checked the restraints that held my wrists.

"What happens now?" I asked, "What are you going to do with me?" I choked back tears, my body once again seized by crushing pain.

"If I leave you here as you are now you shall die, I might add, in excruciating pain. I could also leave you to my friends," he purred. "What they would do with you, the mortal mind cannot even grasp. Or," he came close to me and fixed me with his gaze, "you can accept that you are mine and learn to live with the situation as it is."

"Let me get this straight," I struggled to retain my grasp on reality," you think you are a vampire and you drank my blood and now you want me to become a vampire and live with you forever, right?" I shook my head, adding ruefully, "Where is Anne Rice when you need her?"

"I can assure you that I have never met this Anne Rice, though her fiction has done much to confuse the reality of our existence,

5

and for that we are grateful. And," he added as he bent over me once more, "I not only think I am a vampire… I am. I know you may have a hard time believing this, but over time you will accept it."

"And," he paused to smile almost ruefully, "I have not offered you forever."

"So, I'm stuck here with my fate in your hands and if I accept you, I'm what, damned? Cursed?" I reasoned.

He chuckled," I don't think you fully understand yet. Your fate was sealed the day you were born. Only I can end your pain," his voice dropped to a whisper. "You are either mine or you are gone, only very, very, slowly."

"No," I screamed, "No, no! I don't believe this. You're insane! Let me go!"

He clutched my upper arm painfully and hissed, "I could take you any time I desire but that might affect your mind and it would surely shorten your life." His voice changed again to a purr, "Now that you know what's at stake, I want you to ask for my help. You must ask for me to save you." He chuckled, "And you will…"

He disappeared in an instant. I was once more alone and, this time, relieved to be so. His words echoed in my mind. My future rose before me like a black void. Tears streamed down my face and my nose ran. I shook my head to clear my mind, with little success.

"No," I said to no one, "I'm not helping any by crying myself silly. Time to calm down and think. Think of how to get out of here, how to get away from this psycho." No plan would present itself since I had no idea where I was or where safety might lie. I didn't even know if I was still in Louisiana, let alone Lake Charles. Oh, how I longed to see my little rental house on Enterprise Boulevard.

I prayed. I prayed to God to save me, then to send death to claim me, to release me from my life, which now might very well be Hell. My prayers disintegrated into whining, then ranting and raving. My body ached in every conceivable manner. I smelled of sweat and illness and I could feel myself weakening with each exertion. Help did not come. I struggled to remember how I came to be here. It was as if memories of my previous life had been imprisoned as well, as though they were locked far away from me. I had no recollection of the past, very little understanding of the present and even less hope for the future. That I even knew my name, I realized, was remarkable.

As I started to slip once more into oblivion, I had the impression that there were things passing through the room, some shuffling, some padding, and some slithering. Refusing to open my eyes, I would not let myself think what they might be and sought the escape of sleep…

Chapter 2

The air was warm, but a slight breeze caressed my face and whipped my hair into my eyes as I left the club, that night. I carried my violin in its hand-tooled leather case and my stage clothes in a black zippered gym bag. Our band, Hunter's Moon, had been performing at Club Psyche for a week now and we were developing a small but devoted group of fans. A crowd of maybe twelve or fifteen teenagers asking for my autograph had stopped me at the back stage door. I had been a practicing violinist for twenty years but it took a change from concert violinist to Celtic band fiddler to make me a "star", however tiny. It was a wonderful feeling to be asked for an autograph, though it was strangely disconcerting, too. I kept thinking "this can't be real," even as I smiled and signed my "Cat Alexander-Blair" on various napkins, scraps of paper, and one honest-to-goodness old fashioned autograph book. My parents, both fiercely liberal, had saddled me with the hyphenation when my mother retained her maiden name and they determined that I should bear both their surnames. It was a ponderous moniker but made for an excellent autograph. My mother had always called me Catherine or Cathy and my father affectionately called me "Kit." When they both died I could not bear either name and so became Cat.

My little blue Mazda was parked near the end of the employees' lot. Thanks to the ever-increasing crime rate the place was brightly lit by overhead vapor lights. But as bright as they were, those lights just made the shadows along the walls and between the cars seem that much darker. Having signed my last autograph, I crossed the now empty parking lot. Normally, the boys in the band escorted me to my car, but tonight there was a bevy of beauties in the club and the likelihood of one if not all of them getting lucky was too promising to ignore. Assuring them that I would be alright on my own, I had plowed through the remnants of the crowd feeling somewhat depressed that there were no men of a suitable age waiting backstage for me. Shaking off the self-pity, I steeled myself and pushed open the heavy exit door then stepped into the night. The autograph seekers had heartened me and lifted my spirits for a brief time. Afterwards, I had set my gym bag down to fish the keys out of my front pocket when the breeze picked up and whirled around me. I turned, looking at the stage door, the dumpsters, and the other parked cars. There was nothing. I sensed furtive movement, then sudden pain hit me…

I awoke chuckling. I had done it. I had remembered, in my dreams, how I had come to be here, wherever "here" was. My body still ached but perhaps because of the dream, my head felt a little clearer. I had been kidnapped after our last set Friday night. That must surely be what happened. How long ago could that have been?

There was not much light in the room, but I could just make out the shadow of the loop of leather on my wrist restraint. It had been buckled then doubled back on itself and if I maneuvered carefully I might just be able to release that loop. The leather of the strap was fairly new and thick and I knew that if I could get it loose I could probably push it off of the buckle and release my right hand. Knowing that patience and determination might be all that stood between a lunatic and me, I set to work slowly and methodically to free myself. As to what I would do once I was free, I had no idea. I only knew that I had to try to escape this maniac that was holding me captive. Bending my hand painfully back, right index finger over right wrist, I managed, while holding my breath, to catch the doubled loop and pull it free. Taking a deep breath, I leaned back and relaxed for a moment, feeling quite pleased with myself for my meager accomplishment. Now came the hard part…managing to get my index and middle finger on the loosened strap, I pushed gently backward, rhythmically popping the leather beneath the buckle frame and loosening the buckle tongue. It was frustrating going so slowly, but I knew that if I pushed it the leather would soften and I'd never get it loose. I had just managed to get the buckle free and was sliding the whole wrist restraint free of the bed when I heard movement or something.

Suddenly my skin was tingling and my mouth went dry. I was, once again, not alone. In the corner was a darker-than-shadow shape and it was creeping toward me. I could feel my heart pounding and I think I stopped breathing when what appeared to be an arm extended itself toward my foot. An icy yet blistering sensation encircled my left ankle and fear swallowed the scream in my throat. I was literally frozen with fear. In my mind I was screaming so loud I thought surely God himself could hear me.

The flames in the wall sconces burst to life, showering the floor with sparks and a voice so powerful and so commanding boomed into the room. "Release her," it demanded and the icy hot grip was gone. The lights on the walls had dissolved the shadow and I could breathe again.

I was still working my way back to sanity when Sin strode into the room and began releasing the straps on my ankles. I was about to deliver a roundhouse to my captor's jaw when he raised his hand and caught my wrist with deadly precision. My whole arm felt like I had slammed it into a concrete wall and Sin didn't as much as flinch at the impact.

"No, no, Cat. That would be," he looked at me pointedly, "unwise." Lowering my arm, he released the restraint from my wrist, then moved across me to release my left hand.

I was rubbing furiously at the welts on my wrists and, without thinking I tried to sit up...too fast. The world tilted and swam and pitched sideways, landing me hard on my left hip and elbow at his feet on the marble floor.

"Damn," I yelled as the pain of the impact jarred my whole body.

"Please, do not try to move," Sin said softly as he bent and lifted me effortlessly from the floor. I'm six feet tall and, though I'm not heavy, I'm no feather, so his strength both surprised and frightened me. "You are still weak and in no condition to move so suddenly." He sat me on the edge of the bed from which I'd just been freed. Reading the look of distaste on my face, he lifted me once more and, carrying me as you would a baby, he crossed the room and laid me on a burgundy velvet sofa, propping my head on a pillow.

"I must apologize for what just happened. Leitha knew she was not to touch you and she will be punished for her affront," he explained as he lifted my left ankle. I could see ugly white blisters surfacing above my anklebone until Sin wrapped his long slim fingers around the injury. The pain was gone. I saw a shadow cross his face as he closed his eyes and licked his lips. He seemed to be absorbing my pain. "I'm afraid you may have some scarring, but the blisters will heal. And please, no more thoughts of escape." He brushed a stray lock of hair from my face and gazed intently into my eyes. His touch was gentle and the look he gave me made me squirm.

"What was that thing, that Leitha?" I asked, though I really didn't want to know.

"Leitha is what you might call a Ringwraith. Do you know what that is?" he arched his eyebrows.

"Sure, I've read Tolkien." I snapped as I brushed his hand away and rubbed my ankle. "Ringwraith, sure, next you're going to tell me that fairies, elves, and dragons exist, but that's right, because you're a vampire." I looked up into his impenetrable eyes, thinking he was teasing me, and suddenly I felt despair as I had never felt it before. He was not teasing.

"Let me go?" I whispered, my throat dry and painful.

"No, no, Cat," he smiled as a crystal goblet of water appeared out of nowhere, "You are mine now, remember? You cannot go."

The water was icy and clean and felt like heaven going down my parched throat. I choked and coughed trying to drink too fast and he gently pulled the goblet away and pushed me down into the pillow.

"Help me, please. Save me? I can't stay here anymore," I rasped, "I think I'm losing my mind." I smiled and smacked my forehead with the palm of my hand, "What am I saying? I just explained to a vampire that I think I'm losing my mind! Evidently it's too late, I'm already whacked, gaga, loony tunes."

"You have asked that I save you and I shall. I assure you that you are not insane and that I am, indeed, a vampire. I can take you out of here if you promise to cooperate and not hurt yourself," he explained as he inspected the welts, now disappearing from my wrists.

"You kidnap me and you expect me to cooperate?" I gasped.

"Cat," he smiled patiently as he lifted me from the sofa, "I did not kidnap you. Apparently you don't remember the mugging. You were attacked behind Club Psyche. My people and I rescued you from the hospital where you had been in a coma for several weeks. Another cause for your current weakness."

"I was mugged? " I marveled, "How did you find me, no, for that matter, how do you even know of my existence? I should be no one to you."

His laughter was melodic and genuine, "Cat, I heard your music the moment you were born. I have been following your life all these years. I knew when you lost both of your parents, when you graduated from college, got your first job, got married and divorced. I know everything about you."

"You mean if I hadn't taken up the violin this wouldn't be happening?" I reasoned.

"No," he smiled as he carried me from the room of my imprisonment and down a long and elegant hallway, "not your violin music. The music of your heart beating, your blood coursing through your veins, your chest rising and falling with each breath. I heard your thoughts like whispers when you dreamed. It took every ounce of self-control I had to keep my distance from you."

"So what changed?" I sniffed, "why did you come to me now?"

"Your life was in jeopardy," he answered as he kicked open a door and carried me into an exquisitely decorated bathroom. He sat me gently on delicate little wrought iron stool beside a glistening white round marble tub. Steam rose from the foamy froth-covered water. "Can you get out of those things by yourself?"

"I've been dressing and undressing myself since I was two," I answered indignantly, "or didn't you know that?"

"I meant, are you strong enough? "He added as he laid two large fluffy looking white towels on a small table beside the tub.

"Oh, uh, I think so," I nodded, embarrassed, "if I can stand long enough to get in."

"Very well, I'll be just outside if you need assistance," he smiled as he left the room.

I took a moment to survey my surroundings. The room was large with curved walls covered in elegant French-looking patterned tiles of teal. There was no mirror anywhere to be seen. The floor was black lustrous marble and covered in places with deep soft rugs probably made in some part of the world I'd never even heard of. There were no windows or other doors so escape from this room was out of the question even if I was strong enough. I discovered when I unbuttoned my shirt and tried to remove it from my arms that I was weaker than I had thought.

After looking longingly at the warm water in the tub for several minutes, I determined that I wasn't going to let false modesty keep me from it and called out to Sin on the other side of the door.

"You called, My Lady?" he bowed as he came through the door.

"Yes," I sighed, "I can't seem to get undressed by myself, but the bath looks so good that if you can be polite and not make any snide or derogatory remarks regarding my physical accouterments, or lack thereof, I will accept your assistance."

"Of course," he quickly stepped behind me and removed my shirt, "and I would never say any snide or derogatory remarks about any part of you. I think you are beautiful."

"Right, I'm a thirty-seven year old aging violinist who couldn't even keep a husband when she was twenty. Oh yeah, I'm beautiful," I snickered.

There was one awkward moment when Sin had to pull me to my feet and support me within the circle of his arms, leaning my back into his chest, to unbutton and unzip my jeans. I bit my tongue and prayed that I could make it into the tub without embarrassing myself when familiar, though lately unused, stirrings moved through me.

Perhaps sensing my embarrassment, Sin continued, "Your husband Michael left you because he was a coward and couldn't deal with your leukemia and seeing you going through such difficult treatments."

I stopped breathing and turned my face up to his, "My God, you really do know everything about me. That was twelve years or more ago when I went through that. I hardly ever think about it now."

The bra and panties came off without comment.

"I told you I did. I also know that you braved that time with grace and courage," he said soberly as he lifted me and gently lowered me into the tub, wetting the cuffs of his fine shirt.

I leaned back against the cool marble and relaxed in the wonderfully warm bubbles.

"I don't know about that," I murmured as I closed my eyes to enjoy the sensations, "I thought the bone marrow transplant would kill me. And going through all the transfusions, and platelet infusions... I felt like a pincushion before it was all said and done."

"You've had a hard life, Catherine, Cat, and you've born it well. Please, relax and enjoy the bath. I'll get something for you to wear," he said as I heard the door quietly open and close. Alone. I stretched my muscles in the water and stirred the bubbles with my hands. I reasoned that if you had to be abducted by a vampire, still having a little trouble grasping that, you couldn't find a more delicious looking one. Why were the good-looking guys always gay or nuts? Or

13

vampires? Okay, so he'd done his homework, but a lot of stalkers probably did things like that when they became totally obsessed with someone. Didn't Jodie Foster go through something like this? I wondered if he knew that I still got up early on Saturday mornings to watch Warner Brothers' cartoons, or that gingersnap cookies dipped in icy cold milk were my favorite guilty pleasure. I giggled as my mind took a much more whimsical path and I didn't, for a moment anyway, care about what peril might lie ahead. I closed my eyes and listened to the quiet of the room. It was relaxing. My breathing became deep and regular. Sleep took me.

The water was a bit cool when I woke and realized that my fingertips, normally hard and callused from my violin playing, were wrinkled and puny. I thought I should get out of the tub, though I didn't trust my legs to hold me, so I crawled out onto the marble floor. The cold hit me like something solid as I grabbed for a towel, missed, and knocked over the table. I lay on the cold floor in the fetal position with a towel draped over my shoulders as a series of spasms tore through my body. I quivered all over and was surprised to hear the low feral moan that escaped from my throat. I looked down to see blood seeping from my pores and fought the urge to throw up by wrapping the towel as tightly as I could around myself.

Soft footsteps sounded in the doorway behind me and I swear I heard sniffing. Suddenly I was jerked up from the floor and lifted toward the ceiling. Motion and gravity unfolded my body, legs dropping and arms flailing, as Sin lifted me then brought me down to his chest level and clamped his mouth on my neck. First sharp, searing pain flared from my neck down my arm, then, as he gently sucked my blood, a feeling of euphoria, abandon, arousal stole through me. So what if I was food- it felt wonderful. I didn't care.

Chapter 3

I awoke without opening my eyes and lay there assuring myself that when I did open them, I would find myself in my own sadly under occupied double bed. My ancient air-conditioner would be coughing and wheezing, threatening to die yet again, and the neighbors would be yelling at each other over the sound of their greasy-smoke belching lawn mower. Traffic on Enterprise Boulevard would be noisy and constant, and all would be right with the world.

When I peeked my left eye open a crack, I saw rich blue walls with pristine white trim, not a good sign. My bedroom was sage green. I peered secretly down at the comforter that covered me. It was crisp white eyelet and had to be down-filled. More bad news, mine was a poly-filled rose floral thing that I had bought at Kmart years ago. Above me was a white canopy and I had never had a canopy bed in my life. I considered the possibility that I had become the victim of a drive-by interior decorator, but could not maintain the illusion, so it was safe to assume that I had not yet returned to the real world.

Secretly inspecting my surroundings, I noticed Sin sitting silently and still across the room in one of two occasional chairs. Though his eyes were open, he did not appear to be looking at anything. He was either deep in thought or maybe vampires slept with their eyes open, what did I know? He had one booted ankle resting across his knee and he rested his cheek against one long, pale, slim hand. A black long-sleeved tee shirt shimmering of some fine material stretched tautly across his considerable pectorals and coordinated beautifully with his charcoal gray trousers. His silver hair was drawn away from his face and worked into a thick braid, which lay down his back. When his eyes slowly closed, I spotted thick, lush, black lashes that would be the envy of any woman. He was drop-dead gorgeous, I had to admit. There were women in the clubs I played who would crawl across broken glass on their lips to get this guy's attention and yet here I was. What on earth could a man who looked like that want with me?

I suffered no delusions, readily admitting to myself that I was one of those women who only start looking pretty good around "last call." Pretty boys such as this one seldom noticed that I was alive until they did something to incur my considerable wrath, at which point I would verbally rip them a new one. I had to admit that I did enjoy that, nothing like a good character assassination to get your blood stirring.

"Damn," I thought sadly, "why did this guy have to be a psycho? He had to think he was a vampire!" With that, the memory of last night's episode in the bathroom flooded my mind and I gingerly brought my hand up to my neck and touched it. Reality tilted for a moment when my fingertip brushed the two raised, sore spots on my throat, then righted again when I remembered that some Goths were so devoted to the lifestyle that they had porcelain fangs implanted surgically. That had to be it, the guy had implants! Okay, my reality was still intact.

It was pleasant just to lie there and look at Sin. I imagined myself loosening that braid of his and running my fingers through that silky-looking silver hair. What must that feel like? Probably like running your fingers through water.

"Stop that," the little voice in my head screamed, "don't even let yourself go there. Obviously the man has certain attributes, but remember that he's nuts! He is forbidden. We are not falling for his tricks."

Instantly, Sin was sitting on the edge of the bed, looking down at me with those unbelievably dark eyes.

"How are you feeling, Precious?" he purred.

"I'm no one's Precious," I pouted, " and what happened to me?" Self-consciously, I fingered the marks on my neck, again.

"You had a seizure, Cat," he answered gently as he brushed a few hairs from my face. "I found you on the bathroom floor then brought you back here. Are you feeling better?"

"I'm not sure," I answered truthfully, as everything seemed so disconcertingly real and unreal at the same time. "You were sitting over there in the chair," I added, "I thought you were asleep. How did you get over here so fast without me seeing you?"

"I move very quickly and silently," he answered matter-of-factly. "Are you up to eating something?"

"I could try," I swallowed as my stomach rolled at the mere suggestion of food, "I really don't have much of an appetite, but I could use a drink."

A glass of water appeared in Sin's hand and I took it gratefully and drank deeply from it.

Choking and coughing, I found my throat was so sore that I had trouble swallowing and realized that eating would be out of the question.

"No food," I coughed again, "a cup of tea?"

"Of course," he smiled as he stood to leave, "Should you think to leave, all exits are locked and barred. I would always find you, anyway." He disappeared, he didn't leave the room, he just disappeared.

Closing my eyes, I rolled over on my side, drew my knees up and rocked gently back and forth, trying to calm myself. I hadn't really had enough time to consider escaping and I didn't know where I was or why I was here. Sin's words planted a seed of fear in my subconscious and I found myself considering the possibility that he might always be able to find me. Would that be possible?

Only moments passed before he returned with a cup of hot peppermint tea and a saucer of little sugar biscuits. The aroma was heavenly, but I knew the minute I smelled it that I would be unable to keep it down.

"Thank you for your effort," I smiled weakly, "but I can't."

"Can't?" he looked uncertain, "or won't? I assure you that there is nothing wrong with the tea, or the biscuits."

"I hadn't even considered that," I murmured, disappointed with myself that drugs or poison hadn't even occurred to me, "it's just that my stomach won't take it. I won't be able to keep it down. It smells wonderful though."

"You should try something," he insisted, "you need your strength."

"No," I shook my head, "please, just let me sleep. Maybe I'll feel better after more sleep."

"Very well," he put the tea tray on the bedside table and turned to leave.

"Sin?" I called softly from beneath my covers, "or whatever your real name is?"

"Yes?" he looked back over his shoulder then turned back to face me. He really was beautiful.

"You're really a vampire?" I dared.

Smiling sadly, his long sharp teeth glinting in the light, he nodded, "Rest well, Cat."

17

In my dream, I was running through the woods, low branches whipping by my face and arms, underbrush threatening to tangle my feet. Behind me I heard the unmistakable sound of someone running after me, heavy footfalls pounding closer and closer. As I bounded forward, propelled by a surge of adrenaline, the sound following me became that of a beast, heavy paws hitting the ground very near me. Though the forest was dark, I tried to turn as I ran to see what it was that was chasing me. As in every B movie I had ever seen, my feet tangled when I looked back and I fell forward on my hands and knees. Breathing hard, I waited expectantly for my attacker to pounce. When I at last turned to search the dark woods, I saw only a pair of golden-green eyes peering at me from the shadows. The scene dissolved and I found myself kneeling uncomfortably on a dusty stone floor. Powdery grit covered my hands and made my skin crawl when I realized that it was caked beneath my nails. My knees, bare, were also dusted with the grime. In the room beyond, I could hear angry powerful voices raised in alarm. Architectural columns, wide and dark marched in a line ahead of me and I got up and hid behind the nearest one. After catching my breath, I stole forward quietly from one column to the next until I could see the room ahead and the source of the voices. The chamber beyond was large with stone walls, floor, and low stone ceiling. Torches burned brightly on the wall and a crowd filled the center of the room. In the distance, on a raised platform of some sort, sat Sin, his bearing regal, his clothing rich and luxurious. His silver hair hung loose about his shoulders and bands of some unknown metal wrapped around his biceps. As he suddenly stood and bellowed something in some unintelligible language, he drove the point of his sword into the stone floor before him. His power and force were enough to leave the sword standing upright in the rock, and he angrily turned and strode away, the sword quivering slightly in the floor. Suddenly, the faces of all Sin's audience turned and their eyes fell on me. As fear and panic swept over me, I dropped to the stone floor…

Pain wracked my body and brought me screaming awake. Sitting bolt upright in the bed, I grabbed fistfuls of comforter and squeezed my eyes closed against the onset of the seizure. As my muscles spasmed and contracted, I drew in a ragged breath and sobbed. Before I knew what was happening Sin was beside me, unfolding me and pushing me back down onto the bed.

"It's all right," he whispered as he moved my hair aside and licked my neck. Pain blossomed there and I realized that he had his fake teeth in my throat again. After a moment I found that the pain had subsided a bit and that I could indeed feel Sin drawing my blood into his mouth. Erotic sensations began to course through me and my body relaxed and began to tingle. With uncharacteristic abandon, I cradled his head in my hand, holding his mouth to my throat and the feeling was, whoa, incredible. He released my neck, licking it again, then looked deeply into my eyes as he placed his lips on mine. Suddenly my thoughts scattered and took flight like empty Wal-Mart bags in a windswept roadside field. The sensations were incredible. Sadly, I lost consciousness with his kiss on my mouth, feeling regret as I was swept away.

Chapter 4

For an instant, when I awoke, I thought I was lying beside a dead man. Sin's skin was so pale and he was so still. Then I realized that he was warm beneath my hand, which lay across his near-perfectly-hairless chest. I touched my fingertips to the bite marks on my neck. They were still there. Believing him asleep, I let my curiosity get the better of me and lifted the covers to look down the length of his body. Though he wore satin pajama pants, a considerable bulge caught my attention. "No Ken doll, this one," I thought, "anatomically correct in every way." When my gaze returned to his face he was smiling and fixed me with those ebony eyes. I felt the heat of a blush rush up my neck and burn in my cheeks.

"Oh yes, it's there," he grinned, "and it works," he proceeded to prove as his member rose unassisted beneath the loose fabric of his pants. "Refreshing to have found someone that is still capable of blushing in this day and age," he added

"You kissed me," I marveled as I remembered, "Just before I lost consciousness, you kissed me. Why would you do that?"

"I do not know," he answered simply, "were you offended?"

"No," I admitted truthfully.

"Were you angered?" he smiled.

"No," I added.

"Were you aroused?" he purred wickedly.

Before I could reply his mouth was on mine, his tongue probing between my teeth, seeking, and finding that magic which made my hunger rise to meet his. He threw off the blanket covering us and leaned over me, his hands kneading my breasts, his mouth moving from my mouth down my neck with fluttering kisses. Though every fiber of my being was screaming "No!" I couldn't help myself as he deftly touched those illusive places no mortal man can find without help… or lots of practice. He parted my legs with his knee. Sensations rippled across my body and through my mind and I moaned with

20

abandon as his fingers entered me, roughly. He fixed me with his gaze as he probed and prodded, his touch wetting and widening me. Finally, he rolled on top of me and, teasing, rubbed his hip up and down my abdomen. At last he drove his formidable length into me and began a leisurely rhythm of thrusts. His smile was almost cruel as he intentionally slowed, then stopped his movement. I squirmed beneath him, "Please, don't stop," I cried, as every muscle ached for him, "I can't take it. I feel like you're turning me inside out." His smile widened and his pace accelerated. I was finally, gloriously released in a world-spinning, spine-cracking orgasm. Sin lifted his head up and back and growled like some great rampaging beast. He lay on top of me, still inside me, both of us spent.

"What the hell was that sound?" I asked as I rolled his weight to one side.

"You almost answered your own question," he laughed wickedly as he tossed that magnificent silver hair over his shoulder and winked. "Just me."

"Now that we are," I stumbled on my own thoughts, "whatever we are, can I know your real name? Not that Sin isn't terrifying and impressive and all. Very effective."

"To know a thing's real name is to have power over it," he smiled, running his fingers up my upper arm

"Is that true? I thought that was an old wives' tale," I added as my hand found its way back to that magnificent chest.

"Not, perhaps, in this case, no. My real name is Amon, though those who share this place with me do not know it, to them I am only Sin. You must be careful not to use my real name in front of the others. It has been so long since I had need of a proper surname that I no longer remember it. As the owner of this home and for what dealings I must have with mortals, I am known as Stephen Montjean," he explained, "I am, of course, older than I look."

"Amon, hmm, interesting name," I murmured, "and just how old are you?"

"I was born at the start of the thirteenth century, the year 1201 to be exact, and yes, I have seen much in my time," he smiled ruefully as his fingers brushed up my arm. Electricity rode along my skin and my breath caught in my throat. Could this all be true? It was, alarmingly, starting to feel believable to me.

"So, are you going to make me one of you, now? Isn't that the way it goes?" I teased, "And we live, or not live, happily ever after for all eternity?"

"Alas, my use for you is not of that nature, but that is for later. Right now," he growled, "I have other things in mind."

He caught me up in his embrace and locked his mouth on my neck. He entered me once again just as he started drawing blood from my veins. In a whirlwind, the most incredible orgasm shook me to my very soul. Such intimacy of feeding and mating at the same time could never be matched by mere sex. He left me quivering and gasping, muscles clutching and releasing, all my nerves tingling.

"Amon," I whispered, "what do you want with me?"
"Much," he replied, as I fell asleep in his arms.

Waking to find my head resting on Sin's, Amon's shoulder, I realized that I was cradled in his arms, sitting on his lap. I raised my head to look at him, his silver hair, pulled back from his face, glowing in the moonlight. Moonlight, I marveled as I took in my new surroundings, I was outside in a night-shrouded garden. Lights twinkled from graceful trees and the fragrance of night-blooming jasmine and nicotiana drifted on the warm breeze. White blossoms nodded their heads in a ghostly dance. Surely, I was still in Louisiana.

I looked at Amon, his face was hidden in shadow but his eyes were shimmering. He had apparently dressed while I slept and his crisp light-colored shirt stood out in the darkness. Glancing down, I found myself wearing a silky satin robe and gown, the color unrecognizable in the darkness.

"I can't believe you brought me out here," I gushed. "It's beautiful."

"You dreamed of being outside," he explained gently. "I thought it the least I could do to introduce you to my garden."

"Wait, you can read my dreams?" I stopped to think, then remembered the forest in my dream. "And this is your garden? Is this your house?" I added nodding toward the shadow-splashed stone structure behind him. Soft lights glowed in tall arched windows.

"It is where I live," he answered.

I gingerly stood up from his lap. Surprisingly, my legs held and I took a few tentative steps toward the small fountain that gurgled quietly in the center of the garden. Perhaps inspired by the beauty surrounding me, a tune suddenly filled my mind and I started first humming, then singing as I made the motions of caressing my violin with its bow. "All Souls' Night," came unbidden to my lips and I swayed and played my imaginary instrument uncaring what Amon thought. He rose from the bench and walked around me, studying me from a distance.

"You have power," he announced with awe in his voice.

"Right," I laughed, "the power to entertain somewhat. The power to play an imaginary violin, and apparently the power to get myself into impossible situations."

"No, I mean you have real power," he gestured with his palms out as if feeling heat," I can see it around you like crimson-colored electricity, circling and surrounding you. It's coming from your singing and your music."

"Wouldn't I already know about it if I had any powers?" I asked as I continued to do my weak little dance on the cool grass.

"Perhaps not," he shrugged, "I think we should find out what your power is and maybe we can find someone to help you learn to use it."

"My future seems rather grim," I reasoned, "Would there be any point?"

"There is always a reason, for power is not bestowed on just anyone. You must be meant to use it for some purpose," he answered as he stopped my dancing and touched my cheek with his hand. "Your body has absorbed the energy and your skin is kissed with a crimson light."

"I do feel better, stronger, than I have in a while," I smiled as I touched his hand with mine. "You never did explain why you were warm when I woke up in bed beside you. And your heart was beating. And," I paused, "though you've done a fairly good job of providing for my needs, I must admit that I am ravenous. Does your house have a kitchen?"

"It does," he nodded, "and I have my assistant, Bishop, preparing a meal for you even as we speak." He took me by the elbow and led me slowly across the lawn into the expansive entry of the parlor at the back of his incredible home, "As to why I was warm when you woke, I had just fed. I also made my heart beat because I didn't think you were ready to wake next to a corpse."

"I appreciate that," I smiled into the darkness, thinking he'd never know how loudly I would have screamed or how quickly I would have bolted if I had awakened next to his inanimate corpse. "Inanimate corpse," I chuckled inwardly, "such a short time ago that would have been a redundant term. Who knew that living in the midst of vampires would alter your use of the English language?"

In the parlor, candles flickered in silver candlesticks on the marble mantle of the huge fireplace. Exquisite, old portraits adorned the flocked velvet wallpaper-covered walls. Everywhere silver and crystal gleamed and glistened. Gray velvet sofas and chairs were arranged in a cozy, comfortable conversational setting. Black shining tables held silver and crystal lamps and objects d'art.

"Please," he said as he lowered me onto a sofa, "be comfortable and rest for a moment while I see to your meal." He turned and strode from the room. For the first time, I had the opportunity to really take him all in from a distance. "Wow," is all I could think. His broad shoulders, narrow waist, slim hips, and long legs momentarily transfixed me. His long silver hair hung gracefully down his back. He moved like a cat, smooth and sinewy.

"I heard that," he called as he disappeared, "and thank you."

"If you heard that I'm taking it back," I smiled.

Moments later a young dark-haired man carried a silver tray laden with numerous dishes and glasses into the room and lowered it to the black lacquered table before the sofa. He smiled as he looked up and I found myself gazing into the most unusually blue eyes I had ever seen.

"I hope I am not disturbing you, His Lordship instructed me to bring your meal quickly. I trust you are hungry," he added as he uncovered white china plates bearing meat, fish, and vegetables that made my mouth water. He placed a steak paired with a beautifully prepared lobster tail and a few shrimp before me.

"Surf and turf," I observed as I picked up expensive-looking silverware, "my compliments on your choice of entrees."

"I trust it is prepared to your taste, if not let me know. I had thought to serve some crawfish, but His Lordship said that you don't care for it," he explained as he poured a fragrant Pinot Noir into a crystal wineglass.

"I was born and raised in the Midwest," I admitted between bites, "I have never been able to acquire the taste for crawfish, they taste like the floor of the ocean to me."

"They are not to everyone's taste, I agree." He grinned as he turned to leave, "His Lordship wanted me to tell you that he has some things to attend to and that you will be dining on your own. He hopes you won't mind."

"I'm fine, uh, Bishop, is it?" I added, "By the way, His Lordship? What's that about?"

"Yes, My Lady," he bowed, "In his time Sin was truly a lord and I have served him. He will always be "His Lordship" to me and now I suppose that makes you "My Lady," though it may be an unfashionable title for this time."

"No," I said soberly," whatever I am to him, I am not his lady, nor yours, I'm afraid. Please, just call me Cat."

"Of course, Cat then," he agreed as he took his leave.

I dined quietly on succulent lobster, juicy steak, and delicately spiced shrimp. The wine was warm with a heady bouquet. I got comfortable and became sleepy before I finished and curled my feet beneath me, leaning my head on the arm of the sofa.

Amon was holding my hands in his, running his thumbs across the scars on my wrists, when I opened my eyes.

"You were so bereft, so devastated when your parents were killed," he whispered," I felt your grief, your anguish. Thank the Goddess, you were unsuccessful in your attempt at suicide."

"Yeah, then I wouldn't be here for you to gnash on," I quipped. "Sorry," I grinned, "fleeting moment of self-pity."

I looked around the room. Either Amon or Bishop had carried me back to the bedroom tastefully decorated in sapphire blue and crisp white. The pristine comforter cushioned the bed beneath me and I ruefully noted that I would never have had the courage or the excess of funds to purchase a white comforter. "And, if you have always watched over me, to keep me from harm, where were you when I tried to kill myself?"

"I was there," he murmured as he kissed my scars and looked up into my eyes, "I watched over you until I knew you were out of danger."

"Why didn't you come to me then?" I marveled, "why not then and why now?"

He released my hands and stroked his fingers gently down the side of my face. He played idly with a lock of my hair.

"Let me see if I can explain this properly," he mused. "If your life had not been in true jeopardy, as it was after your mugging when you were in coma, I might never have come to you until the end of your natural life span. When you attempted suicide, I saw to it that you would recover and stayed away. I have always watched from a distance and would have continued to do so, but you would have died if I had not stepped in and spirited you away from that hospital. I felt you letting go, felt your spirit weakening. The doctors were unable to find the cause of your coma. By my feeding on you, I tasted it and knew that you were bleeding, ever so slowly, internally. I brought you here and you were healed. Now I cannot let you go, Cat."

"Why not?" I cried," what am I to you? What do you want from me?"

"For now I only want to take care of you, to make you comfortable, safe, and perhaps happy," he said softly, but I didn't miss the "for now". He was being intentionally cryptic and I didn't like it, but I had no power to force a more forthright explanation. He stood and crossed the room to an overstuffed chair, from behind which he drew a violin case. He smiled as he turned and presented it to me. "I hope you will like this, I know it isn't your old one, but as quality goes it should perhaps even be superior. I know you miss your music."

I smiled with delight as I ran my fingers over the beautifully detailed leather case of burgundy leather. I flipped the latches and gasped as I saw the exquisite violin that lay within. I could never in my life even imagine owning such a finely fashioned instrument. I was almost afraid to touch it. Its wood shone and glistened in the soft light of the bedroom. I couldn't help myself and I drew it gently from its case. I could tell that this instrument had been much used and much loved. The delicate bow was already rosined, though I drew it a few times across the crystal block, which had been secreted away in the case. It sang as I drew it across the strings. The violin felt like it belonged on my shoulder beneath my chin, like we were two parts of the same being. I smiled as I played a soft Celtic melody, a pagan folksong that lifted my spirits and made my heart soar.

"There it is again," Amon marveled. "The power is all around you. Its light is almost blinding. The crimson is changing to nearly purple. It's beautiful. You are drawing it into yourself."

"I wish I could see it," I nodded as I continued the melody to its conclusion. "Thank you so much for the beautiful instrument. I did really miss my music and I hate it that my old violin was lost. I hope they catch the guys that attacked me."

"Rest assured that your attackers have been dealt with. Unfortunately, your violin was already gone when they were intercepted," Amon smiled ruefully as he took the instrument from me and put it reverently back in its case.

"Intercepted," I raised my eyebrow, "interesting choice of words."

"Please, be still and get some rest," he said as he returned the violin to the overstuffed chair, "already I can see your power being absorbed and fading. You are still weak. You need rest."

"I am tired, exhausted really," I admitted, "You know what's causing this?"

"I told you, I am aware of everything about you. I knew you could not survive without blood-builders to strengthen your system, as well as sedatives to help you remain calm," he added as he laid me back against the crisply covered pillows. He pulled the eyelet-edged fine woven sheets up to my chin then kissed me on the forehead, as you would a child, "Now you need time, good food, and light exercise, perhaps a walk in the garden when you are a little stronger. For now, just rest."

"But the seizures," I insisted, "you know what's causing them, what they are?"

"Ssssh," he whispered, as he turned out the lights and stood to leave. My mind was spinning from the information I had just received. So much to think about. Some of it made an odd kind of sense, some of it was still unfathomable. I couldn't even comment as he left the room. Did I expect him to stay? Did I want him to? Why did he sometimes feed on me and other times not? Was the sex, amazing as it was, an aberration? Would I ever experience anything like that again in my life? The biggest question loomed large in my mind, what did Sin, Amon want with me and what would be my fate? In romance novels the heroine always either escaped or, more commonly, fell in love with her captor and accepted his lifestyle, becoming what he was. Apparently that avenue was not open to me. For some reason I fully expected to die at Amon's hands, though he had never said anything to make me think such a thing.

Chapter 5

Blinding pain, cramps, and spasms sent me screaming from the bed at some time during the night. I ran crying into the adjacent room, which as luck would have it, was the bathroom. I banged the lid of the toilet up just in time to be violently ill. Tears ran down my face and dropped from my nose as I sobbed into the porcelain. Muscle spasms wracked my spine and legs. I curled myself up into a ball, trying to escape the pain. What was this? What was happening to me? I had no more time for questions as Amon, accompanied by Bishop, instantly was there lifting me from the floor, and soothing me. He returned me to my bed, straightening the covers and removing my gown. He wrapped my naked body in a blanket of the softest material and laid me back. Bishop appeared at my side and, before I could say anything, plunged a needle into the vein in the crook of my arm. Sudden warmth and stillness hit me and the pain was gone. All was gone.

I was running down a long hallway of indeterminate color. Doors, closed and undoubtedly locked, stood on either side of the corridor. I was alone, lost, and scared. I called out in that dream-muffled voice, "Amon, where are you? I don't know where I am. Help me!" A force like a gust of wind drove me into one of the doors and, miraculously, it opened. Suddenly I was standing in the middle of a bloody, smoke-drenched battlefield. Corpses lay scattered and raw. Weapons gleamed dully in the gray cloud-lit day. Vultures wheeled and turned, screaming their delight on zephyrs of putrid air. I coughed and choked on the horrible stench. I heard the pounding of approaching hoofbeats and turned just in time to throw myself from the path of a huge black war-horse, adorned with burnished silver and blackened leather. The rider, tall and dark, face hidden by helmet, didn't even break his steed's stride to avoid me, or stop to acknowledge me, but kept pounding on into the distance. I stood and backed slowly away from the carnage, unable to look away but wanting not to see any of it. Finally, stepping gingerly one foot behind the other I backed against the door, again. I turned, grabbed the knob, and leapt through the doorway. Once more in the hallway, I could hear Amon's voice from a distance, "She's dreaming, fighting the drugs, and she's calling me. She's in my head. How can this be?" I could not hear an answer but his voice resumed," I overheard her thoughts once before, this evening, but I thought it was just the connection brought about by feeding, and yes, sex. Now, I think she is somehow in my memories, my past. I can't say why I feel this, but I do." The sound of voices faded. The hallway dissolved.

I found myself on a wet cobblestone street, steam and smoke emanating from doorways and sewers. The sidewalks were littered with bodies wrapped in every manner of clothing, some no more than rags, some fine and expensive looking. I was running, panting and stumbling, I realized that I was somewhere in Eastern Europe and that I was fleeing in imminent danger of capture. As I ran headlong around a corner, I collided with a horse-drawn cart piled high with bodies. I cursed as I tumbled to the ground, corpses landing on top of me. I stilled my heart, I stopped my breathing, no mean feat as I was winded from running, and I lay perfectly still. I could taste the wagon owner's confusion as he bent to stack the bodies back on his cart. I clouded his mind so he could not remember what had caused the collision. "Damn pot holes," he muttered as he hoisted me unceremoniously on the top of the pile. At least now I could breath above the smell of rot. After what seemed like hours of bumping along on my dismal mode of transport, the undertaker, if you could call him that, stopped the cart in an alley, presumably to take his break in a local pub. I slid down the pile of cadavers and walked quietly down the street. There, at the end of the block, the door once more shimmered before me. I took one step through and fell...

Amon was calling my name when I fought my way to consciousness.

"Cat, Cat, can you hear me?" he called and softly patted my cheeks, "you're dreaming Cat, you were screaming. Can you hear me, Cat, wake up!"

I gasped as reality slammed into me and I could breathe again. I had never before had such vivid dreams, no nightmares. Even when my parents were killed, and perhaps it was because I didn't see them at the crash scene, my dreams were normal, though full of sadness and loss. No nightmares and nothing like what I had just experienced.

"I was dreaming?" I asked as I searched Amon's silvered-black eyes, "That was just a dream?"

"Apparently it was quite a nasty one from the sounds you were making," he nodded and he poured a glass of water from a crystal pitcher on the night table.

"I heard you talking," I challenged. "You were telling someone that I was in your head, your memories. Oh my God," I cried, "those weren't dreams. Those were your memories. I relived part of your past. How can that be?"

"You must have imagined that," he smiled calmly, "I do not know what your dreams were but I am sure you do not have access to my memories. Such things are not possible, even in my world. And," he added," I spoke to no one telling them that you were in my head. I have been out this evening and Bishop was down in his room, I assume."

"That's right, Cat," Bishop offered from the other side of the bed, one hand having swept aside the canopy drapes, " I was downstairs and I haven't seen His Lordship since we brought you in here. Remember? You had another seizure and I gave you a sedative and Sin tucked you into bed. We left once you were asleep and only now returned when he heard you call out."

"He heard me call out," I murmured, looking Amon straight in the eyes. Oh yeah, someone was 'Gaslighting' me, trying to convince me it was my imagination or a dream.

"I have especially sensitive hearing," he smirked, his dark eyebrows forming a mock-sinister glower. "I have lived in this house for many years, I am used to the sounds it makes and the sounds of those who live here with me. Your call stood out quite keenly."

"What time is it?" I changed the subject, "What day is it for that matter?"

"It is near nine o'clock in the evening and you have slept the clock around. Our little trip to the garden and your violin solo was last night," Amon admitted as he swept aside the covers and, exposing my nudity, which I had forgotten, handed me a robe. I saw Bishop quickly turn his head. I wondered if he would be in trouble if he saw the boss's girl nude. Wait, surely he had seen that when he and Amon rescued me from the bathroom floor. And besides, it was more like seeing the boss's dinner nude ...why the modesty or embarrassment now? I put those things out of my head as Amon guided me by the arm to the bathroom, where he ran a tub of water warm enough to steam up the mirror.

"You added a mirror," I nodded toward the vanity newly parked against the far wall. It didn't truly fit since the walls were concave.

"As you might imagine," he said as he adjusted the water pressure, "we have little need for such things, but I thought you might find one useful."

"I look that bad, huh?" I teased as I pushed myself off the side of the tub and stood clumsily. I wobbled as I made the trip across the room and was relieved to put my weight against the solid marble-top cabinet. He was right, boy did I need a mirror! My usually blonde hair looked greenish and dark and was in severe need of washing. My eyes were rimmed in red and purple hollows accented their sunken appearance. My skin looked pasty and wan, my lips cracked and dry.

"Why, in the name of all that's holy, would you want me for anything?" I exclaimed as I turned to look at his beauty.

"First of all, do not use that phrase," he grimaced, "and I want you because you are beautiful and warm and sexy and talented."

"And old and dried up and graceless and plain," I chanted.

He was behind me in a flash, his hands spinning me to face him. Anger burned in his eyes, "Do not ever say that again. You are a well-spring of hope to me. My future depends on you. You have suffered much in this world and have done so with grace and dignity. What age has done to your face and body, you have earned. You should wear it with pride." He hissed as he swept my hair from my neck and kissed my throat. I could hear my pulse pounding and dizziness swept over me and I thought Amon would sink his teeth into me. He did not, though he kissed along my shoulders and across the nape of my neck. Gently he bent and lifted me into his arms. Three or four of his large strides and we were at the tub once more. He lowered me into the extremely warm water.

"Is there more I can do for you, or would you like some privacy?" he cocked his head and appeared to be studying me.

"I'm fine, why are you looking at me?" I asked warily

"Nothing, Cat. Please enjoy your bath. There is shampoo and rinse there on the corner shelf and your choice of fragrant soaps, including your favorite, Satsuma," he stood and dried his hands on a towel.

"Your knowing everything about me is fast becoming annoying, you know. I don't even think my best friend knows my favorite fragrance of soap," I mused as I traced warm circles in the water with my hands. "Oh no," I suddenly sat upright and stared at Amon, "what do my friends think happened to me? I just disappeared from the hospital, what must they think? My bandmates, Kevin and Bob, and the guys, my buddies. Do they think I'm dead?"

"There was an investigation at the hospital after your disappearance. Nothing much came of it because there was no evidence, fingerprints, DNA, anything like that. The coma ward was not guarded, as it is an unlikely place for a disappearance, but now that has changed. Hospital security is tighter than ever, as I am sure that they are aware that the only way they avoided a law suit over your abduction from their care was the fact that you had no family, no one to sue them on your behalf. And the sheriff and his men and a couple hundred volunteers searched the surrounding areas on foot and horseback and no sign of you was found. They called a halt to the search just last week. You are officially "missing, presumed dead," he explained as he headed for the door.

Tears suddenly sprang to my eyes, "I'm never going back, am I?"

"Cat," he shook his head sadly, "try to enjoy your bath."

When I was finally alone, I leaned back into the tub and sank below the comforting water. My hair floated around me, the water filled my ears. "I should just stay under until I drown," I thought, "Wouldn't that throw a monkey wrench into Amon's plans, whatever they are. Or, if I can make it that far, I could break the mirror and slit my wrists again. I can do it, I've done it before." I knew I was just kidding myself, whatever madness I had gotten myself into, I could not help but see to the end. I felt like a character in some fantasy, sci-fi novel. I had to follow the story to its conclusion.

I looked down the length of my body and took mental roll call of my faults. Spider veins, varicose veins, childhood scars, sagging skin, poor muscle tone...I was a plastic surgeon's dream. At least my breasts, small and still perky, were okay. I was truthful enough with myself to admit to my sagging fanny, which used to be round and firm and sadly, one of my best features. Now it lay deflated and dejected, much like my ego. Had my parents had a huge insurance policy when they died, I might have used some of it on surgery. I knew enough of the world to know "looks open doors." However, part of my inheritance paid my tuition to the school of music and the rest was squirreled away for my retirement. "Huh," I snorted, "that was a mistake." Images of columns of numbers, my money, disappearing into some unscrupulous accountant's pocket danced in my head. "Oh well," I whispered, "maybe his kids have rotten teeth or his wife needs a hysterectomy. Just my luck, a vampire that looks like Adonis abducts me and does he show up when I'm in my twenties, maybe not beautiful but a little striking? No, he dawdles around until I'm in my late thirties and the only way I can get a man's attention is to set my hair on fire. Even then I'm not sure a man would stir enough to put out the flames." I said out loud, "Enough pity party!"

Closing my eyes, I summoned the memories of my boys and wondered at what they must have gone through when I was attacked. Being one of the founding members of Hunter's Moon had been one of my greatest experiences, and I missed those guys. Bob, our drummer, was the sweetest and most genuine soul and I knew that he had always felt particularly protective of me. When one night in Baton Rouge an inebriated would-be lothario confronted me outside the ladies room door, Bob practically pummeled the poor guy and he had only made a few lewd suggestions, certainly nothing I hadn't heard before. I cared for Bob deeply, but let's face it he was only twenty-eight years old and I wasn't up for the role of Mrs. Robinson, though the occasional fantasy did run through my mind.

Kevin and Sean were brothers who, like myself, had migrated to Louisiana from "Up North," so spoken with something like disdain down here in the south. Kevin played bass and Sean played acoustic guitar, and both were talented, fiery-spirited Irishmen from a predominantly Catholic neighborhood in Boston. As Catholics they fit right in here, much more so than little ole' agnostic me. Kevin had reddish blonde wavy hair, bright inquisitive blue eyes, and freckles all over his pale skin. Sean, on the other hand, had smooth dark-brown hair, skin the color of caramel and eyes as brown as nutmeg. Looking at them, you would never guess that they were brothers and their personalities were as different as their looks. Kevin was studious, focused and very into his music. Sean was into wine, women, and song and not necessarily in that order.

Our keyboardist, Brian was the quintessential prankster, always ready with a bawdy joke or a gag of some sort. But when you got him by himself, he could be rather sweet and disarmingly forthright. The boy had a soul of poetry and would make some woman a wonderful husband someday, provided she had the patience to wade through all his shenanigans and still smile. His thick wavy black hair and dark blue eyes attracted the ladies like crazy, but with him it was only for a good time, at least for now.

Hunter's Moon's lead male vocalist was Kurt and he was every woman's wet dream. Tall and muscular, yet lithe, he towered over the microphone during his solos. His curly blonde mane and well chiseled face put you in mind of Roger Daltrey of 'the Who', or Robert Plant of 'Led Zeppelin', though at 6'3 he was taller than either of them. Kurt was very intellectual and was finishing his degree in psychology. We often teased him that we would be his only patients when he became a therapist.

We had only been on the road a few times but we did have one sound man/roadie named Brutus. His real name was Tim, but he was just bigger than that name in every way. He was a huge mountain of a young man who knew amps and electrical wiring, wore a roll of duct tape as a bracelet, and was not afraid of hard work or long hours. Bless him, when we played late into the wee hours he would even drive us to the next place while the rest of us slept. He saved us tremendous amounts of time doing that and we were never able to pay him sufficiently to compensate him for the added effort. Sadly, we were just making a name for ourselves, our fortunes looking up, when my nightmare began and I hoped that the boys had kept the band going without me. Melancholy and self-pity threatened to choke me again and I shook my head and took a deep breath. Enough!

I scrubbed my hair and lathered and rinsed myself. With some practice I was able to pull the plug on the drain with my big toe and lay back to rest as the water washed away from me. My skin rippled with goose bumps as the cooler air caressed me and the water gurgled its last gasp. After a few moments my skin began to dry and the goose bumps disappeared, leaving me weak and naked in the empty tub. I closed my eyes.

Chapter 6

"Cat," a voice called and a fist banged on the door, "are you alright?" Amon breezed into the room, releasing the heat and returning my chills. "I heard the tub drain long ago. I expected you to come out or at least call me for assistance," he added as he grabbed a towel and draped it around my shoulders. Sliding one arm beneath my knees and the other around my shoulders, he lifted me and carried me into the bedroom where he lay me on the bed and covered me with a second towel. "You should have called me," he admonished, as he rubbed my skin dry with the large, warm towels, "I was standing right outside the door, more than happy to help you."

"Please," I trembled as I took the towels from him, "I think I can do this. Could you get me something to wear? Maybe jeans and a light sweater, panties, etc."

"Already done," he pointed at the folded clothes piled at the foot of the bed. "Can you dress yourself or would you like some help?"

"Let me try," I nodded, "but don't go far. I'm not sure how long my strength will hold out."

Amon stepped away from the bed, though he didn't turn his back as I began dressing. I managed the panties, decided the bra was too much trouble and slipped the sweater over my head. My arms got stuck in the sleeves and before I knew it Amon was beside me, pulling it down. I looked helplessly at the blue jeans.

"I guess you're going to have to do most of the work," I admitted, as I lay back on the bed and he started drawing the jeans up my legs. I squirmed my hips to help him get the seat into position then lifted my head to watch him raise the zipper and snap the button. His cool hands rested on my waist beneath my sweater.

"Is that alright?" he smiled as he caressed my skin and looked deeply into my eyes.

"Yeah," I answered breathlessly, "that's okay. I think I can forego the shoes and socks." I raised myself up on my hands and abruptly kissed him full on the lips.

He pulled back, an amused look on his face, "Are we feeling better?"

"We had a momentary burst of strength and we didn't want it to go to waste," I laughed as I drew him to me and wrapped my arms around his neck. "You can either kiss me or you can take me out for a walk. The choice is yours."

"Both," he breathed into my mouth just before his lips found mine. His kiss was firm, purposeful, yet tender and rhythmic. It made places, other than my mouth, squirm and move involuntarily. His right hand moved up to the nape of my neck and he pushed his tongue into my mouth as he lifted me from the bed. He leaned my body against his and I felt his member hard and unyielding beneath his trousers. Thoughts of carnal pleasure crossed my mind as Amon drew his mouth from mine, "Is that what you want, Cat?" He looked at me seriously, and the spell was broken. I remembered that this man, this vampire, whatever, was my captor and would possibly be my murderer. "I want to go outside again," I inhaled deeply to catch my breath.

He lowered me to my feet and helped me to straighten my sweater. I took his arm as he led me from the room. I gasped a little as my feet took the chill of the marble floor. He glanced down at my feet and, without warning, swept me up into his arms.

"You know, you carrying me around like this is also getting monotonous. If you can scrounge me up a pair of socks and shoes or at least sandals, I think I can give your back a rest," I said as he bounced me into a more comfortable position for him.

"Carrying you around, as you put it, is no trouble to me," he grinned. "You are a feather and it pleases me to be of use to you."

"Of use," I nodded, "well, I'd like you to get used to being of less use to me. Surely I'll be getting my strength back soon and we can cut out this 'Gone with the Wind' business of sweeping me up into your arms every time I stumble."

"Gone with the Wind? Ah, another movie?" He nodded then added, "I am sure your strength will be returning soon and I have taken the liberty of providing some diversion for you until that time. Tomorrow you will meet the one who will help you to understand and wield your power." Carrying me effortlessly, he walked from the hallway, past the candle-lit parlor and through the French doors. He stepped out onto the stone veranda and I once again saw the magical moonlit garden. The night air was warm and heavy with humidity. Bugs hummed and swarmed around decorative votives, placed tastefully throughout the garden. The fountain water gurgled and chuckled as it splashed from its stone ewer to the pool below.

Amon set me down, my feet taking comfort in the warm soft grass. I hesitantly took a few steps around the fountain and aimlessly wandered through the garden. I lifted my face to the sky and reveled in the glorious stars. The sky was black and the stars shimmered in the heat. I felt like I was moonbathing. The warm humid air was quickly drying my wet hair.

"Sing me something, Cat," Amon suggested from his seat on the bench.

"Do you really want to hear me sing or do you just want to see my magic, my power?" I asked softly, doubtful.

"I love the sound of your voice and, I admit, the sight of your power moving around you intrigues me," he agreed.

I cleared my mind and the words to "The Old Ways" came to my mind, then my lips. We had been performing a lot of Loreena McKennitt's work at the club and much of it was permanently stuck in my brain. I found it romantic and sadly nostalgic, much of it having to do with magic, hauntings, and Celtic folklore. I crossed my legs and sat down in the warm grass, closing my eyes to concentrate on the lyrics and the melody. Once again, I felt better, stronger than I had only moments ago. Maybe Amon was right, maybe my music did somehow have power for me. I sat quietly after the last words were sung, trying to make out Amon's expression in the dark. Only his hair and his shirt were visible.

"So," I finally broke the silence, "tell me about this person you found to help me with whatever power you think I have."

"Her name is Arathia," he answered as he rose from the bench and came to where I sat, "and she is very old and very knowledgeable."

I held up my hands and Amon gently pulled me to my feet.

"What, given your age and, uh, species, would you consider very old?" I teased, at least I think I was teasing.

38

"Arathia was once a Goddess," he answered quietly, letting the enormity of that statement sink in to my poor mortal mind.

"You mean," I stammered, "a real Goddess, like the Romans and the Greeks had? That kind of Goddess? The real thing? She hung out on Olympus, ate grapes and drank wine, and debauched young virgins?"

"Actually, Arathia was a Goddess before the time of the Druids and I wouldn't make fun of what they did. It would be considered rude," he patted the back of my hand as he drew me from the garden and back into the house.

"So what am I supposed to say to this Goddess? Wait, is she still a Goddess?" I marveled at how far from reality I had come that I could even ask such a question.

"Now she is a seer or sorceress. The time of the Gods has passed, though not the time of all immortals. As to what to say to her, treat her as you would any older and respected woman. Learn from her all you can, she has information, first hand I might add, which some scholars would kill for. She will help you identify your power and will teach you all of its possible uses," he smiled as he held the big French door open for me.

As we entered the parlor I saw that Bishop had put out a silver tray of cheeses, crackers and breads, and fruit. Someone did not want a repeat of what last nights' rich meal had done to my weakened system, apparently, and I mentally blessed him. The snacks looked wonderful but were obviously chosen with my current health issues in mind. Red wine glimmered like a ruby from a crystal goblet set on the end table where I had sat last night. Obviously, he was trying to build up my blood, too. "Oh drop it," I thought as I plunked down on the wonderfully soft sofa and picked up a cracker. So what if I was being tended to like the proverbial fatted calf, I might as well enjoy it.

"I have a few things to attend to while you eat," Amon said, as he turned to go, "I'll rejoin you when you've finished."

"Wait," I coughed on the cracker, as a notion hit me, "it bothers you to watch me eat. Why, why is that? Am I so disgusting or is it something I couldn't possibly be aware of? You attend to my most personal needs without blinking and yet when it comes to me eating, you can't bear it. Why is that?"

He spun and was upon me in a blur, hands on the cushion on either side of my thighs and eyes close enough to bore holes into me.

"Tsk, tsk, tsk," he hissed, "you overstep your bounds, Kitty Cat. Some things you do not really want to know, am I right?"

"Uh," I gasped at his intensity, "I, uh, guess not." Squirming a little deeper into the sofa, I dropped my gaze to the sofa cushion. "But I really do," I whispered.

"Do you not know that your hunger awakens mine?" He breathed, "Any of your yearnings stir me and I find it difficult to control the desire. I would like nothing more at this moment to plunge my teeth into you and not stop until I devoured you. Is that what you want to hear?"

"No," I quivered, "and yes. I don't know. Somehow I knew that. I couldn't put it into words, but I knew it. How can this be? I am so far out of my world here I should be chewing my way out of a straightjacket and yet it all makes some kind of obscenely weird sense. I wish you could tell me what the Hell is happening to me."

His eyes suddenly softened and he touched the side of my face with the backs of his fingers.

"We are in new territory here, Cat," he whispered as he sat beside me. "I am not sure anyone could tell you all that is going on. Arathia, and perhaps some of the other Old Ones may help, but I am not sure any being has all the answers to our situation."

"Huh," I smiled, "we have a 'situation'." I made quotation marks in the air with my fingers.

"I think it is safe to say that," he agreed as he leaned over and kissed me on the cheek. "Now, if you think you have poked the bear enough for now, I shall leave you."

"By all means," I laughed, "don't want to poke that bear any more tonight. Will you be rejoining me when I've finished eating?"

"Of course," he nodded, "and we shall see about dessert." He stood and, without hesitation, left the room.

"Whew," I thought, "note to self...Don't piss off the vampire! What was I thinking? Wait a minute," I mused, "Piss off the vampire? Now what am I thinking? I know, I'm in an insane asylum and I'm delusional, hopped up on hallucinogenics, strapped down in a rubber room. Wait, what if he was telling the truth but, instead of being rescued by a vampire, I'm still in a coma in a hospital with my brain in bandages and tubes running in and out of every orifice? Oh yeah, that's it. That must be it" I giggled and downed some of the warming red wine from the goblet. "Gotta have more of this stuff,"

I smiled, "I'm trying to make too much sense of this nonsense. One minute I believe all this and the next minute the impossibility of it all is smacking me in the face. Let's just get good and numb and stop thinking about anything. I'll just float."

I finished the bottle of wine and ate enough cheese and crackers to take the edge off of my hunger. I felt warm and safe and content. Amazing how wine will do that for you, no wonder it had been delighted in throughout history. My eyelids were feeling heavy, though I was trying to stay awake for Amon's return. Suddenly, though I heard no sound, I knew I was not alone.

"It's safe to come back in now," I murmured through my wine-induced fog, "I'm done eating and I've had enough wine to make me all comfy."

A warm hand caressed my neck and trailed down my arm. I struggled to open my eyes and was startled to see Bishop sitting beside me when I finally did.

"His Lordship wished me to accompany you to your room," he spoke quietly and with a slightly unrecognizable accent. His blue eyes glowed and his teeth were perfect pearls. His black hair lay in ringlets and framed his face perfectly. His lips, light red and bow shaped, gave him the appearance of a cherub. Suddenly, I wanted to touch his face and my expression must have given my thoughts away because he smiled and nodded as if I had asked permission. Lifting my left hand, I touched his right cheek very softly. It was as smooth as any I'd ever felt. I suddenly had this mad compulsion to kiss his tender lips but, shook the cobwebs from my mind and reached for sobriety instead. He closed his eyes and bowed his head. I thought I heard him purr.

"Was that you?" I whispered, "Did you just purr?"

"I am not feline at the moment," he shook his head, "but your touch may cause a small expression of pleasure to escape me. A woman's touch has been long missing in my existence. I had forgotten its power."

"Can I ask you some questions?" I suddenly realized that perhaps he could be an ally, "just between the two of us?"

"Ask," he smiled, "I will answer what I can. Don't, however confuse civility with ignorance. My loyalty lies with Sin and always will. As you are his consort I am happy to assist you in any way, allowing of course, that it would not displease him."

"Whoa there, boy, rein in that galloping paranoia," I gasped at his uncanny reading of my intentions. "I just thought I could ask you because you seem, well, sort of normal." I intentionally let that 'consort' thing pass.

"Very well," he nodded, "I apologize if I mistook your meaning. Ask me what you will."

I leaned back into the couch cushions, temporarily foiled in my plans for an insider on my side.

"Are you, well, maybe I shouldn't ask, but are you what Sin is?" I searched for the most politically correct phrase.

"You mean Master Vampire?" he smiled, "or vampire, powerful immortal, or even killer?"

"Yeah." I chuckled weakly, "I guess that's what I mean."

"Yes," he smiled broadly, showing razor-sharp, incredibly white incisors, "and no. I am Vampire, but I am no Master. Sin's power is formidable and he is a leader. Me, I'm a youngster and no leader. I was born in 1845 and would have died in the Civil War had my sire, my maker, not rescued me. He was later destroyed in a battle for territory and I would have been destroyed as well if Sin had not stepped in on my behalf. Since then I have served him in any capacity necessary and he has treated me well."

"Where were you born? Where is your family?" My mind raced, "Do they have any idea what happened to you? Where you went?"

He favored me with an angelic little smile, "I was an orphan on the east coast when I was little. Later a farm family in Missouri paid to have me sent to them and probably would have adopted me if I hadn't been such trouble. I just never really took to farm chores and ran away after a couple of years. After that I just drifted, making money doing odd jobs just long enough, then moving on. I think I was actually relieved when the war started up. Gave me a job and a way to take out my anger. I was a very good soldier until I was almost killed. Geryon, my sire, found me dying on the battlefield and made me Vampire. I served him until he perished, then I was about to be destroyed when Sin saved me. He had me educated, trained and I have served him now for over one hundred years. I have learned much. One thing I have learned is that I will never be the powerful being that Sin is, even if I last as many years."

As he spoke I was fascinated to watch his sharp, white incisors and marveled that he could speak without cutting his mouth to ribbons.

"This might be incredibly rude," I hesitated, "but, can I touch them?" I motioned toward his mouth.

"It is not rude, though perhaps dangerous," he explained, "they are as sharp as they look."

"I was just curious," I nodded.

"Please, suit yourself, but do not cut yourself," he added, "His Lordship would not like me tasting his lady."

"Yeah, well, I don't know about his lady, but I promise I'll be careful." I added as he smiled and opened his mouth.

The candlelight shone off the tip of his left incisor and I gently touched the edge with the pad of my index finger. I felt a slight puncture on my fingertip but because of my calluses, I drew no blood.

"Wow," I marveled, "you're right, they are sharp. If my fingers weren't so toughened by my violin playing I'd probably be bleeding right now."

"What is this?" his voice boomed as Amon strode into the room.

I was so startled by the sound that I turned to look before I dropped my hand from Bishop's mouth. The back of my hand dragged painfully across the sharp tip of his tooth and immediately blood dripped down my wrist. I grabbed my left hand with my right and squeezed while tucking it under a loose pillow on the sofa.

"Bishop and I were just talking," I smiled, "you know, history, things like that. He said that you sent him to escort me to my room but I was so comfortable here I thought I'd just relax and hang out."

I put on my best poker face and pretended no discomfort while I distracted him, hoping that the pressure I was exerting would staunch the flow of blood. I didn't want Bishop to get into trouble on my account, and for some reason, I didn't think Amon would be very understanding or forgiving of the situation, even if it was of my own making. I made the mistake of glancing at Bishop who was licking his lips and rubbing his mouth with the back of his hand. Of course, Sin caught it all

"What have you done?" Sin hissed as he smacked Bishop across the face with the back of his hand.

"Hey," I jumped up to Bishop's defense, "wait just a minute! He didn't do anything and if you hadn't burst in here bellowing at the top of your lungs, I wouldn't be bleeding."

He turned and looked down at me with such vehemence. "You are bleeding?" he stammered.

"It's nothing," I said, offering the back of my hand, "see? It's just a scratch."

He took my hand and turned it over in the candlelight. He seemed to be studying it, as a growl rose from somewhere deep inside. Suddenly he was on Bishop, one hand around his throat. He leaned close to Bishop's face and whispered some threat in a language I could neither hear clearly nor understand. I saw Bishop blanch and lower his eyes. I had no idea what was going on but I was suddenly so angry at the display of testosterone that I simply got up and walked out of the room. It was a great dramatic move, the only problem being that I had no idea where I was or how to get to my room. The only way I recognized was the French doors to the garden so, without even thinking, I opened them and stepped out into the still humid night.

I paced across the flagstone patio, muttering and gesticulating.

"Men," I swore, "doesn't matter how old they are, whether they're human or not, you get two of them together and it's always the same, "This is mine, no, it's mine. Mine is bigger, no mine is. Touch mine and I'll beat you up." I was so mad that I didn't notice the doors opening or the fact that I was not alone until, in the midst of my pacing, a strong arm grabbed me around the waist and lifted me off my feet.

"Put me down," I yelled and writhed furiously.

"Be still," Amon commanded as he put his other arm across my chest, effectively ending my flailing. "If you calm down and be quiet, I will attend to your wound."

"I told you it's just a scratch, he didn't mean to hurt me, it was my fault," I gasped for air, "You had no right to hit him or threaten him. He was just being nice to me."

Amon took my hand and held it up in front of my face. Blood still ran freely down the back of it and I was shocked to see it look so pale in the moonlight. He looked me straight in the eye and told me quietly to look away. I started to do so and then that little obstinate voice that always gets me into trouble silently yelled "No!" and I turned back to Amon just as he was closing his eyes and licking my wound. There was such rapture, such tenderness in his demeanor that I was entranced. I just stood there, realizing that I had no pain in my hand, and that there was something disturbingly sensual about the scene before me. I closed my eyes to enjoy the sensations.

Suddenly Amon had his hand on the back of my neck and his mouth was very near my ear.

"I realize that you were upset and probably did not think before stepping out of the house, but do not ever, *ever think* to escape or to leave me," he hissed. "I will always find you, and I am not always as beneficent as I would like."

"Beneficent," I snorted. "There's an understatement. Look, I don't understand what is going on but yes I was upset that you were angry with Bishop. I didn't think about escape, I just wanted to get away from you. You didn't hurt him did you?"

"Bishop knows what is and what is not allowed. You need not be concerned for him, he has been dealt with," he nodded as he kissed the back of my hand. The bleeding had stopped. He bent and gently kissed the side of my neck.

I spun away from him, stepping out into the grass, "I don't like your use of that 'dealt with' phrase," I insisted, "and nuzzling my neck is not going to get you back into my good graces."

"I could force my way into your good graces, as you put it, at any time I choose, but I know your grasp on this reality is tenuous, so I am being kind and patient. Do not think, however, that my patience is unending. Come," he snapped as he extended his hand to me, "it is time to be inside. Morning is near and you should be in bed."

I snapped my mouth shut, cutting off the smart-ass comment that rose unbidden to my lips, and took his hand, letting him lead me in. I realized in that instant that I had come close to danger, a peril that I not only did not understand, but probably couldn't even imagine. Common sense, not my strongest attribute, rose to my defense, and I mentally agreed to play along with whatever Amon would ask of me, for a while anyway. We walked in silence back into the house, and I took no pains to hide the fact that I was looking for Bishop in the parlor. Amon simply looked at me without comment. The room had been destroyed, furniture over-turned, crystal broken, pillows shredded. I couldn't speak. I was dumbfounded. Apparently there were rules that governed this world that one simply did not break, for punishment was severe. My mind reeled and I forced myself to not pull away from Amon's touch. How could I be so attracted to him one moment and so utterly repulsed by him the next? I made a decision to try to stay as far from Amon as I could. He had made it clear that I was not to be his "mate" or to become one of them so whatever my purpose, it seemed prudent to put as much distance, physically and emotionally, between us as possible. I knew that with his looks and his moments of tenderness, I could easily fall for him and, though I suspected I might lose my life to him, I was determined not to lose my heart. Hopefully, Arathia's arrival tomorrow would allow me a way to avoid him, after all, I had to study didn't I?

Amon walked me down the maze of corridors. He stopped in front of a door, opened it for me, and without comment, I went in and closed the door behind me. I wanted to punish him and at the time it was all I could think to do. I turned away from the door and was about to fling myself on the bed when I realized that I was not alone. Across the room a young dark woman was turning down the bed and fussing with the pillows. I took an instant dislike to her.

"Get out," I snarled as I launched myself across the bed.

"Mr. Montjean asked me to see to your needs," she said meekly, "I only wish to please you."

"Mr. Montjean can go to Hell and if you really want to please me, you'll join him," I mumbled, burying my face in the pillow.

"I'm sorry, I didn't hear you," she added as she started to move the covers, "what can I do for you?"

"Please," I choked, "just get out. Leave me alone."

Chapter 7

I felt a little bad for my outburst. After all, it wasn't the maid I was mad at, she just happened to be in the line of fire. Once she had scuttled out the door, I lay tossing and turning on the bed, still seething with anger. My mind was reeling. I was sure that I would be awake for hours but the energy it took to sustain such emotions quickly drained away and I was soon sleeping, still fully clothed.

Once again I dreamed I was in the corridor, doors closed, wind blowing. A door banged open and I stumbled through. I found myself in a crowded town square, surrounded by people carrying bundles of wood, wheat, fabric, and baskets of food. I followed the attention of most of the crowd till I spied the gallows near the stone wall of what must have been a governmental building. Five empty nooses swung limply in the gentle breeze. I was amazed to realize that most of the onlookers were in a rather celebratory mood, talking loudly, laughing, and exchanging what must have been jokes.

A hush fell on the crowd as first one, then another, then three more people were led out onto the raised platform in front of the gallows. Inwardly I groaned as I realized what I was about to witness. The first victim, for I could not help but think of them that way, was a tired looking older man, his gray wispy hair playing around his wrinkled face. His hands were tied before him and he looked only at his feet as he was led into position before the first noose. Behind him came a youth, freckled and dirty, who stared blatantly into the crowd with an air of defiance, no doubt false bravado. Following him was another youngster, whom I first took to be a boy of about fifteen, until the wind blew the cap from his head and I gasped to see a beautiful blonde-haired girl. I could not imagine anyone looking more out of place up there on that platform. She swept the crowd with huge cornflower blue eyes, as if she was looking for some-one, perhaps someone to save her. Behind her came a couple, a man and a woman, both wearing tatters of clothes, both filthy, looking as if they had neither eaten nor bathed in months. "What an unusual collection of victims for the hangman," I thought, as each was encircled with a noose. Somewhere a drum started pounding a ponderous rhythm and I could feel the anticipation of the crowd growing. I started backing out of the crowd and, just as I bumped into the facing of the doorjamb, I heard the crack of the wood as the floor beneath the gallows dropped.

I woke gasping, my heart pounding. I fought my way out of the bedclothes, no easy feat since I was still in my jeans and sweater. I was sweating, burning up with a fever, and wracked with chills. I stood weakly leaning against the bedpost, determined not to call out for help, especially for Amon. I stood quietly letting my heartbeat slow to normal, my breathing calm down. I still had a fever and felt clammy and tremble but for a moment I thought I was going to be okay. Pulling the sweater over my head, I leaned back on the bed to remove my jeans. I had them unbuttoned and unzipped and had pulled them nearly down to my ankles when a muscle spasm tore through my spine and sent me to my knees beside the bed. I moaned quietly, holding my breath, waiting for the pain to subside. I squeezed my eyes tightly shut and, hugging myself, rocked back and forth, humming some mindless tune. I heard the door open slowly and heard Bishop whisper my name.

"You're still alive?" I whined with relief when I saw him enter the room. It must have been daylight somewhere because, though there were no windows in the room, I could see him clearly in the available light.

"Of course," he smiled, "come now, let's get you off the floor." He leaned down and lifted me by the elbows and laid me gently back on the bed. "Oh, no," he added, "you're burning with fever. Sin is not going to like this."

"As if I care what he likes," I giggled, delirious. "I got this fever just to piss him off. Do you think it'll make him happy?"

"Please, don't say things like that. You don't understand the whole situation," he explained as he removed my jeans and covered me with the blankets on the bed. "I know that he is only looking out for your best interests. You may not realize it but he has gone to great lengths to see to your comfort, and Arathia will be arriving this afternoon, though it doesn't look as if you'll be up to meeting her."

I felt so bad that tears escaped from my tightly closed eyes and I grabbed Bishop's hand.

"Please," I whispered in desperation, "please help me. I'm afraid. He scares me and I don't want to be here anymore."

He pulled his hand from my deathgrip and patted my shoulder, "Don't worry, I'll take care of you." He took a syringe from the drawer in the bedside table and deftly stuck it into the vein in my arm. I couldn't look at him and turned my head, sure that the look of betrayal would be clearly printed on my face.

The fever was like a tidal wave and I was tossed, turned, then pushed down into the depths. Occasionally, I must have almost surfaced as I overheard hushed voices and felt cool hands touching me. I could not muster the strength to wake to full consciousness, though I sometimes must have been semi-coherent. I don't know how long I was in that state but when I finally woke shivering and clutching myself I found Amon lying beside me, his long graceful hand on my chest. I took note of the fact that he must have fed for his hand was warm and felt good.

"You have been gone long, Cat," he whispered as he stroked a lock of my hair off my forehead, "We have all been worried about you."

"All?" I croaked, my throat dry and voice raspy.

"All," he nodded, "Arathia arrived a few days ago and she has been helping tend to you with her special skills. Her assistance has been invaluable," he looked deeply into my eyes. "Tell me Pet, how do you feel?"

I pulled the covers up tighter under my chin and drew my knees up to my chest, moaning, "I am so cold, I feel like I will never be warm again."

He pulled me closer to him so I was snuggled into the concavity of his torso and wrapped his arms around me. "Rest assured, Cat, you will be warm again," he murmured into my neck, "I promise you."

I closed my eyes and tried to relax in Amon's embrace. Chills still shook me and I felt a little foolish trying to rock gently in his arms.

"Forgive me," Amon breathed beside my ear as he stroked his hand down my arm and cradled my hand in his. He gently bent my arm back towards his mouth and before I knew it he was kissing my wrist. I felt his tongue lick my scar, then he exerted steadily increasing pressure until his teeth broke my skin and he drew my blood into his mouth. He took long, lingering pulls on my flesh and, though part of me was repulsed, I was mesmerized by both the sight and the sensation. Suddenly I had trouble drawing breath and found myself gasping for air. I clawed at Amon in a blind panic, my chest tight, my throat constricted. He released my wrist from his mouth and grabbed both of my hands in his. He rolled me over onto my back and leaned over me. He locked his eyes on mine and brought his mouth down as if to kiss me. He opened my mouth with his and breathed deeply into me. I felt my lungs expand and relax. I was calm, my chills gone, and I was breathing normally when he pulled away. I drew a few deep breaths and looked up at Amon.

"What did you do?" I marveled. "You knew that was going to happen, didn't you? You do know what is happening to me don't you?"

"I had an idea," he grimaced. "I think your body was building up toxins again, so I just took some of them away for you." He leaned into me and kissed the shell of my ear. "How do you feel now?"

"I feel surprisingly well," I realized even as I said it. I rolled over onto my side so I could face him, "You know I should still be mad at you."

"But you're not, are you?" he smiled and kissed my fingers. He batted unbelievably long lashes at me and touched my chin with his hand, "I did not intend to anger or hurt you."

"Well you did, but seeing that Bishop is still with us, I guess I'm not so mad anymore," I snuggled closer to him. "Can I ask you something?"

"Of course," he answered, nibbling my fingers once more.

"Both you and Bishop are, let's see how do I put this," I thought out loud, "unnaturally good looking. Preternaturally beautiful, even. Is that a part of being Vampire? Are your looks somehow enhanced by what you are, or were you both this beautiful before you became vampires?"

"I thank you for the compliment, and though we both look, for the most part, as we did before we were transformed, the vampire blood does seem to, as you say, enhance our looks. Before I was made a vampire my hair was black, but little else was changed by my transformation. Apparently a pleasing look is part of our ability to attract prey," he explained as he moved from my fingers to the inside of my arm with his kisses. "I do not know how Bishop looked before his Sire transformed him."

I rolled onto my back again and just lay there enjoying the feeling of Amon's lips on the tender and sensitive flesh of my inner arm. I smiled, probably looking much like the Cheshire Cat, relaxing under his attentive ministrations. For the first time in what must have been days, I was comfortable and happy just to be lying there, not thinking, and only feeling. I stretched my legs and my one free arm. Amon laid his hand on the side of my ribs and slowly moved it down my waist, my hip and down to my thigh. I felt a growl growing in my throat and turned to face him just in time to squelch it by kissing his mouth. I bit his lower lip, sucked his tender upper lip and gently pried his mouth open with my tongue. Suddenly I wanted to swallow him. I drew him into me as I rolled my tongue over his razor sharp incisors.

"Careful, Kitty Cat," he panted, "Do you have any idea what you're starting?"

"Oh, I have all sorts of ideas," I purred, "and just now, at this very moment, I think I have a very good one."

I rolled him over onto his back and kissed the smooth taught skin of his beautifully muscled chest. I fluttered kisses across his pectorals and down to his waist. He was wearing silk warm-up pants and I made him draw in a gasp as I ran my finger under the waist-band across his stomach. Crawling up on my knees and straddling his legs, I took a moment to simply sit there and enjoy the view. He was magnificent, an exquisitely formed man, and for a moment at least, he was mine. I rubbed my hands up and down his chest, dug my fingers into that glorious silver hair, and kissed him hard and long. He threw his arms around me and rolled us both over. Being 6' tall has certain advantages, and I smiled as I wrapped my long legs around him and hooked my feet, effectively trapping him. He was now on top of me and the view was just as good from this perspective. He kissed my collarbone, then started moving down my body. My nipples hardened as I anticipated his mouth on them and I was not disappointed as he suckled and pulled on first one then the other. My whole body was beginning to thrum and writhe as my need started to grow. I unlocked my legs because they were starting to quiver. His mouth continued its exploration down my abdomen, his hands parting my legs. He kissed that warm wetness and cupped my bottom in his hands.

"Enough," I growled, my voice thick with need. I put my hands on either side of his face and drew him up. He pulled away from me long enough to remove the silk pants, then he was with me, opening me, driving deeply into me with long, expert strokes. I luxuriated in the rhythm, the physical grace he exuded, the power he gave off in waves. As the tempo increased, I had this unbelievable need to be with him, in him, part of him. I felt as if I needed to crawl inside him. He shoved his tongue deeply into my mouth, rhythmically counterpointing his stroke between my legs and I cried out in ecstasy. His muscles clenched and spasmed. Waves of orgasm rode over me and I clutched him tightly, wanting it to never end. The thought of an eternity of nights such as this suddenly sobered me as I remembered that such a fate was not to be mine. I lay still beneath him, my breath suddenly quiet. "When did I become an emotional sap?" I wondered silently, "I'm not like this!"

He leaned back and looked at me, "Cat? What is it? What's wrong?" he asked with furrowed brow.

"Nothing," I whispered as I turned my face from him. I couldn't bear the thought of him seeing me cry and I knew that stinging in my eyes meant it was imminent. "Stop this nonsense," I silently scolded myself. Hot tears escaped from my tightly closed eyes and I rubbed at them, trying to cover my foolishness.

"Cat," he demanded as he caught my chin in his hand and tried to turn my face to him. I resisted as long as I could, but he was much stronger than I, and I was soon looking up into those obsidian eyes, tears trickling down the sides of my face. "Cat, tell me."

"No," I sniffled, "it's just my silliness, nothing really. Please, forget it."

"I don't like to see you unhappy," he murmured as he brushed the tears from the side of my face, "tell me and I will fix it."

"You can't, no one can," I added as I wrapped my arms around his shoulders and pulled him to me, "just hold me. That will be enough for now."

He leaned farther away from me and smiled a little, "You're glowing."

"My magic?" I grinned, "Or just good sex."

"My humility won't let me say what I'd like, so I'm guessing that it's your magic. You're surrounded by a blue pulsating light."

"You're a stallion and you know it, and so far this is the first sign that you have any humility," I leered, "But blue is good, we blondes look good in blue."

"You are beautiful," he whispered, "whether it's your magic or the sex. Whether you're glowing or not."

I lay back, leaning my head against his arm and released a long, deep sigh. I had just had the best sex I had ever known, probably would ever know, and here I was ruining the moment by lamenting over the fact that it wouldn't be forever. No one else got forever, either. I closed my eyes and relaxed, letting the echoes of sexual reverberations run through me. It was delicious, I grinned, then quickly stole a look at Amon. Of course, he had those intense silver-black eyes trained on me. I blushed.

"Feeling better?" he smiled lasciviously.

"Oh yeah," I breathed, "just enjoying the moment."

"Try something for me?" he asked as he raised himself up on his elbows, then propped up a pillow between his back and the headboard.

"Since you caught me in a good mood, sure," I teased.

"Okay, concentrate with me, this is an exercise Arathia told me about," he further arranged himself, then fluffed a pillow behind me. I struggled into a comfortable position and pulled the covers up under my arms.

"Close your eyes and breathe deeply," he intoned calmly, "visualize your power as I see it, streaks of crimson or purple light that encircle and surround you. Hear your music in your mind, watch the light change in direction and speed as your music changes."

I heard the gentle strains of my violin in my head, I imagined my power as little bright fireflies bouncing and weaving around me. I watched them dip and change direction as my music changed keys and they changed color when the tempo changed. I opened my arms and held out my hands and the fireflies landed on my skin.

"Imagine your power touching you, engulfing you and becoming part of you," Amon directed even as I imagined my fireflies sinking into my skin, being absorbed by my flesh. I knew what to do. It was as if it was second nature, something that I had once known but forgotten, being remembered. I looked down at myself and, for the first time, I could see my power, see the colors crimson and purple glowing and pulsing under my skin.

"Oh my," I gasped as I witnessed this magic, this wonder. "What do I do with this?" I marveled, as I looked at Amon.

"What does your magic tell you?" he asked as he ran his right hand down the length of my arm, "does anything come to you?"

I smiled, "Apparently my magic, as you call it, is not talking. I have no idea." I closed my eyes once more and thought, "help me, Amon, help me wield this, direct this."

He gasped and looked up at me as I opened my eyes, "You need my help?" he looked startled, "Cat, I heard that in my mind."

"What?" I asked in disbelief, "What did you hear?"

"You called for me to help you wield and direct your power," he answered, "and I heard it as clearly as you are hearing me now." He rolled over and laid his palm against the side of my face, "You're doing it, Little One, and you're learning and developing your power. Your natural ability is incredible."

"It feels strange, and yet it feels perfectly natural," I admitted as I stroked his hand with mine. "So what do I do with this force?"

"Absorb it if you can," he murmured. "Its power will fortify you. Take as much of it as you can and mentally disperse the rest, simply visualize it dissipating around you."

I did as he instructed and found that I was able to accept most of the power into myself. What little remained I simply shook off as you would dust.

"I'm sure this will all become second nature soon," he added as he leaned into me and kissed me on the lips. I kissed him back and snuggled against his chest once more.

"Tell me," I suddenly thought, "is it day or night? How long have I been here with you? And, by the way, can you walk around in the daylight or will you spontaneously combust if sunlight hits you?"

"Kitty Cat, Kitty Cat," he sighed, "Does all that matter?"

"Well, only if you want to bolster my sanity," I explained, "I think it would help if I had some idea of time passing, day into night, that sort of thing."

"Very well, it is now near four in the morning, you have been with me now for several weeks, and no, I will not spontaneously combust if sunlight touches me," he shook his head, grinning.

"Can you walk around in daylight?" I prodded further.

"No, it is uncomfortable for me to be out in the sunlight, so I sleep during the day or stay inside. My eyes are so sensitive to light that I'm practically blind in the daytime so it's easier to avoid it. I have had hundreds of years to adjust," he added, "I hardly think about it anymore." He looked down at his hands. His expression was rather sad, but that may have been my imagination.

"It was a dangerous inconvenience to wait while you were in the hands of those incompetent doctors at the hospital," he looked at me pointedly. "That took almost all the will power I had to remain patient while I waited for the sun to go down. Of course, I had sent my people to insure your safety, but I insisted on being there when we brought you out."

I shook out my hair and bounced against him, my hands catching his face, "My white knight in shining armor," I smiled and kissed him on both cheeks, "rescuing me from those bumbling buffoon physicians who were oblivious to my peril or intent on my demise."

"If not your demise, Cat," he nodded and took my hands in his, "at least your undoing."

That phrase brought me up short. I suddenly had no words…

"Wow," I thought, "don't like the sound of that." I sat quietly considering what he might have meant by such a statement. I turned to look at Amon once more as I realized that I was growing warm, comfortable, and sleepy. My eyelids were drooping, it was very hard to see him, but I felt his hands lift and move me so my head was resting on the pillow and the blanket warmly surrounded me.

Chapter 8

The smell of hot black coffee woke me. Very black, very hot... and with chicory, the kind so favored here in Louisiana. I opened my eyes to find that I was lying on my stomach, my right knee bent and asleep, my right arm extended with my hand dangling off the side of the bed. The worst thing was that the left side of my face was scrunched into the pillow and felt practically numb. "Probably look like that chick that played the ADA on the Big Easy," I mumbled as I wrestled into an upright position.

The sound of clanking china and tinkling silverware drew my attention to the far side of the room. The maid, whom I'd blistered with my verbal tirade yesterday, had her back to me and was busying herself pouring coffee and setting a place for breakfast at the small table between two occasional chairs.

"Miss Cat's awake," she announced, for it was not a question. "Mr. Sin had me bring you breakfast. We got bacon an' eggs, grits, coffee, juice, and beignets, chocolate of course. You know, Miss Cat, I've been workin' for Mr. Sin for over two years and it still feels odd to call him Sin. He told me once that he had a younger sister when he was little and she couldn't say Stephen. Sin was as close as she could get," she smiled and turned to look at me, "Funny to have such a handsome man called Sin, though, isn't it?"

Her voice was clear and melodic, her posture upright and proud, and a braid of dark coarse hair lay on milky chocolate skin between her shoulderblades. When she turned toward me, a loaded tray in her hands, I saw that she had lovely high cheekbones, a generous mouth, large unnaturally green eyes and beautifully sculpted eyebrows. She was stunning, and it intensified my dislike for her. I resented being waited on and, damn it, I resented her presence here.

"Would you like your breakfast in bed or would you care to have it over here in this area?" she motioned toward the table and chairs.

"I'll come over there," I tried not to snarl, "go ahead and pour my coffee, I'll get my robe and help myself. I'm sure you have better things to do than stand around waiting on me."

"No, Miss Cat," she smiled broadly, "I am here for you. Anything and everything you want, I'll see to it. Mr. Sin said you'd be staying with us for a while so if you'd like some books or something. Lousy reception this far out, there is no television."

She was so sweetly disarming that I was having a hard time holding on to my dislike for her. I made it to my feet and threw an emerald silk robe, which had been lying at the foot of the bed, around my shoulders. Muscles ached where, before last night, I was unaware I had muscles. Perhaps my vampire lover should have chosen a more athletic or at least younger, more muscular partner. I was sore all over, and I luxuriated in the pain.

"You're hungry," the maid quipped, "I'll fix you a plate, some o'the best cookin' in Louisiana. My grandmama taught me to cook and I'm good at it." Her Cajun accent came and went, probably like my Midwestern drawl.

Steam rose from the coffee served in a delicate china cup on a saucer, I'm usually a mug girl, myself. I poured cream into the thick bitter-smelling stuff and stirred it briskly with my spoon. Though I loved coffee, I had never been able to adjust to, or develop a taste for, coffee made with chicory. It smelled good, it tasted bad. I sipped tentatively…not horrible was the best rating I could give it, besides, I knew I needed the caffeine.

"So if you are, as you put it, here for me," I said between sips," I guess I should know your name."

"My name is Lily, Miss Cat, and I'm pleased to meet you," she smiled once more and extended her hand.

I shook her hand and held it for a moment to get her attention, "I'm sorry about last night, what I said to you. I didn't mean it, I was just mad and you happened to come in at the wrong moment. I hope you'll accept my apologies,"

She chuckled, "Please, Miss Cat, you don't owe me no apologies. Shoot, I hear worse than that everywhere. You're gonna have to work on your badmouthin' for me to know you're mad." She patted the back of my hand and turned to pick up her tray, "Now, you eat all you want and I'll be back for your dishes in a little while. Enjoy!"

I was half way through my scrambled eggs and eyeing the delicious looking beignets arranged on a pastry tray when the door opened and in shimmered a vision. This creature, this woman, was unlike anyone I had ever seen. She was not tall, but she was so lithe and moved with such grace that she seemed to tower over me. Her hair was ebony, shiny and smooth, and yet it somehow flowed around her shoulders. Her skin was alabaster and flawless. Her eyebrows arched dramatically over pale blue eyes, which were fringed with incredibly long lashes. Her narrow waist and broad hips gave her the appearance of a spider and I couldn't help but feel like a fly trapped in her web. She was so beautiful, and yet she exuded such an air of threat and danger.

"You are Cat," she smiled with lips drawn back so wide that it was almost a snarl. She did not offer her hand, but merely nodded and proceeded to seat herself in the chair across from me. Her perfectly manicured hand, blood red nails of course, appeared from within the black gossamer sleeves of her gown. She poured herself a cup of coffee and leaned back in her chair. She seemed to study me.

"You must be Arathia," I nodded. "Sin told me that you helped tend to me when I had the fever. I thank you for that."

"It was nothing," she waved that hand dismissively. "Now tell me, Cher, your power, your magic, Sin has told me something of it but I wish to hear about it from you. How has it manifested?"

"Well, Sin was the first person to notice it," I began, "Apparently it appears as a crimson or purple electric-looking light that swarms around me when I play my violin or sing. I realized that I felt physically better after that first time that I played. At first I thought it was just that I was happy to be playing my music again, but later I thought that maybe it was the magic that had improved my health, for a little while anyway."

"Go on," she said, as she sipped her coffee and crossed her legs.

"Though Sin doesn't believe me, or doesn't think it's possible, I seem to be dreaming his memories," I grimaced as I remembered those vivid images. For some reason I felt reluctant to tell her about the telepathy between Amon and I.

"You have seen his memories?" she leaned forward, obviously quite interested.

"I think that must be it, or I'm having nightmares of monumental proportion suddenly," I explained.

"I see power around you," she announced, "but the energy is blue. Is this your magic, or does it come from something else?"

I blushed and shook my head, "I wouldn't know. This magic business is new to me." I had no intention of discussing my sex life with a total stranger, and I chuckled as I thought, "and there's no one stranger than this." I somehow knew instinctively that the power Arathia saw surrounding me was Amon's and was residual from our lovemaking.

Though I expected her to question my answer a little further, she simply sat her coffee cup down on the table and turned her eyes on me. "You tried the exercise I told Sin about. You were successful," she didn't sound happy.

"I guess you could say that," I nodded. "It seemed to work and it felt good and natural. In fact, I had gone past Sin's instructions before he could tell me what to do. It was like an instinct."

"Good," she said as she stood and smoothed her gown. "We have much to do to teach you how to use your magic. I know that you are still weak, so I won't tire you now. Please get some rest. Oh, and I want you to consider coming with me to New Orleans. I have a lovely home there where you will be safe and we can study more conveniently."

"Would that be allowed?" I asked in surprise.

"My dear, I do as I will," she quipped as she nearly floated to the door, "And, I think it would be wise to get you away from Sin as soon as possible. Don't you agree, Cher?"

"I, uh, I don't know," I stammered, "I haven't even considered that."

"You think about it," she smiled knowingly, "You must know I'm right."

With that she was gone, and I sat back with my mind both a whirlwind and a blank. The only cohesive thought that surfaced from the maelstrom was that I was relieved that she was gone.

I must have sat there in a stupor for an hour or so, not really thinking. Lily startled me when she came in to collect the dishes. I nearly jumped out of my skin.

"I'm sorry if I startled you, Miss Cat," she said as she started putting the plates and cups and silverware on a silver tray, "You were in another world."

"Truer words were never spoken," I laughed, "Tell me Lily, is it still morning?"

"Yes Ma'am, bout eleven o'clock. We had a powerful storm go through here last night, lots of thunder, lightning, and wind. Sun's out now though, air is warm and thick enough to cut with a knife."

"I'd like to go to the garden, Lily," I announced as I stood.

"Oh, Miss Cat," she chuckled, "You don't want to go out there right now. Sun's high in the sky and would seer the skin right off of you. Humidity's so high you'd be soakin' wet after just steppin' out the door."

She must have seen the disappointment in my face because she sat down her tray and patted my shoulder, "How 'bout you get some rest for a while, must be exhausting' talkin' to that Arathia woman, and I'll come back with a snack in a few hours. We'll go outside after four o'clock, when the sun's gone down a little and it'll be cooler, okay?"

Seeing the logic in her reasoning, I went to the bed and, removing my robe, stretched out. As I lay there looking at the canopy above me, her words came back.

"Lily," I added as she turned to leave the room, "What do you know about Arathia?"

"I only know that I get a bad feeling when I'm in the same room with her," she nodded. "I think she's up to no good. If I were you, Miss Cat, I'd watch my back."

"Funny," I murmured, "I had that same feeling."

I closed my eyes and stretched my arms up behind my head. It was so quiet I could almost hear the minutes ticking by. Without realizing what I was doing, I suddenly could see the lights dancing around me, as I had inadvertently called my powers. I relaxed and watched them dive and climb. As I willed it, they changed colors. Now they were not only purple and crimson but also pink, green, and gold. I followed a tune in my head and found that the lights bobbed and weaved with the rhythm. When I reached the crescendo of the piece the lights intensified and grew bigger. As I neared the end of the tune the lights landed on me, entered me. I felt like I had been slammed in the ribs with a two-by-four when I absorbed the energy of the lights. My skin began to tingle and burn, my hands started trembling, and my legs quivered. I could feel my heart pounding and my breathing became ragged, almost panting. I knew I had taken too much power, I was overloading, but I didn't know how to get rid of it.

"Cat," Amon's calm, powerful voice swam up out of my panic, "Be calm. You must release some of this power before it destroys you. You have taken more than you can just dissipate."

"I don't know how to release it," I whined, and hated myself for doing so.

"You need to concentrate on directing the force to a specific spot. Focus on one place and push with your mind. I will help guide you," he spoke confidently.

I glanced around the room, and in my panic saw only swirls of black spots swimming before me. How could I concentrate on a specific spot when I couldn't see, couldn't distinguish one spot from another? I sat up on the bed and shook my head, trying to clear my mind and my vision. It didn't work, the black spots were still thwarting my efforts. My skin was really beginning to burn and I was having trouble breathing.

"Relax," Amon's voice was like a cool breeze in my fevered mind. "Just concentrate."

I pulled in as much breath as I could and tried to let it out smoothly. I suddenly felt Amon's hand on the back on my neck, strong, reassuring, and supporting. The black whorls left my vision and I could once more see. I focused on the farthest corner of the room, pointed my right hand and pushed with all the might my mind could muster. Electricity, or something like it, jumped from my hand and shot across the room to the spot where I pointed. There was no fire, but the force left a charred mark the size of a human head on the wall above a dresser. I could smell ozone in the air.

I turned and looked behind me. No one was in the room. Amon had not physically been with me at all. I glanced down at my hands. They still trembled. I wasn't sure if I could stand, but at least my heart rate had returned to normal and I could breathe. I was surprised to find that my skin was neither blistered nor even red. Apparently I did have a lot to learn about this power, this magic. I lay back on the bed and willed myself to stop shaking, of course with no effect. Almost impossible for me to will myself to calm down. The more I think about it the shakier I get. I closed my eyes and thought of Amon. I smiled as I just conjured up a vision of him, eyes piercing, hair shining, mouth inviting.

"Pretty proud of your little fledgling, aren't you?" I mumbled, sensing his smile as I fell asleep.

Chapter 9

I was just stretching and opening my eyes when Lily came in carrying another tray loaded with silver domes and, I spied happily, a tall pilsner glass of what I hoped was an ice cold beer. She stopped dead in her tracks when she saw the charred mark on the wall. Her eyes grew wide, her lips pursed and she looked at me.

"Lord, Ma'am, I don't even want to know," she shook her head as she put the tray down on the bed across my legs.

"Snack in bed?" I grinned.

"Why not, Hon? You lay back there and enjoy these chips and dip and that fine cold beer. I'll go draw you a bath. Then," she added as she bustled from the room, "we'll see if you're up to going out to the garden for some fresh air."

I sat back and dug into the spicy hot salsa with the crisp salty chips. I realized how much I had missed junk food. The beer was wonderfully cold and a perfect complement to the snacks. I moved the tray aside when I was finished and swung my legs off the bed. I was still a little wobbly from my earlier exploits but was feeling pretty good. Slowly I stood, waiting to see if my legs would hold me... they did!

Lily had just turned off the water when I entered the bathroom. Steam rose invitingly from the sunken tub and soft, thick towels were stacked on the table beside it. The mirror on the far wall cast a cloudy reflection but every other surface in the room gleamed.

"I've laid out a fresh robe and I'll have a nice outfit for you when you're done with your bath," the little maid quipped as she left the room, abruptly. I hoped seeing that mark on the bedroom wall hadn't spooked her.

I hissed a little as first one foot then the other touched the almost too-hot water. I sank into the tub and smiled. First a cold beer then a hot bath, what more could a girl want? After lathering and rinsing, washing and scrubbing, I finally noticed a razor, safety of course, on the shelf beside the tub. Shuddering at the thought of how long I had been growing the hair on my legs, I shaved them with care. The skin had so softened from not being exposed to a razor that it was easy and smooth. "Shaving easy is not worth going Bohemian," I thought. Splashing water over my shoulders, I finally stood to exit the tub. A sudden wave of dizziness hit me. I threw out my hand to the wall to steady myself.

"The heat," I said to no one, "and the beer. That's all. I just got up too fast. Just take a minute and a breath and I'll be okay."

After a few normal breaths and no further dizziness, I stepped out of the tub. I dried myself on one towel then wrapped myself in a fresh dry one. A third towel went wrapped around my head for my wet hair. When I stepped into the bedroom it was empty, but as Lily had promised, there was a fresh new white satin robe lying across the foot of the bed. On a hook on the back of the door was a mint green floral sundress with a full skirt, spaghetti straps, and buttons down the front. Though it looked cute, it so did not look like me.

"Beggars can't be choosers," I sighed as I took the dress down and tried it on. It felt cool and crisp and made me feel uncharacteristically feminine. I twirled around the room a few times, wishing for a full-length mirror. A pair of tan leather sandals caught my attention, as they peeked from beneath the towel I had discarded on the floor. They fit, of course. On the dresser I found a set of silver brushes and combs and managed to detangle my wet hair. Just as I was wishing for a blow dryer, Lily returned and began picking up my wet towels. "There's a dryer in the bathroom, under the sink," she said when she saw me. I didn't know if she was reading my mind or if it was just obvious what I was thinking.

The garden was still warm in the late afternoon when we arrived, but I was just happy to be out in the sunlight. Though this far south air conditioning was necessary for survival, I had always felt better breathing real fresh air, even if it was humid and warm. Muggy breezes wafted the scents of roses, lavender, and jasmine around us. Water bubbled and gurgled in the fountain. Lily had thoughtfully provided me with a pair of sunglasses, so I wasn't forced to squint or stay in the shade. I took off my sandals and walked in the cool grass, mindful of any fire ants. Clouds skittered across the horizon and the sun was darkened from time to time. On a whim I climbed up on the low wall of the fountain and walked around it, as I had every wall when I was a child. I extended my arms and curled my feet on the edges of the stones pretending I was a tightrope walker, another holdover from my childhood. I was on perhaps my fourth trip around the fountain when Lily cleared her throat and looked at me.

"Don't you think we should go in now, Miss?"

"Do we have to?" I favored her with my most winning smile, "Can't we stay a little longer? It's been so long since I've been out in the sun."

"Which is exactly why," she nodded briskly, "we should go in now. Your pale skin is gonna' be redder than all get-out if we stay out here much longer."

"Alright," I pouted as I stepped off the fountain. It was one of those stupid moments when you know something's going wrong, and though time slows to a crawl you know you are helpless to do anything. As my right foot touched the grass it turned painfully as my weight came down upon it. I was startled to hear a snap and collapsed on the grass. My hand instinctively went to my ankle, but I couldn't bring myself to touch it. My foot was actually pointing the wrong direction, and I looked at it with detached amazement.

Lily screamed when she saw my foot and wrung her hands as she knelt beside me.

"Oh, Miss Cat, what have you done to yourself?" she chided, "You stay right here and I'll go get help." She stood and turned to go.

"Help from where, Lily?" I shaded my eyes with my hand as I looked up at her, "Neither Sin nor Bishop are around at this time of day. Just help me to my good foot and I can hop into the house."

"Nonsense, I'll just go get my brother Lucius from the stables. Won't take me but a minute. You just stay right there and don't move," she called as she ran between two bushes, out of the garden.

"There are stables here?" I called out to her disappearing form. "Doesn't look like I'm going to be getting on a horse for a while," I admitted as I looked again at my rapidly swelling ankle.

I wrestled myself into an almost upright position with my back against the fountain wall. Stretching out my right leg, I found wisdom in Lily's suggestion to not move. Where before my ankle must have been numb, when I moved it sharp screaming pain tore through it. I gritted my teeth and closed my eyes tightly until the pain lessened

Eventually, I heard movement and opened my eyes to see Lily returning to the garden with her brother in tow. He was dark skinned, tall, and muscular. His eyes were as green as Lily's, you could tell they were related. He crouched down beside me with concern on his face.

"Sorry to be meetin' you like this Ma'am. I'm Lucius, Lily's brother. Looks like you've hurt yourself," he said as he gently touched my shin above my ankle. As he examined my leg, it occurred to me that, caring for horses, he had probably done this many times before. "You just put your arms around my neck and I'll carry you into the house."

"No, no," I shook my head, "That's silly. Just help me to my left foot and with your help I'm sure I can hop into the house."

"Miss Cat," he said looking into my eyes seriously, "If I help you to your good foot and you let your injured foot down, all the blood is going to rush into it. It's going to swell faster and worse and you won't believe the pain. I broke my leg playing football in college and I can tell you from experience you want to avoid that at all costs."

"This is just a whole lot of fuss over nothing," I complained, "I'm sure it's just sprained. I'll put some ice on it and it'll be fine tomorrow. I don't need you carrying me around and I'm sure your back doesn't need it either."

Without comment, he bent over and wrapped one arm behind my shoulder blades and the other behind my knees. He lifted me effortlessly and looked me in the eye, face to face. "Miss Cat, I've been working with animals all my life and for a short time after school I was a volunteer fireman and a paramedic. I know what I'm saying when I tell you that ankle of yours is broken. My guess is you'll be in a cast for four to six weeks." He carried me briskly into the house, following Lily. When she started down the corridor to the bedroom I called out to her to stop.

"Please, Lily, just put me on the couch in the parlor. I can't stand the thought of going back to that bedroom already."

When Lucius laid me gently on the couch, my right foot propped on the arm, I caught his face in my hands and, looking him in the eye, I kissed him on the cheek.

"Thank you," I whispered.

He grinned and left without a word. I laid my head back on the arm of the couch and tried not to think of Amon. I didn't want him reading my thoughts and tearing in here in alarm. Lily had disappeared and I was surprised when she returned not only with ice packs but with a scotch in a crystal glass. "Just what the doctor ordered," I thought as I took the gleaming crystal from her. She gently put the ice packs on my foot as I sipped the scotch and let it burn down my throat. With any luck I'd be good and numb by the time Amon or Bishop showed up.

I didn't realize that I had been sleeping until I woke stiffly, still on the couch. Amon was standing beside me in front of the sofa, and as I looked up at him, he pushed my shoulders gently forward and sat down behind me. He positioned me so that I was leaning into his chest. He brought his head down beside mine and whispered, his lips brushing my ear, "It's alright, Cat."

"What's alright?" I whispered back to him, as I noticed Bishop at the other end of the couch. He had removed the ice packs and was studying my foot. "What are we doing, guys?" I asked with growing alarm.

"Your ankle is broken, Cat," Bishop explained as he examined my foot. "I need to manipulate the bone back into position for it to heal." He looked up at me pointedly, "It's going to hurt, a lot."

"Okay, well, let's just consider this," I stalled, "I don't suppose there's any way around this so we should probably do it before I have a chance to think about it, right?"

Amon put his arms around me, beneath my own. He clasped my hands in his. "I've got you, Little One, don't worry, I've got you."

Bishop looked up at me once more. I nodded. Quickly, he lifted my foot between his hands and, pulling, he snapped it back into position. It all happened so quickly that it took a moment for the sensation to radiate up my leg. I screamed as the enormity of the pain registered and tore from one end of my body to the other. Amon held me tightly as I cried. He whispered soothing words to me and rocked me back and forth. When the pain had subsided a bit Amon lifted me forward and got out from behind me. Bishop moved aside from the other end of the couch and Amon took his position. He gently placed his hands on either side of my right foot. Heat radiated from his touch and the pain disappeared. He massaged my foot for a while, then turning it ever so slightly, he noticed the tattoo on the right side of my calf, just above my ankle. He looked up at me and smiled, "Two roses entwined on a single thorny vine, very nice."

"Seemed like a good idea at the time." I shrugged.

"Is that symbolic of the union between you and your husband?" he suggested.

I smothered an outright laugh and managed to chortle, "Oh, aren't you the romantic one? And no, my tattoo is definitely not symbolic of my marriage. I suppose if it were to symbolize me with anyone it would be my violin, or that special someone I've not yet met, and never will."

"How do you feel, Cat?" he asked, changing the subject. Perhaps he spied a pity party on the horizon.

I took a moment to consider the answer, "I feel pretty good. The ankle aches, but not as much as it did. I'm just a little stiff. What now, crutches?"

"For now, bed rest," he answered quickly, "then we'll see." I watched as Bishop wrapped an ace bandage around my ankle and secured it with two clips

"I don't mean to be a bitch," I pouted, "but I hate to think of going back to that bedroom. I feel like I've spent an eternity there, okay, slight exaggeration. I'm feeling rather confined in there. I need a change of scenery."

"Very well, Pet," Amon smiled as he came back and lifted me from the couch, "tonight you will share my room and my bed."

"I can think of worse suggestions," I leered at him as he carried me down the labyrinthine corridors. He stopped at one point in our journey and, pressing me between the wall and himself, kissed me deeply and slowly. I drove my tongue into his mouth and gingerly brushed it against one of his incisors. Feeling it cut like the sharp edge of a paper, I tasted the salty flavor of blood. He inhaled deeply and drew my tongue deeper into his mouth. The sensations were so erotic I squirmed in his arms.

"I do not know if I can wait until we get to your room," I breathed, when his mouth finally released mine. I wrapped my legs around his waist, careful to support my right ankle on my left. Still wedging me between himself and the wall, he freed his hands and slowly unbuttoned the front of my dress. I felt goose bumps rise and my nipples harden as he leaned back and looked at me. Once again, I wanted him inside me and I wanted to be inside him. It was almost a primal urge, one that I had never felt with any other man. Softly, I stroked my hand down one side of that beautiful face. I ran

my fingers through that silky smooth silver hair. Prickles of anticipation touched me like quicksilver. He reached beneath me and tore
off my panties. I knew I was already wet for him. He hiked my
weight higher on his torso and unzipped himself. Kissing me hard,
he shoved my back against the wall. In one smooth move he drove
himself into me. I gasped as he thrust into me fast and hard, meeting
my every desire just as I thought of it. He touched me when and
where I wanted. His thrusts were timed perfectly to meet my own.
Our mutual orgasm exploded as a crack of lightening tore through
the night sky. I looked at Amon's face, both of us still panting.

"You were reading my mind, weren't you?" I trembled in his arms.

"No, Precious," he gasped, "You were telling me what to do, and
just when to do it. You were directing the show and, I might add,
what a show it was," He kissed me more slowly and tenderly. "And
now I had better get us to my room before my legs give out."

He was still inside me as he carried me smoothly down the hall.
It was incredibly erotic, the motion of his legs pumping back and
forth. By the time we reached his bedroom I was starting to climb
again, and he smoothly dumped us both on the bed. I surrendered to
the sensations, relishing the feelings, both physical and emotional.
We rode orgasmic wave after orgasmic wave as the storm raged and
crashed outside. I lost all concept of time as we made love again and
again. Finally, panting and exhausted, I lay back against the pillows
and sighed. I felt Amon's lips on the inside of my thigh, as I started
to fall asleep. "Help yourself," I murmured. "There's plenty more
where that came from." Feeling the sharp stab of his teeth between
my legs, I smiled as I experienced a new kind of orgasm.

Chapter 10

When I awoke, I lay quietly looking around. The door on the other side of the room was partly open and I heard water running. I assumed Amon was in the bathroom washing up. My attention turned to the room itself. The décor surprised me. The walls were a deep forest green, touched here and there with a frosting of gold. An obviously antique carved marble mantle perched dramatically above the large fireplace. Rich brocade drapes covered what I suspected were light-sealed windows on either side of the fireplace. Two beautifully designed wing-backed chairs stood facing the hearth, a small table gracing each near its outer arm. Artistically designed wall sconces flickered with electric flames. Deep umber marble tiles covered the floor and were scattered with lush, intricately woven Persian rugs. The bed was ornately carved from beautiful cherry or mahogany, I always got those two confused. The headboard bore the carved symbol of a dragon on a coat of arms. I wondered if it was Amon's family crest. All in all, the effect of the décor left me feeling warm, safe, cocooned. I was looking forward to my time recuperating in this room.

The next three days and nights were spent in Amon's bed. vAs intriguing as that idea first sounded, the reality was much more mundane. After that first night of passion, his bedroom was turned into a recovery room where I slept, was fed, sponge bathed (I hated that), and generally watched at all times. Whether it was the first night's sexual calisthenics, my body's way of healing or Bishop slipping sedatives into my food I couldn't decide, but I was well aware that I was sleeping, a lot. In Amon's bed my sleep was mostly peaceful, with the exception of one particularly vivid dream or memory, whatever. Each time I woke, either he was lying in bed beside me, or Lily or Bishop was sitting in the chair beside my bed. I never once woke alone.

Lily was dozing in the chair beside the bed, head in hand, once when I awoke and I just lay there silently watching. Her breathing was deep and rhythmic, her chest rising and falling with each breath. As I lay there, movement caught my eye from the corner of the room. A figure, female and dressed in old-fashioned garb, floated across the room and stood silently at the foot of the bed, merely watching. Her dress had a high neck and long sleeves and, though she had no feet, I assumed was floor-length. She wore her hair tightly knotted into a bun high on her head and she constantly wrung her hands as she stood there. Finally, she turned, rather sadly I think, and floated through the door. I had never seen a ghost before, but considering my current situation, it wasn't difficult to accept. She made no requests of me, nor spoke to me in any way so what her appearance meant, I could not determine. When I told Amon about it he didn't seem surprised or even interested, so I decided it must be rather common place in his world.

The dream I had the third night in his bed was similar in vibrancy to the others. It was very real, very vivid, and, though I couldn't remember all of the details, its meaning was clear. I was riding a horse on a dusty road as evening settled on the land. My left shoulder was suspended poorly in a sling of rough fabric. Blood oozed from the spear wound that throbbed and ached with each hoofbeat of my weary steed. Somehow, I was aware that I was returning from Egypt after having fought in the Crusades. My head nodded forward on my chest as exhaustion claimed me. I toppled, as if in slow motion, from my mount and rolled on to the edge of the rough trail. I don't know how long I lay there unconscious or asleep. When I next opened my eyes I found myself lying on a rough bed of wool-covered straw. An elderly woman spoke an unintelligible language to someone who stood just out of my line of sight. Having no way to understand the conversation, I lay back and closed my eyes, grateful to be out of the weather and safe. Suddenly, I grabbed weakly for my neck as I felt a blinding stab of pain. I didn't have the strength to fight…

I gasped and grabbed for my neck as I sat bolt upright in bed. I knew, instinctively, that what I had just experienced was what had happened to Amon when he was bitten by a vampire. Feeling his exhaustion and his weakness, I thought it was safe to assume that it was also when he became a vampire. The man, warrior though he was, had no power to resist.

On the evening of day four of my convalescence Bishop came in and unwrapped my foot to examine it. He gently turned it this way and that and flexed it. A small gasp escaped my lips before I could bite it off, and he looked up at me with a knowing expression.

"It's just a little stiff from being a bound up and elevated so long," I explained quickly. "I think it will be alright if I can just start putting a little weight on it and maybe take it out for a little walk."

"We'll see," he nodded as he started binding my ankle again. When he was done, he lifted my wrist and checked my pulse, looked at my eyes, and put his hand on my chest to check my breathing. He nodded silently then left. I didn't know if Bishop had any formal medical training but he sure was acting like a doctor. I had always resented the way doctors know things about your body that you don't. Shouldn't you, as the owner, know more than they do? Bodies should be self-diagnosing, if not self-healing, I had often thought.

Perhaps an hour or so later, Amon came in followed by Bishop. He bowed rather theatrically and presented me with a lovely black walking cane with a silver dragon's head handle. Bishop stepped up behind him and produced a boot-like brace contraption and smiled as he fastened it together on my foot.

"Now," Bishop smiled, "you can take it out for a little walk, if you feel up to it."

Amon sat down beside me on the bed. "Have you ever used a cane?" he asked as he lifted my left hand to his lips and kissed my fingers.

"Never had cause to," I smiled and turned his hand over and kissed his palm.

"The brace Bishop has put on your foot will help support it and protect it as you regain your mobility and your strength. I'm sure that with a little practice you will be using the cane properly in no time," he explained.

"Sounds great," I admitted, "but first, before I go patrolling the grounds, I really would like a shower or a bath. I feel kind of grungy, no offense to those wonderful sponge baths. So if you would be so kind as to remove this contraption?"

Bishop silently stepped forward and removed the brace and unwrapped my foot. I wiggled my toes in the freedom.

"I'm afraid I only have a shower in my room," Amon admitted, "But I would be happy to take you back to your room where you can stretch out in a warm tub."

"No," I answered as I scooted my legs across the bed, forcing him to stand. "Just help me to your bathroom, show me where the towels are, bring me a fresh change of clothes, and stand back out of the way." The idea of standing upright in a scalding hot shower, the water beating on my hair and skin sounded too good to resist.

"I'm sure I can manage on one foot. I can steady myself with my hands on the walls," I quickly added when I saw the look of doubt on his face.

"You may be right," he nodded, "but I think to be on the safe side I should stay in the bathroom with you. I would never forgive myself if you fell."

"Fine, whatever," I snapped as I stood on my left foot and took his arm for support. I half-walked, half-hopped across the room and into Amon's bathroom. I had not noticed the all-enclosed shower when I had previously used the room. It was in the wall behind the door and was hidden behind a very ornately carved panel. It looked like wood but, given the location and purpose, it was probably some other less porous material. I leaned against the wall as Amon opened the shower door, switched on the light inside, and turned on the water. I peeled off my clothes while he fetched towels and shampoo.

"I'll be right outside the shower door," he promised as he helped me hop into the shower, "I'm not totally convinced that I should allow this."

"Lighten up," I grinned as I bounced into the stall and under the spray, "this will make me feel like a thousand bucks."

He nodded and closed the shower door. I could hear his weight settle against the frame and knew full well that he was leaning on it, listening for the slightest sound of trouble.

"You know," I called out over the sound of the water, "If you were really concerned about my welfare, you would be in here with me."

"I fail to see how joining you in the shower would expedite your leaving it in one piece," he called through the door.

"Who said anything about one piece?" I shouted, "I was hoping for more than that." I admitted defeat. Apparently I wasn't going to entice him into my shower today. Pity...

After washing and shampooing, I had to admit that my left leg was getting a little wobbly. I wrung the excess water out of my hair and turned off the faucets. The minute before the last drop fell from the showerhead Amon opened the door and wrapped me in a large bath towel. I hopped forward out of the stall and into the bathroom proper.

"Just stand there for a moment while I dry you off," he directed as he grabbed another dry towel and started rubbing my arms. "I am not sure what we can do about your wet hair."

"Okay," I instructed, "just hold me around the waist while I bend forward and twist a towel around it. It might be awkward but I think it will work."

He turned me so my back was against his chest and put his right arm around my waist. He handed me a towel with his other hand.

"Here goes," I laughed as I threw my head forward, bending at the waist. My momentum almost caused me to lose my balance, but Amon's strong arm was there to catch me and I was able to wrap the towel around my hair and right myself without incidence. He helped me into a robe and was escorting me toward the door when my left leg finally decided it had enough. My knee buckled and I started to go down before he swept me up in his arms.

"I told you that this was not a good idea," he said as he carried me to his bed.

"And I told you that I would feel like a thousand bucks, and I do," I smiled and kissed him on the cheek.

"You are not as strong as you would like me to believe, Cat. I think we should postpone your walk until you have regained your strength."

"If you care at all about my mental health," I explained, "you'll let me rest for a little while, then when I'm dressed, you'll come back and take me at least to the parlor if not the garden."

He looked deeply into my eyes as he laid me down on the bed. It was as if he was searching for some sign of deception or, at least some measure of my resolve. Finally, he turned away from the bed and went to the other side of the room. He returned momentarily carrying my brushes and combs.

"I will send Lily in to help you dry your hair and get dressed," he nodded. "I shall return in a half an hour and we shall see how you are then. Bishop will be in shortly to put your brace back on."

When he had gone part of me was relieved, and a larger part of me felt sad, as if I had disappointed him. What was going on in my head? Or my heart? This was not like me at all. I had seldom in my life cared about what anyone thought of me, or how I was perceived. This whole situation was getting to me.

73

Chapter 11

A few minutes later Lily bustled into the room and went straight to the bathroom. She returned with a blow dryer and, bending down beside the bed, plugged it in and turned it on. She tossed my hair one way and then the other as she aimed the warm air at it. After a while, she turned off the dryer and took the brush out of my hands. She started humming as she began to brush the tangles out of my hair.

"You need some curls, Miss Cat," she suggested.

"I'm afraid curls are beyond me at this point, Lily," I shrugged.

She tossed me the brush and disappeared out the door without a word. Before I knew it she was back brandishing a curling iron. Across one arm she had draped a simple black dress, which she handed me.

"Might not do too much good in this humidity," she agreed, pointing at me with the curling iron, "but at least it feels better when you know you've done it."

She began sectioning and curling my hair and she once again hummed a familiar, yet unknown tune.

"Miss Cat," she whispered quietly after a few moments, "I overheard something and I've been trying to decide if I should warn you. I decided I should."

"Go on, Lily," I urged, as I shook out the dress and slipped it over my head. It was an elegantly understated dress of some softly draping fabric that I did not recognize. It was sleeveless and the scooped neckline flowed smoothly into a princess waistline then fell into an incredibly full mid-calf length skirt. It was both beautiful and comfortable, like wearing a tee shirt that went the length of my body.

"I heard that Arathia woman tellin' His Lordship that she wants to see you again. I don't know if she's comin' now or if that's for later, but she aims to see you again soon."

"Thank you, Lily, the warning is appreciated," I nodded, "I don't know what she really wants with me but I have taken your warning to heart. I'm keeping my back covered."

She had just turned off the curling iron and set it down to retrieve the brush when the door opened and Bishop came straight to the bed and checked my ankle. He felt my forehead and checked my pulse again while Lily arranged my hair.

"How are you feeling now, Cat?" he looked with concern into my eyes.

"I'm fine, my left leg got a little tired in the shower, that's all that happened. I really, really want to take a walk and get out of this room," I complained.

"I don't think that will do you any harm," he nodded as he retrieved the brace from the floor beside the bed. "You do have to promise not to put any weight on your foot unless it's in this brace. You understand that normal healing time for a fracture like this would be six weeks or so. Sin's ministrations have shortened your recovery by several weeks, but your body must still adjust and we may need to start some physical therapy for you to recover completely." He had finished fastening the boot brace and was leaving as Amon came through the door.

"Doc here says I can go ambulatory," I grinned as I stood for the first time with my cane and brace.

"Indeed?" he raised an eyebrow to Bishop as he was leaving.

"A short walk, no taking off the brace, and maybe the change of scenery will do her good," he admitted as he strode away.

Amon offered me his arm and we made our way slowly down the halls and the stairs. It seemed like it took an hour to get to the parlor and though I was tired, I had no intention of stopping there. When Amon paused outside the parlor doors, I shook my head and nodded towards the French doors leading to the garden. We stepped out into the night and I stopped to take a deep breath of the warm air. Stars glimmered and danced between blue-black clouds. The air was humid and though we were miles from it, I was sure I could smell the Gulf of Mexico. There's a very unique smell that I connect with that body of water and, though I could never put my finger on what specifically it was, I knew it like an old friend.

"There's Gulf on the air tonight," I murmured wistfully, "what I wouldn't do to walk barefoot on the shore and wriggle my toes in the sand."

"What would you give?" Amon asked as he led me forward and settled me on the bench in the garden. He placed his hand on my thigh and gave it a gentle squeeze, as if to get my attention. I turned my face to his, but in the semi-darkness I couldn't see his expression clearly.

"Let me think about that," I mused, " I have no money, no home, no job, no car, no stuff… Hmm, I think I can safely say that I'd give all that I have to walk on the beach."

At that moment, the clouds in the dark sky parted and the moon shone brightly into the garden. Amon's face was lit by the moon, and I saw one corner of his mouth curl up into a cryptic if not cruel grin, then the smile blossomed and he leaned forward and kissed my cheek. He stood and, taking both of my hands into his, pulled me up. I hopped on my good left foot, stumbling into him. He steadied me in his arms, then lifted my chin with his hand and looked deeply into my eyes.

"Close your eyes," he whispered with his mouth very close to my ear.

I closed my eyes and felt his lips touch mine. He wrapped his left arm around my waist and cupped the back of my head in his right hand. He breathed into me and the world became hushed and still. Cold surrounded us. I felt power building and surging from my feet, up my legs, into my abdomen and chest, till it reached my head. I felt light, weightless, and free. This was not my power. This was power that Amon was giving me, breathing into me.

"I accept," he whispered, as I lost my equilibrium and the world spun out of control. I risked a glimpse and, when I opened my eyes, it was as if I was looking at a film negative. That which should have been lit was dark and that which should have been dark was bright. Bitter cold streaked by me as my mind registered that we were moving. I quickly closed my eyes again, trying not to panic. Amon kissed me once more and it grew more demanding and more passionate. He was obviously distracting me. Before I knew it, my feet were touching down on cool damp sand, my foot brace blocking the sensation on my right foot. Amon smiled and stepped back from me.

"You owe me all that you have," he whispered, "and I may collect someday."

I looked around me in awe. We were standing on the beach in the moonlight, the Gulf waters lapping at the shore. Reflections of the clouds skimmed and skidded across the rippling surface of the water. Rich, pungent, salt breezes assaulted my nose. I felt like I was home. Without warning my legs collapsed, and I sat rather awkwardly on the cool sand.

Amon knelt beside me and looked into my eyes. "Is this not what you wished for?" he asked.

"Oh, uh… yeah, this is what I wished for, but you could have warned me," I laughed weakly, "I had no idea what you were doing when you kissed me, the next thing I know we're flying. Oh, my God, oh my God, oh my God. We were flying!" I looked at him in utter disbelief, "You can fly!"

Amon smiled and offered his hands to me. He gently pulled me to my feet and I limped down the length of the beach, my mind still reeling. I found a log that some kids must have used for a seat at a party. The ashen skeleton of a fire lay before it littered with beer cans and hotdog packages. I sat down on the log and stretched my legs out in front of me. Bending over, I unbuckled the foot brace and unwrapped my right foot.

"Bishop will be very disappointed," Amon nodded as he watched me disobey doctor's orders.

"We don't have to tell him." I suggested, "I just wanted to feel the sand with both feet. I promise, I'll wrap it back up and put the brace back on before he sees me."

Amon sat down beside me. Only the sound of the waves broke the silence.

"Tell me, what else can you do?" I smiled into the darkness as a cloud blocked the moonlight.

"What do you mean, what else?"

"Obviously, you can fly. You're immortal. You can't go out in daylight, though you say you won't combust. What else should I know? What else did Anne Rice get wrong or right? Oh, wait," I added, "Anne Rice's vamps were, if not impotent, at least disinterested in sex. We've already determined that she was way off base there. Tell me, though, what else should I know about your existence?"

"We are immortal in that we will not naturally die, though we can be destroyed," he said. "Some of us can fly and all of us actually enjoy sex very much. It fulfills a need which we feel most keenly, the need for human touch, human closeness. Master Vampires, those of us who choose to anyway, can also shape shift when we need to."

"You can become an animal?" I gasped.

"A few animals actually, depending on what the circumstance requires," he nodded as the clouds broke and the moonlight bathed his silver hair.

I looked up at him and touched the side of his face with my hand. My fingers traced their way down his silky smooth tresses.

"Tell me," I whispered as I kissed the side of his mouth, "what animals can you become?"

"Hawk, wolf, panther. It depends on whether I need strength, speed, or stealth."

"What, no bat?" I laughed.

"I suppose if I needed to I could change into a bat, but I have never felt the desire to become a bat. They are rather small, after all. It is easier to shift into something closer to your own physical size."

"Are you really dead? Do you have to sleep in a coffin?" I blurted out without thinking.

"Though I have tasted mortal death, I do not think of myself as dead and I do not have to sleep in a coffin," He nodded patiently, "but I do need to sleep over my native soil. That part of the folklore does seem to be true."

"Where was your native land?" I asked, as it occurred to me that from his accent, very light and sporadic, I could not discern his heritage.

"My native land, in this instance anyway, is not where I was born as a mortal, but where I was transformed into a vampire. The soil I sleep over is from Yugoslavia. I fought in the Crusades in Egypt and when I was wounded I was sent home, my wound was considered fatal. I sailed from Alexandria to Greece and had made my way as far as Yugoslavia when I collapsed. I was taken in by a peasant family and was recovering when my Sire found me. I suspected that my rescuers had reported my whereabouts to the vampire, Cesare, as he was their Lord and Master of their lands. Once I became a vampire, I was in the grip of a bloodlust for so long that I could not bring myself to return to my native Friesland. I knew that I would destroy the people I loved," he spoke calmly, almost wistfully.

Though the mention of Egypt and the Crusades stirred the memory of a dream, I shook off the odd feeling of déjà vu and filed the issue in my head for later consideration.

"Friesland," I searched my memory of geography, "In the Netherlands? Is that where you were born?"

"It is, though I left it when I was barely eighteen, and once I became a vampire I never returned. I couldn't witness my family aging, mourning their missing son. I'm sure once the Crusade was over and I didn't return they assumed I was killed. Once I had control over myself and my need to feed, I could have gone back, but I thought it would be torture to see my family and friends and not be able to approach them. I come from a very pragmatic, practical and instinctive people. They would have taken one look at me and known that I was no longer human," he explained.

"I wish I knew that much about my roots," I mused, "as far as I can remember there were only my parents and me. I never knew my grandparents, any uncles or aunts, anything like that. Whenever I asked about our family my parents changed the subject. Once, my Father told me that my relatives were all dead and that it made my Mother sad to think about it. Of course, I never brought the subject up again after that. I assume that with a name like Blair, we were probably from England or Wales, but I never had the time or resources to do a genealogy search. My mother's people, the Alexander's, they could have been from anywhere."

I rather awkwardly tried to make it to my feet and had to sit down abruptly. I put my hand on Amon's and turned to him.

"Could I press the bounds of your chivalry by asking for your help?" I smiled in the darkness.

"Of course, ask what you will, Cat," he replied, his eyes shimmering at me.

"Would you help me to hop down to the water so I can stand in it and dangle my foot in the cool?" I asked.

"Better than that," he stood and lifted me from the log and carried me down to the water's edge. "I will put you down on your good foot, but please don't put any weight on your right one." He let me slide slowly down his body and gently down on my left foot, holding me around the waist and under my right elbow. For a moment I felt like a ballet dancer standing there gracefully in the arms of my partner. The cool water startled me, but it felt good. I dipped my right foot in as a wave approached the shore. It hurt a little, but it was, oddly, a good hurt. I risked putting the ball of my foot down ever so gently in the water to the ocean floor. Pain radiated up the shaft of my calf and I quickly lifted it out of the water. I took hold of Amon's arms and turned in his embrace. Putting my hands on either side of his beautiful face, I pulled him down to me and kissed him deeply.

"Thank you for bringing me here," I whispered. I put my arms around his waist and just stood there hugging him, resting my head on his chest. The salt breeze stirred my hair and melancholy settled on me as I realized that I was no longer part of this world. I felt real regret that I hadn't spent more time here, watching the waves and listening to the sea birds.

Glancing down I realized that we were both standing in salt water up to our calves. Of course, I was the only one barefooted.

"I'm sorry I made you ruin your boots," I sighed as I watched the water gently slapping against the shafts of his beautiful leather boots.

"I have others," he answered simply, "don't worry."

Listening to the sound of the tide and feeling the sand shift and curl around my left foot was so relaxing and peaceful that I hated the thought of leaving, and stood silent and still in the hope of freezing the moment.

"Ready to go back?" Amon looked down at me.

"Just hold me here a few minutes longer?" I begged, "I just want to remember this."

We stood there, holding each other in silence. After a few moments he bent and lifted me out of the water and returned me to the log. Though my foot was still damp, I rewrapped the bandage and put the brace back on. Managing to stand on my own, I turned and faced Amon, sliding my arms around his neck. When eventually he leaned down and once more breathed his power into me, I called my own power to meet his and we shot skyward with startling velocity. It seemed only a moment before we were touching our feet back down in the warm grass of his garden. As my weight settled upon me my body crumpled and bent double as a violent spasm wrenched pain up and down my spine. I landed on my side, my knees drawn up, my fists clenched and my eyes blinded by the agony. I trembled and gasped for air.

With startling speed, Amon stretched me out on the lawn and, locking his mouth on my neck, drove his teeth deeply into my flesh. After he had drawn the second or third mouthful of my blood, my pain subsided and my muscles began to relax. I tilted my head towards his so I could rub my face in his hair. He looked up at me questioningly, dark clouds mirrored in those black eyes.

"Much better," I moaned as he rose on one elbow then leaned over me for a kiss.

The thought occurred to me at that moment that his mouth should taste of my blood, that I should be sickened or even repulsed. Strangely, I was not the least phased by those qualms. If Amon's kiss tasted of anything, it was just Amon. I could detect no coppery or salty flavor.

"You met my power with your own," Amon said with perhaps a touch of awe in his voice.

"You gave me your power when we first flew. I felt it. It was a rush," I added. "It just felt natural to give my power to you."

"Yes," he admitted, "I filled you with my power to make it easier and more enjoyable for you to fly with me. Apparently though, when you released your power to mingle with mine it left you defenseless, depleted physically. The toxins were overloading your system, again."

I smiled into the darkness that was his face and wrapped my arms around him. I feather-kissed first the left then the right corner of his mouth. I lifted my face and kissed his eyes. My lips found his and I pressed hard against his mouth. After a moment, I forced his mouth open and drove my tongue deeply inside, then sucked at first his lower lip then his upper. This was so unlike me. I'd had the occasional lover, sure, but I was honest enough to admit to myself that I would never be a sexual dynamo. Yet what I was feeling was a wild and reckless abandon. I was, at that moment, the personification of lust.

He pulled back from me, breathing deeply, and looked at me seriously as the moon breached the clouds' edge. "You play with fire, Kitty Cat," he breathed in the light of the moon. Curtains of silver and gray wavered across the irises of his eyes.

"Burn me," I replied in a throaty sultry dare.

In answer, Amon just stared at me, not moving. I should have felt self-conscious, but I didn't. Meeting his gaze, I intentionally held it, a wicked smile playing on my lips. Though I felt something foreign inside of me move under his scrutiny, it wasn't me. It felt like some force that stirred deep within me had turned away, though I had no idea what the sensation meant. Again, his eyes flickered and reflected the moon.

"Your eyes," I remarked gruffly, "they've gone shiny silver."

"Yours are lit also," he nodded, "but they are glowing bright emerald." He rolled on top of me and straddled my hips, a knee on either side. He sat up and looked down at me as if from a huge distance. He rubbed his hands up and down my chest, stopping briefly to knead my breasts. He gently pulled down the top of my dress, exposing my skin to the moonlight. Moving his cool hands up my ribs, he devoured me with his eyes. Gooseflesh rose on my arms as anticipation clouded my thinking. He leaned forward and laid his head on my bare chest, his hair spilling down my sides. The sensation was delicious. He planted a line of delicate kisses from my navel up to the underside of my breasts. I gasped as he rolled my right nipple between his finger and thumb, and drove his teeth into the delicate tissue of my left breast. I reached beneath him and tugged at his belt buckle. He raised up and smiled as he opened his trousers. His fullness spilled out. Taking him in my hands, I rubbed the length of him. Rolling my body sideways so he could move, Amon lay back on his elbows and watched as I crawled down the length of his body. Gently, I took him into my mouth, lowering his pants as I went. Thunder rumbled in the distance as I ran my tongue up and down his member. The wind picked up as I gently massaged him and traced finger marks up and down his thighs. He shivered as I ran my hands up his hips and across his abdomen.

Abruptly he pulled me off of his body and nearly threw me onto the ground. He shoved my skirt up and raked down my panties, breathing hard. I opened my legs for him, anticipating the sensation of his touch. Just as he entered me a bolt of lightning tore open the sky and the rain whipped and raced around us. Clouds roiled in the inky sky and thunder pounded at the horizon. Amon set a hard, steady rhythm between my legs and I thrust my hips up to meet his, taking him as deeply into myself as I could. The storm intensified with each movement until I was deafened by the barrage. When, unable to resist any longer, we gloriously climaxed the sky was torn apart and blinding white clouds churned and vibrated. Winds tore limbs from the trees and rain shimmered in glistening sheets. Amon and I lay quivering and panting, and untouched by nature's tantrum.

"Amon, what is this?" I turned to look at him, amazed that both he and I were dry, though a gentle breeze did stir in our hair.

"Our power," he answered simply, as if I should know what he meant.

"What about our power," I insisted," What do you mean?"

"Our power, yours and mine, and the power of our sexual union has called the old ones from their slumber. We have awakened the Elders. They stir," he explained.

"What, are they looking down at us or something?" I gaped.

"The Elders are not in human form, or at least they have not been for many centuries. I believe that the mingling of our power has stirred them, but I am unsure as to the reason why."

My heartbeat was slowing down and my breathing was returning to normal. As Amon too relaxed, the fury of the storm passed. The clouds broke and hurried toward the horizon. The moon shone bright and clear as the sound of night creatures' stirring returned.

"Come," Amon whispered as he rose and helped me to stand, "we should go in. Tomorrow Arathia wants to start your training and you need your rest."

I didn't complain as he lifted me off my feet and carried me into the house. I wasn't totally sure that my one good leg could support me after the work out we had just enjoyed.

Chapter 12

Morning came too early for me when Lily swept into the room with a tray full of clinking china. I moaned and stretched and tried to bury my head under my pillow. In truth, I hadn't done that since I was in high school, but I just felt so wiped out. Every nerve sang, every muscle thrummed, every bone ached.

"Miss Cat," Lily sang as she set out breakfast, "your coffee's going to get cold if you plan on hiding in those covers. It might work for a little while, but Miss Arathia is plannin' on being here shortly. I'd say if you want to eat in peace, you should come now."

"I'm coming, I'm coming," I moaned as I made it into an upright position. Thankfully, I noticed that I had somehow made it into a nightgown when Amon and I returned last night, though I had no recollection of changing clothes. Moving to the edge of the bed, I glanced down and contemplated wrapping my foot and putting on the brace. "Screw it," I mumbled as I grabbed the cane and hobbled across the room using my heel to support my weight. I dropped into a chair as Lily poured my coffee. She handed me a saucer with a pecan Danish on it.

"Thanks, Lily," I nodded and took the delicious looking morsel. "Could we maybe splurge and buy some Folger's coffee and skip this stuff that smells so good and tastes like tar?"

Her laughter was like bells tinkling, "You bet, Miss Cat, Folger's it is from now on. Now, is there anything else I can do for you?"

"I don't want to sound high-handed, but would you draw me a hot bath? If I have to face Arathia, I'll need all the strength and calm that I can get."

"Yes ma'am," she saluted as she went into the bathroom and started the bathwater running.

I finished my coffee and pastry, wiped my mouth on a lovely linen napkin, and wobbled into the bathroom. The room was shrouded in warm mist, the mirror fogged, and condensation trickled down the tile walls. Perching on the edge of the tub, I stripped off my gown and panties and gently lowered myself into the steaming water. It was glorious, my muscles relaxed immediately. I leaned back in the tub and closed my eyes. I could have very easily gone back to sleep but was startled when the door swept open and Arathia came in a swirl of steam and cool air.

"I see I have perfect timing, as usual," she announced.

"Hardly perfect," I sneered, "As you can plainly see I am taking a bath. Can't our training wait until I get out of the tub?"

"Are you uncomfortable being nude in front of me?" she smiled that crimson smile. "Do you think of your clothing as a form of defense? Something of a protection?'

I thought about it for a moment. "I guess I do think of it that way," I admitted, "and I'm used to bathing either alone or with a man. I'm not used to having a woman in on my bath."

"I understand, Cat," she nodded as she traced one perfectly manicured nail in the water, "But be aware that in magic, clothes are often a hindrance. That's why you have probably seen pictures of witches dancing naked under a full moon. What is a defense to our self-esteem is also a barrier to magic. Once you have developed all your skills, it won't matter whether you are dressed or not. For now, so I can ascertain your ability, I thought to catch you bathing, and to have a clearer idea of your gift."

"Fine, whatever," I slapped the water with my palm "but don't expect me to drop my clothes anytime you want to work on my training. If I can't learn to use this "gift" with my clothes on I'm probably not going to get much use out of it anyway."

Arathia sat on the edge of the tub and looked down at me. "Now, Cat, concentrate on speaking to me, to my mind without using your voice. Let's see if telepathy is part of your magic."

I closed my eyes and concentrated on screaming my defiance at Arathia, but after a few moments, I opened one eye as she sighed, "It appears telepathy is not one of your gifts."

Part of me expected her to pull out a clipboard and start checking off all the things that my magic wasn't doing for me, like some demented pencil-sucking secretary.

She leaned over and looked me straight in the eye, "Can you move things with the power of your mind?"

"I don't know," I grimaced. "I've never tried."

"Relax, and try to concentrate on something, say that sponge on the shelf there," she pointed to the scrunchy sponge on the shelf beside the tub.

"Alright," I sighed as I lay back and stared at the sponge. I saw it moving in my mind's eye. I willed it to move. I saw it tremble. When Arathia gasped, I was startled and swept my gaze across the room to see what had caused the sound. For an instant I caught sight of the mirror on the far wall. My gaze apparently paused there too long for the mirror suddenly bulged then splintered and crashed into a thousand tiny pieces. Shards of mirror, like confetti, fell into the sink and scattered across the marble floor.

Arathia stood abruptly with her mouth gaping open as she looked at the mirror. I looked at her then at the mirror and broke out laughing. I splashed bath water and giggled.

"What, may I ask, is so funny?" Arathia demanded, as she crossed the room and bent over the shards of broken mirror. She picked up a dangerously sharp-looking piece and turned it this way and that, inspecting the edge.

"Oh," I chuckled, my laughter dying in my throat, "It just occurred to me that a broken mirror is seven years bad luck and it doesn't matter a bit. I won't be around for another seven years anyway."

"And this you find amusing?" she cocked her head in confusion.

"Well, in a rather sad, sick, and somewhat pathetic sense of humor way, yeah, I find that amusing." I agreed, noting that she had not tried to dispute my assumption.

She approached the tub and held out her hand.

"Give me your hand," she commanded.

I lifted one dripping hand out of the water. She grabbed it and drove the sliver of mirror into the pad of my index finger. Instantly a bright drop of blood surfaced and she lifted it to her lips. She licked the blood and seemed to roll it around on her tongue, tasting it. Her eyes shimmered with a touch of amber for a moment, then returned to normal.

"Wait a minute," I stammered, "You're not a vampire!"

"No, I'm just tasting your power," she smiled with my blood smeared on her lips, " Now I have some idea of what it is, it will be easier to train you to control it." She started for the door, "We shall continue tomorrow."

With that she was gone and my bath was once more my own. In only a few moments, Lily came in and shook her head at the mess the broken mirror had made on the floor.

"You just stay in that tub, Miss Cat," she ordered, "while I clean up this mess. Did that Miss Arathia do this?" Bending over, she opened the cabinet door beneath the vanity.

"No," I smiled, "I get the credit for this mess, Lily. I'm sorry."

"Did you try to throw something at her and miss?" she chuckled, as she crouched under the sink, her upper torso disappearing into the cabinet.

"Something like that," I nodded.

"Well, maybe next time you'll hit the target," she added as she brought out a broom and dustpan and began sweeping up the mess. Bishop was waiting in the next room when I finished my bath. I had put on a robe and hobbled out of the bathroom with the aid of my cane. I was startled to see him sitting beside the bed with the foot brace in his hands.

"Before you say anything," I held up one hand, "I saw no point in putting that thing on just to make it into the bath. I put almost no weight on my foot when I made it in there and, as you can see, I'm using my cane."

"That's fine, Cat, just sit down here and let me put your bandage and brace on now, and you can get on with your day, or evening as the case may be."

"I thought it was morning," I admitted, "But seeing you here, I assume the sun has set."

"It's near 10 o'clock. This probably is rather confusing for you to have your days and nights mixed up like this. You've slept through the day after last night's storm," he nodded.

"Last night's storm," I thought, "if he only knew." I sat down on the edge of the bed and let him wrap my foot and put the brace on. After he left I found myself alone, awake and feeling restless. Amon didn't put in an appearance so I got my violin out and played anything I could think of. It felt good to lose myself in my music. My fingers tingled with each caress of the bow and my speed increased as I got caught up in the joy. I had been playing with my eyes mostly closed to concentrate. When I finally opened them I was shocked to see that the whole room was pulsing with a purplish blue light.

87

My violin fell silent as I sat there dumbfounded by the display. I put down the instrument and held out my hands. Balls of light the size of grapefruits landed gently on each hand. There was no heat, no sensation of burning or cold. They just vibrated quietly, then they disappeared. The light in the room returned to normal.

After returning the violin to its case, I paced around my room for a little while. It got old fast. I quietly opened the door to the hall and, looking both directions, decided that I was alone. I grabbed my cane and set off to see if I could find the parlor on my own. I tried to not think about where I was going, rather to go by instinct and memory, and after a while I was rewarded. The parlor lay candle-lit to my right and the French doors to the garden lay straight ahead. The parlor appeared empty so I opened the French doors and stepped out into the cool night air. Clouds obscured the moon and stars. The night sky was absolute darkness. A high pitched scream sounded in the distance. It was a bird, I was sure, and though I couldn't identify it, it was familiar. I heard snorting, which I assumed came from the stables. After taking a few tentative steps into the garden I found that my cane was useless, since the ground was so soft. I sat down heavily on the garden bench and breathed in the night air. It felt odd to be alone and outside. The thought of escaping did flutter across my mind momentarily, but given my current physical situation, I didn't think I had much of a chance at success. Stretching my legs out and resting my head on the back of the bench, I closed my eyes and just listened to the night sounds. Whispers of living things whizzing, scuttling, hopping and buzzing soon caused me to open my eyes. Indistinct forms moved in the distance as a fog moved into the garden. Suddenly I was cold, and grabbed my cane and headed back into the house.

I entered the parlor and poured myself a glass of red wine from a crystal carafe. Sitting down on the sofa, I propped my braced foot on the coffee table. Suddenly, I realized that I didn't like being alone here. As much as this world was strange and even sometimes frightening, I found those strange creatures that inhabited it interesting and wonderful. Realizing in that moment that I had been irrevocably changed, I knew that whatever became of me, my life would never be what it was. Having apparently emptied the first without realizing it, I poured myself another glass of wine then lay back on the couch. I stared at the beautifully decorated room and blinked, as my eyesight grew hazy. Crossing my arms on my chest, I sighed as I got comfortable and drowsy.

When I awoke, I found that I was no longer in the parlor. I wasn't in my bedroom or Amon's, either. This room was unfamiliar, though tastefully decorated, and smaller than the other rooms I had seen in Amon's house. Peach walls glowed warmly in the lights from delicate porcelain lamps. Floral drapes hung from the windows and deep green carpet covered the floor. A creamy colored down-filled comforter lay folded at the end of the bed. I sat up and stretched, my head feeling the after-effects of the wine.

"Hello," I called, "Is anybody out there? Lily? Bishop? Sin?"

There came no answer. I swung my legs off the side of the bed and bent to remove my brace and bandage. I wiggled my toes and moved my foot around without pain. Gingerly stepping down onto the carpet, I was pleased to find that not only would my foot support me but there was no pain. Apparently my healing was complete. Now I just needed to find someone to share my good news with.

I went to the door and turned the knob. It wouldn't budge. It was locked. I rattled it one way then the other. I pounded on the door with my fist.

"Lily! Someone! My door is locked. I want out," I banged, "Is there somebody out there?"

"There is," a distinctly masculine voice answered.

"Open this door! Tell me what's going on." I demanded

"I cannot," the voice answered succinctly.

"Cannot or will not?" I yelled and pounded again.

"Both."

"I can't talk to you through this door," I called, "Can't you come in here and tell me what's happening?"

"I can enter if you invite me," the husky voice replied.

"Fine, you're invited," I called and stepped back expecting the door to open.

A gentle sound, like a branch soughing, whooshed by a moment before an arm as strong as steel slipped around my waist and a hand clamped painfully across my mouth. I was lifted off the floor. A voice hissed against my ear, "That, Kitty Cat, is the last time you will invite anyone you do not know into the room, right?"

The hand across my mouth forced my head to nod in agreement.

"And when I remove my hand you will not scream or try to run, right?"

I shook my head and drew a deep breath when the hand suddenly released me. My feet gently returned to the floor. I took a step forward and turned to face my attacker. The beauty of the man before me froze me in my tracks. He towered over me, though he probably wasn't quite as tall as Amon. His broad chest and shoulders sported an exquisitely tailored black suit jacket. A diamond stud earring glistened from his left ear. Hair so black that it shone blue in the soft lights of the bedroom shimmered down his shoulders and reached almost to his waist. His eyes were such a remarkable pale blue that they almost seemed white, creating the illusion of blindness. His features were perfectly proportioned and well defined with an aquiline nose and delicately bowed lips. His chin sported a small black goatee. I was struck dumb by his looks and the number of questions spinning through my head. For an instant I thought that he looked like a drug lord, but that was probably because he was so menacing. It wouldn't explain how he had entered the room, either

"Who are you?" I demanded as I idly rubbed my ribs where he had grabbed me.

"My name is Chimaera," he answered with no emotion behind those frosty eyes.

"That doesn't answer my question. Who are you? What are you doing here?" I snapped.

"I am one of Sin's men," he nodded, "I am here to guard you."

"Guard me? What is this some kind of punishment for falling asleep by myself in the parlor?" I asked, my anger building.

He stood, shoulders squared, feet spread, purposefully between the door and me. He did not answer.

I turned and paced away from him in exasperation. It was clear that Mr. Monosyllable guy wasn't going to volunteer an explanation. Something had changed in my situation and I really needed to know what it was.

"Okay," I rubbed my forehead as I paced from one side of the room to the other, "Sin sent you to guard me, so obviously he's not available to be here himself. I'm guessing that, given your looks, you're a vampire so that means it's after sundown. Sin isn't just off somewhere sleeping the day away. Surely he knows that, even though I was alone, I did not leave or try to escape. What is going on?"

He stood silently, hands clasped in front of him, eyes regarding me calmly. I was right, no answers from this guy.

"I can say this," he finally said, "I, and another of my kind named Winter, will be guarding you from now on at night. During the day it will be two men named Bear and Dodge."

"That's catchy," I snapped, " aren't any of you guys ever named Bob?"

My attempt at sarcasm fell flat, Chimaera didn't crack a smile. My patience with this guy was quickly being depleted. I marched to one of the windows and threw open the drapes. Frosted, mullioned, panes nearly hid the iron bars mounted across the exterior of the window.

"We bear the names our Sires give us," he said simply from across the room.

That was clearly the end of his contribution to conversation. Apparently he assumed that I knew what he meant though I had only the vaguest idea.

"I can't believe that Sin thinks I need a bodyguard in here," I grumbled, turning back to the window, "I'm not trying to escape and no one could get to me in here, if he's thinking someone might try to rescue me. And besides, it's not like I'm helpless."

Chimaera moved forward with blinding speed and grasped my throat in one large powerful hand. There was no time to take in breath, I choked and clawed at the air as my feet once more left the floor. He pulled me very close to his face so he could look straight into my eyes. He stared at me for one heartbeat, then two. "You think you can protect yourself from the likes of me and my kind?" he snarled as he roughly released me.

Stumbling back a step, I clutched my throat and drew in a deep gasp of air.

"So," I coughed, "Did Sin tell you it was okay to abuse and threaten me? Is that part of your job description? "

"He told me to do what was necessary to make sure that you understand the gravity of this situation," he paused, "though he probably won't appreciate the bruise that's forming on your throat." He resumed his position in front of the door. "Understand this," he announced, "You are in danger." He obviously did not intend to expound on that statement. I would have to wait until Amon showed up for an explanation.

"So, what am I supposed to do now?" I asked.

He raised one eyebrow, comically. The gesture mocked me. He clearly could not believe that I would dare to ask such a foolish question, as if he cared to answer. I threw up my hands and returned to the window. I slid up the sash and let a cool breeze waft in. At least this room, for a change, had real functioning windows, no tromp l'oeil or boarded and sealed remnant of a window. Since it seemed that I wouldn't be visiting the garden for a while, I leaned my elbows on the windowsill and peered out into the darkness. There were few lights burning on the grounds, but I could make out a rectangle of yellow illumination spilling from a wooden structure several hundred yards away. It had to be the stables. It lay past the garden in the direction Lily had taken to get Lucius. Something was happening out there. I heard shouting and the banging of what sounded like metal on wood. Maybe one of the horses was having a colt. "Was that called foaling?" I thought idly.

Time dawdled and hiccupped and almost refused to pass at all. I had never waited well, and being forced to remain in this room was giving me a screaming case of claustrophobia. I was too angry and upset to play my violin so I did the only other thing I could think of, I practiced my magic. In my mind, I was playing a violently intense piece of music and I opened my eyes to see that the lights dancing around me were orange, as if in reflection of my mood. I sat quietly maintaining the power, letting it roll and build with each movement of the music. When the tune in my mind ended, I held out my hands and the orange lights converged on my palms. I closed my eyes for a moment as the sensation of heat and prickling ran from my hands up my arms and into my chest. I flashed them open and the world swam red for a moment. I knew that, could I see them, my irises would be orange. Glancing at the door, I thought I heard Chimaera let out a gasp of surprise, but his face gave away nothing.

I was bored. Bored, bored, bored! Finally, I tossed myself diagonally across the bed, landing on my stomach. Crossing my arms above my head, I rested my forehead against my forearms and closed my eyes. I wondered where Amon was, why he wasn't here with me. If I could force or fake a seizure I was sure that he would be right here. "No, that's nothing to be messing around with," I thought. I forced myself to calm down and thought of Amon. I called him with my mind. He did not answer me. Either our telepathy only worked in extreme situations or he was busy or ignoring me. My frustration continued to build.

Though I clearly heard the snick of the lock turning in the door handle and the gentle squeal of the hinges as the door opened, I remained face down on the bed. Obviously it was Amon who had entered, I felt it, but I would not acknowledge him until he understood how mad and upset I was. Granted, my reaction was perhaps a bit childish, but I was feeling powerless and I wanted him to apologize and beg my forgiveness. It's a girl thing.

Standing beside the bed, Amon cleared his throat and asked, "Do you wish to know what has been happening, Cat, or would you prefer to continue pouting?"

I considered this for a moment, then rolled over onto my side and looked at him. Lily had bustled into the room behind him and was busy setting a tray of fruit and wine on the bedside table. She bowed her head and disappeared without comment. As she went through the door I noticed that Chimaera had disappeared, too. Good riddance!

I sat up on the bed and folded my arms across my chest. Amon leaned over and examined the bruising on my throat. He shook his head, and I swear he almost smiled, but he made no comment on my injury

"You are angry," he nodded, as he settled himself on the edge of the bed.

"Doesn't take a rocket scientist to figure that out," I snapped, awaiting further explanation.

"Your skin is shimmering orange. Anger is fairly consuming you," he grinned.

"Fine, I'm angry," I admitted, "now, are you going to get on with it?"

"I am," he answered, as he stood and poured a flute of white wine. He handed it to me and sat back down beside me. "I will tell you all that I can, but please do not interrupt me with questions. It is very close to sunrise so my time for explanations is limited. I will tell the tale, then if there is time I will answer your questions."

The instant I swallowed my first sip of wine a vision popped into my head, only for a moment but it was clear and vivid. I saw Bishop putting three drops of clear liquid into the bottle of white wine that now stood on my night table. A voice spoke very clearly, "She'll be easier to keep safe if she sleeps through the day." A female voice added, "And easier to control." I stared at Amon, for I knew his voice had been the first I had heard. I took another swallow of wine.

"Am I going to be able to stay awake long enough for this story?" I smiled bitterly, nodding at the glass in my hand.

He raised an eyebrow, but did not answer.

"Suffice it to say," He started, eventually, "that earlier tonight two trespassers were discovered on the estate. In their possession they carried a large canvas duffel bag, two ropes, and a roll of duct tape. After some 'persuasion' they admitted that they were here to kidnap you and, though Arathia put a spell on them to elicit the truth, they refused to tell us the identity of the one who sent them. In fact, after a time, their fear of their boss so consumed them that they ended their lives rather than face him. So, though the immediate threat is over, the danger still remains. That, my dear Cat, is why you shall be guarded, night and day, until the threat is gone."

Silently sipping my wine, I took a moment to process this information.

"Persuasion?" I glanced his way, "was that the screaming I heard earlier? And why, if they knew that you're a vampire, did they try it at night? Why not wait until daylight?" I reasoned as I got up off the bed and began pacing.

"They did not scream, no, that must have been the peacocks. And I did not say that the interlopers were human, Pet," he smiled dryly, "They were vampires, though not very powerful ones."

"Let me get this straight," I tried to shake the approaching drowsiness out of my head. "You are a "Master Vampire" whatever that means, right?"

He nodded silently, apparently now willing to let me ramble.

"So whoever sent these two vamps, or thugs, is either as powerful if not more powerful than you, or they are so desperate to get their hands on me that they'd risk pissing you off. Am I missing anything? Is that how you see it?" I asked, pausing in my pacing to face him.

"It is," he nodded again.

"So," I stifled a yawn, "It all comes back to the crux of the biscuit, doesn't it? I don't know what you want with me, but someone else does. And they want me too, right?"

"Cat," he smiled, looking down at my feet, "You are not wearing your brace or using your cane."

"Oh, that," I waved my hand dismissively, "The healing is evidently complete. I was about to find you and share that good news when I found stone boy outside my locked door."

Well aware of the fact that he had smoothly changed the subject, I returned to the bed somewhat crestfallen. I handed him my wine-glass and lay my head down on the pillow. I was still angry but perhaps even now more confused. There were so many scenarios playing out in my head, so many unknown elements clouding my thinking that nothing really sang true. Struggling to make sense of things, I murmured, "No time to ponder now," as I fell asleep.

Chapter 13

The dream landed me in near-total darkness. I leapt up abruptly, broke my constraints and threw off the wooden boards that hindered my escape. Tearing down long, dark, stone tunnels I pounded around corners and through arched doorways, heading for the outside. I did not pause to contemplate where I was or how I had come to be here. I was moving on instinct alone. Realizing that after several minutes of blind running I was not even winded, I continued till I found the heavy iron embellished wooden door. Without even pausing, I shoved my arms out ahead of me and shattered the door out of the way. I paused in the fresh air and looked about me. Dark clouds moved slowly across the night sky, momentarily revealing the moon then obscuring it again. I glanced back at the doorway, now devoid of a door, and wondered from what type structure I had escaped, for I truly felt that I had escaped something.

Sudden pain flared deep within me and my throat constricted and lips quivered. My mouth felt oddly disjointed, as if my teeth were too big. Instinct once more took over and I ran, blindly and as fast as I could, across open fields and down dirt paths. As I fell and tumbled down an earthen hill, I caught sight of a house, really nothing more than a hut. Lights burned in the windows. Though I didn't know why, I was drawn to those lights. I heard sheep and cattle lowing as I approached the place, quietly. I peered in through glassless windows to spy a woman rocking a baby in a cradle, as her man lit his pipe near the fireplace. Suddenly I burst through the door and, pinning the man's arm behind his back, I sank my teeth into his throat. The woman screamed as she stood, uncertain whether to escape or save her babe. I backhanded her and she fell into a pile against the far wall. I went to her and, picking her up like a limp doll, drove my teeth into her jugular vein. I drank and drank, but my thirst would not be sated. I dropped her empty body on the dirt floor and returned to the man. Though he was nearly dead, his blood still flowed. I clamped my mouth on his neck once more and swallowed all that I could get out of him. I discarded him as I had his wife. Looking around the room in a blind rage, I spied the infant still asleep in its cradle. Hardly a mouthful, I remember thinking, but it's better than nothing. The hunger was not lessening. In fact, it was growing. I approached the sleeping infant...

The sound of my heart beating wildly, my pulse racing, and my ears ringing woke me...or had I screamed? Sudden nausea grabbed me and I bolted from the bed and into the bathroom. I heaved over the white porcelain but nothing came up. I panted and quivered weakly, leaning on the toilet seat. After I caught my breath, I stood uncertainly and tiptoed across the cold marble floor to the sink. I noticed that this room too had been thoughtfully equipped with a mirror above the vanity. Running the cold water and filling my cupped hands, I was about to splash my face when I caught sight of my reflection in the mirror. I was pale, big circles under my eyes, hair a mess, but what caught my attention was my tears. They stood, in the corners of both eyes, in stark contrast to my skin. One tear trickled slowly down my cheek alongside my nose. It was blood.

I was dumbfounded. Touching one tear with my fingertip, I looked at it closely then lifted it to my lips. It tasted like blood, warm and salty and rich. "Where did that notion come from?" I thought, turning to look around the empty bathroom. Memories of my dream surfaced and I shuddered at the images that were, most likely, permanently etched there. Filling my hands again, I splashed water on my face and wiped and rubbed until the tears of blood were gone. Drying my face, I made my way into the bedroom and was turning out the light when I noticed that I was not alone. In front of the bedroom door stood, presumably, another of my bodyguards. He was about my height, maybe a little taller, so a little over six-foot and had hair so blonde that it was almost white. From the balance and subtlety of his features, I knew immediately that he too was a vampire. His eyes, large and lushly lashed, were the golden color of a cat's. He wore a brown leather jacket, white shirt, and jeans. Judging by the looks of his leather boots, he had money as well as taste.

"Who are you?" I croaked as I threw myself back on the bed.

"Winter," he answered not unkindly.

"Great, another conversationalist," I sneered as I tucked my head under the pillow. He probably wasn't going to be anymore interesting than Chimaera, and I figured the best thing that I could do was just avoid the both of them as much as I could.

Sometime later, Lily came in bringing bagels, cream cheese, fruit, juice, and coffee. She had remembered the Folger's.

"I take it that since this is breakfast, it's morning out there?" I smiled as she poured the juice and coffee.

"Well, let's just say that it's breakfast for you," she nodded, "not necessarily morning out there/"

"Damn it Lily, I think I'm losing my mind. What time of day is it?" I insisted.

"Bout nine o'clock in the evenin'," she smiled and patted my hand as you would someone you didn't want to get upset.

"Any idea what's happening around here?" I mumbled around a bite of bagel.

"Lots of bustlin' around. Mister Sin's been talking with Lucius out at the stables. We got all kinds of security standing around and getting in the way. Tell you the truth, Miss Cat, they make me nervous," she lowered her voice with this last admission.

"It's okay, Lily," I smiled and took a sip of the deliciously normal coffee, "they make me nervous too, standing around all serious and brooding. They seldom say anything. Let's face it, they're about as social as house plants."

We both laughed. I realized that it was probably an unkind thing to do, they were, after all, only doing their jobs. But that they couldn't be at least civil, I figured that was a vampire thing and I wanted them to know that I expected more.

When I had finished eating, I went into the bathroom to wash up and dress. After closing the door and turning the lock, I heard the door creak gently and knew that Winter had just leaned on the jamb. Damned annoying having someone follow your every step without saying a word. I stepped into a fresh pair of blue jeans and pulled a cotton tee shirt over my head. My face washed, hair combed and teeth brushed, I released the lock and turned the door-knob. Winter took two silent steps forward and turned to regard me as I exited the bathroom.

"You have no shoes," he observed, startling me with the unsolicited remark.

"I go nowhere," I retorted.

"My instructions are that you are to go nowhere unprotected," he offered.

"So I'm allowed to go out of this room?" I asked with renewed hope.

"As long as I am with you, to protect you," he nodded, "but you have no shoes."

"This is Louisiana in the summer, Winter, who needs shoes?" I took his arm and headed for the door, "Let's go for a walk."

We paused at the door long enough for him to unlock it then we stepped out into the silent hallway. I looked first one way then the other. Both views were identical to me.

"Which way?" I asked, hoping he knew where we were.

"Depends on where you wish to go." He smiled sweetly.

"Can you get me to the garden? Or better yet to the stables." I suggested.

"This way," he nodded to the right. Once more I took his arm and we set off at a leisurely pace. After a few moments walking on the marble floors with my feet bare, I was beginning to feel the cold. My toes wanted to curl up and I had to concentrate to keep myself from tiptoeing. Winter occasionally stole a glance at me and at my feet so I worked at not making a face that might give my discomfort away. We had been down two long halls and had taken two right turns. I expected to reach the parlor and the French doors to the garden at any moment. We kept going. I was not, apparently, where I thought I should be. Involuntarily, I drew in a sharp breath when we turned another corner, this time to the left, and came face to face with Arathia. Winter drew up short and we froze like deer in high-beams. From Winter's pained look, I realized that he had no more regard for her than I did. This guy was growing on me.

"Arathia," I nodded a greeting, "Lovely to see you."

"Cat," she purred, "and who is your friend, here?" She ran her fingers down the front of Winter's shirt. He looked stricken.

"This is Winter, one of the many bodyguards who now dog my every step and observe practically every breath. Sin is being overly protective," I added, "we're going for a walk."

"How nice," she murmured as she locked her eyes onto Winter's. Neither moved for a moment, but I sensed a challenge in that look

"It's been nice Arathia, but I have to be going. I'm sure I'll see you tomorrow, or tomorrow night," I smiled a false smile and nudged Winter forward.

Having stood still on that marble floor long enough for this social farce to unfold, my feet were now really turning blue. Winter shook his head, hair whipping one way then the other, and blinked as if to clear his mind. I detected what was almost a shudder. He glanced down, his expression now alert.

"Your feet are turning blue. I told you these floors were too cold," he declared.

"I'm fine," I lied, "Let's just keep moving."

With that almost imperceptible vampire speed, he turned, grabbed my arm, crouched, and came up under my ribs. He hoisted me over his shoulder into a fireman's lift.

"This is so not necessary," I giggled as my feet kicked gently, my thighs encircled in his powerful arms. My left foot bumped something solid near his waist, under his arm.

"Winter," I shook my head in disbelief, "are you packing heat? Armed? Packing a rod? Are you carrying a gun?"

"Hush," he swatted gently at the back of my calves, "Yes, I am armed and I'm not afraid to shoot you."

"Why would a vampire carry a gun? Can't you pretty much kill anyone with your teeth or your extraordinary strength and speed?" I teased.

"I have found that sometimes, it is more efficient to drop your adversary before he or she can get too close. Saves you from surprises, and saves on messy clean-ups," he explained as he continued our journey.

He let me gently down on the grass once we arrived in the garden. I straightened the bottom of my shirt and stretched my arms back until they snapped.

"What kind of weapon do you carry?" I asked. I had taken a course on firearms and gun safety and had learned how to shoot several years back when a serial rapist was running loose in Lake Charles. In truth, I had enjoyed it and had earned enough points at the range to be considered an expert marksman. "I carry a Les Baer 9mm," he answered, pulling back the right side of his jacket and removing the handgun from its holster. I noticed that he must be left-handed if he wore his gun under his right arm.

"Have you always been?" I looked at his gun hand inquiringly.

"What? Good with a gun?" he smiled.

"No," I answered sarcastically, "Left handed. How would I know if you're any good with a gun?"

"I managed to clear my holster without shooting myself or you," he offered brightly.

"Oh yeah," I laughed at his unusual vampire humor, "that's the criteria I use when choosing a bodyguard."

He laid the pistol gently on the palm of his right hand and turned it over for me to see. It was a beautiful piece. I lifted it and held it in the normal shooting position, left hand supporting the butt, right hand in the grip. The balance was incredible and, though it had some weight, it didn't feel unwieldy, just solid.

"You know weapons?" he raised his eyebrows.

"I know a little," I smiled cryptically. No man, or vampire for that matter, needs to know all a girl's secrets.

He returned the gun to its holster and we started across the garden on our way to the stables.

"And yes," he admitted, "I have always been left-handed."

The night was clear and breezy, and the circulation was returning to my feet. Lights glowed in the stables and as we approached I could hear horses gently chuffing and stamping their hooves in the dirt. A low, calm voice was soothing them.

"Lucius?" I called softly as we entered, the smell of warm hay, dirt, and horses tickling my nose.

"Miss Cat," Lucius appeared from behind a stall door and smiled broadly, extending his large bearpaw of a hand to me. I beamed back at him and shook his hand in genuine pleasure.

"Good to see you, Lucius. Thought I'd come down here and meet your friends," I nodded at one of the horses poking its nose out of its stall.

"My, my, you do heal fast, Ma'am," he shook his head slowly, "Thought you'd be out of commission for several more weeks."

"I am a quick healer, and I had a great doctor. Who's this?" I patted the nose of a tall leggy-looking rich brown mare, eager to change the subject.

"That's Bella," he answered, "Or Belladonna to be more proper. She's a beauty of an Andalusian, great racing stock, hell of a jumper. Mr. Sin's never raced her, though I don't know why. She's got a little temper. Miss Arathia has ridden her a few times, I believe."

"That would explain her bad temper," I chuckled under my breath.

He moved on to the next stall, "This is Abraxis. He's the master's favorite, a Frieslander stallion." He patted the horse's nose. "They have a very old and distinctive bloodline. I've never seen Mr. Sin ride, but I have come out here occasionally to find Abraxis winded and sweating, still saddled and foaming at the bit," he smiled at the huge horse standing quietly in the straw. It was jet black with huge black eyes and a massive thick mane that lay down its neck and on its forehead. I touched its nose and it looked at me impassively, not moving.

"Okay, it's clear that Abraxis doesn't like me," I turned and clapped my hands together, "who else do we have?"

"This big buckskin is Shiloh," he pointed to the next stall, "past him we have Nightshade, he's Belladonna's brother." He walked to the other side of the stable and spread his arms, "And over here, we have Avalon, a gorgeous appaloosa, Fox, which is short for Foxglove, and Daedalus. These three are newcomers to the stable. The boss just acquired them a few weeks ago. They seem to be fine horses though. Mr. Sin has an eye for horseflesh. If you were to want to ride, Miss Cat, I'd recommend Shiloh or Avalon. They're both even-tempered with great speed, and they'll give you all they got."

"I'll keep that in mind if I ever get the opportunity," I smiled as I went from one stall to the other. They were all beautiful creatures, though of course, Abraxis was the most magnificent of them. That was only right and proper, I supposed. "As you can see," I nodded at Winter, "after last night's excitement I don't think I'll be allowed far from the house."

"Yes, Ma'am," he agreed quickly, "best to keep you safe. But when you are ready, we'll be here."

I wondered idly if Lily and Lucius knew that I had not come to this estate of my own free will, that I had in essence, already been kidnapped.

By the time Winter and I returned to the house, my feet were both dusty and damp from the stable floor and the dewy grass. I stepped into the parlor and walked brazenly across those beautiful Persian rugs with my filthy feet. Lily came in directly with, of all things, a cheeseburger, fries and a beer. It felt absolutely decadent to be eating such common fare in such exquisite surroundings. Winter stood silently behind the sofa with his back turned to me. Perhaps my eating stirred his hunger too, so I didn't bring up the subject.

I was beginning to learn a few things about vampires. I ate with hands still dusty from petting the horses and I really didn't care. Funny how freeing it is to know that you're probably not long for this world. Why wash your hands if you could die tonight? What's a little bacteria, a few germs?

I finished my meal and emptied the bottle of beer just as Lily came in to clear the dishes.

"Lily, I think I'll go back to my room. Or whatever room I've been in today," I amended, "Would you bring me another beer? And, what the hell, see if you can scrounge me up a pack of cigarettes." I had quit smoking years ago, but felt a sudden whim to try it again. No point in worrying about my health.

"Yes Ma'am, Miss Cat," she beamed a smile at me, "I think you're getting the hang of this place."

"Ain't it the truth," I drawled as I nodded at Winter and left the parlor. Though he moved silently, I knew that he followed me.

"No point in putting this off," he said as he came up behind me and hoisted me across his shoulder. Carrying me once more, he set off down the long hallways at a brisk pace.

He took me not only to the bedroom, but through it and into the bathroom beyond. He put me down rather unceremoniously and pointed at my feet.

"Bath," he commanded sternly.

"Yes, Sir," I nodded and threw him a mock salute. I was really beginning to like this guy. At least he was way ahead of Chimaera in the personality department.

I turned on the faucets over the tub, mostly hot water. This tub wasn't quite as ornate as the one in the blue room where I had previously stayed, but it was an oversized claw footed antique and it did possess more personality than the garden tub. I poured in a couple of caps full of bubble bath and stood, flicking soapsuds off of my fingers. I looked up to find Winter standing just inside the bathroom, leaning on the doorjamb. I had expected him to make an exit while I was busy, but here he still was.

"Are you planning on staying there?" I allowed the surprise to be heard in my voice.

He said nothing, only turned to look at me soberly and nodded.

"Okay, suit yourself," I quipped, "But I must insist that at least you turn your back while I undress and get into the tub."

Once more he said nothing, but he did turn to face the door. I peeled off my jeans, tee shirt and panties and stepped quickly into the tub, sinking in the bubbles up to my chin.

"Okay, you can turn back around, I'm covered. At least until the bubbles burst, that is," I added. "What's going on Winter? I can tell something's up."

"I have an uneasy feeling," he answered simply and quickly, as if he couldn't talk for listening. He closed his eyes and crossed his hands in front of him, squaring his shoulders and spreading his feet in that familiar "bodyguard" stance. I could see the tension in his body, suddenly I was becoming uneasy.

Trying to settle back and relax, I closed my eyes and let out a sigh when the door opened and Lily came in with a tray bearing a bottle of beer and a glass. She also had a pack of cigarettes, lighter and ashtray. She sat it down on the vanity.

"You want the bottle or a glass?" she turned with the beer in her hand.

"Bottle's fine, Lily, Thank you,"

"You don't have a table in here so I guess if you want to set it down you'll have to put it on the floor," she glanced at Winter, "Or you can hand it to him."

"No problem, Lily, and thanks for the cigarettes. I think I'll have one later after I dry off," I grinned.

"You let me know if you need anything else," she nodded as she left the bath, tray in hand.

I leaned back and took a long swallow of cold beer. The bath water was hot enough that I was turning red and my forehead was perspiring. I touched the cold bottle to my face. It nearly took my breath away.

Suddenly the door flew open again and in came Arathia in a swirl of red chiffon. Her black hair flew about her shoulders and her eyes sparkled in amusement.

"My my, Cher, you do surprise me," she smiled and glanced at Winter. "I know you said that you prefer men in your bath, but I never expected this."

"Knock it off, Arathia," I refused to take her bait. "You know he's a guard. And what are you doing here?"

"I just wanted to check in on you and see if you were well," she said as she leaned on the edge of the tub, "and to see if you wished to work on your training before the sunrise. Your friend here would have to leave, of course."

I looked at Winter, who stood solidly still and would neither look at Arathia nor acknowledge her comment. His eyes met mine. I read something disturbing in that look.

"To tell you the truth, I am a little tired," I admitted and yawned for proof, "I think I'll just finish my bath and my beer and go to bed. I haven't seen Sin tonight so he must be busy with something else. Guess he'll have to see me tomorrow night."

"Very well," she said as she stood, "we'll work tomorrow then. I'll let you sleep and then send Lily to wake you by, say, 4'oclock. That will give us girls a chance to chat before the boys," she nodded at Winter, " wake up."

"Suit yourself," I smiled and took another swig of beer. Her referring to the two of us as "us girls" made me want to change my gender and possibly my species. She made my skin crawl. I couldn't understand why Sin would befriend her, if they were indeed friends. Whatever else they might be or might have been, I didn't want to consider.

When she left I sighed, and felt suddenly calm. Winter turned and stepped out of the room, quietly closing the door behind him. It occurred to me, before the beer and hot water completely fogged my mind, that Winter would only leave me after Arathia had come and gone. Perhaps he sensed that she was dangerous, too.

Setting my empty beer bottle down on the floor, I pulled the plug on the tub and stepped out to dry. I pulled on panties and a camisole and threw my robe over my shoulders. As I was leaving the room, I remembered the smokes and rescued them from the moisture of the steam-filled room.

Winter was leaning with his back against the bedroom door when I came out of the bath. He looked decidedly more relaxed.

"Night, Winter," I murmured as I tossed the robe across the end of the bed and put the cigarettes and ashtray on the bedside table. Though I turned off the table lamps, soft electric flames still danced in the wall sconces so we weren't thrown into complete darkness.

"Night, Cat," he answered and went back to his silent vigil.

Stretching out under the crisp sheets, I lay my head back on the pillow. It was an odd feeling knowing that Winter was standing silently across the room while I was trying to fall asleep. I was keenly aware of my own breathing, and hoping that I didn't snore. I listened to the moments ticking by in my head. The silence was deafening. Finally, I rolled over onto my stomach and buried my head under the pillow.

Chapter 14

Gusts of wind pushed me down that hallway in my dream. Once more, most of the doors on either side of the corridor were closed to me. As I moved along clumsily, the door to my immediate left banged open and through it I tumbled. On the other side of the door all was calm, the wind suddenly still. Kneeling on the floor, I waited with my head bowed until I received the order to look up. When it finally came, I witnessed a figure swathed in sheer raiments of gold and silver being escorted into the room by two brown-robed priests. This being, this Oracle, for I could not determine if it was male or female, was seated ceremoniously on a large heavy-looking chair of dark carved wood. It would surely have been considered a throne, for its back was unusually high, save its lack of decoration. I kneeled in silence as the priests disappeared.

"I have seen," a voice spoke clearly, "the means of your salvation." The sound was so even and so unemotional that it did not give away the gender of the speaker. Knowing that I was not to speak, I remained still.

"One will come, a mortal touched by magic," the voice intoned. "You shall know it the moment she is born and you shall always be aware of her. It is her Life's Blood that will allow you to walk in the daylight. You will no longer need to sleep on your native soil. Her blood will satisfy you, that you need never feed on human blood again. You will find this mortal and obtain her Life's Blood. Bring it to me for I must bless it to fulfill the prophecy. Once it is blessed, you will drink and your curse will be lifted. You will still be Vampire, still immortal, yet free of the constraints of your species."

"You have the wages of my sight?" the voice continued.

I nodded and set about putting my offerings on the floor at the Oracle's feet. Fruit, twigs, feathers, stones, coins, and bones formed a rough circle and I placed a drop of my own vampire blood in the center. Looking up, I noticed the Oracle cock its head to one side in an almost bird-like movement. Were my offerings not enough? These were what I had been instructed to bring. The Oracle stood and stretched an arm out toward me.

"Your hand," it commanded.

Still kneeling, I stretched my arm out and reached my hand as far as I could. The Oracle's touch was hot. Through the shimmering raiments, it bit my finger and drew my blood gently into its mouth. Nodding, the Oracle seemed to be satisfied and turned to go.

"Do not forget," it added, "She alone is the vessel of your salvation. Protect her. Let no harm befall her. Her magic will be the one thing in this world that will save you."

I sat up straight in bed, fully awake, with the echo of those words bouncing around in my head. The implications of this dream, this memory of Sin's, were staggering, but I was too overwhelmed to consider them at the moment. Looking around the still semi-dark room, I realized that I was alone. Winter was gone. I had no idea what time it was, my fault that I hadn't requested a wristwatch with a.m. /p.m. indicator when Lily asked if I needed anything else. Turning on the bedside lamp, I pulled a cigarette out of the pack and lit it. Marlboro Lights, wouldn't have been my first choice but they weren't bad. I drew in the smoke and held it a moment, bringing back memories. Propping the pillow behind me, I leaned back and sat there smoking, my mind reeling. Amon had told me that he had known the moment I was born, that he had heard the music of my soul, or something like that. So, it was all finally coming clear. It was my Life's Blood that Amon was after, to cure him of his vampire curse.

"Man, oh, man," I chuckled softly to the empty room, "Anne Rice would never have come up with something as lame as this. Note to self," I added, one of the foibles of living alone is that you talk to yourself, "find out, surreptitiously if possible, what the hell 'Life's Blood' means. Sounds so not good, especially for little old me." Instinctively I knew that I should not admit to Amon, or anyone else for that matter, that I knew about the prophecy until I understood its meaning more fully, as I feared I might be hastening my own demise if I tipped my hand too early. Apparently, my sense of self-preservation was not only making itself known, but was honing itself to a fine razor's edge. I liked that thought.

I had just stubbed my cigarette butt out in the ashtray when the door burst open and a large swarthy complected man stood in the doorway with a look of surprise on his face. He wore a black tee shirt tucked into black pleated trousers that were cinched at the waist with a belt bearing a brushed black metal buckle. His shoulder-length coarse black hair hung loose on the sides and was drawn back on top, hanging in a ponytail down the back of his head. He smiled broadly exposing a dazzling set of perfectly straight white teeth.

"I'm sorry," he shrugged, "I smelled smoke."

"Indeed you did, Reverend Davis," I nodded, "And you are?"

"Oh, uh, they call me Bear, Ma'am," he stammered, "Reverend Davis? "

"Don't mind me, Bear," I shook my head, "I'm just being a smartass. Up until about five minutes ago I hadn't had a cigarette in almost twenty years. Thought it was time to jump off the wagon. Anyway, I take it you're the daytime shift. Any idea what time it is?"

He looked at the watch on his wrist. It was a dark fabric band with a matte finish face. "Looks like nearly 2 o'clock, Ma'am."

I nodded at the watch, "Military?"

He flashed that brilliant smile, "Ex-marine, Ma'am."

"Bear," I grinned, "I know that here in the south it's a sign of respect to address a woman as Ma'am, but you keep doing that and I'm going to spend all my time looking over my shoulder for someone's mother. My name is Cat, please."

"Sure, Cat," he seemed a little more at ease, "Lily said she wasn't to wake you until 4 o'clock so I didn't expect you to be awake and, well, and smoking. Mind if I ask? Why did you jump off the wagon after so long?"

"Nothing to lose, Bear," I smiled sadly, "nothing to lose."

He looked at me curiously for a moment then, seemingly accepting my explanation, nodded and straightened his shoulders. He turned toward the door, looked back as if to say something, and then shook his head.

"I'll be just outside if you need me," he started to say Ma'am, then recovered, "Cat."

Nearly 2 o'clock, I thought and Arathia would be darkening my door sometime around four. I was trying to find an excuse or somewhere else to be when Lily came in carrying a tray of food with a few paperback novels tucked under one smoothly dark arm. She wore a crisp white wrap skirt and matching top and had her hair hidden in a white twisted scarf. She looked marvelously fresh and bright, like she had just blown in from Jamaica or Barbados.

"Hungry, Miss Cat?" she stopped beside the bed to observe me.

"Yes, I am. Oh, Lily," I had a sudden idea, "Could you have Lucius saddle a horse for me? I think I need to go for a ride today."

"Mr. Sin okay that, did he?" she smiled conspiratorially as she began pouring coffee and setting out plates of shrimp, rice, and biscuits.

I jumped out of bed and pulled on my robe. Snatching a shrimp off the plate with my fingers, I took a bite and smiled at the familiar Cajun spice. Lily shoved a napkin at me as I flopped down in the chair and threw one leg over the arm.

"Not specifically, no," I paused and looked up at her, "but according to Winter I can't go anywhere unprotected. As long as I can get Bear to go with me..."

"You lookin' to get yourself or one of us in trouble?" she looked at me pointedly.

"Between you and me, Lily," I leaned forward and lowered my voice, "I'm looking for a way to avoid Arathia. She's planning on coming around 4 o'clock so," I made quotation marks in the air with my fingers, "we girls can talk before the boys wake up."

"My God in heaven," she waved her hands in the air, "She actually said that?"

"She did," I laughed, as I shoveled a fork full of rice into my mouth. Another shrimp followed it. Suddenly I realized that I was ravenous. Wherever it had been hiding, my appetite had returned with a vengeance.

"I'll tell you what, you get Bear to agree to this scheme, Lucy, and I'll see what I can do," she nodded as she turned to leave.

"Thanks, Ethel," I laughed as I took another bite of the delicious fare. Nice to find someone whose cultural references were the same as my own. "And ask Bear to step in here, if you wouldn't mind," I added.

She gave me one last look of exasperation as she left the room. Now, if I could only convince my bodyguard without having to lie to his face. One of my weaknesses, I was more than capable of fabricating a story if necessary, but I simply never had been able to lie to anyone to their face. My guilt always gave me away and I assumed that a man trained by the military and working as a bodyguard was sure to detect any attempt at prevarication or even subterfuge.

Looking up from my meal, I smiled and swallowed as Bear stepped into the room.

"You wanted to see me?"

"I did," I nodded and downed the last bite of shrimp. "Tell me, Bear, do you ride?"

"Ride Ma'am? Uh, Cat?" he asked, confused.

"Ride, Bear, horses," I clarified, "do you ride horses?"

"Oh," he smiled broadly, "Yes, Cat, I ride. Sort of born to it, if you know what I mean."

I had no idea what he meant, but I was willing to let that go for the moment since I had gotten the answer I was searching for. "I'm going to have Lucius saddle a couple of horses for us and we are going for a ride," I announced, as I stood to begin dressing.

He looked at me dubiously.

"What? Did Mr. Sin specifically forbid it? Did he say that I was not allowed to ride?" I challenged, recalling Lily's objections.

"Well, no," he shook his head slowly as he considered this, "he didn't specifically instruct me to not allow you to ride, but then he didn't even mention that it might be a possibility."

"Trust me when I tell you, he knows me so well that I'm sure he must have assumed that at one time or another I would insist on going riding. He probably just didn't think to mention it to you. Anyway, Winter said I could go wherever I wanted as long as I was protected. If you'll go with me I'll be protected," I explained and, though it might not have been the complete truth, it wasn't an outright lie.

He seemed satisfied with my reasoning and, nodding, said, "Okay, I'll take you. Do you want me to go to the stables and talk to Lucius while you're getting ready?"

"That would be great," I smiled coyly, hating myself for it, "I'll be ready in twenty minutes. Come back and get me?" I hated acting like a girly-girl, but sometimes it's what the situation calls for, so you do it.

"Yes Ma'am," he smiled at his gaff, "I mean yes Cat. Uh, could I call you Miss Cat? It just seems more comfortable for me. You know, bein' a southern boy?"

111

"Well, okay, though only because you're a southern boy, Bear. You can call me Miss Cat if it's more comfortable for you," I agreed, even though it made me feel like a schoolmarm. Obviously he wasn't getting the hang of calling me by my first name, anyway.

He left and I set about getting dressed and getting out of there before the wicked witch of the west showed up, or was it east? I wriggled into a pair of jeans and grabbed a white cotton blouse out of the closet. Shoving my arms through the sleeves, I was buttoning the front of the shirt even as I was tucking it into the waist of my jeans. I grabbed a pair of white socks and was pulling them on as I walked around the room looking for a pair of shoes. Finally, under the bedskirt, I found a pair of tennis shoes, my size, and pulled them on without untying them. My panic to get out of this room was mounting. Sprinting across the floor to the bathroom, I grabbed a brush and ran it through my hair. I raked it into a ponytail and secured it with a scrunci. After brushing my teeth, I ran a washcloth across my face, tossed it in the sink, and ran for the door. Remembering the heat and the sun, I grabbed my sunglasses and a bandana off the dresser. Without a cowboy hat this was the best I could do. I opened the door and stepped out into the hallway, apparently the door wasn't locked during the daytime or Bear had inadvertently left it that way when he left. Somehow I didn't think men like Bear made mistakes like that so it probably was unlocked during the day. After a moment I heard footsteps and was relieved when Bear appeared from around the corner, smile on his face and cowboy hat in his hand.

"Let's go," I commanded, grabbing his arm and pulling him back the way from which he'd come.

Once we were away from that room, I began to relax, knowing that my plan was going to be a success.

Chapter 15

When we arrived at the stables, Lucius was waiting, holding the reins of Shiloh, I think it was, and another great gray horse. He shot me a questioning look. I raised both hands and shook my head, "Don't give me that look, Lucius. We're going for a ride." He didn't say a word, only handed the appaloosa's reins to Bear and turned to help me mount my horse.

"This is Shiloh," he said as I hoisted myself into the buckskin's saddle, "He's a gentleman, knows how to behave himself." He handed me the reins and patted the horse on the rump as I turned him around. "You two be careful," he called as I gave Shiloh a gentle kick and he took off across the field. Looking back, I saw Bear spur Avalon forward as he raced to catch up.

As Bear rode up beside me I glanced over at him. He had put on his cowboy hat and when he looked at me and smiled I realized what he had meant when he said that he was born to horseback riding. Seeing him in this situation, in these surroundings, it was obvious. The man was at least part, if not all, Native American. Amazing, after all the political correctness of the world these days, I didn't even consider calling him an Indian, though I'm sure twenty years ago that was the term that would have come to mind. I smiled and nodded and kicked Shiloh in the haunches to outrun Avalon. Though he was certainly a beautiful and spirited horse, Shiloh simply didn't have the desire or the temperament of Avalon and the appaloosa outdistanced us without even breaking a sweat.

"Okay, Okay," I called as I reined in my mount, "I give up. Uncle. Unconditional surrender, and all that."

Bear slowed his mount and turned him to trot back to us. "Thought you'd lose us, huh?" he asked as he drew up beside me. Avalon snorted and danced nervously.

"Nah," I smiled, "Just giving you a run for your money."

He nodded and pointed toward the horizon, "There's a forest just over that rise, should be cooler in there and I think there's even a little stream where the horses can drink"

We started at a leisurely pace towards the woods. I was marveling at the landscape, the fields, hills, and small hollows. I had always considered Louisiana to be a rather flat state, but I thought I might now have to change that notion, unless...

"Bear," I said abruptly, "Do you know where we are? I don't mean where we are right now, I mean where the estate is geographically. This doesn't look like any part of Louisiana that I've ever been to."

His face suddenly turned to stone. My query was obviously a forbidden one. He regarded me silently.

"Never mind," I brushed the question aside, "it doesn't really matter, just curious."

"I'm sorry," he finally said at length, "I was told not to discuss such matters with you."

"Doesn't that make you curious," I prodded, "why something like that would be forbidden?"

"I'm paid to not consider such things, Miss Cat," he answered soberly as we crested the gentle slope and started for the shade of the forest.

The woods were alive with noise, which stopped instantly as we entered. I took the lead, letting Shiloh pick his way through the trees, and Bear followed, always keeping me in sight. After a while the noise of the forest resumed, having accepted our intrusion. Birds screamed, insects chirruped, and small-unseen creatures scurried about in the leaves and sticks carpeting the forest floor. In the distance, I could faintly make out the sound of water, babbling and gurgling. I nudged Shiloh in that general direction and looked up at the canopy of trees. The bright blue afternoon sky stood in stark contrast to the cool almost black green of the foliage.

I was just thinking that this looked like a forest from a fairy tale, when Bear called out at the same instant Shiloh rose on his hind legs. Leaning forward I tried to hold on as I realized what had startled him. Someone had intentionally stepped suddenly out from cover and was still standing in front of the horse, now beneath him I assumed, almost sickening at the thought. Shiloh's hooves came down forcefully and he danced up and down in alarm. I caught sight of Bear bounding from Avalon's saddle and tearing off through the trees after someone dressed in black. As Shiloh's panic piqued, he reared again, and I toppled from his back, my hip and elbow taking the brunt of the impact. I heard footsteps crashing toward me and just made it to my feet when I saw a man dressed from head to toe in dark clothes, wearing black face paint, gloves, and a black cap. He was racing at me and drawing his weapon at the same time. It gave me one moment to grab a fallen branch that had been lying nearby. As he neared me, I pulled the branch free and, with one smooth move, swung for the bleachers. The impact caught him just under the chin and, with every ounce of strength and a bit extra from the adrenaline I was pumping, my follow through lifted him off of his feet and tossed him backwards. He landed several feet away with a painful and satisfying "Hrumph." Letting the branch hang at my side, I stumbled around in the leaves looking for any sign of Bear or the horses. I was just starting to feel pretty proud of myself, noticing that my assailant was not moving, when a loud thunk reverberated behind me. Blinding pain blossomed in my head and my vision was suddenly filled with bright splotches of color. Falling forward I lost consciousness.

When I came to I tried to open my eyes but they didn't seem to want to move. Someone was gently patting my cheeks and talking to me but I couldn't understand what was being said. I finally managed to open my left eye a little, though the right one still refused to open, and squinted against the bright daylight above me.

"Miss Cat," Bear was calling as he tried to rouse me. My hearing had returned once my ears stopped ringing. I raised my right arm and wiped at my right eye with the back of my hand. A tacky substance had seemingly glued my right eye shut. I inspected the back of my hand and was surprised to find it smeared with blood.

"Who's bleeding," I croaked as I struggled to get up. Pain shoved me back to the ground with a whimper.

"You are, Miss Cat, looks like you've got a cut near your temple. Scalp wounds bleed a lot," he added as he brushed my hair out of my eyes. "As bad as that is, I think you might have a concussion. You've got a pretty good-sized knot on the back of your head. I was behind the guy that whacked you by maybe two steps, but he got to you first. I'm so sorry."

I tried to make sense out of what he was saying, but it hurt too much to think. Suddenly, nausea clutched at my stomach and I rolled onto my side and threw up. When the nausea had passed, I rolled back toward Bear and looked at him levelly.

"Do you think you can move?" he asked.

I tried to think of the appropriate answer, but one wouldn't come to mind. I took his right hand in mine and placed it on the back of my neck. Putting my right hand in his left, I whispered, "Gently lift."

He seemed to understand and slowly lifted my head and back, supporting me with his hand. I screamed suddenly when my head felt as if it had exploded and I cried, "No, no, put me down, put me down."

Lowering me gently back to the ground, Bear stood and straightened. He put two fingers to his lips and whistled loudly. Almost instantly I heard the sound of hooves. Bridles jingling brightly, Shiloh and Avalon both trotted into the clearing. Bear tethered Avalon to a tree then turned and gave Shiloh a sharp whack on the rump. He whinnied and took off at a gallop.

"Why did you do that?" I groaned, as I struggled to understand.

"He'll go back to the stables," he answered as he squatted down beside me, "Lucius will find him, figure something's wrong, and come looking for us."

"Bad guys?" I whispered, looking around but not daring to move my head. "Gone?"

"I got one," he smiled grimly, "One got away, and the one you took down is lying over there in a heap."

"Dead?" I murmured weakly.

"Don't know, I haven't checked," he admitted, "as long as he wasn't moving I didn't care."

"Check for me, please," I moaned, squeezing his hand to plead my case.

"Okay, I'll check. You don't move," he added as he stood and moved away. I heard his footsteps muffled by the leaves, then silence. Footsteps again, then he was kneeling beside me, looking into my eyes. I read the expression in those eyes. The man I had hit was dead and I was a killer. I knew that I should feel bad about this, but I couldn't. There was simply just no regret in me at the moment. Maybe sometime in the future I'd have to deal with this, but not now. I closed my eyes and a tear rolled down the side of my face. The tears weren't for the dead man, they were for me. The pain in my head was pounding, keeping time with my heartbeat and pulse.

"You'll be okay," Bear murmured, "I'll get you out of here soon."

"When is sunset?" I breathed roughly. Pain was radiating down the back of my head, my neck and into my shoulders and back.

He looked at his watch, "An hour, maybe two."

The idea of lying out here in the woods with my brains possibly leaking out of my ears stirred what little resolve I had. I took Bear's hand in mine again and looked at him beseechingly.

"Try again," I managed to get out.

He once more placed his hand on the nape of my neck, this time moving it slightly higher on the base of my skull, and lifted. My vision swam, the pain reasserted itself, but I managed to grit my teeth and hold my breath until I was sitting upright. I took a couple of deep breaths and slowly released them.

"Should I let go?" Bear asked.

"Not for a minute," I answered quietly, letting my brain readjust to its new position. I continued breathing slowly and calmly and, after a few minutes, could open my eyes without dizziness. The pain was still there, but it had lessened a bit. I was afraid to turn my head or move, but at least I could maintain this position.

"Okay," I smiled weakly, "You can let go now."

He looked relieved when he moved his hand away and my head didn't tilt at a hideously violent angle or pop off and roll away. Standing to look around, he went to Avalon's saddlebag and withdrew a bottle of water. He offered it to me.

"It's not too cold, but it's wet," he smiled

"Not just now," I groaned as I tried to move my legs and body into a more comfortable position without moving my head. "Just give me a minute to think," I added, holding up one finger and closing my eyes.

Through the pain in my head I tried to summon the image of Amon. I envisioned his dark glistening eyes, his sensual lips, his beautiful silver hair. "Amon," I called weakly with my mind.

"Cat," his powerful voice rippled through me like a breeze. I felt his power touch me like a warm hand on my heart. The pain in my head receded. "I will come for you," his melodious words calmed me.

I opened my eyes. Bear was pacing back and forth in front of me. Worry was etched across his face.

"Clouds are moving in," he nodded towards the edge of the woods, "I think it's going to storm. Sky is turning black as night. I'm not sure how things could get any worse."

117

"You know that you should never make such comments," I answered, "You're just inviting the Gods to show you how things can indeed get worse. Look, I'm okay for now. Why don't you take Avalon and go for help?"

"No," he shook his head, "No way am I leaving you out here by yourself in your condition. No, we'll stay put and Lucius will be here with help anytime now."

Bear was right. The sky was growing darker by the minute. I watched the colors of the day change as he continued to wear a rut pacing the forest floor. The haunting calls of the night birds replaced those louder, more abrasive screams of their daytime counterparts. From a distance we could finally hear the sound of horses' hooves, and the sound was growing louder.

"In here," Bear called to the distant riders.

The sound of the approaching horses was like thunder through the trees. Unlike Avalon and Shiloh, these steeds were not picking their way gently between the trees. These were bounding through the woods at us at a full gallop.

I unwisely raised my head up to see Lucius, Winter, and Chimaera rein their mounts to a halt in the clearing. Winter leapt from the saddle and was kneeling before me in a heartbeat. Chimaera was engaging Bear in what looked like a rather heated discussion, with much gesticulating and head shaking. Lucius was gathering Avalon's reins. Finally, I heard Chimaera give Bear an order, "You will return to the estate with Lucius. He'll take care of Avalon. Winter and I will see to Miss Cat. You will go home and report to the house tomorrow for debriefing. Is that clear?" Finally, Lucius and Bear mounted their horses and rode quickly out of the clearing.

"Cat, what happened?" Winter asked with eyes full of concern.

"We were attacked by three men," I pointed across the clearing. "Bear took down one, one escaped, and I," I closed my eyes, "I took out the other."

He smiled and stood up. "Chimaera," he called, "Little Sister's one of us now."

"One of us?" Chimaera asked, as he strode across the clearing to the body of one of my assailants.

"She took out that guy over there. She's a killer, just like us."

"Knock it off, Winter," I snarled, "I'm not up to it right now."

"Oh, sorry," he grinned. "Just kidding. How are you?'

"Not good," I grimaced, wiping fresh blood from my temple.

"Give me your hands," he said extending his hands down to me.

"You've got to be kidding," I croaked in disbelief, "I can't stand up."

"I'll help you," he added, "and it will only be for an instant."

I took both his hands in mine and he pulled me to my feet. The world swam and the bright colors returned for a moment, then strong powerful arms were holding me and Amon was breathing into my mouth, kissing me. The silk of his shirt felt like a cool breeze surrounding my hands as I encircled his waist and touched his strong back. I felt his power enter me, and my power weakly twined around his. As I lay my aching head against his chest, we rose gently skyward and I closed my eyes in relief. I was safe and in the arms of the man I loved. In the dark recesses of my mind, that little tiny voice screamed, "Arms of the man I love, my ass! How about the arms of the man that will someday take my life and possibly my very soul?"

Chapter 16

I realized that I was awake when I heard myself whine, "I'm cold." My eyes fluttered open to find that Amon was lying beside me, looking down at me with worry in his eyes. When I reached up to touch my wound, I found that he was holding an ice pack against the back of my head, supporting me with his hand.

"How long have you been this way?" I smiled weakly at him.

"A while," he admitted. "How do you feel?"

"Cold," I answered, pulling his hand and the ice pack away. The throbbing resumed almost immediately, faded, then disappeared completely. "Isn't that numb?" I nodded at his hand, which had a decidedly blue pallor.

"We do not feel the cold," he answered as he laid the ice pack on the nightstand and turned back to face me. "If I were not so incredibly relieved to have you back and in close to one piece, I would be very angry with you."

"Really?" I smiled mischievously, "would I be punished?"

"Undoubtedly," his lips curled into a smile, though his eyes remained serious. "Your punishment would be," he hesitated, "exquisite."

"I'd probably deserve it, too," I murmured breathlessly, my pain forgotten. His beauty, I realized was surprisingly intoxicating, taking my mind places it had no business going.

He suddenly leaned down and put his lips on mine. His mouth tasted and licked mine, his teeth nibbling my lips, one at a time. He wrapped his hand gently around the back of my neck and held me tightly in his caress. His hand vibrated with heat. For a moment I felt trapped, panicked, then my power rose and my body writhed with the passion and delight of his touch. My head no longer ached.

"Do not ever," he whispered into my mouth, "ever do such a foolish thing again."

Kissing him slowly and deeply, I paused and looked up into those shimmering black eyes.

"I'll try not to," I murmured, as I moved my mouth to the side of his neck and planted delicate, moist kisses along his throat.

"Do you think this is wise, Pet?" Amon pulled away and looked me in the eye. "You have a head injury, possibly a concussion."

"Wise?" I grinned, "Well, if I throw up or lose consciousness on you we'll know this was a mistake, but I feel fine."

Unbuttoning his shirt and following that progress with my mouth, I kissed slowly down the length of his chest, pausing to tongue lazy circles on his washboard abs. He hooked one finger beneath my chin and lifted my face to his. He shook his head.

"Tsk, tsk, tsk, Kitty Cat," he chided, "no, no. Tonight, at least, you should lie still. Doctor's orders."

I pouted, pursing out my bottom lip, and he kissed me and pushed me onto my back. "Stay still," he commanded as he began unbuttoning my blouse, slowly. He nuzzled my neck, my chest, down my ribs, and the tender flesh on the inside of my arms as he removed my blouse. Lifting me slightly, he pulled the garment from behind my back and tossed it towards the end of the bed. He ran one finger beneath the bra strap on my shoulder and I shivered. Kissing my shoulder, he slowly lowered the strap and pulled down the cup of my bra. My nipples, hard as pencil erasers, ached for his touch. He traced invisible designs on my breasts with his fingertips, but was obviously delighting in denying me his mouth. I looked up at him with a mixture of desire, anger, and determination, and he nodded and smiled.

"My punishment is," he grinned wickedly, "severe."

"If you don't make mad passionate love to me right this minute, I swear I'll run a stake through your heart," I hissed.

His laugh was deep and rich, his amusement at my frustration genuine. Finally he placed his lips on my nipple and sucked gently. I sighed and wriggled beneath him.

"More," I demanded, laughing in delight. He obliged.

He ripped the remainder of my bra to pieces with his fingernails and flung the fragments into the air. Rising onto his knees, he unsnapped and unzipped my jeans and pulled them down my legs. Then he ran one fingertip beneath the edge of my panties and my abdomen quivered at the sensations. Slowly, he pulled my panties down my hips, pausing to kiss my navel and just below it. He ran his strong hands down the front of my thighs as he tugged the fabric

121

further down to my knees, my calves, the finally over my feet. He held my panties up with one finger and smiled down at me. Wadding them in his hand, he drew the panties to his nose and inhaled deeply.

"I love your scent," he breathed huskily.

"Shut up," I snapped, grabbing his face between my hands and bringing his mouth down to mine. Suddenly my power flared and electricity coursed through my veins. Any residual pain vanished, leaving only the intense yearning to be with Amon, inside him, a part of him. I pulled him roughly on top of me and opened myself for him, encircling his waist with my legs. His power rose and he inserted himself deeply within me. The air crackled with static and sparks as we set a frenzied and frantic rhythm. My magic and my hips rose to meet his thrusts. Every fiber of my being was vibrating with passion and with power. When I could hold on no longer, he thrust so deeply into me that I thought my body would split, but it didn't. It opened anew and he and his power reached a place in me I didn't know existed. For an instant, the briefest of moments, I found myself looking down into the emerald green eyes of a blonde mortal woman beneath me. Concern, lust, anger, and a deep resentment over the hold she had on me swarmed in my heart and in my head. Regret that my future would eclipse hers crossed my mind. Blinking, the moment passed, I looked up once more into those wonderfully black eyes as a force so powerful, so intoxicating, rolled over me and we climaxed at the same moment. The lights flickering in the wall sconces dimmed as lightening lit the night skies. Thunder echoed beyond the walls of the estate. Amon collapsed on top of me, panting, resting his head on my chest. I lay there quivering, muscles still rippling, stroking his hair and running my fingers down his arm. He started to rise and I stopped him.

"No," I whispered, "no, stay. Please." I didn't want the moment to end, didn't want to face the next one. If eternity could be encapsulated into one perfect moment, I knew that this was it. It took a moment for my head to clear enough to realize that I had been inside Amon, privy to his thoughts and feelings, part of him. I had seen myself literally through his eyes. It had been a brief but enlightening experience. Each time we made love we had reached new heights of passion and pleasure and I could not imagine how we could equal, let alone surpass, tonight. I closed my eyes and listened to the storm crashing about outside. Amon rose and moved up to lie beside me, kissing me tenderly on the edge of my mouth.

"I understand that you have been blooded," he said cryptically.

My mind was not on small talk and I struggled to grasp his meaning. I looked down at my hands and then my body. There was no blood.

"What do you mean, blooded?" I asked, "Wait, isn't that what they do to you when you've killed your first fox in a foxhunt? Oh, I get it, you mean the bad guy in the woods." Suddenly I didn't like the way this conversation was going.

"Yes, Pet, your first kill," he smiled and touched the side of my face with his fingers.

"That's not funny," I snarled and brushed his hand aside. "That was an accident and it was self-defense. It was not my first kill, as you so blithely put it." I struggled to sit up and dizziness engulfed me. The room spun slowly as I tried to make it to my feet. I slid down the side of the bed and landed unceremoniously on the floor on my bare ass. Leave it to a man, even a vampire, to ruin a beautiful moment by opening his mouth. I covered my face with my hands and wept. The regret that I had been unable to feel this afternoon in the woods swept over me and this time I did cry for the dead man, whoever he was. However nefarious his intentions, no one deserved to die. I realized that I might not be able to live with myself and my actions, when that little voice once more cut in, "What are you blubbering about? You're not going to live that much longer, anyway. Spank your inner moppet and get over it! Your time is limited. Do you want to spend what little time you have left wallowing in regret and self-pity? The guy was there to either kill you or kidnap you, he doesn't deserve your pity."

Suddenly, Amon reached down and jerked me roughly up off of the floor. He yanked me back onto the bed and threw me down, leaning over me. Lowering his face to within inches of mine, he hissed, "In this world, Little One, its kill or be killed. You are either the predator or the prey. Right now, as can be witnessed by this, the second attempt on you in forty-eight hours, you are prey. Your continued existence may very well depend on your instincts, your power, and your will to survive. Do not get so wrapped up in sanctimony and human emotion that you lose yourself."

I blinked, swallowed hard, and nodded very slowly. The intensity of his anger startled me. I didn't know how to respond.

"Now, why don't you get some rest?" he suggested as he lay back against the pillow, crossed his arms on his chest, and closed his eyes. Looking at his still body, so pale against the white sheets, I was reminded that I wasn't dealing with a human and that this was his world, not mine.

"Nice effect," I smiled at the pose, "The only thing you're missing is the white lily between your hands."

He opened one eye and peered at me, grinning, "You think?"

"Definitely," I nodded.

"Hush, please," he murmured, "Get some rest."

"You can't expect me to nap at night when you've got me sleeping all day, thanks to your vampire schedule," I complained.

"I didn't tell you to go to sleep," he opened his eyes and rolled over to face me. "I asked you to get some rest. You've had an eventful day, not to mention a head injury."

"Oh," I sighed, "Okay. I'll try to rest but I am not going to sleep."

"Fine. Quiet," he commanded.

Lying there, trying to be quiet, I found it hard to resist drumming my fingers together or twiddling my thumbs. The thought occurred to me that vampires, besides being pushy, had very volatile moods. Probably didn't get enough fiber in their diets, I snorted. Pulling a sober face, I turned to peek at Amon. He was giving me a dirty look so I put one finger in front of my lips and nodded. I rolled away from him and onto my side. When I had first tumbled into this fantastic world of vampires and magic, I felt like I was Alice in *Alice in Wonderland*. It didn't take too much imagination to see Arathia as the Queen of Hearts, running around screaming, "Off with her head." I wasn't sure what role Amon would play in this little fantasy, definitely not the white rabbit. He was probably closer to Grace Slick's white rabbit than the long-eared fuzzy guy with the waistcoat and pocket watch! I suspected he was or could be lethal, anyway. After a bit I decided that I was more likely Dorothy in *the Wizard of Oz*. Amon was the Wizard, hiding behind the curtain pontificating cryptic verses and Arathia was the Wicked Witch of the West. Though I hadn't met him yet, I cast Dodge in the role of the cowardly Lion, Winter was the scarecrow, and Bear was the tin man. Chimaera was undoubtedly the captain of the flying monkeys.

However, lately I was beginning to suspect that I was really the hapless heroine, Pauline, in the *Perils of Pauline*. Considering that I had been mugged, kidnapped from the hospital, bitten by a vampire, suffered seizures, broken my ankle, been thrown from a horse, and knocked unconscious by a thug, I was waiting for the director to yell, "Cut." I wouldn't have been at all surprised to wake up and find myself bound with ropes and lying tied to a railroad track. Whether or not it would be Amon standing beside the rails sporting a black coat and top hat, twisting the end of his handlebar mustache and chuckling maniacally, I had not decided.

Opening my eyes, I lay perfectly still and looked around the room. Enough exercising my imagination, I had to devise a plan to find out what Life's Blood was without tipping my hand that I knew about the prophecy. My eyes came to rest on the short stack of books that Lily had brought in. Thankfully, she had stacked them on the dresser with their spines facing out, so I could just make out the titles from this position. It looked like three of them were either romances, yuck, or mysteries, but the one on the top was titled, "Madame Olga's Book of Shadows." I knew that a book of shadows was another name for a book of spells and an idea bloomed in my head. I could use that book as an excuse to ask a question about Life's Blood. Bishop would be the least suspecting, so he would be my first target. I was betting that he would have no idea about the contents of that book, just in case it was some bodice-ripping story of carnal confessions.

A tremor rippled through me and I rolled over to look at Amon, lying still with his eyes closed.

"Amon," I whispered and touched him on the shoulder.

He opened his eyes and looked over at me, "Yes?"

"How long has it been since you've fed?"

"Fed?" he raised an eyebrow.

"You know, fed off of me. How long has it been?" I probed.

"Two, maybe three days. Why do you ask?"

"Well, I was just thinking," I explained, "Over time the toxins that cause my seizures build up in my system and you have to feed off of me to siphon them off, right?"

"Right," he looked skeptical.

"Could you feed regularly so that I don't have anymore seizures? Kind of launch a pre-emptive strike?"

"I don't know, Cat," he considered, "I will have to ask Bishop about that. For some reason I don't think that is possible, but I may be mistaken. Why, do you feel another seizure is near?"

"Maybe," I admitted, "I just felt something, but maybe it was my imagination."

"Bishop should be along shortly to check on you," he added as he got out of bed and began dressing. "I need to check with the security staff before sunrise, so I'll do that now. As with Bear, you will be de-briefed about this afternoon's incident tomorrow evening. We need to get as clear a picture of what happened as possible."

"Right, de-briefed," I mused, a mental image of a dingy cell lit by a single bare bulb, rubber hoses, and being grilled by unseen authorities popped into my head.

Just then there was a knock on the door and Bishop came in, muttering apologies for disturbing us.

"It's okay, Bishop," I smiled, "Sin was just leaving."

Amon nodded silently at me and turned and left the room, quietly closing the door behind him.

Pausing at the nightstand to set down a leather pouch, Bishop bent over me and looked into my eyes with a tiny penlight. He gently pulled my hair away from the laceration at my hairline and touched it with his fingertip. Lifting and supporting my head with his left hand, he tenderly explored the bump on the back of my head with his right hand. Releasing me, he gently laid me back on the pillow.

"I have a question for you Bishop, well," I paused, "actually I have two questions for you."

"I will answer them if I can," he nodded and pulled a syringe and a vial of clear liquid from the leather pouch.

He leaned over and wrapped a tourniquet around my arm then, smacking the flesh a couple of times to raise the veins, he pushed the needle of the syringe in and depressed the plunger. The sensation of heat briefly flared up my arm, then was gone.

"Um, oh yeah," I struggled to remember, my mind already growing foggy, "Could Sin feed off of my blood regularly so that I don't have to have anymore seizures? You know, kind of maintaining a lower level of toxins rather than waiting for them to reach the point of causing a seizure."

"Unfortunately, that is not possible," he said soberly, "By removing the toxins when they reach the critical level, Sin can return your system to normal and relieve the seizure. If he were to feed before the toxins reach that level it would just cause them to increase more rapidly. Your system would be bombarded, as it were, with strengthening and rapidly multiplying toxins until it could not withstand the attacks anymore. It would eventually kill you."

"Wow," I breathed, "Bad idea, huh?"

"Indeed," he nodded as he turned to go, "very bad idea. And your second question?"

"Um, oh, I can't think right now," I murmured as my eyes had already begun to close. My plan would have to wait.

Chapter 17

Images flittered through my mind as I slept. They were more like still photos than normal dreams. In one instant I was lying on the battlefield bleeding, when a hand surrounded by a nimbus of gold light touched me. The next moment I was facing my enemy, reaching out in an almost tender gesture to touch my hand to the side of his face, though I knew my intentions were not kind. Suddenly my enemy screamed and disappeared in a shimmer of flames. I saw, once again, the Oracle cock its head then bite my finger, drawing my blood into its mouth. Next, the familiar image of a hospital room with an empty bed, I.V. stand, tubes and bags appeared then dissolved. Finally, I heard the deep and resonating thud as the branch I swung connected with my black-clad attacker's chin and I watched him sail backwards in slow motion, landing in a pile of leaves and twigs.

A lance of sheer agony brought me screaming to my senses. Pain roared up my spine, down my legs and through my brain. Drawing my knees sharply up to my chest, I rolled from the bed and landed on my side, naked and cold on the bare floor. I clutched my hands into fists and gritted my teeth against the spasms that swept through me. The door burst open and Chimaera, of all people, came in. He crouched down beside me and I growled at him. Chuckling gently, he leaned forward and easily lifted me from the floor.

"His Lordship must like his women scrawny," he remarked as he put me back into bed.

"I'm not scrawny," I complained through gritted teeth, "and why should you help me?"

"Relax, Little Witch," he smiled, "I am not so fond of you that I would incur Sin's wrath on your account."

"Some charmer," I whimpered and moaned and tried to think through the pain. The fact that Chimaera was standing placidly beside the bed watching and enjoying my agony was starting to tick me off. As my anger grew it caused my magic to stir and tiny sparks of electricity popped and crackled in the air.

"Either make yourself helpful," I hissed, "or get out now."

"Helpful how?" he shrugged. "And by the way, that's a very nice touch," he added.

"What touch?" I asked more out of reflex than from any desire to know what he was talking about.

"Your skin," he indicated with a nod of his head, "Your pores are oozing blood and your eyes are bleeding." He bent over and laid one long tapered finger at the corner of my eye. He turned his hand over and showed me the drop of blood on his fingertip. "See?"

"Chimaera, you and I are going to have words one of these days and they're going to be four-lettered," I warned between gut-wrenching spasms, "Please, at least you could bring me a wet washcloth."

"What?" he protested, "Now I'm your butler? What's next? Wash your hair? Powder your wig? Shave your legs?"

"Either do it now, or get your slimy smartass vampire butt out of here," I screamed. The pain in my head and back was causing my magic to increase and fill the air with static. The smell of ozone was getting thick around me.

Though it was not likely my threats or any fear of me that got him moving, Chimaera did step out of the room then return shortly and hand me a damp washcloth. Struggling to hold onto it while enduring another painful spasm, I touched the corner of the cloth to my eyes and wiped away the blood. This was the second time that I had now experienced tears of blood and I was no closer to understanding what, if anything, it meant than before. I tried to wipe the blood from my arms and legs but the pain was growing and the trembling was intensifying. Squeezing my eyes tightly shut, I visualized my power. In an attempt to soothe my pain I imagined the energy as blue and peaceful. It quivered and shimmered as a living, throbbing thing. Abruptly the blue pulsing light dove at me and a shaft of pain coursed through my body. I fought to hold onto the power, to rein it in and control it as the agony threatened to engulf me.

At that moment Amon rushed into the room, gasping as I turned my eyes toward him.

"Goddess save us," he muttered as he approached me, a look of disbelief on his face. He looked exquisite in a fresh white silk shirt and wonderfully tailored linen trousers. I wondered for an instant if all vampires had such a flair for fashion. Though it seemed an eternity, it was only a moment before he had his mouth locked onto my neck and his teeth deep into my vein. Relief was sudden as he drew my blood into his mouth. Wisps of smoke and tendrils of electricity curled and slithered in the air around me as my power moved. Out of the corner of my eye I saw Chimaera, his expression a mixture of distaste and perhaps jealousy, turn and leave the room.

"What was that cursing about?" I looked up at Amon when he released my neck from his mouth.

"Your eyes," he said, licking his lips, "your eyes were glowing bright blue and shedding radiant tears of blood. It was startling."

"I had been trying to control the pain through my power and had imagined it as blue and calm. It must have surfaced in my eyes when it reached its strongest point," I reasoned. "I have no idea what the tears of blood mean but it's the second time it's happened. Same thing with the blood oozing from my skin, I've had this before too. Any idea why or what this means?"

"No, not at this moment. Have you asked Arathia?"

"In truth," I admitted, "I've kind of been avoiding her. She gives me the creeps."

"Cat, please trust me when I tell you that she has vast knowledge and her instruction will be invaluable to you. She may very well know what these precious tears of blood mean," he smiled as he kissed the edge of my eye and paused to lick off a drop of blood.

"They aren't stopping this time are they?" I sighed as I felt another warm trickle run down my cheek.

"Apparently not," he murmured as he leaned down and caught the tear with his tongue, "Hope you don't mind. I hate to let this go to waste. Your blood is delicious." He continued to kiss and lick the blood from my face. It put me in mind of having my face washed by an overly friendly dog and I giggled when it began to tickle.

"Okay, okay," I snickered, "If I promise to make nice with Arathia will you stop giving me a tongue bath?"

He pulled away and regarded me with an odd expression on his face. Moments ticked by and still he just looked at me. Finally, he drew his eyebrows together in a look of confusion and shook his head.

"You have no reason to be jealous of Arathia," he announced

"What are you talking about?" I gasped, "I am so not jealous of that, that witch! And my, don't we have a rather grand opinion of ourselves, assuming that I would be jealous of her over you?"

He just looked at me calmly and offered a smug smile that I had an urge to slap right off his face.

"I do not understand it," he spoke quietly, "but I can smell the jealousy on you when you say Arathia's name."

"Well, don't let it go to your head," I grumbled, "if there's any jealousy, and I'm in no way admitting that there is, it's a female thing. In the zoo they don't put two big cats in the same cage."

"I have no idea what you are saying," he looked amazed.

"You're a man and a vampire," I shrugged, "there's no way you could understand."

"But you will, as you say, make nice with Arathia?"

"I'll do my best," I nodded, mindful not to promise what I might not be able to deliver.

"Would you like to go to the parlor, get out of this room for a while" he suggested, "I know you feel a touch of claustrophobia if you have to stay in one place for too long."

"Wait," I caught something in that statement, "how long have I been in here? Wasn't it just this afternoon that Bear and I went for our ride?"

There was something like pity in his eyes when he answered, "No, Cat that was two days ago. You have been sleeping since then."

I flew off the bed, incensed, and grabbed a pair of jeans that had been folded and placed neatly on the dresser. Snapping on a bra, I pulled a tee shirt over my head and paused to fume at Amon.

"If there's any reason for my sleeping through the last two days I'm sure that it was that little injection Bishop shoved into my arm. And what happened to that de-briefing business that we were supposed to do? I can't believe you," I seethed as I slipped my tennis shoes on, I was too angry to look for socks,

"You hold me against my will then, because I'm an inconvenience, you keep me hopped up on drugs to keep me out of trouble, out of the way."

In a flash he was off of the bed and had me pinned against the wall, leaning his weight into me. I struggled against him and would have slapped that beautiful face if he hadn't grabbed both of my wrists in his hands and yanked them above my head. Anger was making me reckless.

"Make no mistake, Little One," he breathed anger and threat very near my face, "I will do whatever I deem necessary to keep you safe."

"To keep me under control," I sneered and tried to wriggle free of his grip. He stepped smoothly aside as I tried to bring my knee up to cause him the maximum guy pain.

"Kitten's got claws," he chuckled at my feeble attempt, and of course it just made me more furious.

"Let me go," I hissed through gritted teeth. The air around us started shimmering and twinkling.

"I will let you go when I chose to do so, Precious," he murmured. "Remember you are mine." He leaned his face into my neck and placed a very hot wet kiss on my skin.

"Stop that, vampire boy, and I am not your Precious," I tried to move again but he held me fast. The idea of somehow using my power against him occurred to me and I stopped struggling and looked into his eyes. There I saw his power and the futility of my anger, and I dropped my head onto my chest, weeping tears of frustration. "Please tell me what you want with me," I sobbed, "what do you mean by that "you are mine" thing?"

"Just that, Pet," he looked at me levelly, "you are mine." He brushed one long pale finger up my cheek and caught a tear, sticking it in his mouth. Yep, it was blood again.

It was clear from his expression that he had no intention of explaining what it was that he wanted with me. He kissed me hard on the mouth then released me. In that moment I realized that I had foolishly been holding onto the notion that I could find a way to if not escape, at least survive, that "happily ever after" was still a possibility. That notion suddenly fled. I absently rubbed my wrists where he had held them so tightly.

He straightened his silk shirt and brushed his hair out of his face. Smoothing the pleats in his trousers, he moved toward the door and turned back to me. "Now," he half bowed with a flourish, "shall we go to the parlor, My Lady?"

I was defeated and emotionally exhausted and only nodded mutely. Utter despair swept over me and threatened to take me away. I bowed my head and walked silently beside Amon as we made our way to the parlor. The realization that I both loved this beautiful man, this seductive vampire, and loathed him with equal passion shimmered into my mind and I resented the emotions that he stirred in me.

"Lily will bring you something to eat," he stated as he led me into the candlelit room where soft music played in the background.

"I'm not hungry," I pouted as I dropped onto the sofa.

"You will eat," he insisted, quieting my protests with a look.

Just then Arathia blew into the room and sat down beside me on the couch. Her black silk sheath shimmered smoothly in the candlelight. She had her ebony hair pulled away from her face and knotted into a sleek bun on the back of her head. Her makeup was, as usual, flawless, lipstick blood red and deftly applied. I realized that my face hadn't seen so much as a mascara wand in weeks and I felt unarmed.

"Something of you has changed," she observed, looking at me closely.

"Yeah," I admitted, "I guess it has."

"Your power is changing. You have been using it?" she arched one perfectly drawn eyebrow.

"Not exactly," I hedged, "but it has been making itself known."

"How so?" she purred, running one finger down my arm. I hated people who seemed to have to touch me when they talked to me.

"It's been raising its ugly head now when I get angry," I sighed and rubbed my eyes with the heel of my hand, "Oh yeah," I added, "and I've been crying tears of blood."

"Remarkable," she smiled, "Though they seldom have the emotion to do so, it is generally accepted that only vampires cry tears of blood. Sin has fed off of you but you are not a vampire. This is unheard of."

"Great," I shook my head, "and I was hoping that you could explain it."

"I will look into the matter, but I doubt that anyone knows why this is happening to you," she sighed.

"Tell me Arathia," I interjected, the question having popped fully formed into my head, "where is my magic?"

She looked confused, "Where?"

"I mean where in my body is it?" I spread my hands, "Is it in my heart, my head, my blood?"

"Your blood, Cher?" Her eyes widened in surprise, "no, no. Let me explain this as clearly as I can. Your power, your magic, is a

133

living thing with a will and a purpose all its own. You do not have power, you have received it. For whatever reason, the Gods have found you worthy of receiving and wielding this power. You are a witch. You have been gifted, be thankful."

Though I should have been both amazed and insulted at being called a witch, I felt the truth of her words, and recalled that Chimaera had once referred to me as such. At that time however, I'd been in too much pain to react or question his words. How quickly I was becoming accustomed to accepting the fantastic as natural!

"Sorry," I shrugged, "I'm not feeling particularly thankful just this very moment."

"Come, Cat," she smiled and took my hands in hers, "show me your magic. Call your power."

"I'm not sure I can right now," I said weakly, "I'm feeling kind of wiped out."

"Relax Cher," she insisted, "The magic is yours to call as you wish. You can do it anytime you chose. Close your eyes and concentrate and it will answer your call."

"Wait," I hesitated, holding up one hand, "before I do this answer me one more question."

"Oui?" she waited expectantly.

"Is this magic black or white?" I asked, "Good or bad?"

"Child," she shook her head slowly, "magic is neither black nor white. It is neutral, gray. Whether it is good or evil depends on the witch that wields it. You are now that witch and I will give you one word of warning," she added leaning over to look me seriously in the eye. "With magic, as with many things in this world, the devil is in the details."

"Meaning what, exactly?" I nodded, fully expecting further explanation.

"Just that, Cher," she answered without answering, "the devil is in the details."

Lily bustled in at that moment pushing a trolley full of fragrant and delicious-looking goodies and I wished I had an appetite. She parked the trolley behind the sofa and, no doubt noticing that the conversation had died as she entered, she gave me a meaningful look of helpless sympathy, turned, and left the room.

"Okay let's do this thing," I huffed as I closed my eyes. Imagining my violin cradled gently beneath my chin, I drew the make-believe bow across the strings, then picking up a tune, I dropped the bow and plucked the strings with my fingertips. Energy danced like an electrical discharge around my hands. Opening my eyes, I smiled as bright blue sparks jumped from my fingers into the air.

"Focus," Arathia intoned from beside me, " and control your power. It is yours, a tool of your will."

As I watched calmly, the lights morphed into one orb of white energy. I held out my hand and it landed gently on my palm.

"This is just a manifestation, Cat," Arathia spoke quietly, "take it into yourself, where it belongs. Breathe it into yourself."

I was afraid she was going to say something like that. When I had previously played with these things, they had ended up shoving their way into me rather painfully. My only hope was that maybe with Arathia here to guide me, it wouldn't be quite so uncomfortable. Opening my mouth slowly, I gently drew in a breath and the orb stretched and lengthened into something like a rope. In the blink of an eye it had slid down my throat. Instructor or not, the power still felt like a battering ram running through me and I fought not to scream. As the sensation of bodily intrusion subsided, the energy flowed throughout my body and I found that my vision was being assaulted by a riot of colors, changing the normal world into a psychedelic one. Scanning the room with my new sight, my eyes came to rest on Amon, leaning casually against the fireplace, wineglass in hand. In the instant it took to remember my anger at him, without intention, I hurled a small mass of energy at him, shattering the wineglass and sending shards of crystal cascading to the floor. Drops of red wine gaily splattered his pristine silk shirt and expensive linen pants.

Looking at the shock and surprise on his face, I started to grin and mumble some sort of apology when his eyes froze my smile, then killed it completely. Fury seethed in those eyes and before I knew what was happening, I was flying headlong across the room, landing painfully against the wall, my back sliding down it to the baseboard. The lever on an air vent ripped my jeans and drove sharply into my calf, and dull bone jarring force took the air from my lungs. I sat there, dazed, for only a moment before rising stiffly and gracelessly to my feet. My power flared behind my eyes and a thought, not my own, paced through my mind like a restless jungle cat. "I will have a piece of him," it hissed. I took two or three lurching steps in his direction before Arathia placed herself in my path.

"No, child," she screamed. I paid her no mind. "You must not challenge a Master Vampire, especially in his own lair. This is suicide." She struggled to stop me, but I pushed by her.

With a slight brush of Amon's hand I once more went tumbling backwards, this time regaining my footing as I landed. I observed in horror, as if from a distance, as my bruised and battered body once more staggered forward. I was going to confront Amon. "No, stop, get down or he's going to kill you!" the familiar voice of reason and sanity was wailing in my head, but I wasn't in charge of my body's movements. I was watching a marionette making her way to her destruction. Looking at me with something like awe or amazement, Amon made a barely perceptible motion with his index finger and I watched as a bright gash opened on my face, running from below my right cheekbone to my chin. It spread like an opening mouth and blood gushed in a torrent. Suddenly, sharp burning pain and the sensation of heat on my face brought me back to myself. I stood mutely clutching my cheek, trying to figure out what had just happened. Without warning Amon appeared before me, clutched my throat in his left hand, and easily hoisted me into the air, holding me at arm's length. He looked into my eyes. "You dare to challenge me?" his voice boomed. Of course, I was unable to answer. I was vaguely aware of Arathia screaming and jumping around Amon like a yipping little dog. Funny what goes through

your mind when you're being deprived of oxygen. Looking once more at Amon, my eyes widened in panic and disbelief when I realized that he was indeed going to kill me, then and there. Suddenly his expression softened and instead of killing me, he merely tossed me onto the sofa and strode from the room.

Gasping and clutching my throat, I struggled to regain my breath.

"What," I coughed roughly, "what the hell just happened?"

Arathia smiled calmly, looking like the Cheshire cat.

"You just challenged a Master Vampire in his own lair," she beamed, "It's amazing that you are still alive."

"Okay," I admitted, "I accept that I did do that first little bit, with the wineglass, but it was an accident. I was just angry at Sin and it happened. But I had nothing to do with that last part about challenging him. That was not me! I might be a little rash occasionally, maybe a little headstrong, but I am not stupid. It would never even occur to me to challenge him, I don't know what that means."

"I believe that your power was challenging his for control," she explained like this sort of thing happened every day. "Control of him, his power, and all he commands."

"Yeah well, I don't suppose that offer to take me to New Orleans with you is still valid?" I muttered as I pressed my palm to my cheek to control the bleeding,

"Too late for that, Cher," She smiled as she sat on the sofa beside me, "There is too much affection between the two of you, he would never let you go now."

"Affection?" I cried indignantly, "The guy just threw me across the room! That is not affection in my book."

"If he didn't care for you so deeply," she shook her head, "you would not still be alive, Cat."

"Yeah, well," I hissed, rubbing my backside, "Remind me to be grateful when the pain stops."

Amon entered the room with a glass of ice and clear liquid in one hand and a cloth in the other. He knelt in front of me and laid the cloth against my face, then handed me the drink. I took a recklessly large gulp of what turned out to be straight vodka and tried not to choke on the fire.

"The other possibility is that your power is quickening Sin's powers," she nodded sagely.

I had watched every Highlander show and movie, where they were always quickening something, and could still not understand what she meant.

"Explain please," Amon suggested.

"You, Sin, have powers, abilities, that you have not used for centuries. Powers that you hide even from me," she added, "it's possible that, for some reason, Cat's magic is challenging yours to quicken those abilities, to reawaken them, if you will. If I knew which God bequeathed Cat these powers perhaps I could discover why this is happening, or to what ends it may lead. As it is now, I have no idea what her magic intends."

"Enough explanations," I moaned as my muscles began to tighten and stiffen, "I'm tired and I hurt everywhere."

"You should rest," Amon stood and offered me his hand.

"I realize that this power, this magic," I waved absently, "I know that I don't always have control of it but, please, no more drugs."

He stopped in midstride and turned toward me.

"Oh God," I stammered, "that's just what you had in mind isn't it? You were going to toss me into bed and shoot me up again, weren't you?"

"You need your rest," he said soberly.

"With all the drugs you and Bishop have been pushing on me it's a miracle that I have any functioning gray matter left," I whined shamelessly, "Please, no more. I promise. No magic, no power stuff. Just let me sleep. I won't even twitch my nose, promise."

"Twitch your nose?" Amon lifted one eyebrow.

"Bewitched? It was a TV show," I explained as we made our way out of the parlor and down the corridors, "Samantha Stephens was a modern witch and whenever she wanted to use her magic powers she just twitched her nose."

"I see," he murmured, "but to be sure I think you will sleep with me."

"Not like last time?" I smiled.

"No," he shook his head, "this time you will sleep with me."

Maybe it was an indication of just how complicated my life had recently become or how jaded I was becoming, but I really didn't like the inflection in his voice when he said, "sleep".

Amon ended up carrying me most of the way to the sapphire bedroom as the cut on my calf started bleeding rather profusely. He took me through the room and into the bathroom where he placed me gently on the side of the tub and ran the bath water. I sat unmoving with my eyes closed until I heard the water stop. As Amon pulled the ruined tee shirt over my head I gave a little whimper when my muscles protested the movement. Luckily, the bra removal took no motion on my part so it went more smoothly. I groaned as he stood me up and removed my jeans and panties. He stopped and bent down to look at the cut on my calf.

"A rather nasty wound," he observed, "and you are going to have some bruises."

"I don't care, I'm too tired to deal with it," I mumbled as I stepped into the tub. Hissing and sobbing a little as the heat assaulted my injuries, I managed to lower myself into the water and breathe a sigh of relief. The bath water turned pink as my blood washed away. Leaning my torn cheek on a warm washcloth, I rested my head on the side of the tub.

Chapter 18

I must have fallen asleep as soon as I hit the warm water, because the next thing I knew Amon had dressed me in a satin gown and was carrying me away from the sapphire room, down a long set of stairs.

"Where are we going?" I yawned.

"My room," he said simply, though I did not recognize this as the way to his room.

Closing my eyes, I relaxed and leaned into Amon's arms, marveling at how I could be so furious with the man one minute, then so perfectly comfortable in his arms the next. When I felt a gust of cool air rush around me I opened my eyes and tried to take in what I was seeing.

"Oh, no," I murmured as my eyes came to rest on the coffin in the middle of the large candlelit room. Every mental image Anne Rice ever gave me ran through my mind in a blur. "I'm not going to sleep in that, am I?"

"Don't worry, there's plenty of room," he said as he put me down and lifted the lid. Of course it was lined in plush, tufted white satin. "You will sleep in my arms."

"As truly romantic as that sounds," I shuddered and began shuffling backwards, "maybe drugs would be better."

"Too late," he warned as he scooped me up in his arms, "The sun is rising and Bishop has already retired." He laid me down in the coffin and moved to get in beside me. I noticed briefly that he must have changed clothes at some point as he was now wearing a butter soft gray tunic over tight black pants. His feet, like mine, were bare.

"I thought you said that you didn't have to sleep in a coffin, since you're a Master Vampire," I complained.

"I don't have to," he nodded, "but I prefer to."

"The devil is in the details," I sighed as Amon wrapped me in his arms and closed the lid of the coffin. "Is there any air in here, can I breathe?"

"There is air," he answered as he leaned down and placed his lips on my forehead, "Hush."

Panic attacked momentarily as it dawned on me that I was stretched out in a casket embraced by a corpse. Amon must have read my thoughts, for his heart started beating beneath my hand. I lay my ear against his chest and fell asleep listening to the strong, steady rhythm.

Whether it was the security of Amon's arms or just the lack of space for tossing and turning, I slept deeply and without dreams. When I woke, the lid of the coffin was open and I was alone. I stretched my arms above my head and yawned loudly. Discovering that, unlike those vampire movies where everyone floats, there is no graceful way to climb out of a coffin without assistance, I tumbled from it in something like a disjointed somersault. "The last thing in the world I need is another bruise," I muttered as I stood and brushed dirt from my gown. It was then that I noticed the floor was smoothly packed dirt. "Yugoslavian dirt, I bet," I nodded.

At that moment winter opened the door and entered with a bemused look on his face.

"Heard I missed some excitement last night," he smiled. He came near and gently touched the skin around the wound on my cheek.

"Yeah," I snorted, pulling away from him, "I guess you could say it was exciting."

"Did you really challenge His Lordship?" his eyes widened.

"Yeah," I smiled weakly, "I did, or my power did."

"Wow," he whistled, "I knew you were something else, but ...wow!"

"Winter, can you just take me back to the sapphire room so I can dress?" I asked, impatiently taking his arm. "I'm starving."

"You know that's going to leave a really cool scar, don't you?" he grinned, indicating my face.

"My life just keeps getting better and better," I grumbled and shoved Winter out the door and down the hall.

An exquisite deep emerald satin tunic with matching pants and shoes lay neatly arranged on the bed in the sapphire room. Black embroidery formed an elaborate dragon on the left breast of the tunic and continued down the left leg of the pants. Though it was a very feminine thing, which I usually hated, I couldn't wait to try it on. Winter had followed me into the room and was now leaning, his usual position, against the doorjamb. I shot him a dirty look from across the room and he held up both hands in the universal sign of surrender, and turned to face the door.

I pulled the shoulders of my gown down my arms and discovered that Winter was peeking when I heard a gasp from behind me.

"Winter," I snapped, "You're not supposed to be looking."

"Sorry," he stammered, "But whoa! Your back, Cat, you've been playin' with the big dog, huh? He do that to you?" he murmured as he came up behind me and touched my back and left shoulder.

"Yeah," I snorted, "You immortal boys play rough, don't you?"

"You are one ugly bruise from end to end, '*tite soeur*,'" he shook his head slowly.

"What does that mean? '*tite soeur*?'" I turned to face him, holding the tunic up in front of me, "and you haven't even seen my end."

"Little sister, Cat," he smiled and stepped back to the door shaking his head and waggling his bushy blonde eyebrows, "and anytime, *Cher*." He turned his back politely to allow me to dress.

Still aching from last night's activities, I knew that there was no way I could maneuver my arms into a bra and hook it, so I slipped the tunic over my head with as little movement as possible. Cringing as I slipped on the pants, I continued the conversation with Winter.

"I'm just grateful that he didn't insist on shooting me full of drugs to make me sleep all day today," I called out, my back turned. Realizing that the central air was cool enough to give me problems, I crossed my arms over my breasts until the cool satin fabric reached my body temperature

"You slept in His Lordships coffin, right?" he snickered, "there was no need to sedate you."

I heard him chuckling behind my back and turned to find him holding his hand in front of his mouth, obviously to cover a smile.

I walked very slowly and very deliberately to him and, planting my feet and squaring my shoulders, I gave him my most serious and determined expression.

"What aren't you telling me, Winter?" I insisted. "Tell me now."

"I'm so sorry, Cat," he shrugged, "I assumed Sin would have told you. If I tell you now he'll kill me."

"If he doesn't," I snarled as I grabbed the lapels of his leather jacket and stretched up to put my mouth near his ear, "I will. Now, tell me."

"Alright," he pulled away from me and straightened his jacket, "For the time that you shared in his coffin?"

"Yes?" I asked with a growing sense of unease.

"You were tasting death for that time," he admitted, "that's why he didn't have to drug you."

I turned and paced away from him, my hand going to my mouth as if to chew on a nail.

"How can that be?" I cried, "I'm mortal, I can't, as you say, taste death! Are you sure?"

He nodded grimly, "Ever heard of "sleeping like the dead? In your case it was a temporary state, you were just visiting if you will, sharing Sin's death. If he hadn't been with you, you would have just slept very deeply."

I cringed, unwilling to admit to sleeping perhaps the most peaceful time in my life in Amon's coffin.

"Please," Winter shook his head, "if you have to mention this to His Lordship, please make up something. I don't know, tell him you dreamed it or something but please don't tell him that I told you. His anger and punishment..."

"Yeah," I nodded, "I know. Don't worry about it. If it does come up, you won't be implicated."

"Thanks," he smiled broadly, " *'tite soeur.*"

It occurred to me that I had made an ally and I decided to take advantage of the situation while the time was ripe. "Winter, do you know what Life's Blood is?"

Immediately a look of suspicion came across his face, "Why do you ask?"

"Lily had brought me a book," I embellished what almost wasn't a lie, "it was a book of shadows and there was a spell that called for the Life Blood of a virgin. I'm not planning on casting a spell or anything, but nowhere in the book could I find what Life's Blood meant. Is that, like, the last few drops of blood in a human's body?"

"The last?" he looked relieved, "no Cat, not necessarily the last. It's more like those drops of blood that mean the difference between living and dying. Spill those drops," he shrugged, "death. Save those drops, you survive."

"So how would a person, say a witch, know if they had those few specific drops?" I continued to push.

"I don't know how they do it but we," he grinned, "we vampires, can see them. To us they glow, almost like liquid neon, they glow kind of amber."

"So if I were a witch, not a vampire," I reasoned aloud, "the only way to be sure to use those exact drops would be to use the complete blood supply, right?"

He looked at me uneasily.

"Relax, Winter," I grinned, "I'm just thinking. And even though Arathia says that I'm a witch, I'm not casting spells. I'm just trying to figure out all that I can." I patted his arm and stepped into the bathroom to finish my morning ritual, which I supposed was now my evening ritual.

Brushing out the tangles in my hair, I gathered it up into a pony-tail and secured it with a black satin scrunci, moaning only slightly from the exertion. I paused before the mirror to inspect myself, noting that the rich emerald of the outfit did bring out the green of my eyes and accent my hair very nicely. Unfortunately, it also brought out the angry red that had developed around the laceration on my cheek. The effect was Frankensteinian. After brushing my teeth, I stepped out of the bathroom, washcloth in hand, to find that Chimaera had replaced Winter as my bodyguard.

"Great," I sighed, "It's you." Hoping that my questions hadn't caused any undue suspicions with Winter, I wiped my face, gingerly avoiding my wounded cheek, and tossed the cloth back into the sink.

"Okay, Chimaera, go ahead and make your snide comments about what happened last night, get it out of your system," I demanded. Expectantly, I waited and looked up at the usually surly vampire. His eyes, glowing frosty blue, examined first my face, then my body, coming to rest on my nipples that had just made their presence known anew thanks to the air conditioner.

I caught that familiar look in his eyes and huffed, "Oh, get over it, Chimaera." I stepped into the satin slippers and headed for the door. "Let's go to the parlor. I haven't eaten since," I paused and looked at him, "I don't know the last time I ate."

"Nor I," he murmured cryptically as I brushed past him and headed down the corridor. I was both startled and surprised when he caught up with me and took my arm, a very gallant gesture from someone who, up until this moment, had shown nothing but contempt for me. Fear and confusion kept me from engaging in idle chitchat with him and we walked the whole way to the parlor in uneasy silence, at least I was uneasy. Until today Chimaera had been a known quantity, now something had changed and I did not want to consider what that might mean.

Amon stood staring out the window and turned to look at me as I entered the parlor. He wore smooth black leather pants, a crisp white shirt with slightly billowing sleeves, and a sapphire and black paisley vest. A stud in the shape of a polished bar of silver secured the throat of his shirt and gleamed softly. His thick silver hair lay glossy and perfectly smooth on his shoulders and down his chest. This vampire was stunning and his eyes sparkled when he appraised me.

"You look beautiful," he nodded, "the ensemble suits you." His words were more of an announcement than a compliment and it was obvious that I need not reply.

Tension vibrated in the air. Neither Amon nor Arathia smiled or approached me. Alarms were going off in my head as I took a seat in one of the damask occasional chairs. I was afraid to speak, which admittedly was a rare occurrence. Amon walked cat-like to me and touched my cheek.

"I regret that you forced me to do this," he purred as he caressed my wound.

"You suck at apologies," I remarked, secretly reveling in his touch.

"I did not," he said pointedly, "apologize. Now, would you care for a drink?" He offered and moved to the liquor cabinet against the wall.

"Am I going to need one?" I asked warily.

"Perhaps," he quipped, as he turned to pour the drink. I sat silently looking at his back, his broad shoulders and perfectly proportioned derriere. It was a pleasant diversion as I waited for the axe above my head to fall.

When Amon stepped over and handed me a glass, I spied Winter and Chimaera standing across the room like silent sentinels, one on either side of the big French doors. I had no idea what they could be doing there, surely I was safe with Amon around and neither he nor Arathia could possibly need a body guard, unless…God, I prayed that Winter hadn't squealed about my questioning him.

"Arathia and I have been discussing the matter," he began, taking the chair beside mine.

"Discussing me?" I choked, having just taken a sip of brandy, I hated brandy. My mouth tasted like cough syrup now.

"Yes, discussing you," he smiled stiffly, showing that he already had little patience with me, "and we think it most important that we find out where your magic is coming from, what deity is empowering you."

"That doesn't sound so bad," I shrugged, "why are you all acting like I'm to be burned at the stake?"

"We don't mean to alarm you unduly," Arathia cut in, "but your power is, forgive me, considerable. Your inability to control it is troubling. We are concerned about your safety as well as our own." She sat quietly on the sofa, inspecting her manicure. Tonight her couture was totally Asian. A canary yellow sheath touched with black butterflies accented her beautiful mane of black hair, which tonight she wore straight and smooth. Her eyeliner was drawn into sharply elongated points at the corners of her eyes and the lipstick she wore was true Chinese red.

"Arathia has suggested a Sheih Na Rah, a ritual to help us determine the origins of your power," Amon leaned toward me and touched my hand with his own. That little voice in my head screamed, "that translates into She'd Rather Not!" He added, "There are however, some troubling aspects to this ritual."

"Wait," I demanded holding up my hands, "Before I hear what is almost guaranteed to ruin my appetite, I insist on being fed. Anything, I don't care, but I really need food."

Perhaps forty minutes later I wiped my mouth on a linen napkin and downed the last of my Perrier. The steak and salad had been perfectly delicious, though I couldn't help but think, "... and the condemned ate a hearty meal." Okay, so part of me was a drama queen. I knew something serious was afoot because, for the first time, Amon had not disappeared while I ate. Something serious had his mind so distracted that it didn't bother him to watch me eat. Things were so not going well.

"Okay," I sighed, "tell me about this Sha Na Na thing."

"Sheih Na Rah," Amon corrected.

"Whatever," I tossed my napkin on the table and returned to my armchair in front of the sofa. Amon returned to his chair beside mine.

"Basically, *Cher*," Arathia leaned forward and patted my hands, "I will call forth a demon and he will tell me who has given you your powers."

"And still," I waved my hand in a circle, "I'm not hearing that other shoe drop."

"The demon," Arathia explained, "will demand a price for the information we seek. I can force him to disclose the information once he has it, but he will want payment for seeking it."

"And?" I was losing my patience with this dance.

"You are that price," she admitted without meeting my eyes.

I turned to look at Amon, whose expression I could not read. His ebony eyes regarded me calmly.

"Most demons delight in the sexual favors of mortal women," he said at length. "He may demand to ride you."

Even I wasn't willing to admit the mental imagery that statement called forth. Again, the alarm bells were going off in my head.

"I'm guessing that you don't mean riding like a horse," I challenged his gaze.

He absently rubbed his temple with his index fingers, "Only as a stallion rides a mare."

"Yeah, that's what I was afraid of," I nodded. "What do you mean that he might demand? "Why does the demon get to demand anything?"

"We will be forced to barter with the creature," Arathia explained, "and it is not unusual for a demon to crave a mortal woman. We shall of course, try to barter for something less than this, but it is a possibility. We thought you should be warned."

I stood and walked around the sofa. Tossing down the last of the brandy, I grabbed a bottle of scotch and poured a couple of fingers into a shot glass, then tossed it back too. Internally fuming that one moment Amon was saying that I was his and the next he was only too willing to pimp me out to a demon, I turned and faced the vampire. Moving slowly and purposefully, I stopped before his chair.

"Go ahead," I dared, leaning down to touch the fine line of his jaw and meet his eyes, "tell me the rest."

"Your magic should protect you, but there's a chance the demon may destroy your mind," he looked down at his hands, "Or should the demon not wish sex, he may want something else."

"Which would be...," still leaning forward, I lifted his chin.

"It could demand an ear, your tongue, a nipple, a toe, anything as payment," Amon admitted.

"What, and it will knit little things with my body parts?" I yelled, "Is there nothing else that you two can think of that might lead us to these same results? Wait, wait." I added, seeking an alternate escape route, "Can you drug me so I don't have to experience this, you know, I could sleep through it? You could make sure I wouldn't wake up until I was healed."

"Unfortunately Cat," Amon rose to face me in my pacing, "for your power to be summoned, you must be awake."

"But you're not going to allow my powers to protect me or themselves, am I right?" I leaned up to him and breathed my question against his smooth firm cheek, "how willing you are to sacrifice me. Will it be worth it?" I kissed his cheek and his chin tenderly. "When the demon has had his payment he will nonchalantly turn to Arathia and say, this power comes from Bob of Fleugalworld and Arathia will know who Bob is? She will know what Bob intends?"

"Most likely," Amon nodded, "and if she doesn't know this entity she shall seek the counsel of others to discover his or her intentions."

"Damn," I seethed, "and this is all because my power challenged yours? Is this really such a big deal?"

He pulled me roughly into his embrace and fixed me with his stare, "No one, no thing, has challenged my power in centuries. Yes," he breathed, "it is a big thing."

Pulling away from him for the benefit of the audience, I turned to regard him coolly, *Could I speak to you out on the veranda, Your Lordship?* I asked with my mind, a little show of power and control.

His eyes lit up as he acknowledged my gesture. *Of course, Miss Alexander-Blair!* He answered without words.

No one in the room spoke as we both rose and silently walked out of the room. I thought I glimpsed a barely hidden grin on Winter's face. Chimaera was unreadable as ever.

Once outside in the night air, I couldn't stop myself pacing across the veranda. The satin of my outfit swished noisily as I walked back and forth, considering all that I had just heard. All the intensity of our making love, of our mental connections, all of that meant nothing to this man when his authority had been challenged. I was merely chattel, to be paid to the first entity that could provide the information he was seeking.

"I can't believe you'd be willing," I started when Amon scooped me up in his arms and quelled my ravings by putting his mouth on mine. His tongue probed its way into my mouth, doing a sensual tango with my tongue.

"No you don't, Buster," I shrugged out of his arms, "You're not getting out of this that easily."

Disappointment, betrayal, fear and loathing at the situation roiled inside me. My emotions were a whirlwind and my anger was threatening to unleash something very bad. In an effort to calm myself I began humming as I paced, smiling, as Blue Oyster Cult's "The Reaper" popped into my head. It was always in my subconscious, just below the surface, and I pulled it out and used it for comfort whenever I needed it. I closed my eyes and concentrated on the words to each verse.

"Cat, stop this," I heard a warning in Amon's voice and paused in my pacing to observe him. He was standing still, arms across his chest, hair slightly stirring in the soft night breeze, and eyes flaring in anger at me. At first I didn't know what he meant, then I saw the faintly glowing, pulsing pattern of light quietly throbbing in front of him, between us. It resembled a Celtic symbol of some sort.

"You are weaving," he announced. "You must stop this!"

"Weaving, huh?" I looked at him, bemused, "And this, what, bothers you?" I knew I was playing with fire, baiting him like this, but I couldn't resist.

"You are weaving a ward," he shook his head. "You know it will not hold or keep me from you." He started to move slowly and deliberately toward me.

"I know," I answered stubbornly, not really understanding myself why I was doing this. I folded my arms across my chest.

"And yet you defy me, knowing that you will only anger me, knowing that my power is greater than yours and that you will be punished," he marveled.

"Considering the fact that you and Arathia have already decided to let some demon fuck me," I noticed he winced at my crude language and was delighted, "and possibly destroy me either physically or mentally, I don't think you could dish out any punishment that could compare."

Ripples of energy rode up and down my arms as Amon said, "You have no idea," and I sighed and let the ward drop. It shattered like silent glass then disappeared. His energy had brushed against the satin of my clothes and my body reacted against my will. Things deep inside me coiled and tightened, and my breath caught in my throat. Amon grabbed me by the wrists and pulled me into his arms, pinning my arms behind my back.

"This is your last warning," he glowered, "you will not defy me or challenge my will again."

Leaning away from him, I moaned, "There is nothing I can say or do to change your mind about doing this ritual?"

"I know no other way," he sighed, "Of course if you could tell me the name of the one who has given you these powers, the one who may be challenging me…"

"Which you know very well, I can't," I cut him off before he could finish the statement.

I pulled away from him and walked to the edge of the veranda, looking out over the darkened garden. No moon lit the flowers tonight, the dark was near absolute. Only the soft lights from the house made any dent in the shadows.

"Sin," I called over my shoulder and he moved forward to stand beside me.

"You seldom call me that," he spoke gently, taking my hand in his.

"Tonight the name fits," I smiled grimly, "Something just occurred to me."

"Yes?" He moved silently behind me, leaning his body protectively against mine, resting his chin on my shoulder. Denying myself the luxury of leaning into his firm frame, I held my head up and maintained my posture.

"That night that we made love here in the garden," I reasoned, "you said that we had wakened the elders, right? When it started storming but we weren't touched by it?"

"Yes," he murmured into my hair.

"Could that have anything to do with my power? Could it be the elders?" I turned and looked hopefully into his eyes.

"I don't see how," he shook his head slowly, "the elders have not bothered with the business of man, or of vampires for that matter, for ages. I can't conceive of any reason why they would take a hand in this world now."

"Damn," I lowered my eyes, turned, and wrapped my arms around his waist, burying my face in his shirt. Hot tears rolled down my cheeks and stung when they reached the wound on my face. The pain just made me cry harder. Amon held me silently and let me spend my despair. I wanted to pound on his chest and scream, "How could you?" but I knew that I was so far out of my realm of comprehension, it wouldn't help. This world turned, apparently, on a different axis, different values than the one from which I came and I wasn't sure that I even wanted to truly understand these concepts.

At length he bent down and lifted my chin, kissing me tenderly, then again with more demanding. Finally, he pried open my mouth with his tongue and ground his lips on mine. Rubbing his hands up and down my back, he paused and withdrew from my mouth, "You wear no bra," he breathed heavily, "I approve."

"The only reason I wear no bra, as you put it," I replied, "is because I was too stiff and sore to put one on and I didn't trust Winter to help me without comment. And by the way," I struggled in his arms, "I am way too upset with you to have any of this touchy-feely stuff."

He caught my face between his hands, "You would deny me?" His eyes were serious, but a hint of a smile played at the corners of his mouth. Smoothing my hair back, and playing with my ponytail, he tugged on it gently. "Note to self," I thought, "never wear your hair in a style that may be used as a weapon or means of torture."

"Deny you?" I stretched up on my toes and kissed his neck, digging my hands into his tresses, "You bet. Especially since I have a hot date with a demon in my future, thanks to you."

"Your power should protect you from the worst of the demon's effects," he looked at me with something like concern.

I put both hands on his chest and pushed myself backward out of his embrace. "I don't want should protect, I want will protect, I want is guaranteed to protect," I snapped my fingers as I resumed my pacing, "And just when is this lunacy to take place?"

"Arathia, Winter and Chimaera are preparing even as we speak," he answered somberly, almost regretfully. "We shall perform the ritual before sunrise."

I turned and froze in utter disbelief. Time stood still as I searched my mind for an appropriate reply. There was nothing, my mind went blank, and coherent thought left me. Turning away from Amon, I sat down on the steps of the veranda and dropped my head into my hands. Having fully expected my demise at his hands, I still could not accept that he would throw me away for something so seemingly inconsequential or that it would come so soon. I still believed that my death would be connected to the prophecy, not this madness. This time tomorrow I could be dead, or worse, a raving lunatic foaming at the mouth and trying to chew my way through a straightjacket.

"Amon," I had a disturbing thought, "if when the demon is done with me, when he has given you the information you need? If my mind is destroyed yet my magic remains I'll be a huge danger, right?"

He sat down beside me on the steps, stretching out his incredibly long leather-clad legs, leaning back on his elbows. I noted, with a little evil satisfaction, the bloodstain from my tears marred the beauty of his white shirt.

"You will kill me won't you?" I whispered quietly.

He turned and looked at me questioningly. "I will not lose you in this manner," he murmured, slipping his arm around my shoulder, "there is one protection more that I can offer you, but you must consider it at length for its ramifications are far reaching. Once you accept it, it cannot be removed, returned or denied."

"At this point I'm willing to consider anything," I replied gruffly, feeling the minutes rushing by, the time of my terror approaching.

"You could bear my mark," he whispered seductively into my ear, "but you must accept it willingly and bear it always."

I turned in the darkness and saw that his obsidian eyes were burning. "What do you mean always?" I asked.

"My mark," he leaned over and nuzzled my ear and neck, making me squirm, "is permanent. It is a symbol of your acceptance, your obedience, and your fealty to me. When you accept my mark it means that I am eternally your master in all things, absolute, and that you are eternally under my protection."

Turning away from him, I paused to contemplate the meaning of his words. I noticed heat-lightning etching its way across the black horizon and wondered at its portent. My first reaction to Amon's words were, of course, you've got to be kidding, but I knew that he had little sense of humor and would never joke about something concerned with his power or his control. Whether it was self-preservation or merely sheer mistrust, a thought occurred to me and I turned back to look at Amon, to read his eyes. Oh yeah, there was something he wasn't telling me. My inner voice was screaming so loud that I could hardly hear myself think, and it was screaming, "Nooo!"

"I think not," I shook my head. "Thank you, no."

"You are refusing my gift?" he smiled, his teeth softly glowing white in the darkness of the veranda. "You asked for a guarantee of protection, of survival, yet you refuse when it is offered?"

"The price is too high, Amon," I leaned over and laid my hand on his broad chest. "There are invisible strings attached to your gift, something you aren't telling me, and I feel, no I know, that it's in my best interest to say no to you."

"If I told you all would you accept?" he raised an eyebrow.

"No, probably not. I think I'll take the chance that my own power is enough to protect me," I shrugged, "So now that I have refused, what was it that you wouldn't tell me?"

"By accepting my mark," he leaned up and wrapped one hand behind my neck and pulled me down into a kiss, "you would have relinquished your will, your control and your power to me." The notion that I had just dodged a bullet popped into my head, followed by another question,

"So have you given your mark very often? It doesn't sound like something anyone would accept, it seems a rather one-sided deal."

"I have never offered my mark to another," He blinked and looked hurt, like I had insulted him. Vampires could be so touchy.

"So what, I'd have become your puppet?" I imagined what his words might mean. "I'd be under your constant control and you'd use me to use my magic?"

"You would live at my discretion," he said simply and seemed unwilling to discuss the matter further.

"Eew!" I thought, feeling my flesh crawl at his answer. "Note to self; thank the inner voice in spite of the fact that it's sometimes a smartass."

Thunder rumbled in the distance and a night bird shrieked some-where overhead. The breeze was picking up as the storm on the horizon drew nearer. Amon and I sat in silence, side by side, holding hands or touching or rubbing. It was as if I needed his touch, his nearness, as if I was drawing comfort and courage from him and oh, how I resented it.

Before we went in, I requested my violin, and Amon had Winter bring it to me there on the veranda. I sought solace in my music and played sweet, gentle tunes, their melancholy bringing tears to my eyes. Blood trickled down my cheeks as I finished the last chorus of a tune, but my magic had lit up my fingertips before diving back inside me. I felt as if I had just girded my loins for the battle that I was about to face. Gently I caressed the instrument then, raising it to my lips for one last kiss, I sadly returned it to Amon. He silently returned it to its case and we went inside, the sound of thunder following us through the French doors.

Chapter 19

As Amon apparently had some other business to attend to, Bishop escorted me to the sapphire room where Arathia was waiting for me. He had offered a sedative to calm me during the ritual, but I refused, thinking that my survival might depend on having a clear head. Giving me one long last look, Bishop nodded and silently left the room. Arathia had just stepped out of the bathroom wearing a silvery charcoal gown and carrying two delicate looking bottles of some smoky colored liquid.

"Come Cat," she smiled and turned, going back into the bathroom, "You shall bathe then I will anoint you and dress you before the ceremony." She placed the bottles on the table beside the tub.

Secretly I was relieved when she mentioned dressing me. Figuring that being sex bait for a demon might include some nudity on my part, I relaxed a little thinking that I might not be facing total humiliation. Okay, the thought that this bath might be my last still kind of bothered me, but I had no choice but to face what was coming. Taking off my beautiful emerald tunic outfit and panties, I lowered myself into the warm water as Arathia moved mysteriously around the room, chanting softly and gesturing with her hands. I lay back in the water and closed my eyes, waiting for her to finish her business. When the sound of her shuffling slippers stopped I opened my eyes to find her standing beside the tub, staring down at me.

"You know, Arathia," I rubbed a finger across my eyes and yawned, "If you're done I would like a few minutes alone to collect my thoughts, maybe center myself."

Her eyes lit up and she nodded, "Yes of course, you should do that. I'll give you what, ten minutes?"

"Fine," I waved her away and closed my eyes again, "Ten minutes."

As soon as she was gone I sat up in the tub and began trying to recall the configuration of the ward that I had unintentionally woven when I was on the veranda with Amon. I wasn't sure I could do it, but I planned to attempt a ward for tonight. It would have to be small and not very strong or it would be discovered. Quickly returning my mind to that emotional state, I concentrated my power into my fingertip and drew a symbol in the air. It glowed faintly red, the size of a teacup's saucer. Knowing that it was too big, I caressed the symbol on both sides, applying gentle and steady pressure until the ward began to get smaller. Continuing until it was the size of a dime, I then placed it on my index fingertip and planted it beneath my hair, on my scalp behind my right ear. It was the only place I could think of that it would not likely be discovered and might still afford my mind some protection. I would have preferred to have it in the middle of my forehead but knew that it would not be allowed, so I worked in secret, doing what little I could.

Having dried myself with a huge black towel presumably provided for my use, I wrapped it around my torso and sat down on the edge of the tub. Pulling the scrunci from my hair, I shook out my moistened tangles and was about to go to the vanity for a hairbrush when Arathia returned. She carried what I first thought was a stiletto in her left hand and pointed with it at my towel. "Stand up and remove that please," she smiled pleasantly enough, then dipped the wicked looking sharp thing into one of the smoky liquid filled bottles.

I did as I was told, inwardly groaning that the pleasantries were about to commence, so as not to attract any undue attention. Hoping that my insignificant little ward would not be found, I closed my eyes and held out my arms as Arathia began drawing intricate little designs on my skin with, unfortunately, near invisible fluid. What I had taken to be a stiletto was in fact some exotic paintbrush and she dipped it into first one then the other bottle as she made her designs. I could discern no pattern to her application as she went from one part of my body to another in a seemingly random fashion. She made a little circular motion in the air and I turned around so she could attend to my backside.

"You may turn around," she said at length. She was going over her work, inspecting every inch until finally, she seemed satisfied. "Put this around your neck with the charm on the front," she said as she handed me a cord of leather with a small silver trinket of some sort on it. I obeyed. "Next this one with the charm down your back," she instructed with another leather cord. This continued until I had seven necklaces down my front, the longest with the charm just above my navel, and five down my back. She then fastened three leather straps around my hips and positioned the charms they bore at various intervals on my pelvis. Two strips of leather encircled each wrist, though they bore no charms, and two encircled my ankles. I was beginning to feel like some bizarre Bali dancer when she stopped and left the room. Moments later she returned carrying an amber colored robe made of some delicate gauzy fabric. "Put this on please," she nodded and handed it to me. I was happy to find that it had a fabric belt that could be tied at the waist, since apparently all I would be sporting was the leather and charms, and I did so. Thankfully it was generously cut and draped in thick folds because the material was so lightly woven it would have covered nothing save its volume. Arathia stepped back and observed me then nodded and turned to leave. "Let us go," she commanded as she moved forward and I discovered that my feet were rooted to the floor. Forward movement was suddenly out of the question as I realized that we were actually going through with this, this madness.

Immediately, Winter and Chimaera appeared at the bathroom door, their faces filled with determination and urgency. "Come, '*tite soeur*," Winter smiled sympathetically and offered me his hand. Focusing only on his hand, I concentrated on putting one foot in front of the other. I looked up as we left the bedroom to find that Amon and Bishop had joined Arathia and our little entourage headed into the bowels of Amon's house. The little voice deep in my mind laughed bitterly at the idea that we must look like a condemned prisoner being escorted to the gas chamber, surrounded by guards, a priest, and prison officials. It would have been more amusing had I not been the condemned. No demon yet in sight and my choo choo was already threatening derailment.

Relief flooded through me when I saw that there was no sacrificial altar of stone in the center of the room which had been prepared for this night. Horror replaced the relief when I spied the manacles hanging from the wall on the other side of the room. I froze at the sight, then took two hesitant steps backward until I bumped into Amon. I turned to face him.

"Something tells me you don't have a really big dog, do you?" I whispered. "Those are for me?"

His silence crushed me. He would not look at me and I realized begging would do no good.

Winter and Chimaera once more appeared on either side of me and, each taking an arm, they guided me forward. After a few steps I shook the two vampires off and, straightening my shoulders, strode to the wall where I turned and lifted my arms. "Like this?" I smiled sweetly, secretly planning revenge on all and sundry. Joyfully I realized that the fear I had expected had not appeared but his brother, anger, had ridden up in all his glory. From this position I could see that the room was filled with people I had never seen, my revenge would take a while. Evidently our little ritual was of great interest and all the local vampires had been invited. Chimaera shot me a look of sympathy as he slipped the cold metal shackle around my left wrist. "Little Sister," he nodded. Winter smiled encouragement as he did the same with my right, then they both stepped back behind Amon. Whispers and murmurs stirred around the room. Amon turned to Arathia and nodded and she began to speak in some unintelligible language. She moved about the room burning something in a chalice and once again, gesturing with her free hand. I was mesmerized watching her and was startled back to reality only when Amon's voice boomed, "Stop!"

I held my breath as he glared and strode deliberately toward me. "She is warded," he snarled and stopped only inches in front of me. "Willful girl," he chided, his voice dripping venom, "where is it?"

I turned my head to the left, exposing my right ear. Amon leaned forward and blew on my neck and I felt the ward dissolve. He grabbed my chin tightly in his hand, "You will be punished for this."

"Fine," I snapped, "If I survive you can punish me. You should have known that I would have to try."

He nodded and turned to step away, his motion causing my belt to drop and the robe to fall open. "Yes, I should have known."

Arathia's chanting resumed and I busied my mind imagining vampires as insects that I could mount with pins and pull off their wings. Smoke and some other substance started filling the room. A faint hint of sulfur and creosote assaulted my nose. Though the walls all bore torches burning merrily, darkness slithered into the room and my anger began to flag. I closed my eyes and pulled with all my weight on the shackles in a futile effort to escape. All I managed to accomplish was to hurt my wrists and panic myself to tears. The crowd released a collective gasp as the blood began to roll down my face.

Suddenly Arathia's voice became louder and she began calling some unrecognizable word over and over. The air around me shimmered and stirred as a being, as black as pitch, took form before me. The demon was tall and feline, his skin looked like rubber and his claws and eyes were red. His tail swished nervously as he leaned his cat-like head toward me and sniffed. Nuzzling the right side of my neck where the ward had been, he gently ran his rough tongue up my throat and I swallowed hard and fought not to scream. His paws gently parted my robe and he looked me up and down. Nodding, he turned to Arathia, "I accept," his voice was deep and almost a purr. "A leopard man, that's what the demon is," I thought as he turned back to regard me. "Little witch," the demon hissed and put one claw on my chest as it leaned into my neck. My power did not stir or ripple. I was scared, uneasy, but not threatened. The demon licked a tear from my cheek then, spitting and gagging, turned in anger and screeched, "What is this treachery?" It screamed once more before it dissolved into a puff of smoke and was gone.

Breathing a sigh of relief, I turned to Amon. "Okay, well that was a good try but it didn't work. Come on, let me out of these and we'll go think of something else. Ritual's over," I called to the audience," Sorry it didn't work, but glad to have you. We'll have you all back for dinner sometime soon. Bye Bye."

"Silence," Amon bellowed in anger that I didn't understand. He turned to Arathia and they spoke briefly in hushed tones

"We shall call Agathodemon forth," Arathia called out and the audience suddenly fell silent.

I groaned and started to protest when Amon stepped forward and tied a gag around my mouth. *This just keeps getting better and better,* I touched his mind with my thoughts.

"Hold your tongue, woman," he seethed. *Well I will now,* I snapped back silently, struggling to spit the bitter tasting fabric out of my mouth.

Arathia's words reverberated around the room and took on a different tone as she stepped in front of me. Her eyes shot me a warning and I ceased my struggles. Cocking her head in a bird-like motion, she moved away and continued her incantation. Some memory stirred in my subconscious but had no time to surface, as once more the air became heavy and charged, shimmering in front of me. This time I felt my power coiling and moving deep within me. A combination of fear and anger rose and my vision became tinged with a film of red. As Arathia called out the name Agathodemon for the third time a mist appeared before me and then became a solid form. I tried to gasp through the gag as a dragon appeared in front of me. His eyes glittered gold and his scales shimmered silvery green. Huge wings spread out behind him and I thought, "This guy I can pull the wings off of." He leaned very close to me, his eyes widening in surprise, then took the form of a man. A man, I noticed, very similar in appearance to Amon. The demon must have read my affections for the vampire, though at this very moment I did so not like him, and assumed a similar form. He wore a silk shirt the same color as his scales and black leather pants. His hair, long and thick, was charcoal to Amon's silver. The wings were gone.

"Pretty evil witch," the dragon murmured as it parted my robe and tinkered with the charms on my girdle of leather strips, "Do I get to keep her?"

"Do my bidding," Arathia answered, "and she is yours for a time."

"How much time?" he turned to face Arathia and scanned the room, noticing the crowd for the first time.

"An audience," his eyes lit up, "shall we give them a show, Little Witch?"

"Do what I ask of you and you may have her for," I expected twenty minutes, an hour at most, "twelve hours." Arathia answered. My heart fell.

"Twelve of my hours or of yours?" the demon asked suspiciously.

"Twelve of our hours," Amon stepped forward and answered.

"The Master Vampire has affection for the little witch?" the dragon cooed.

"Careful, demon," Amon warned, "you overstep your bounds."

"Yet what you desire is worth parting with your little morsel here," Agathodemon insisted, touching my hair as if to pet me, "it must be very valuable to give up such a treat." I pulled my head away from his hand and would have hissed at him if I hadn't been gagged.

"We seek the author of her power," Arathia commanded.

The dragon turned back to look me in the eye. My power was writhing and curling in my gut as he moved closer and sniffed the air around me. "Must I return her alive?" he asked.

"We have further need of her so yes, she must live," Arathia answered lightly. My mind was spinning.

"And must she be," he breathed very close to my ear, "sane?" His hand slipped beneath my robe and slithered around my ribs, making my skin crawl.

"Preferably, " Arathia nodded, "but we understand if her mind breaks in your service."

Real nice! With friends like you guys who needs enemies? We understand if her mind breaks in your service, I mean really! I hissed in my mind and noticed that Amon had moved away from Arathia and was now standing with his back to me, as if he couldn't face me. *Serves you right*, I added vehemently, *hope your guilt eats you up like this guy's likely to do to me*. Though I knew that Amon had heard my thoughts and felt my dismay, he shut his mind, succinctly raising his mental shields before turning back to look at me.

"Just for the record, and for the benefit of the audience," the demon smiled and bowed graciously. "When I determine the author of this little witch's power, after disclosing this information to you," he bowed to Arathia, "I will have her to play with at my leisure for twelve of your world's hours. Is this correct?"

"It is," Arathia agreed.

"I agree to your offer," Agathodemon smiled wickedly and I closed my eyes and turned my head. A hand that felt remarkably like a claw slithered under my robe and stroked a fiery line up and down my ribs. My power was uncoiling, building, and I fought to hold on to control. My vision swam as I felt the charms bouncing and moving on my chest. The dragon slipped his arm around me and pulled me into an embrace. His skin was cool, smooth and taut. He leaned his head forward and breathed fire on my neck His tongue snaked out and burned the flesh beneath my ear. I whimpered as he released the gag, moved his mouth onto mine and kissed me deeply. My power suddenly burst forth, rocketing into him. The dragon screamed and leapt back, reverting to his true form. His reptilian eyes were filled with panic, the pupils contracting to slits, and he put one claw to his mouth as he turned and strode away. Small puffs of smoke curled and rose from his ears, marking his path of departure, and his wings fluttered anxiously.

"Wherever her power comes from," he hissed, obviously in pain, "it is not for me to disclose. I will not risk destruction for a mere slip of a mortal. Even if you gave her to me outright, the cost would be too dear. I leave you to your witch, Master Vampire. Sorceress," he snarled at Arathia, "trouble me no more."

Turning to pin me with his angry stare, he sniffed haughtily and raised his chin in defiance. "You," he muttered nearly beneath his breath, though even from a distance I knew what he was saying, "the next time we meet, one of us shall not survive!"

With that he vanished and my hope returned. My power settled comfortably once more and my vision returned to normal. Sagging against the wall, my knees buckled and the shackles were the only things holding me upright. I must have fainted for when I came to the manacles were gone and I lay in a heap on the floor against the wall. Chimaera came forward and lifted me in his arms, shaking his head in something like disbelief.

"Put her in my coffin, Chimaera," I heard Amon order, "I will tend to her later."

"Great," I murmured beneath my breath, "now comes the punishment for the ward."

"Shh," Chimaera whispered, "that, at least, is for another time."

I closed my eyes and leaned my head on his shoulder. My eyes were still closed when he laid me in Amon's coffin but I swear I felt him lean down and kiss me on the forehead. "Something else to figure out," I mumbled to myself as he shut the lid and sleep, or death, took me. At that moment I didn't care which it was.

Chapter 20

Though I expected dreamless release in Amon's coffin, I was disappointed to be assaulted by images of people, the sensation of my mouth filling with gushes of hot, sweet blood, and swallowing what my mind refused to admit. A parade of Amon's victims marched through my dreams, earlier ones bathed in violence and pain, later ones washed in sexual tension and sensuality. Darkness, a shadow shape I recognized as Leitha, moved to embrace me in my dream. Tossing and turning, I fought sleep, at last emerging gasping and crying in Amon's embrace. His chest, beneath my ear, was silent and I knew that he had not bothered to make his heart beat for me. Suddenly his hand shot out and grabbed one of the leather strips that still encircled my pelvis. He twisted it sharply and pulled me against his body, as if I could have gotten any closer. Feeling the smooth fabric of his shirt, I realized that someone had removed my robe and that all I wore were the leather cords and charms from last night. Releasing the strap, Amon straightened his arm and opened the coffin, then turned to look at me. My bloody tears were beginning to dry and he looked longingly at them.

"I am relieved that you were not harmed," he whispered, licking his lips. "I regret that I put my own need to know of my possible enemies before your physical and mental welfare." He followed the tracks of my tears with his eyes, his expression rapt with desire.

Looking at him somberly I shrugged, "Go ahead," and closed my eyes and offered my bloodstained face. His lips were moist and hot as he licked the precious tears from my cheeks. Other parts of my body were becoming moist as his lips and tongue sent ripples of delight across my skin. Cool air touched my bottom and goosebumps rose on my flesh. Lust uncurled deeply in my abdomen and I slid my knee between his legs and mounted his thigh.

"You were crying in your sleep, Precious," he ran his hands up and down my arms as he rested his head back against the satin pillow, "What caused your sadness, your pain?" His ebony eyes were lit with desire and came to rest on my breasts. They were covered with gooseflesh from the cool air and I ached for him to touch them and make me warm. My pulse quickened from just his look, the nakedness of his hunger.

"It's not important," I brushed away his comment, "but what is important is why was I dreaming? The last time I slept with you here I had no dreams and slept peacefully." I leaned forward and unbuttoned his shirt, my rear end squirming on his thigh.

"I did not arrive back here and join you until just moments before sunrise. You slept alone for several hours. Without my influence, your mind was free to dream," he explained, finally reaching up to cup one breast in his hand. He lifted its weight, softly squeezed it, then pinched the nub of my nipple between his fingers. When he gently pressed the stiffness of that nipple back into the soft firmness of my breast I gasped and glared down at him. Leaning forward, I opened my mouth to brush my lips up his smooth, taut chest. The firmness of his member moved beneath my ribs and I sat up and released his zipper. I did not hesitate for a moment, but moved up and positioned myself above his hard, throbbing length. His expression changed subtly as he grabbed my hips in his hands and moved smoothly and expertly into me. We made love leisurely, languidly, and I marveled at how comfortable we were becoming with each other. As our passion mounted, our rhythm increased, my breathing grew ragged, and I longed for release. Having closed my eyes to relish the sensations of Amon touching me, arousing me, I was startled when I opened my eyes to find his hands reaching presumably for my throat. His eyes were suddenly different, no longer ebony but a feral gold, and his expression was one of hunger but of a different kind. Fear choked me for a moment, striking me dumb. At last I was able to draw breath and croak my alarm.

"Amon?" I tried to get his attention, "Amon, what are you doing? Amon?" I noticed in that moment that in addition to his eyes changing, his hands had become longer, his nails sharp and claw-like. It may have been my imagination, but for a moment his jaw appeared longer and more canine. Grasping his wrists in my hands, I leaned forward the instant our orgasm rocketed through the two of us. "Amon!" I demanded firmly and his eyes finally focused and returned to their normal black. He drew in a startled breath and his eyes widened in surprise as he returned to himself.

"What was that?" I released a tension filled breath and shook my head, "I don't know where you were, but it wasn't here with me."

"Goddess save us," he whispered as he rubbed his now normal appearing hands gently up and down my arms. "I cannot believe that this happened. I was beginning to shapeshift. This cannot happen!"

"What do you mean this can't happen?" I smiled ruefully, "You told me that you can shift into a wolf, a bird, and what was it, a panther? Surely it can happen."

"No," he insisted, "what I mean is that I cannot unintentionally shapeshift. It takes a tremendous amount of power and concentration to transform into another creature. It cannot just happen accidentally."

"What were you going to do if you had transformed all the way?" I leaned my head down and rested my ear on his chest.

"What do you mean?" he looked at me with dismay.

"I mean what would have been your intentions?" I insisted, "What would you have done if you had become a wolf? Would you have torn me to ribbons, feasted on my flesh?"

"I assure you I had no such intentions," he replied indignantly. "My beast has not raised its head uninvited since shortly after I was made Vampire. Several hundred years have passed since my emotions called it forth. I do not know what its meaning is but I am sure I would not have made a meal of you." He lifted me by the elbows and pulled himself to sit upright beneath me. His arms encircled me and he buried his face in my neck.

"Oh my god," I whispered as a thought rang true in my head, "I was giving you my power again. That's how you were able to almost shift completely without knowing it! You were channeling my magic. Am I safe? Could this happen again?"

He shook his head. "Now that I know this is possible I will be constantly vigilant against it," he reasoned. "Please do not fear me. I would never intentionally hurt you."

"But Amon," I whispered as I recalled his eyes, "It wasn't you that was looking at me through those bright golden eyes. If there was human, or even vampire, intelligence behind those eyes it was surely hidden." I crawled off of him and curled into the edge of the coffin. He stood and dressed quietly, unable or unwilling to meet my eyes.

Bowing his head, he turned to leave. "I promise you are safe," he murmured as he left.

"Damn," I hissed as I sat upright in the coffin and smacked my forehead with my palm. "Vampires are so freakin' touchy. I can't believe that I just hurt his feelings after he almost made a human Poo-Poo Platter out of me! I have GOT to start watching what I say!" I raised my head and looked around the empty room. In the corner, deep in the shadows, a darkness moved and I heard whispering, a plea, a sob. The creature Leitha shuffled forward then hesitated, stepped back, and disappeared.

How long I sat there in the silence, listening to my heart beating, I don't know but it seemed an eternity. What Leitha's appearance meant I had no idea, but I was sure that it meant something.

By the time Amon returned I had given up trying to make sense of anything and was just happy to see him composed and apparently willing to forgive me for yet another human faux pas. And my, did he look good! His thick lustrous hair shone in the soft lights, a leather braid holding it neatly away from his face. That lovely face was so well chiseled, so perfectly wrought in its beauty. How could I, after what had just happened, feel such desire for this creature? Instead of being terrified I was still enraptured by him! The tiny voice in my head was ranting violently and all I could do was notice how his black satin shirt dramatically enhanced the silver of his hair and perfectly matched his crisply pleated trousers! Across his shoulder was draped a garment of some sort, white and shimmering. A belt of black leather encircled his waist and bore a silver dragon's head buckle. He leaned over me and I involuntarily drew my arms tightly around myself before I could stop it.

" I regret that your defiance and my own newly stirring emotions called forth my beast and I lost control. Without the addition of your power to mine this would not have been possible. I assure you that my creature has not stirred unbidden in centuries. I hope I did not frightened you." He offered me his hand and I took it, forcing myself to think only of the man, not the creature that lurked inside him. Offering me the garment from his shoulder, which turned out to be a delicately woven white silk robe, Amon slipped it up my arms, drew the belt around me, and cinched it at my waist.

The realization that I could suddenly find myself in such a vulnerable position, vulnerable, hell indefensible, threatened to swamp me and the world swam for a moment. That I was dealing with something that wasn't human, trapped in his world, was a sobering taste of my new reality. Amon wrapped his arms around me and whispered in my ear, "Please understand. When you intentionally warded yourself I got very angry with you. Though I had not expressly forbidden a ward, you knew that you were not to use your magic during the ritual. You willfully defied me, in public, for the meager protection of a sad little ward."

"I had to try," I sighed as I turned and placed my hands on his beautiful satin shirt, "that's just my nature."

"Though roused by my anger," he continued, "it was your passion and your power that brought forth my beast."

"Of course," I shook my head and stepped back, "I knew that somehow this would all be my fault. I'm beginning to think that everything that goes wrong in your world is my fault!" I threw up my hands in mock exasperation.

He took my hands in his and looked at me soberly, his manner suddenly serious.

"I am not assigning blame," he smiled weakly, "I am just trying to explain what happened and why. Please do not hate me or fear me."

"I saw your eyes change," I nodded, "I guess maybe I knew it wasn't you anymore." I hugged him and breathed, "Okay, let's just let this episode of errant emotions go, just put it behind us."

"Punishment for your defiance still awaits you," he said remorsefully, "and if you cannot or will not change your nature, I fear there will be additional punishment in your future. I take no pleasure in your pain."

"Again, you suck at apologies," I smiled and looked up at him.

"Again," he raised an eyebrow, "I did not apologize."

On the way upstairs, Amon tried to convince me to eat something but I insisted on showering first. He drew me through his bedroom into the bathroom beyond. As I dropped the lovely white robe I realized that, though I could draw the leather necklaces over my head, I had no way to remove the girdle of leather straps from my hips.

"Amon?" I asked, after studying the knots at my hips with no hope of freedom. He stepped out of the shower stall where he had been turning on the water. When he saw my dilemma he smiled broadly and, with those black eyes twinkling, stepped up behind me. He placed one smooth powerful hand on each of my hips and growled deep in his throat, "Whatever shall we do about these?" He ran one thumb beneath the lowest strap.

"How about remove them?" I grumbled.

"Very well," he breathed heavily on my neck as his front brushed against my backside. With no real effort, he snapped the leather cords with his fingers and the charms fell tinkling to the floor. Completely naked, I turned and put my arms around Amon's neck then stood on tiptoe and kissed him chastely on the lips before stepping away and into the shower. Hearing his wistful sigh, I smiled and adjusted the water temperature to sluice away the oils and demon fluids from the Shieh Na Rah. Nice to know that at my age I could still excite a male even if he was an eight hundred-year-old, lusty, sex starved vampire.

Shampoo was dripping down my face and stinging my eyes when the shower door opened and Amon stepped in, muscles gloriously firm and naked, under the spray. I watched hypnotized as the drops of water cascaded down his chest, rock hard abdominal muscles, and regions below. He smoothed his hair back out of his face then began to massage my scalp.

"You may not believe this but, I think this is the first time I've ever had a man wash my hair," I murmured in delight. To give him better access, I propped my forearms against the cool tile and leaned my head back. When the last of the shampoo lather had washed down my back, Amon rubbed a fragrant sponge over my shoulders, pausing to touch my injuries gently.

"Your bruises are many," he observed.

"Yeah well," I answered dryly, "I'm not accustomed to being hurled across the room by someone with superhuman strength."

He took his time and massaged the flesh all over my body. I was relieved that sex was apparently not on his mind, for though I had not suffered physical injury in tonight's drama, my mind was still reeling. When I tried to take the sponge to wash him in return he merely smiled and shook his head. Wrapping his arms protectively around me, he just stood quietly holding me as the water washed away the magical debris and the steam purged the demons from my pores. I turned and wrapped my arms around his waist, pressing my cheek against his smooth chest, and we stood silent and unmoving beneath the pelting spray.

"So what does last night's fiasco mean?" I asked as it occurred to me, "Why did the leopard demon disappear when he tasted my tears? And why did the dragon demon bolt when he tasted my power?"

"Apparently the author of your gifts is powerful enough," he explained, "that disclosing his or her identity might mean risking destruction for the demons. And I believe that your power actually injured Agathodemon, whether or not you intended it."

"I did nothing," I admitted, holding up my hands and shaking my head. "Whatever happened it was my power reacting to the demon, not me. Though I will confess to feeling rather pleased when dragon-boy yelped in pain. If he only could imagine what punishments I was concocting in my mind he would have fled instantly."

Amon laughed with genuine delight, "I have no doubt, Little One, no doubt."

We stood peacefully together a while longer then at last I looked up at him and smiled, "Shall we adjourn to the other room?" The water was still warm, but I was beginning to feel a little pruny.

"As My Lady wishes," he leaned down and kissed my forehead as we moved apart and stepped out of the shower. The air was cooler in the bathroom and my skin immediately rose in goosebumps. Amon wrapped me in a towel then pressed himself against me, exuding heat.

"How do you do that?" I gasped as his warmth rolled over me. Apparently being a vampire didn't necessarily mean being cold-blooded.

"I have all sorts of tricks," he grinned and rubbed his hands up and down my arms till the chills subsided.

Amon wrapped a towel around his waist and disappeared, promising to return shortly. I tucked my towel in above my breasts and pulled a blow dryer out from beneath the vanity. As this room had no mirror above the sink, I didn't have to worry about primping. Plugging the dryer in, I leaned over so my hair was spilling upside down to dry it. Through my legs I saw Amon return with his arms full of garments. I snapped off the dryer and stood up to look at him. He had dressed in a sapphire blue shirt with a black leather vest and black jeans. His hair he had left loose and flowing. Once more he sported the belt with the silver dragon's head buckle.

"You look good enough to eat," I purred, looking him up and down.

"Woman, do not do that," he said gruffly, favoring me with a roguish smile. "If you have any hope of leaving this room anytime soon you will not tease me." He moved forward and handed me the stack of clothes. Roughly he grabbed the back of my neck and forced his mouth onto mine. His kiss was demanding, hot, wet, and electrifying. Abruptly he released me, "Dress quickly, we have guests for dinner."

Of course, at that statement, my mind instantly conjured the image of well dressed dinner guests trussed up like Thanksgiving turkeys and stretched out on really large dinner plates, waiting for us to dig in. I giggled helplessly when I recalled the vampire episode of "Gilligan's Island," where Gilligan played Dracula and the Howell's were unsuspecting tourists about to become dinner. Something about that phrase, "guests for dinner," touched off such a memory. "I am so a child of TV Land," I chuckled to myself.

Putting the folded garments on the edge of the vanity, I lifted one item after another and found that he had brought me a lovely black crepe sleeveless sheath. There were also black panties and a pair of three-inch heels, though I could find no bra. I had to laugh out loud at the sight of the shoes. Being six feet tall, I had never in my life worn anything taller than a one-inch pump. These heels were so tall and so tapered that they were practically stilettos. Never having even tried on such instruments of torture, it was doubtful that I could walk in them. The black silk panties were exquisite and felt, when I slipped them on, like I wore nothing at all. I slid the sheath over my head and smoothed it down my body. Very high slits ran up either thigh almost to my hips and I was relieved to think that at least I would be able to move and sit down in this dress. As I pulled the shoulders up, I realized why Amon had not brought a bra with the other things. This dress was backless, sporting a scoop that rested on the small of my back just above my panties. Unfortunately, this meant that everyone who saw me tonight would also see my bruises. I was sure to be the topic of whispered speculation, if not outright conversation.

"Oh well, there's nothing for it," I sighed to myself and slipped my feet into the heels. I teetered for a moment, unused to balancing and the additional height, before I took a few stiffly hesitant steps. There was a little wobbling at first, but I soon felt comfortable enough to hope that I could make it through the evening without falling on my face. Using an ornately decorated hairbrush that I had found on a shelf above the sink, I brushed the tangles out of my mane and swept it back off of my face. A tube of umber-red lipstick lay on the shelf, so I assumed it was for me and applied it as carefully as possible. Without the aid of a mirror, I just hoped that I was presentable.

Chapter 21

Amon was waiting, leaning up against the fireplace mantle when I stepped out of the bathroom and into his bedroom. His eyes lit up and he smiled broadly, showing his pearly fangs, when he saw me. I turned and made a little circle, modeling the dress and shoes, and he nodded approval and stepped forward, offering his arm. With such tall heels on I was much closer to his height and it felt odd to not have to look up to see his eyes.

"I wonder about the wisdom of wearing a backless dress tonight, Amon," I sighed and took his arm, "You yourself said that my bruises are many."

"Don't worry about that," he smiled and patted my hand, "Our guests will be expecting it."

I froze in my tracks and looked at him, his face a mask of calm innocence. A really ugly thought occurred to me and I almost bolted, probably would have were it not for the heels, at the disgust I felt.

"Your guests?" I waved my hand in anger as I started to rave. "You have me wearing this dress so they can see how you've punished me? What is this some kind of sick macho, testosterone-induced vampire thing?"

He turned to face me, his hands firmly holding mine. "Our guests know that it was your power that challenged me. If you arrived without a visible mark on you I'm afraid they would insist on seeing proof of my reprisal. That might include one, if not all, of them watching you undress. Assuming that you would wish to avoid this," he shrugged gallantly, "I chose this dress."

"Oh," I smiled weakly. There were moments, frequent actually, when I felt so out of my element. I knew I could never hope to grasp all the subtleties of political and power machinations apparently inherent with being a vampire

"Also, the fact that I would inflict injury on you is proof that you are not a weakness of mine," he grinned, "though of course you

172

are. But, those at dinner tonight must believe me impervious to your witchly ways."

I moved into his arms and laid my head on his shoulder. "Oh you vampires say the sweetest things," I cooed. Amon looked at me out of the corner of his eye and sighed deeply.

He turned me and took my arm again and we resumed our stroll through the corridors at a leisurely, even ponderous pace. "I should," he began, "explain about this evening. What is going to happen and why."

"I so do not like the sound of that," I said warily, "or the tone of your voice."

"Our guests," he continued patiently, "are not just guests. They are the Council of Five."

"Council of Five," I parroted with proper reverence in my tone.

"Let me finish, woman, unless you would prefer to go in there unprepared?" He regarded me soberly and I dropped my flip attitude. I donned a mask of solemnity and he began again. We moved gingerly down the grand staircase toward the magnificent foyer below.

"Regrettably, I did not discover your ward until we had entered the ritual chamber and were in the presence of witnesses. Had I found it earlier, the punishment would have been mine and, well," he leered, "private. As the offense was discovered publicly, the punishment must be decided and meted out publicly. The Council of Five is a body of vampire government, if you will, and they determine what is just and dispense that justice. I, as Master Vampire, must remain objective and neutral. I can influence their decisions, but I do not vote. Though Arathia is not a member, the Council often seeks her advice so she will be present After the failed ritual, I do not know if this is a good thing or a bad thing." He took my chin in his hand and turned me to appraise the wound on my cheek, "I am hopeful that seeing the marks you already bear, this and the wounds on your back, that the Council may be moved to mercy."

"Mercy?" I stuttered, "Wait a minute. Just how bad can this be?" In my imagination the Howell's evaporated and it was me, I was the one who was running around screaming, trying to escape the vampires. Reaching the foyer, we strode on, and I found myself leaning heavily on his arm for support.

"Your body will recover from whatever punishment is inflicted," he said simply, as if he were giving me the weather forecast. "Please, take my signals and follow my lead tonight, as any protests will only make things worse."

With that we came to the wide doorway leading into the dining room. Winter and Chimaera stood sentry on either side of the entrance. Inside, huge chandeliers cast soft drops of light onto the magnificently appointed table. Black bone china glimmered on the deep burgundy tablecloth and bright gold flatware gleamed beside each setting. Crystal goblets, filled with ruby liquid twinkled in the light. Our guests, apparently, had already arrived and were seated. Whether it was because I was human, female, witch, or the subject of punishment, I don't know but no one stood when we entered. Amon nodded at those seated then seated himself at the head of the table, indicating for me to take the chair to his left. It was evident that these vampires either had no manners or thought me undeserving of such common courtesies. Arathia, I noticed, occupied the seat to Amon's right. He was right, I smelled the jealousy on myself, tonight! Looking around the room, I noted that Arathia and I were the only two who weren't vampires. Everyone else in the place had that hyperbeauty that I now recognized as a preternatural glamour. The vampire to Arathia's right was a delicious looking young man with hair and eyes the color of dark caramel. His skin was smooth and his lips full and crimson. He wore a "give my eye teeth for it" creamy brocade jacket over a shirt the color of summer wheat. He looked at me indifferently, I couldn't tell if he was friend or foe. Amon introduced him as Kasimir, though I thought from his looks that Cashmere would have been a more appropriate name. He fairly oozed smooth sensuality.

To Kasimir's right was an angelic vampire, if that's not an oxymoron, with curly hair the color of spun gold falling well below her ample bosom. Her eyes were startling blue and her cheekbones high and well defined. Pink lipstick decorated her cherubic mouth. She wore a gown of white gossamer with a deep plunging neckline and long tapered sleeves. The effect was hideously startling when she smiled and her fangs appeared. The angel's name was Nephthele.

The vampire at the end of the table, Amon told me, was called Thammuz and he was perhaps the most aged looking member of the Council. He looked like a mortal man would near fifty. His hair was white and drew straight back from the widow's peak on his brow and his eyes were dark. The vampire exuded an air of intelligence and power. Something in his manner, nothing I could put my finger on, made me fearful of him. He wore an elegant black suit cut in the European manner with a crisp white shirt and expensive looking white tie. His movements were precise and efficient, spare even. My sense of self-preservation was setting off alarms just looking at this guy.

To Thammuz's right sat a flamboyant female vampire named Chesmne. Her hair was wild and sparkled with a riot of different hair colors. Red, white, blonde, black, and brown, they were all there in her mane. She looked very much like a calico cat and her green eyes sparkled with feline intelligence. She wore a gold lameȼ beaded gown and amber crystals twinkled at her neck. Her hands were long and delicate with dramatically painted black fingernails. It was clear from her looks that she would not be the type to hang out with a lowly mortal witch and would not likely be an ally to anyone of our shared gender.

To Chesmne's right, and my left, sat Mastiphal who was introduced as the newest member of the Council. He looked very much like a Viking, with long thick reddish blonde hair, which he wore loose, and a goatee. His complexion was ruddy and his eyes were the color of sapphires. The creases at the corners of his eyes made him look like he was smiling, though he wasn't. He wore a leather jacket the color of ox blood and beneath that a shirt of candlelight satin with a jabot at the throat.

Arathia, as perfectly turned out as usual, was resplendent in a gray satin gown sporting quite a décolletage. I suspected that if she stood we would all be treated to a view of her navel. Her glossy black hair was woven into an intricate pile on the top of her head and her graceful neck was adorned with a solid collar of silver. I resented like hell the fact that she was wearing Amon's color. For a moment jealousy stirred my power, then I willed it to calm. The last thing I needed was another little display of my magic, or my lack of control thereof.

Lily brought in food for Arathia and me and refilled the ruby liquid in the crystal goblets in the others' hands. Why we were enacting this farce of dining was never explained, nor could I figure it out on my own. Arathia ate leisurely, though I could find no appetite for what lay on my plate. It smelled like crab etouffe, which I normally loved, but I knew that eating it under these circumstances would likely ruin it for all time for me. At length, Amon cleared his throat and addressed his guests.

"Council of Five," he nodded, "You know why we are here tonight. The witch, Catherine Alexander-Blair," he turned to acknowledge me, "defied my orders and now must face the punishment for that defiance. It is you who will determine the means of her discipline and though I show her no favor, I would ask that you consider the marks and injuries she bears already. Her power has brought many wounds down upon her." At this he turned to me and mouthed "Stand up and turn around." I started to object, but he shot me a venomous look and I reluctantly stood and turned my back to the table. I pulled my hair to one side so everyone could get an eyeful of my bruises. No one made a sound. Turning back around, I turned my cheek so the council members could see that too, then I sat back down.

"Winter," Thammuz called my bodyguard and ally from his post at the door. Winter stepped beside me and pulled my chair out, leading me away from the table, though not out of the room. I gave him my shrinking violet look and he whispered, "Be strong, *'tite souer.'*" I glanced back over my shoulder at Amon and noticed Arathia leaning over to speak quietly with Kasimir. She drew back and cocked her head in a bird-like manner and bells went off in my head. As sure as I was that Arathia was the Oracle that gave Amon the prophecy, I was equally certain that Amon didn't know it. Though it wasn't immediately clear why, I knew that this was important.

"A finger," I heard one of the male vampires demand.

"She plays the violin," Amon answered, "it would be a pity to kill the music. Remember, this is chastisement not dismemberment. She must be able to recover from her punishment." There was silence for a moment then a female voice suggested sequestering me. "That doesn't sound so bad," I whispered to Winter, moments before it was mentioned that my mind would not likely survive intact. Apparently sequestering in this world meant something different than it did in mine. I had envisioned a hotel suite in Miami.

"She should bear the Mark of the Penitent," one of the male vampires announced and there were murmurs of agreement around the room. I looked up at Winter with a questioning expression. He shrugged with a grimace, which I took to mean that, though it wouldn't be pleasant, it could have been worse. I was fully aware of the Machiavellian maneuver of discussing my possible torture within my earshot. This could have all been very easily decided before I came into the room. The Council wanted me afraid and intimidated by what might happen. I hated politics and apparently vampire politics were no better than those of my fellow man.

"Bring her," Amon called and Winter guided me over to the table. He stood me beside Amon's chair. Evidently, I was about to be sentenced.

"It has been decided by this, The Council of Five, that you should, for your defiance, bear the Mark of the Penitent. As this is a fair and just punishment I declare that it should be carried out immediately," Amon announced to the room.

A very uneasy feeling came over me when Winter stepped in front of me and bound my wrists together tightly with a leather strap. He then led me across the room and bade me stand near the fireplace. A cloth of black fabric was tied across my eyes and when I started to lose my balance in the dark, Winter placed my hands against the wall. I hoped it was only to steady me. Standing blind and bound for countless minutes, I was forced to shift my weight uneasily from one foot to the other to maintain my equilibrium. I didn't wait well and my power was beginning to rear its ugly head. "Come on," I silently pleaded, "if we're going to do this, lets do it before my magic brings down this whole freakin' house."

Finally I heard the scraping of a chair being moved away from the table and the sound of boot heels approaching. Metal rattled near me and my stomach dropped as my mind registered the possibilities. Someone pulled my hair off of my back and laid it on my left shoulder. I heard Winter whisper to turn my head to the right and I silently obeyed. After a moment I felt a presence behind me, then a bolt of white-hot pain hit my shoulder just at the base of my neck and I screamed until I thought my lungs would burst. Never in my life had I felt such incredible and unrelenting pain. It did not let up, in fact the searing agony increased for a moment as pressure was applied, then at last I was released. I gasped a lung full of air and then screamed again as the pain reasserted itself. Finally it reached a plateau and I could breath. The burning sensation was constant and I realized that I had been branded just to the right of my spine on my shoulder.

Winter removed my blindfold and I noticed that it was wet with bloody tears. My vision swam red with the power that my anger called. He looked at me uneasily, then past me to Amon. I didn't know what to do with this power but I knew that it wanted revenge. "Please calm down," Winter whispered to me as he untied my wrists.

I heard chairs scraping the floor as apparently the night's entertainment was over and the crowd was dispersing. Amon stepped in front of me and I fixed him with a bloody look that would have wilted a lesser man. In his eyes I saw compassion and concern. Closing my eyes tightly, I directed my power outward and suddenly outside a bolt of lightning ripped through the sky, thunder crashed, and the house trembled. The wind rose and howled through the trees and rain sliced through the night. I was fury, I was tempest, I was chaos itself and I fought to keep from striking down my enemies. Unseen things exploded in the distance and I could feel the showers of sparks as they rained down upon the land. At last my anger was gone, my power vented. I looked once more into Amon's eyes for the briefest of moments before I fainted.

When I came to, I found myself draped over the sofa in the study. My arms dangled over the side and my head rested uncomfortably on the armrest. Immediately, the stinging pain in my shoulder radiated down my back and up my neck. "F---ing vampires," I muttered when the memory of my punishment returned. Amon crouched down before me and looked into my eyes.

"Did you say something?" he asked with knitted brow.

"I'm not sure if I actually said it or if I was just thinking it, but I think I said F---ing vampires," I grumbled.

His eyes lit up with relief, "How do you feel, Precious?"

"You have the nerve to ask?" I exclaimed at his audacity, considering his role in my current situation. "And I'm not your Precious."

"I can take away your pain, Cat," he said gently, "but you must admit subservience. You must show penitence for your defiance."

"No," I growled, "No, no, no!" The pain roared through me.

"You would suffer this agony rather than submit?" his voice rose in disbelief.

"I submit to no one," I snarled, then whimpered, "even if I wanted to, and believe me a good part of me does, I cannot. I will bear this pain. Please, go away before I start entertaining thoughts of staking you out on an anthill at high noon. Leave me!" I felt warm tears brimming in my eyes and whispered, "Damn, here we go again".

"Cat, please," he grabbed my face between his hands and looked me straight in the eye, "The Mark of Penitence will remain burning and painful until you become penitent. Once you accept, I can take away your pain and the mark."

"You would blackmail me with this torture?" I gasped at the concept.

"It's not blackmail," he insisted, "it's the way the mark works. I have no hand in the matter and am powerless until you submit."

"I can't, my power won't let me," I pulled roughly away from him. "So this thing is going to feel like this for the rest of my life?"

"The mark will remain active for one phase of the moon," he stood and straightened, "one week, more or less. After that, it is accepted that you will never be penitent and the mark will heal and scar as a regular wound would."

When I leaned over to remove my heels, the motion caused the mark to stretch and a fresh bolt of heat rushed down my arm. I gasped and winced. "Damn," I hissed, " this promises to be a great week! Can I see Bishop?" I moaned as I straightened, forcing back the tears.

"Of course," Amon nodded, "an ice pack will relieve the worst of the pain, at least as long as you keep it on. I warn you though, the minute you remove it, the pain will return with a vengeance." He turned and left the room. I closed my eyes and waited helplessly, seething with rage and pain.

Bishop came into the parlor carrying a folded square of white gauze and an ice pack.

"I don't want to risk having the tissue get infected," he explained as he laid the gauze across my brand, "so this should keep it dry under the ice pack. The Mark of Penitence is rarely given to a mortal and, of course, infection is not an issue with most of us. We feel discomfort but probably not true pain as you do. I can give you a sedative to help you relax, but I'm not sure that it will have any effect, since your mark bears magic." His curly hair framed his face and those blue eyes expressed sympathy and concern. He really was a beautiful being, as well as obviously moved to compassion and tenderness. "Someone could sure take a lesson," I thought acidly.

"Bishop," I smiled weakly at him, "do you know how to make a martini?"

"I do," he beamed, "dry? Olive?"

179

"Perfect," I relaxed on the sofa and closed my eyes, careful to hold the ice pack in place. "Do you know Leitha's story?" I asked seeking a mental diversion from my pain.

"Leitha? Why do you ask?" he shrugged as he brought me the drink. He carefully lowered the offered glass so I did not have to stretch or move my brand.

"I've noticed her around, here and there," I accepted the drink and took a sip, letting it burn down my throat. "Something about her bothers me, I don't know. It's like she's trying to talk to me or something."

"Really?" he grinned and leaned his head to one side, "I didn't realize that she was able to communicate."

"I wouldn't call it actual communication, it's more like whispers or chitters or something," I nodded, "but I feel like she's trying to tell me something."

"I do know her story, as you put it," he admitted, "but I don't feel that it is my place to tell you. You should ask Sin. It is His Lordship's story as well."

I patted Bishop's hand, as he touched my wrist and took my pulse. "Maybe I will ask him, if I ever speak to him again," I smirked.

He smiled as he stood to go, "You will, there is much ahead between the two of you."

"Why Bishop," I drawled, "Prophecy from you?"

"If that is what you wish to call it," he bowed and turned to leave, "Keep that ice pack on your wound until it is no longer cold. I will check in on you later. Winter will be in soon to take you to your room."

Closing my eyes, I downed my martini in three gulps, leaned on the couch and sighed. Winter came in and I looked at him through bleary eyes "I'm not going to my room, Winter. The martini cured me and I'm perfectly comfortable. I'll stay right here," I grinned.

"I think not," he huffed and lifted me off the sofa. "You just relax and I'll get you to your room where you can have a nice nap and sleep it off."

He had lifted me, cradling me as you would a child, but his forearm brushed by my mark and I yelped and jumped to my feet, not as gracefully as I would have liked. I hissed and winced and paced a few steps then looked at Winter's aghast expression. "It's okay, Winter, you just got a little too close to my brand. I'm okay now.

Why don't you just walk with me?" He looked relieved as he took my left hand in his and we went down the hall toward the bedroom.

"Little Sister," Winter smiled amusedly, "can I ask you a question without fear for my life?"

"You can ask," I paused and looked at him meaningfully.

"The storm was yours, wasn't it?" he nodded. "When I removed your blindfold I saw your eyes, your power. You made that storm."

I said nothing as I turned and looked straight ahead. He chuckled and nodded, "I knew it. It was you."

He had no idea how close to the truth he had come. Though I had not made the storm, I actually had been the storm until my rage had diminished.

After perhaps fifteen well-intended steps my knees gave out when the pain in my mark suddenly intensified. My ice pack had thawed and I was helpless against the torment of the burn. It was an odd sensation when my eyes rolled back in my head and the agony ripped my consciousness away.

Chapter 22

In my sleep I heard voices. My mind was clear and I was alert, though my body refused to be roused so I lay silently still, listening. Amon and Bishop were speaking in somewhat hushed tones, though I could clearly make out all that was being said.

"Can you believe this woman's incredible stubbornness?" Amon asked.

"Stubbornness Sire?" Bishop answered.

"She is so headstrong that she would suffer the pain of the Mark of Penitence rather than to submit. It's nothing but foolish obstinance," he added.

"But Sire," Bishop reasoned, "Did you not hear her say that her power would not allow her to submit?"

"I do not believe that the author of her powers would have her suffer this agony. No, she is doing so willingly. This is her own determination," Amon grumbled.

"Perhaps it is her strong will, her refusal to submit, that caused her to become the recipient of these powers," Bishop suggested. "It seems not so long ago you told me that you admired her strength and her will. Am I mistaken?"

"Of course I admired her strength, her ability to persevere," Amon snapped, "but that was when I was observing her from a distance. She is in our world now and I am powerless to make her understand what a dangerous place this is. For some reason, she will not accept that I am acting in her best interests, that I am trying to protect her."

"Forgive me Sire, but she is long accustomed to protecting herself," Bishop replied. "I sense that you have feelings for this woman. Is this wise?"

"After so many centuries I thought that I had lost the ability to feel emotions such as these. Of course, under the circumstances, it is not wise to become involved with her but I seem to be powerless to stop myself. I don't like the power she seems to have over me, but I am amazed at the feelings I am experiencing. Even knowing what bringing her into my world means, I find myself intrigued and, yes, infuriated with the woman."

"The fact that you care for her has made you angry and impatient with her ways?" Bishop suggested.

"I admit that I am at a loss to understand Cat," Amon sighed, "My experience dealing with women is limited, and a modern woman...the way she thinks!"

"Like a woman?" Bishop interjected, "if I may hazard a guess."

"Of course, in some instances she thinks very much the way a woman thinks," Amon agreed, "but in other instances she thinks exactly like a man. Now I ask you, how do I deal with a woman who thinks like a man?"

"Might I make a suggestion, Your Lordship?" Bishop asked.

"Of course, Bishop," Amon answered, "You are certainly closer to her time than am I. Speak your mind."

"Sire, Cat is like a wild, spirited horse. She would be destroyed before she would be broken. I would suggest that you give her her head. Let her run herself out, exhaust herself and she'll be easier to handle. If you force her, you'll only strengthen her resolve," Bishop spoke earnestly, though I was beginning to resent being compared to a horse.

"You may be right, Bishop," Amon replied, "though it is not in my nature to accept willful defiance and I do not like feeling powerless."

"Nor is it, I believe, in Cat's nature to admit subservience to anyone," Bishop retorted, "and it's clear that she does not take feeling powerless well either. There you have the stalemate."

Though the conversation continued, the volume began to diminish. Either Amon and Bishop were leaving or sleep was claiming me yet again. After a few moments of straining to make out what was further being said, I gave up and sank once more into oblivion.

The pain of my mark stinging, burning and aching brought me back to reality and I found that I was lying on my stomach on a bed, a pillow propped beneath my ribs, wearing only the black silk panties. The air conditioning was blowing across my skin and I gingerly wrestled my way under the sheets, pulling them up to my waist. Restless and uneasy, I paused to recall the conversation that I had overheard and wondered for a moment if it had all been a dream. No, it didn't feel like a dream, it clearly felt like a memory. Though the insight into Amon's feelings was touching, and somewhat gratifying except for that business of being likened to a horse, I failed to see how this information could be of use. It was just another tidbit to be stored in my mental file cabinets for consideration at another time.

A murky gray rectangle of light crawled across the deep green carpet and I realized that I was in the peach room. Unable to determine the time of day from the light filtering into the room, I looked around and found that I was alone. *Amon*, I called in my mind and heard his *Cat*, resound as both an answer and an invitation.

The black sheath lay in a heap on the floor beside the bed but I couldn't bring myself to put it on, so I pulled the flat sheet off of the bed and wrapped it around my torso. I had neither the time nor the patience for finding shoes, so I opened the door and padded down the hall in my bare feet. Odd, I thought as I started my search, there were no guards on the door and it had been unlocked. I wondered what that meant.

Unerringly I found my way down the hallways, down two sets of stairs and around myriad corners until I reached the room in which Amon lay asleep. Tiptoeing across the dirt floor, I placed my hand firmly on the lid of the coffin and it opened silently. Amon lay still within, wearing a soft billowy-looking white poet's shirt and gray sleep pants. His eyes did not open as he smiled and murmured, "I don't think your sheet will fit in here, Pet."

Without hesitation, I dropped the sheet and climbed into the coffin and into his embrace. His arms were warm and his heart beat strong and steady as I lay my head on his chest.

"Sleep, Little One," he whispered as he stroked my hair, "the sun will set soon and we will have much to discuss."

Upon waking, I discovered that I was still surrounded by Amon's arms but that the lid of the coffin was open and so were his eyes. He looked at me only fleetingly, then moved to get up. The void that remained when he moved left me feeling both cold and empty. I was almost relieved when the mark on my shoulder resumed its searing pain.

"We have much to discuss," I reminded him as I cleared my throat and grabbed for the sheet, which was still lying carelessly, piled on the dirt floor. Amon glanced over his shoulder in my direction but would not meet my gaze. With his back still turned, he stood and strode toward the door.

"Amon, "I called and he froze but did not turn around, "what's going on? Why don't you look at me?"

He turned and favored me with his profile, "What do you mean?"

"You can't look me in the eye can you?" I marveled, "why not?"

He turned and walked back to the coffin with his gaze held steadily on the floor.

An idea popped into my head and I paused in arranging my sheet and looked at his face, still bowed.

"Who gave me this mark?"

"The Council of Five, of course," he answered without moving.

"And who on the council actually does the punishments?" I insisted.

"Thammuz administers the punishment," he said soberly.

"But not this time, right?" I raised my voice and reached out to take his chin in my hand. I turned his face toward me, "they made you do this, didn't they?"

He looked at the floor and nodded, saying nothing.

"I'm sorry," I whispered, searching for his eyes.

"You? For what?" he turned his eyes finally to meet mine.

"I'm sorry that you were put into this position," I stroked the side of his face, " I'm not sorry that I tried to protect myself at the ritual, but I am sorry that you were forced to do this or have your authority called into question. I understand and I don't blame you. Now what I'd like to do to the other members of the Council, well, that's another issue. I don't believe that you would willingly hurt me, and I know that you had no choice."

Relief lit his eyes and softened his look as he took my face in his hands and kissed me firmly. He pulled me against his chest and wrapped his arms around me, stroking my bare back with his fingertips. His touch sent a shiver through me and I reached up and pulled his mouth back down to mine.

"Stay here," he commanded, "I will bring you a fresh ice pack and some clothes. We can't very well have you running around here in that sheet."

"We can't?" I smiled coyly.

He just shook his head and stood and left the room. I lay there in his coffin, the sheet wrapped loosely around me and considered how

I was going to bring up the subject of Leitha. There was no smooth segue into the topic. Though I didn't want to put him on the defensive, I wasn't sure I could adequately explain why I needed to know about her. I had to just hope that he would trust me and try to understand.

When he returned, Amon carried a fresh ice pack, a pair of blue jeans, black camisole top and sandals. He laid the ice pack gently on my shoulder and handed me the clothes. The camisole was loose and satin with tiny rolled straps that should easily avoid touching my wound.

"Lily is preparing some food for you," he gallantly turned his back so I could dress, "I have some things to attend to this evening so I will have to leave you for a while."

"Oh, okay," I was scheming as I drew on the blue jeans, "Amon, I need to know something from you and I can't explain why. Will you just trust me that it's important and tell me?"

He drew in a deep breath and let it out slowly, nodding, "I trust you, but it depends on what you ask whether or not I will tell you. What is it?"

Pulling the camisole carefully over my head, I struggled to slip it into place without hurting my shoulder. Amon appeared behind me and slipped his fingers under the hem of the garment and gently pulled it down into position. I slipped the straps up on my shoulders and turned to look at him. He had dressed, I noticed, in a tailor-made crisp white shirt, white brocade vest, and black double-pleated trousers that cupped, and hung very invitingly from, his firm round derriere. He must have at least touched on my thoughts because he breathed deeply and rested his chin on my left shoulder and kissed my neck, "Thank you," he whispered.

"Leitha," I started, "I can't tell you why but I need to know her story. I asked Bishop but he said that her story is yours as well, and that you should be the one to tell me, if you wish."

Slipping his arm around me, he hesitated for a moment while I slipped the sandals on, then guided me to the door. As we stepped into the corridor, he sighed and turned to me.

"I was Captain of the knights in the Crusade, as you know, and Leith's husband, Karl, was one of my men. Leitha was a deeply religious woman and prayed every night and every day for her husband to return safely to her. When he was killed in battle, Leitha became angry and bitter and turned away from her God. Though she had no formal instruction, she took up witchcraft and became a witch of some notoriety. After a time, and a slight taste of power, Leitha sold her soul for just ten minutes more with her beloved Karl. Being naïve of demons, she foolishly believed that Karl would be returned to her for that time. Instead, she was delivered to the Hell where Karl, being a bit of a debaucher, had settled comfortably into the arms of female demons sporting multiple breasts and orifices. Leitha was devastated to discover the truth about Karl and cursed him and the demon with which she had bargained. When she was returned to this world, she was quite mad, forsaken, and unforeseeably, immortal. Now she wanders in an endless void of soullessness, a ringwraith, disappearing more and more into the shadows without hope of redemption."

We had moved steadily toward the parlor, going down the various hallways and the first staircase, we paused on the landing above the grand entrance hall.

"Wow, that's quite a story," I marveled, pausing to look at his eyes, "So you took her in because you felt responsible for Karl's death?"

"Perhaps a bit," he nodded, "but mostly it was out of respect for the woman Leitha had once been."

"Thank you for telling me," I smiled, leaned up and kissed him on the chin.

"Will you now tell me why you needed to know?" he encircled my waist and lifted me, almost off of my feet, to kiss me on the lips.

Grinning wickedly, I just shook my head, "No." There was a seed of an idea in the back of my mind but I knew that if I pushed it, it would simply shimmy away. I had to let this notion come to fruition in its own time.

I wrapped my jean-clad legs around his waist and dug my fingers into the lush length of his hair. Nibbling first his upper lip then his lower, I insistently worked my lips on his until his mouth opened. Sliding my tongue in deeply, I rolled it around his tongue then gingerly touched his teeth. An almost electric shock went through me when my tongue touched the tip of his left incisor and it flashed a tiny pinprick of a wound. Amon growled huskily as he pulled my tongue into his mouth and sucked the blood from that tiny hole. The thought that I might be becoming addicted to this feeling of euphoric, rhapsodic, lust occurred to me and I pushed it away with reckless abandon.

At length, Amon released me and we moved down the stairs, across the huge foyer, and stepped into the parlor. Lily, bless her heart, had already set up a place setting on the coffee table before the sofa. I sat down and investigated the contents of three different sized silver dome-covered platters. Beneath the largest lay what must have been the meat from a whole roasted chicken. The next size sported a vegetable mixture of tomatoes, okra, onions and peppers, and the smaller one bore a pile of white rice sprinkled on the top with chunks of sausage. A linen breadcloth covered an oval wicker basket and held warm, yeast-fragrant rolls. A crystal wine cooler held an open bottle of no doubt, perfectly chilled Chardonnay. Amon bowed, though I was so busy spooning food onto my plate that I barely noticed, and excused himself.

After gorging myself shamelessly, I stretched back and relaxed with my second glass of wine. Amon had not yet returned and I was wondering idly what to do with myself when Lily came in. She began collecting the serving platters and my plate and things on a little wheeled trolley.

"Lily, could you sit down and talk with me for a while?" I offered, patting a cushion beside me on the couch.

"I'd love to, Miss Cat," she nodded, but did not pause in her cleaning, "but I can't tonight. Bishop and I have to get the kitchen straightened up before Lucius gets here to pick me up for church."

Two things went through my mind simultaneously, first that Bishop was cleaning in the kitchen? Second, church? At night, what day of the week was it?

"Church, Lily?"

"Yes Ma'am, its Saturday night," she said like I should know what she meant.

"Are you Catholic?" I dared guess.

"No, not Catholic," she laughed, "Southern Baptist. Saturday night is always Gospel Choir night and Lucius and I both sing in the choir."

The fact that both Lily and Lucius were Baptists and worked here for a man they knew as Stephen Montjean, Sin, led me to realize that though they might have their suspicions about this situation, they surely did not know that they were surrounded by vampires. They must think this house full of strangers and eccentrics. I had to chuckle at that notion, for it was surely true.

"Bishop is cleaning the kitchen?" I asked with disbelief, the mental image just would not materialize.

"Why not? He made part of the mess, he can clean part of the mess," She smiled and directed the trolley through the double doors. "Good night, Ma'am," she called over her shoulder.

"Great," I said out loud to no one, "now what am I going to do with myself?" I stood and downed what wine remained in the glass, then walked around the coffee table to the tall arched windows. Parting the sheer drapes, I peered out into the darkness. The soft twinkling garden lights were barely visible from this distance, but the moon was shining brightly and I could just make out the shadow of the fountain. Unsure of the safety of being outside by myself, I wandered around the room trying to find something to occupy my time. There was a short bookcase, I seemed to remember it being called it a barrister's case, against one wall. I lifted the glass doors, one at a time, looking for a book to read. Choices were extremely limited, as the shelves were filled with classics such as "Bleak House," "Don Quixote," "Moby Dick," and "Pride and Prejudice." I did find a copy of "The Canterbury Tales," on the bottom shelf and thought if I got desperate enough, I might peruse that. "That Chaucer always was a knee-slapper," I murmured, well aware that I was talking to myself again.

Abandoning the idea of reading, I returned to the sofa and dropped into the corner. Refilling my wineglass, I rested one arm on the back of the couch and just looked around. The mark on my shoulder was burning merrily and, of course it might have been the wine but I was having a hard time just thinking. Leaning my head back and closing my eyes, I hummed a tune, the theme song to some '80s show, and imagined my magic. It dawned on me that if this stuff was going to be a part of me, for however long I had left, I might as well make friends with it. I willed the landscape behind my eyelids to be vast black smoothness, then let the magic come forth. Tiny twinkles of every color and shade popped and shimmered in the air of my imagination. I sat comfortably and let them just do what they wanted. They danced and darted, shimmered and hovered, all the while seeming to pulse and expand. This time, when in my dreamscape I reached out my hands, the lights came and lit upon my skin, sliding beneath gently without pain.

Back in the world of reality I gasped and opened my eyes when I felt the magic, the energy, fill me. I was no longer restless, but remarkably calm, centered even. I looked around the room with renewed vision and saw ethereal images, masses of energy, and phantoms. They did not acknowledge me and I rose quietly and took my wineglass out to the garden. I had no fear for my safety, being outside alone now.

Chapter 23

The night was mild, though the humidity was holding on. Reflections of the moon rippled in the water below the fountain and fireflies bobbed through the air. A massive wisteria that had overgrown a trellis at the far end of the garden released its perfume onto the gentle breeze. Looking up, I watched the stars twinkling and my gaze followed the Milky Way from one end of the horizon to the other. Crickets chirped and birds called softly to each other in the distance. I relaxed on the bench, placing my wine down beside me, and took a deep breath of all that was nature. No lights burned at the stables for I would have visited the horses had it not been dark and obviously shut down for the night. It occurred to me that I hadn't even checked on Shiloh since my riding debacle and I felt guilty about that. The stables were so quiet now though, I didn't think I should disturb things.

Standing and stretching my arms above my head, I heard a *thwap* and, out of nowhere, Chimaera stood before me. He exhaled suddenly and threw me to the ground, shielding my body with his. Instinctively my vision followed the sound to its source and without thinking I hurled a mass of energy at the spot. My aim must have been more accurate than my assailant's because I saw the silhouette of a man going down when the magic exploded. Chimaera groaned and rolled off of me.

"Chimaera," I demanded, "are you hurt?"

He tried to move away from me but I would not let go of his arm.

"Its nothing," he growled, "I will heal."

When he sat up I saw the shaft of an arrow protruding from his back just beneath his rib cage. In the darkness I couldn't tell for sure but it looked like the wound was oozing blood. I had never before even considered if vampires had blood, other than that which they drank, of course.

"You've been shot," I insisted, moving his arm and inspecting the injury, "the arrow is short, it looks like maybe from a crossbow. You took this for me, didn't you?"

"Don't get all sentimental, it's my job, remember?" he snarled. "Just pull the arrow out and I'll be okay."

"You want me to pull it out?" I cried in disbelief.

"Don't tell me you're squeamish," he sighed and started to get up.

"No, no," I protested, "I'm not squeamish, but this is going to hurt, you know."

"Just do it," he hissed through clenched teeth.

Placing my left hand firmly on Chimaera's back, just beside the shaft, I grabbed the arrow with my right hand and smoothly and steadily pulled it from his body. His flesh made a wet, sucking sound as the point was removed and my stomach did an involuntary lurch in response. He stifled a cry as I held the arrow tip up to the moonlight. It was metal, barbed, and razor-sharp.

"Hold still," I whispered when Chimaera tried to move. He started to protest but I "shushed" him harshly.

Concentrating, I pressed the palm of my left hand over his wound and directed my power into it. The energy glowed and pulsed in the dark. Heat emanated from between my fingers and I could feel his flesh mending. The tissue, the very cellular structure, was repairing in response to my power. Remaining still, I held him in place until I was confident that the wound, including any damage to his internal organs, was healed. When I removed my hand, he jumped up and looked at me with startled eyes.

"What did you do?" he demanded.

"I don't know," I admitted weakly, "I guess I healed you."

"Why? I would have healed in a few hours," his fingers trembled a little as he examined the hole in his shirt. The hole lay now over smooth and unblemished skin, though he couldn't tell that from the front. "Why would you do this?"

"I don't know," I shrugged, "In spite of the fact that you're surly, mean, and have no obvious affection for me, I kind of like you and I couldn't stand by and watch you suffer when I knew that I could help."

He shook his head again and moved toward the edge of the garden, to where our assailant lay. I saw Chimaera lean down and check on the form lying unmoving in the vines of a honeysuckle bush. He stood up and put his hands on his hips, pausing silently for a moment, then turned back to me.

"Looks like you don't need me anymore, witch," he shrugged, "you are more than capable of taking care of yourself."

"Dead?" my head was spinning at the thought of another death on my hands. But I had been filled with an overwhelming sense of righteous indignation when my friend was injured. My friend? Chimaera? Where would this insanity end?

I saw him nod in the darkness and though I wanted once again to feel remorse, I could not. Inwardly I groaned however, at the ribbing I was going to get from Winter and the admiration from Amon. This world creeped me out at times.

"Come," Chimaera snapped and offered his hand, "let's get you back into the house. I'm sure His Lordship will want to know of this."

He pulled me to my feet and wrapped an arm around my waist, guiding me toward the veranda.

"Do you have to be such a pushy vampire?" I grumbled "Couldn't we just let this slide? You know keep it between the two of us?"

"You have a Healing Hand and you want to keep it a secret?" he chuckled, "You think no one will notice the body decomposing in the honeysuckle?"

"Alright," I agreed, "I guess you have to tell Sin, but please don't, I don't know, take such obvious delight in this situation, ok?" I stumbled up the last stone step and Chimaera caught me. He lifted me in his arms and carried me through the French doors, "Let's get you inside before someone else can get off a shot at you."

Winter was standing by the fireplace and a look of alarm crossed his face when he saw Chimaera enter carrying me. His golden eyes widened in surprise at the two of us, and he started toward us intent on being of assistance.

"Relax, Winter," I smiled at his concern and held up my hands, "I just stumbled up the steps and Chimaera decided it would be more expedient to carry me than to allow me to continue on my own. Right Chimaera?"

"Just so," he nodded and plopped me down on the sofa. Straightening, he regarded me silently for a moment then turned to face Winter.

"Okay, you two," Winter grumbled suspiciously, "what did I miss? What's happened?"

"Another attack," Chimaera said, as he turned to leave, "but kidnapping wasn't what our assailant had in mind. This time he intended to kill the witch. I think I should explain to His Lordship, right away. Will you keep an eye on your Little Sister, here?"

"Of course," Winter turned and came to stand behind me, one hand placed protectively on my left shoulder "You were not hurt?" he peered down at me

"No," I shook my head, "Chimaera jumped in front of the arrow and knocked me to the ground. I kind of defended us and that was the end of it."

"Don't worry," Winter suggested, "Chimaera will heal, we all do.

He must have read something in my expression because he suddenly stopped speaking and moved around to the front of the sofa. Crouching before me, he fixed me with a penetrating look. "What did you do, '*tite soeur*?

I looked down at my hands, studying them. They didn't look any different than usual, nor did they feel any different at the moment. No blisters, burns, or extra digits. For reasons I did not understand, I couldn't look Winter in the face when I answered, "I healed Chimaera." Just saying it made me feel ridiculous.

Winter rose and sat down beside me on the couch and took my chin in his hand, turning me to face him.

"You healed Chimaera?" he whispered, smiling and shaking his head, "I have always known that you were a power to be reckoned with, Little Sister, but I had no idea just how powerful you are. His Lordship is going to love this."

I hesitated, then since I was confessing, I finally admitted to Winter that I had killed our attacker.

"I just hurled some energy in his general direction and," I shrugged, "he went down, permanently." Leaning my head back on the sofa, careful to lean away from my brand, I considered Chimaera's words. I hadn't had time to think about what the attack had meant. The fact that the attacker had intended to kill me was sobering, No more kidnapping attempts, now it would be murder, mine.

Amon and Chimaera arrived just as I was considering pouring myself a drink, so I resisted that temptation and settled back on the sofa for what I was sure would be a "de-briefing." Instead, I was surprised to see Winter and Chimaera leave the room silently. Amon approached and went down on one knee before me in front of the sofa. Taking my hands in his, he kissed each one tenderly. He looked up at me from beneath long thick lashes, his black eyes shining. "I understand we have a Healing Hand," he murmured softly.

I silently nodded and pulled my hands away from him. It was disconcerting having him kneeling before me.

"This is quite a revelation," he smiled as he rose then sat down beside me

"Why do you seem so surprised?" I asked, thoroughly bewildered at his reaction. "You do it. You healed me."

"No, Cat," he shook his head slowly, "I do not have the ability to heal. I can only take pain. I absorb it. That is a small thing compared with what you have done." His voice was touched with sadness and regret, and his expression was one of awe and respect. With a fleeting lustful thought, I noticed that he still wore the custom-tailored white shirt, which he now had tucked into a pair of tight black jeans. The jeans were in turn tucked into a pair of soft, knee-high, black leather boots. His silver hair, lying loose on his shoulders, shimmered in the soft lights of the parlor. The look of admiration on his face made him all the more attractive to me.

"Look," I shrugged, "I didn't plan on it, it was just instinct. Chimaera was hurt, I had my hand on his back, it started feeling warm and, I don't know, vibrating so I put it over his wound and it healed. I could feel his flesh mending beneath my hand and I just kept it there until the healing was complete."

"And this was after you threw a charge of energy at your attacker and killed him, right? Oh, Chimaera told me that you only used your left hand, is this right?" Amon asked.

Replaying the series of events in my mind, I realized that Chimaera was correct. I had only used my left hand as my right hand had been holding the crossbolt. I nodded. "I healed with my left hand but I threw the energy bolt at our assailant with my right."

"Amazing," Amon breathed and pulled me into his arms, "I am relieved that Chimaera was there to protect you. Thank the Goddess that you are safe. You will not, from now on, step outside alone under any circumstances. Winter and Chimaera are now making a sweep of the property. They will make sure that we have no more surprises this night."

Snuggling into his arms, wrapping my arms around his waist, I struggled to turn off my mind. Tidbits of information, questions, unsettling ideas were swirling through my head. What I wanted most in the world at that moment was just to be held, comforted, cuddled, without the cares of this strange New World intruding on my sense of security. At last I pulled away from Amon and stood up, then I started pacing, thinking.

"Wait," I reasoned, "You say that you can't heal, that you can only take away pain. Then how did my broken foot heal so fast? That should have taken what, four or six weeks, yet it was only days, a week at most."

"When I removed your pain, your natural healing ability was allowed to work unimpeded. Also," he nodded, "I believe your power helped your healing."

"No, no, no," I insisted, "when I healed Chimaera I used my left hand and it was hot and tingly. I did not do that to my foot. I didn't even know then that I was capable of such a thing. I would have remembered if I had done that."

"No," he agreed, "I meant your passive power. The magic that is part of you whether you are using it or not." Still sitting on the sofa, Amon stretched out his legs then crossed one booted calf over the knee of the other.

"This is all very confusing," I murmured, "and why is it such an issue that I only used one hand to heal?"

"It is a gift from the Gods," Amon turned that angelic face and beamed at me, "there have been many instances of beings, humans even, who have had a gift for healing. "The Laying On of Hands," I believe it's called. It is a gift, but not necessarily one of such divine authority. The Healing Hand is a legend, a story from the old days, if you will. So the story goes that it is only gifted by the Gods to someone worthy of wielding it. The Hand mends tissue, regenerates bone, draws disease, and restores mental clarity. It is always the left hand and only the left hand."

Inwardly I groaned as I considered what this might mean to my immediate future. If Arathia had been willing to summon demons to find the origin of my power before, what might she do when she found out about this?

"I'm getting a headache," I grumbled as I sank into the couch and rubbed my forehead.

Amon moved over and put his arm around my shoulder, carefully avoiding my brand. I leaned my head against him and closed my eyes. All of this was overwhelming. I couldn't control my thoughts and I was getting upset. He pressed his lips against my temple and kissed me gently. The pain in my head receded.

"I should consult Arathia and the Council on this new development," he murmured, stroking my hair.

"Please," I shook my head, "do me one favor. Tell no one of this for tonight. Just let us sleep on this and we'll take a fresh look at things tomorrow?"

"They should know," he pulled away and looked into my eyes.

"Please," I closed my eyes, "tomorrow."

"That was where I was this evening," he hugged me again, "I was speaking to the Council, and consulting others, about any further steps we could take to discover the origins of your power. We discussed the matter and have, I believe, come up with a new way."

"No," I cried, "No more, not tonight. Please, just take me to bed. Let's just leave the wolf outside the door."

"I have a better idea than that," he smiled lewdly as he leaned over and kissed me firmly. The kiss was full of promises of eminent passion and I growled deep in my throat as I rose to meet his force. Keeping his mouth on mine, he slipped his arms beneath me and lifted me gently, intentionally not breaking contact. "*I could kiss you forever,*" I thought and heard his answer, "*and I you,*" in my mind. Finally drawing my lips from his I looked into those remarkably black eyes and found something unexpected… I saw love. No, surely not that! Quickly, I guarded my thoughts from Amon, for I would never admit to him what I had seen in his eyes, as I was sure that he would never admit his feelings to me. We continued to stare into each other's eyes as he carried me down unfamiliar hallways and up several flights of stairs. "Wherever we're going," I thought, "it's up."

At length we came to a narrow corridor and an attic storage room beyond. Amon put me gently down, my bare feet touching warm, smoothly worn wood. The air was warm and dusty smelling and there were no lights but a rectangle of dim moonlight stretched out on the floor. The light was coming through a tall narrow, multi-paned door at the far end of the corridor. Amon took my hand and drew me toward the door, then opened it and pulled me out onto the roof. As I looked around, I realized that we were standing on a widow's walk fashioned on the roof of this hideously tall mansion. I pulled my hand away from his and stepped back a little closer to the door and possible safety. Amon turned and gently led me forward and encircled me in his arms.

"Look at the night, Pet," he whispered into my ear. "Listen to the wolves, smell the forest, feel the mist."

He was right, the night was beautiful from here. Stars twinkled in the dark sky, the moon played hide and seek with the clouds and a slight breeze stirred my hair. Wolves howled sadly, forlornly, invisible in the distance. A heavy mist, almost fog, enshrouded the land below, the moonlight causing it to glow ethereally. I took a deep breath and let it out slowly, leaning against Amon's chest, relaxing in his embrace. He caused goose bumps to rise on my skin when he gently pulled my hair from my neck and kissed my throat. I moaned and wriggled against him, delighting in the sensation. Suddenly he spun me around and shoved me back against the doorjamb, pinning his mouth on mine. His tongue drove into my mouth and he sucked and pulled on my bottom lip. My heart was beating wildly as he lifted me on one knee so he didn't have to bend down. I wrapped my arms around his neck and licked the side of his throat. His skin tasted clean and wild, deliciously masculine. He shuddered beneath me. His hands moving to my back, he snapped the straps on my camisole then roughly pulled it down. The night breeze was startling on my bare skin and my nipples instantly hardened in the chill. My breasts felt heavy and achy, awaiting his touch. His hands were warm and firm as they gently kneaded my flesh. My clothes were beginning to feel constrictive and I yearned to feel the night air enveloping all my naked skin. I leaned back and pulled the ruined camisole over my head and began to unsnap my jeans. Amon released me long enough for me to shed my clothes, then I stood naked and brazen before him. His gaze held mine as he raked his white shirt over his head, his hair flowing wildly in the wind. As he bent over to remove his boots and jeans, I watched the planes of his muscles move and glisten in the moonlight.

When he stood naked before me I stared in awe at the beauty, the perfect proportions of Amon's body. I did not move to touch him, to rush into his arms, but remained at a distance, observing and appreciating his form. I loved that his chest was almost perfectly hairless, hard and sleek. Smiling wickedly, I looked into his eyes, challenging him to come to me. Recognizing the challenge in my eyes, he stood unmoving, weighing his choices. Finally, he smiled and rushed to me, enfolding me, pushing me once again against the wall. Cupping my bottom in his hands, he lifted me and I wrapped my legs around his naked waist. I could feel his desire moving restlessly beneath me. He parted my most intimate folds with his fingers and gently probed and opened me. My passion was rising unbearably and I started moving purposefully, willing him to enter me. Groaning and whimpering, I leaned up and locked my mouth on his, sucking, pulling and demanding all of him. He growled and moved, then pushed his length deep within me. I gasped and inhaled at his force, then opened to him, my muscles tightening around him, drawing him in. Our passion was driving me into a frenzy and I was oblivious to everything as Amon drove into me again and again, my back scraping up and down on the wall. Grinding my hips on his as hard as I could, I took his length and wanted more. As we reached the penultimate moment, he dug his teeth sharply into my throat. I was released in multiple orgasms as he sucked the hot blood from my veins while spilling his juices deep inside me. It was as if we were completing a circuit, his mouth taking my blood and my depths accepting his seed.

Panting roughly, gloriously satisfied, we held each other and basked the energy that was flowing between us. I loved the feeling of him still inside me. Inevitably however, my back began to feel the abuse we had given it and my brand began to sting and burn in the night air. As the adrenaline went away, the pain intensified and tears began building in my eyes. Amon pulled me away from the wall and carried me to the edge of the widow's walk. Reluctantly, he pulled himself from within me then sat down on the railing and sat me down on his lap. As the tears of blood spilled down my cheeks, Amon caught them with his finger and put them gently in his mouth.

"We've scratched and scraped my back. It's really beginning to hurt. Can you take the pain?" I pleaded.

He leaned over and kissed me, pulling gently with his mouth, and the pain in my back was gone. I could think and breathe again, though the pain from my brand remained. As my heartbeat and breathing returned to normal I could once more feel the chill of the night air. Amon wrapped his arms around me and radiated heat but it wasn't enough. I stirred, seeking more warmth than he could supply and he murmured "Come, let us get you out of this night air." We stood and moved toward the door, retrieving our clothes as we went.

I pulled on my jeans but the camisole would no longer function as a shirt so Amon handed me his beautiful, fine white shirt. It was too large and very billowy, but it covered me and I thought I might look a little coquettish in it. Amon put on his jeans and boots and we went back through the attic and down the stairs. "So, are you going to tell me now about what you and the Council came up with about my power?" I turned to look back at him as we walked down yet another corridor. He looked magnificent in those jeans, tight and low rising, and that bare chest...

"I thought you did not wish to discuss the matter tonight," he raised an eyebrow in surprise, "to save it until tomorrow."

"I don't think I could sleep the day away knowing a sword is once again hovering above me. As much as I don't want to know, it's worse not knowing. Please, tell me," I insisted.

"In here," he paused and opened the door to a room I had never before seen. Within lay the quintessential Master's Library. Shelves of books stretched from the floor to the ceiling on three of the four walls. The fourth wall boasted a fireplace and two twelve foot tall windows covered with heavy velvet drapes. If this was Amon's room, I fully expected that the windows were an illusion purposefully designed to provide balance and maintain the sense of aesthetics the room demanded. A fire burned merrily in the fireplace, the real wood popping and sending showers of sparks up the chimney. Two burgundy leather armchairs sat facing the fire, before one stood an ottoman on curved wooden legs. I pulled the ottoman up in front of the fire and sat down, warming my back in the radiant heat.

"I should be angry with you that you never told me about this room," I pouted and rubbed my hands up and down my arms, displacing the chill.

"I am sorry that my concern was for your physical well-being rather than your emotional health. You are right, I should have brought you here so that you could avail yourself of this room's pleasures," he spread his hands in that gee-sorry gesture and sat in the leather chair closest to me. At this distance our knees were almost touching.

"Okay," I shrugged, "I know I'm not going to like this, so go ahead and tell me what you and the Council of Goons came up with."

"That is Council of Five," he corrected, then shot me a look when he realized that I was baiting him.

"Man," I flipped my hair back and chuckled, "You vampires have got to get a sense of humor."

"Perhaps that would be useful," he admitted, "at least in dealing with you."

"Ouch, touché!" I mimed an imaginary arrow to my heart, "You wound me."

"Are you going to let me explain our plans?" he sighed, then waited silently while I decided my answer.

"Very well," I straightened and pulled a sober face, "Continue." My own pompous tone tickled me and I couldn't contain a snort. I wiped the smile from my face and looked at Amon again. The harder I tried to be serious, the sillier I was feeling. For some reason I had a screaming case of the giggles. I used to get them when I had been working too long and was in extreme need of sleep. Any word, any topic, carried some secretly delicious funny and I would be reduced to gales of laughter until tears streamed down my face and my ribs hurt from laughing so hard. Someone uttering the word "toe-jam" would have me rolling on the floor, cackling like a loon.

Amon just looked at me calmly and I held up both hands.

"Wait," I snickered, "Wait just a minute while I try to pull myself together. I'm sorry. I don't know why I'm behaving this way. The only times I've ever acted like this was when I was so tired that I couldn't sleep. It's like my body is drugging my mind when I get this exhausted. It will pass. Just give me a minute." I closed my eyes and rested my head in my hands, consciously steadying my breathing and trying to control the giggle that still threatened to erupt.

Amon leaned forward and put his hands on my knees.

"You have had quite a night. I should not have taken advantage of you on the roof," he lifted my chin with his hand, "The dawn is approaching. We should sleep now and discuss this matter tomorrow evening. You need rest."

I sat huddled, hugging myself in front of the fire, mentally snickering over Amon's use of the phrase, "taken advantage of," when I realized that I should have been warm. A cold, ugly chill wormed through me and I felt the familiar muscle contractions of a seizure coming on. Looking into Amon's ebony eyes, I called for help with my thoughts as the pain had stolen my voice. Amon! I drew breath raggedly as the spasm rode down my spine and I crumpled to the floor. Amon took me into his arms and, pulling up the sleeve of his shirt, he bit into the vein in the crook of my left elbow. The pain and muscle contractions quieted after he drank only a little of my blood, but the seizure itself had been as strong as those that had required him to take much more. Apparently his feeding on the roof had not lessened the seizure, only the amount required to relieve it.

"I'm sorry," I whispered, as he licked the wound closed and pulled my sleeve down. I touched his hair with my right hand, feeling its smooth silkiness. I marveled at the sensitivity in my fingertips, as my violin playing had previously rendered the pads of my fingers rough and callused, able to feel only the most intense of sensations. Of course, being right handed, my left hand was much more callused than my right. Fatigue had my mind wandering, I realized.

"You will sleep now," he demanded, looking seriously into my eyes.

"Yeah, you would get all pushy and bossy now," I moaned, "when you know that I don't have the energy to refuse you."

"If that is what it takes," he agreed and lifted me in his arms. My body felt boneless, weak, and jelly-like. Resting my head on his shoulder, he stroked my hair with his hand as he carried me from the library and down the familiar staircase to the basement. Though part of my mind rebelled, my body had no energy to deny him and I went silently into his embrace in his coffin.

"Amon," I murmured, "what will Arathia think when she hears about my Healing Hand?

"I do not know," he admitted truthfully, "but I only seek her council. You need not fear her."

"I do," I whispered, as I started to doze off.

Amon kissed my forehead and pulled me closer, my head resting on his chest, my ear over his heart. Once again the steady beating of his heart lulled me to sleep.

Chapter 24

Music woke me. Still lying in Amon's arms I heard a familiar tune and my eyes fluttered open. I sat up, startled to find that the music had been coming from me. I had been singing in my sleep. Amon's eyes were open and he smiled at my confusion.

"What a lovely way to be awakened," he reached over and cupped the side of my face with his hand. I closed my eyes and pressed my cheek into his palm, delighting in his gentle touch and steady strength.

"Has this happened before?" I blushed.

"The singing in your sleep?" he asked, smoothly rising on one elbow. His hand slowly traced a line down my neck, my chest, then brushed up beneath my right breast. I still wore his shirt so most of what he touched was fabric and part of me wished it gone. My breath caught in my throat as his fingers found my nipple. I nodded, unable to speak.

"No, this is the first time your song has greeted me. I rather like it," he added quickly. His hand continued its exploration and moved down my stomach, touching spider-like on my thigh.

"What are you doing?" I managed to croak as his fingers crawled between my legs. Spreading my knees, I offered him access.

"Do you wish me to stop?" he murmured, his calm expression one of absolute knowledge and power.

"I don't believe you can," I smiled as his fingers hit their target and my juices spilled out for him.

"Oh," he leered, "I can stop if you just say the word." The assault continued.

Admitting my weakness, I leaned over and kissed him, careful not to lose contact with his hand.

"If you stop," I whispered into his open mouth, "I'll die right here and now."

Pulling the shirt off over my head, I straddled his hips, his fingers still within me. Unsnapping his jeans and pulling down the zipper, I shrugged them down his hips just far enough to free his throbbing member. He was hard and hot, ready for me. Finally his fingers left my wetness and he caressed my breasts as I sank down around him. My blood was pounding in my ears and my heart was leaping in my chest as I began an intentionally slow and deliciously languorous rhythm. Lifting my pelvis almost as far as possible, I rose to the very tip of him before slowly lowering to his base. He leaned up and took my nipple into his mouth, flicking it with the hot tip of his tongue.

"You realize," I breathed heavily, "starting my day, or rather my night, like this means anything else will be anticlimactic."

"I doubt, my Precious, that anything with you would ever be anticlimactic," he moaned and thrust his hips up, catching me by surprise and increasing our rhythm. He then took control and worked me into a frenzied pace, his muscular chest beading with sweat. I could tell that he longed to take me at his will and intentionally pulled away from his movement. He sought control and I delighted in denying him. Withholding myself, I smiled down at him, teasing and titillating him with my distance.

"Woman," he threatened, then with blinding speed and coordination a gymnast would envy, he rolled me over while rising above me. We ended up still in the coffin but suddenly I was beneath him and his look of conquest said it all. It was my turn for a little teasing and torture.

"Paybacks are such a bitch," I grinned as his left hand pinned both of my wrists above my head and I squirmed for a defensive position. Was sex always this much of a battle for control or was it just the two of us? I couldn't remember any other lover bringing out this need for dominance in me. I relished the thought of controlling this man, this beast.

He leaned down and kissed my mouth, then licked the side of my face, nibbling the edge of my chin then the lobe of my ear. His breath was hot and powerful on my throat, as he feathered kisses along my most vulnerable spots. I realized just how powerful he was, that with minimal effort he could dig those wicked teeth into my neck and I would be dead before I could resist. My pulse pounded in my throat. His mouth continued south and found my chest, then my breasts. He kissed first the right then the left, pausing to caress and knead each one. At last he began moving inside me and my pulse began racing again. Slowing, then quickening, he maddeningly varied the pace, forcing me to adjust to his will. My anger and frustration was beginning to stir when he smiled and drove me onward. His primal force was powerful and magic swirled above us. The air sizzled and crackled, and smoke curled around us. As our passion took us both over the edge, the lights in the wall sconces exploded and sent showers of sparks onto the dirt floor. The house trembled and tiny plumes of dust shot out from the cracks in the walls. I wrapped my legs around his waist as he lay heavily on top of me. His hair spilled across my arms and breasts. My skin was so alive, so sensitive, his silky hair felt like electricity almost burning me.

"I do hope we don't have anywhere to be just now," I purred and stretched beneath his weight, "I don't think my legs are going to hold me for a while."

"I believe you are gloating," he raised his head and grinned.

"Call it what you will," I shrugged, "I only state a fact. Baby, you rocked my world."

"I believe it was you who rocked my world," he murmured, smiling like the Cheshire cat as he stretched his arms above his head. "The Council will not be here until midnight," he added as he untangled himself from me and pulled up his jeans. "We have several hours to ourselves. You need to eat and I should feed before they arrive. I trust you will want to know what is happening tonight, so we will take the time for explanations."

I sat bolt upright in the coffin, once again flabbergasted at his easy manipulation of my life. "Yeah, I think we will take the time for explanations and I think that time is now."

"You seem upset, Cat," a look of confusion furrowed his brow.

"Upset," I seethed, "You're leading me like a lamb to the slaughter yet again and you seem surprised at my reaction."

"Before you start hurling balls of energy around the room, let me explain," he spoke calmly. "There are several levels of power, ranging from the ultimate, the Origin to the least, that of Taroists, Palmreaders, and Astrologers. By administering certain tests, setting forth specific tasks, we can determine your level of power by what you accomplish and by how much effort you expend. If your power is equal to or less than mine, there will be no further attempts to identify it."

205

"And if my power is equal to or greater than yours?"

"The Council will decide if further action is needed," he admitted.

Silence spun out before us and I grabbed the white shirt, seeking some form of defense or protection.

"Amon," I said at length, "Do you feel that I am a threat to you or to your power, your control over your fellow vampires?"

He did not move for a moment, then turned to face me. "You," he shook his head, "I do not feel you are a threat, but I am not certain that it is truly you who controls your power."

"You doubt me," I sighed and dropped my shoulders.

"Not you," he replied quickly.

I looked up into those black, black eyes and whispered with my heart and soul, "Hear me Master Vampire. It's me, Catherine, and I wield this power. Nothing can happen but that it moves through me and I know that the author of this magic would not force me to act contrary to my nature. I am not your enemy, nor would ever I seek to usurp your power. This power may have its own agenda, but I am in control." With that I pulled the shirt down over my head, stepped out of the coffin, and strode purposefully from the room. If my dramatic assertion had the desired effect, Amon should have been left with his chin on the floor but I wasn't sticking around to find out.

Finding his bedroom first, I went through it and into the bathroom. Turning on a scalding hot shower, I ripped his shirt off and hurled it across the room. I was livid, my anger threatening to boil over. No, I would not give him the satisfaction to point out my lack of control. Stepping under the pelting water, I lifted my face and let the anger sluice from me. I stood beneath the spray and cried. Longing for my old existence, I hummed a sad tune as I began washing the weirdness of this world from my skin. The heat from the water was angering my burn and I placed my left hand over it to protect it from the spray. Suddenly my hand began a familiar vibrating and heat caused steam to rise from it. The skin of my brand began knitting, the sensation sharp and alarming. After a few moments, the sensation passed and I removed my hand. It was normal again. With my right hand, I examined the skin on my shoulder. It was perfectly smooth and unblemished. The Mark of Penitence was gone. "Oh man," I sighed, "is the Council going to be pissed about this!"

Finishing my washing, I squeezed the water from my hair and stepped out of the shower, relieved to find myself still alone. Amon had a way of materializing out of nowhere and I really didn't want to have to deal with him at this moment. I wrapped a big towel around myself and pulled the blow dryer from under the sink. After drying my hair, I brushed it smooth but the steam in the room left it wild and unruly. "At least the fullness and length should cover my lack of punishment mark," I thought as I put the dryer back.

Jumping back in surprise, I yelped when I stepped out of the bathroom and caught sight of Bear leaning against the door to the hallway. He smiled broadly and laughed at my alarm.

"Jeez, Bear," I gasped, catching my breath, "You almost gave me a heart attack. Do you have to stand there all silent and broody? You could have coughed or sneezed or even knocked on the bathroom door to let me know you were here."

"I'm sorry, I didn't know you'd be so jumpy," he shrugged. "There are no clothes for you in this room, but I did find one of Sin's shirts that should cover you until we get back to the blue room." He pointed at a black dress shirt lying on the bed. It was huge, would probably reach my knees, but he was right, it would cover me. I took the shirt and indicated to Bear that he should turn away. Nodding, he faced the door and I dropped the towel and slipped the shirt up my arms. I buttoned it quickly and rolled up the sleeves, it would do. I would have wished for panties and a bra, but wishes don't always come true so I would adapt to going commando.

"Tell me Bear," I stepped up beside him and slipped my arm through his, "What are you doing on the night shift? It is night isn't it?"

"It is night," he patted my hand and escorted me down the hall. "Big happenings here tonight. The Boss has all the security team on duty. In fact he even increased the force by two. There are now six of us patrolling the place."

"Big happenings?" I groaned, "Any idea what?"

"No," he admitted, "But there's going to be a lot of people here and security will be the tightest."

"Great," I thought as the image of the last crowd rose unbidden in my mind's eye, "another spectacle starring yours truly." We reached the door to the sapphire room and Bear gallantly opened it for me. I turned and smiled at that wonderfully bronzed human face, "I'll just dress and hang out in here for a while. I don't know when

I'm expected at this shindig so I'll just stay put until Sin calls for me or, better yet, until its over."

"Yes, ma'am," he saluted, "I mean Miss Cat. I'll be right outside the door if you need anything."

The hook on the back of the bathroom door held a garment covered in a plastic bag, as if new or just back from the cleaners. Ripping the plastic off, I smiled at Amon's taste when I saw the gorgeous dress he had chosen. It was silk and obviously hand-crocheted, of natural color with fitted bodice and flutter short sleeves. The hem was scalloped and would reach just above my ankles. The V-neck, front and back, probably would give my mark no cover, so my hair was definitely staying loose. There were no other garments in the room, save a pair of crocheted sandals so I didn't have to worry about bra straps or panty lines. Slipping the dress over my head, I shimmied it into place and marveled at the feel of the silk on my skin. I examined the delicate crocheting. It was an incredibly complicated pattern and I was amazed at the skill it must have required to create it. I stepped into the matching sandals.

Behind the armchair, I found my violin and, with joy and relief, removed it from its case. Taking my time, I rosined the bow thoroughly then began to play. The music was soothing and replenished my soul. My concept of time passing was, at best, poor but judging from the number of music pieces I played it was roughly a half an hour later when Bear knocked on the door and poked his head in.

"I'll be switching stations now, Miss Cat," a smile lit his face. "I'll be on the ground floor. I think Chimaera will be here with you."

"Going to be frisking the guests as they arrive?" I teased.

"You think they'll let me?" his wicked humor warmed my heart.

"Have a nice night Bear," I waved him on, "and keep your head down."

"You too, Ma'am," he paused, "Miss Cat."

When he was gone I returned to my playing and perched on the edge of the bed. As I played I noticed that the lamplight was dimming. Shadows were converging on the room and darkness was moving erratically across the floor. Laying my bow and violin beside me on the bed, I sat silently holding my breath. I could hear my heart beating in alarm and tension froze me to the spot. When at last Leitha shuffled out from the corner, I breathed a sigh of relief. Her I could deal with.

"Leitha," I called gently, "come here. I wish to speak with you." Her shadowy form slowly approached, hesitant and fearful. Sensing her terror, I murmured, "It's alright Leitha, you need not fear me. I wish to help." As she moved forward, I sensed that she was trying to reach me, to communicate, and I opened my mind to her as I did with Amon. Feeling her pain, her torment, I tried to reassure her that all would be well. Her frenzied thoughts quieted when she realized that I had touched her mind and that she had understood me. The madness left her eyes and she looked at me with a mixture of awe and gratitude on her face.

Leaning down, I smiled encouragingly, "It's alright, Leitha. I know your story. I know of your love and great faith, and of your devastation at your husband's betrayal."

Slowly she approached me and stood hunched and huddled within arm's reach. I was vaguely aware of the door opening and someone else entering the room. Concentrating on the task at hand, I ignored the intruder, and reached out my hand to the tortured creature before me. My left hand thrummed and glowed as I touched Leith's wizened, distorted face. Her frightened eyes widened in alarm then closed in acceptance. She nodded and smiled.

"Your deal with the demon was never a binding one, you have been deceived yet again. Finally," I whispered, "your time is finished. I release you." The power in my hand flared and bathed the room in light, nearly blinding me. I heard a sweet angelic laugh as Leitha trembled, her flesh dissolved, then her spirit shot skyward. Her coarse empty robe dropped to the floor. She was free, and rode on gales of laughter to the heavens. I bowed my head and opened my mind to her once more to listen to her joy. "Godspeed," I whispered as I felt her spirit depart.

I got up from the bed and started for the bathroom when I caught sight of Amon and Chimaera standing just inside the door. They both looked stricken, then startled as a blast of some sort sounded in the distance.

Chapter 25

"**S**tay here," Amon commanded, as he and Chimaera turned and bolted down the hall, leaving me standing alone, feeling strangely vulnerable. I walked to the doorway. Straining to hear, I poked my head into the hallway and caught the distant sounds of voices raised in anger and alarm. Doors slammed somewhere. I recognized the sound of running feet. Anxious to know what had happened, I stole quietly down the hall toward the main floor foyer. I had planned to pause on the landing of the staircase that faced the great double front doors, but never made it that far. Three doors past the sapphire room an arm shot out of the doorway and a hand of steel grasped my throat. Another arm grabbed around my waist and I was lifted into the air. Kasimir, his face beside mine, hissed, "This time we shall not fail, Little Witch." There was no time to draw breath as a cord was slipped over my head and brought up tightly against my neck. My hands clutched at the cord but it was too tight, I couldn't get my fingers beneath it. The blood was roaring in my ears as my body fought for oxygen. "Amon! Chimaera!" I screamed in my mind, already sure that they would not arrive in time. My vision was dimming and I could feel my pulse weakening, my heart was struggling to continue.

"Why," I mouthed at Kasimir before the darkness swallowed me.

"I need give you no explanation," he snarled. "Our issues do not concern you."

"It's my death and I don't even get to know why?" I thought, indignantly.

A blur sped by me and I collapsed to the floor, as Kasimir was suddenly airborne, hurtling down the hall headfirst. I raked the cord at my throat and realized that I was too weak, it was too late. My heart had already stopped beating and my eyes froze, staring down the hall at the sight of Chimaera standing over the crumpled form of my assassin. Too late, I thought.

I was standing, and surprised to be doing so, on a rough, rocky spit of land that jutted out into the ocean. The waves rolled and crashed against the rocks, sending a fine spray up into the air. My soft cloak of gray, the hood gently covering my hair, was damp and smelled slightly of sea salt, but beneath it I was warm and dry. All about me, I found, stood others like me. Silent and still, we stood sentinel, watching eternity unfold before us.

"Where am I?" I called out to a molten sky of blue, red, orange, and purple. Clouds, the sun, stars and the moon revolved endlessly in the canopy above us. I witnessed time unfurling like a roll of ribbon across the vaulted sky.

"Welcome Home, Beloved," a voice that was at once powerful and yet tender answered, "Relax and refresh yourself while you are here, for you cannot stay. This is just a respite in your journey, not your journey's end. You have much yet to do in the world."

"Me?" I asked, startled, "I have much to do? Are you sure you mean me?"

"You know it is so," the voice sounded familiar and comforting.

In my heart I realized that the voice spoke the truth. I did have much yet to do. My task was not complete, my promises not fulfilled. Looking about me, I took comfort in being among my own kind. I drew in a healing breath and hung my head, weeping bitterly with the knowledge that I could not remain here. Watching the sun and the moon constantly exchanging places, I understood that time was passing.

"I am prepared," I called to one whom I intimately knew, yet could not name. The mist rose, surrounding and enveloping me.

My heart triphammered then sputtered, before resuming a steady beat. Remembering how to breathe, I gasped and drew in as much air as my lungs would hold. I tried to scream but no noise came to my ears. My hands struggled to reach the cord about my throat, but they could only flail weakly. Apparently my body was not yet accepting directions from my brain. I was finally able to open my eyes and focus on the world before me. Amon's beautiful face swam into view. Smiling weakly, I tried to reach out to touch his cheek but had no energy to move.

The memory of my death came rushing up at me and I panicked as I relived the crushing pain in my throat and the burning of my lungs as I was strangled. I gasped and gasped, struggling to breathe, clawing at the air as the feeling of helplessness settled over me. My heart pounded and beat at my ribcage, protesting the lack of oxygen. Black spots began swirling in my vision and Amon's face dissolved. I knew that I was dying again.

"Cat," a voice called my name in the darkness, "Cat, hear me." Barely able to understand the words over the roar of blood racing through my veins, I answered in my mind.

I'm dying, I'm dying again, I turned around and around, *help me!*

"Hear me, Catherine," the voice demanded and something inside me calmed to listen, "You are not dying. You are trapped in a memory. It is dangerous. You cannot stay there. Follow my voice and I will lead you back."

Who are you? I longed to remain in contact with someone, something.

"You know who I am," the answer reverberated and I moved toward its source, confused by the echo.

Why are you doing this? I raced forward, then paused for the voice to direct my movements.

"It is not I who am doing this, Witch," the voice was stronger to my left and I ran that way, hoping to catch up with my guide.

Am I going the right way? I ran until I stumbled, tangling my feet and landing hard. The breath was knocked out of me.

My eyes fluttered open as I gasped to fill my depleted lungs. Lying in Amon's embrace, my head on his chest, I hesitated to move, unsure if I was dreaming or not. Rubbing my hand gently across the ribs beneath his silken shirt, I assured myself that he was real, though his heart was not beating. I looked up and found his eyes closed, his face serene. He looked as if he was carved from marble and I reached up and touched his jaw to feel its softness. The memory of the voice crossed my mind and I was puzzled to realize that the voice that led me back was not Amon's. As telepathically linked as we were I would have expected it to be him, but it wasn't.

"It was Chimaera," Amon woke, lifted the lid of the coffin and looked at me soberly. His black eyes shimmered in the dim light of the coffin room.

"What are you saying?" I balked at the words even as I acknowledged their truth.

"It was Chimaera's voice that led you back to us," he tightened his embrace and I clung to him. I had never before felt so lightly tethered to the ground, as if at any moment I could simply float away never to return. "It is one of his talents. You have been here in my coffin room for three days and three nights, dead to the world."

I sat up and lifted my hands to the heavens, "He picks this minute to grow a sense of humor?"

"Cat," he sat up beside me and turned my face to his, "You know my understanding of modern humor is limited. I was not joking. You have literally been dead for three days and three nights. It was the only way I could ensure your complete recovery. If we had resuscitated you the minute we found you, you would have suffered brain damage. We had to put you in a type of suspended animation to give your body time to heal."

Closing my eyes, I pulled my knees up and rested my forehead against them, considering if I really wanted to think about having been dead for three days. I drew in a few calming breaths and realized that I was just happy to be alive. Deciding to pull a Scarlet O'Hara, I wiped the matter from my consciousness. That was for another day.

"It was you wasn't it?" I suddenly remembered the blur of speed that knocked Kasimir away from me, "You were the one who flew at Kasimir so fast I couldn't really see you. You tossed him down the hall."

He nodded and slipped one arm around my shoulders.

"And what of Kasimir?" I shuddered, "Did he give any reason for trying to kill me?"

"He is in the Council's custody, but he has admitted nothing," Amon replied, "They think he might be mad, crazy."

"Yeah," I snarled, "Crazy like a fox." Would the Council buy an insanity plea? Would there be a trial? I considered asking these questions but thought better of it. My peace of mind depended on assuming that the vampire community would deal with its own criminals.

"I am not even going to mention the fact that you now bear no Mark of Penitence, nor the scar," he whispered as he caressed my back, "You healed it did you not?"

Nodding, I turned to look at that beautiful face, realizing that I had missed him while I had been away.

"I'm glad you aren't going to mention it," I grinned and leaned against him.

He caught my chin in his hand and turned me to face him, "Not once in history, as far as I know, has anyone healed himself, or herself, of the Mark of Penitence, and certainly no mortal. Your powers are multiplying. The Council would be very uneasy if they knew that you had removed their punishment as well as having released Leitha."

Swallowing hard, I whispered, "And what about you Master Vampire? Do I make you uneasy?"

He leaned toward me slowly, almost menacingly then locked his mouth onto mine. He kissed me deeply and for a moment, all thoughts fled. Pulling away slightly, he murmured, lips still near mine, "You terrify me, Witch". Pulling me down on top of him, Amon cupped the back of my head in his hand and forced me down on his mouth. I drove my tongue through his razor-sharp teeth and sucked at his lips. That need, that yearning to be inside him, a part of him, rolled over me again and I ripped apart his silk shirt so my hands could touch the skin of his chest. Using the tip of my tongue, I licked a line along his jugular vein and up to his ear. He was making his heart beat for me now and I could feel his pulse beneath my tongue. My lips tingled as the thought of driving my teeth into his neck popped into my head. I froze, then pushed myself up off of him.

"What have you done to me?" I hissed.

He smiled patiently at me. "I had to give you a small amount of my blood to sustain you," he explained, "so that you could be brought back whole. It was only a few drops, and the effects will soon wear off, probably as soon as you have your first meal."

"And what would happen if I gave in to this urge and sank my teeth into your flesh?" I murmured, still staring at his neck, tantalized by the thought of tasting him.

"You would be stronger, your blood enriched," he replied, "We might be even more telepathically linked. Other than that, nothing. In order for you to become Vampire I would have to deplete your blood supply then replace it with my own. As I have told you before, this is not your fate. Your system remains intact. You should, however, eat soon."

At that moment the thought of food made my stomach lurch and I decided to let the issue drop.

Straddling his legs, I rubbed his chest and tangled my fingers in his. "If Arathia knew all that has happened, she would summon the Devil himself and have him cart me off to Hell, wouldn't she?" I joked.

He smiled, "She might at that."

"I don't know if I can survive another of Arathia's schemes," I admitted.

"It doesn't matter," he said offhandedly, "The issue is behind us."

I looked at him suspiciously, "What exactly does that mean that it's behind us?"

"Arathia and the Council. They believe that you are either dead or trapped beyond. You rest in that coffin," he pointed across the room where a glossy black casket stood with its lid closed. "You are no longer a threat to them so the matter should be behind us. There will be no more schemes," he answered, his hand moving to caress my cheek. I knew that he was mistaken and that Arathia knew very well that I still lived. She might believe that I was off in some other state of consciousness, but she knew I was still alive.

"That's my coffin?" I peered into the shadows at the exquisite piece. "Did I have a funeral?"

"A memorial service of sorts," he nodded. "Lily, Lucius, and the Council were in attendance, and your guards and I were properly somber."

Mesmerized by the sight of my own coffin, I stared as if frozen until his hand dropped down my neck, slid gently across my shoulder then down my chest. Both his hands rubbed up my ribcage and claimed my breasts.

"You know not what you start, Vampire," I warned, turning to face him. "As tempting as the thought of making mad passionate love to you is, at this moment I could very easily rip your throat out and shake it like a dog does a slipper. I don't think either of us wants that, do you?"

He smiled and removed his hands, "Very well, Pet. What is your wish?"

"Let's see," I smiled and lowered myself to kiss his chest, then swirled my tongue around his left nipple, "I've been dead for three days, I think I need a bath and a meal."

"Only Bishop, Winter, and Chimaera know of your recovery so you will have to be content with Bishop's cooking. I can, however, see to your bath," he rose and pulled me from the coffin. He bent over as if to lift me and I scurried away.

"None of that He-man crap," I warned, "I think I can walk beside you, thank you very much."

"You would deny me the simple pleasure of carrying you in my arms?" he whined sardonically.

"You bet," I nodded, "Let's go."

Grabbing his hand, I dragged him from the room and pulled him protesting up the stairs and down the hall.

"In here," he said, pulling me inside an unfamiliar room. The lights were off but candles flickered from heavy iron candleholders placed on nearly every level surface. In the middle of the room sat a huge whirlpool tub gurgling noisily.

"Wait a minute," I backed up slowly. Considering how many closed doors decorated each corridor, and how surprised I was to find a library upstairs, an idea popped into my mind suddenly. "You're not hiding a swimming pool from me are you?"

Amon sighed heavily, dropped his head and shook it slowly. Looking up at me, he smiled a wickedly wry smile and suddenly stepped before me, hoisting me over his shoulder. As he hauled me back down the corridor and around an unfamiliar curve I laughed as his hands tickled the backs of my knees.

"If you are supposed to know everything about me," I pointed out, "You should have known that I love swimming. It's second only to sex, and eating. Okay, it's third on my list of favorite things to do."

"I am happy to know that it ranks behind sex," he nuzzled my hip through my gown. I wriggled on his shoulder.

He pulled open two ornately carved rolling pocket-doors and carried me into the most unbelievable place. A large rectangular pool shimmered in the soft light of several torchieres that stood against the far wall. Lush velvet drapes hung behind them. Palms growing from dramatically fashioned Grecian urns decorated the area around the pool and black wrought iron patio furniture, an elaborately designed dining table and four matching chairs, sat on a raised platform at one end of the room. Porcelain tiles formed a mosaic of the sun burning over a tropical rainforest on the wall behind it, and twinkle lights decorated the wrought iron banister that surrounded the dining area. I was still taking in the room, amazed at its opulence, when Amon strode forward and tossed me into the water, then laughed.

"You think you're very clever don't you?" I sputtered and coughed when I surfaced. My gown was heavy in the water and when I stood I realized that it had become effectively transparent. The water was quite cool and my skin was covered with goose-bumps beneath the fabric. I splashed at him and he stepped nimbly back. Ducking beneath the water, I pulled the gown off over my head and swam away, leaving it floating and sinking toward the bottom. I swam in long strong strokes, reaching the far side of the pool with little effort. Soft inset lights cast circles of luminescence in the water and I had little doubt that Amon was enjoying the show I made as I sliced naked through the depths.

Surfacing, I wiped the water from my eyes and watched Amon, his pale gray silk shirt still hanging open, walk around the edge of the pool, as if stalking me. His eyes burned with lust and I laughed and rose out of the water before diving below again. The silence beneath the water was calming and reassuring and I luxuriated in the feel of it moving over my skin. Pushing off the other side with my feet, I rolled and swam back to where Amon stood, towering over the edge of the water. I hauled myself up and sat on the edge of the concrete lip, smoothing the excess water from my hair. The cool air touched my skin and a chill crept over me. Amon crouched behind me and laid his shirt over my shoulders, rubbing my arms to dry and warm me.

"You look like you belong in the water, Cat," he murmured as he kissed my temple.

"I used to swim all the time, but they closed the Y where I used to swim, and it was too inconvenient to go to the other pools, so I kind of fell out of the habit. Damn," I smiled and stretched my arms before me. "It was good to be back in the water."

"You may use this pool anytime you wish," Amon smiled, then his smile faltered as he spied something at the end of the pool. His hands tightened on my shoulders.

I turned my head and saw what had attracted his attention. The water at the other end of the pool was bubbling and roiling, moving slowly toward us. As the whirlpool reached my feet Amon grabbed me under the arms and pulled me up from the pool. I stood in front of him, his arms encircling me protectively, watching this hypnotizing water dance as it came nearer. From the foam and froth emerged a man of great beauty and great menace, his hair ebony and slick with water, his eyes yellow and glowing. The muscles of his arms and chest were firm looking and well defined. He stood in the water before us and regarded me with hatred in his eyes. I pulled Amon's shirt up my arms and hastily buttoned it, regretting the little protection it afforded.

"You," he snarled, "You have stolen my prize. Leitha was mine and you took her away from me." He was speaking to me and me alone. "I have waited, biding my time while you wandered in the next world. Now that you have returned, I will have you."

Amon stepped in front of me, trying to drag me behind his back. "She is mine. She is under my roof and under my protection. I will not allow you to harm her."

"If she is yours Master Vampire," the demon bowed, "I will leave this place now as it is your right to have and protect what you will. If she is not yours, I demand satisfaction."

"Hello," I stepped out from behind Amon's back, turning first to him, "I hate it when men talk about me like I'm not here. And I am not a possession, I am not yours!" Then turning squarely to face the beautiful, powerfully built demon in the water before me I demanded, "Your name, Demon."

He sputtered and hissed and I could see the defiance in his face. I had demanded his name and as one more powerful than he, he could not help but answer me. I had no idea how I knew this.

Amon spun me around and grabbed my elbows, pulling me very close he whispered fiercely, "Do you know what you're doing?"

I backed away and nodded, "This is my fight."

"As you wish, Little One," he touched my shoulders as I turned, "But I am here, he will not be allowed to harm you."

"I was counting on you guarding my back, but leave this to me," I said confidently, though I had no idea from where this confidence sprung. "Your name, Demon," I called again.

"I am Arioch, Witch," the demon finally answered as he rose naked from the water and stood on the edge of the pool maybe twenty feet from me. "You owe me a life, as you took my Leitha. I will take you in trade. You will take her place."

"Arioch, your deal with Leitha was not binding and you know it. If she had known to challenge your bargain all bets would have been off," I took a step toward him, "You made that poor creature wander in the shadows for decades, no centuries, for no reason. Her only crime was loving a husband who was beneath contempt. You tricked her into that deal and I only freed her from it. You may take my life if you think can," My power, colored with righteous indignation, was coiling low in my belly and I knew this demon was but a gnat before me. I felt Amon draw a deep breath and seem to swell behind me. Squeezing his hand firmly, I stepped away from his protection and moved to confront Arioch.

"Wait," the demon hesitated, "I need to know that if I take your life, in a fair fight, the Master Vampire will not destroy me. Is this so, Witch?"

I turned to look at Amon, "Well, Master Vampire? You need to promise that if he takes my life you will not destroy him in retaliation. Is it a deal?"

Amon looked at me silently, as if I had lost my mind. Finally, he nodded, "It is a deal."

The odor of sulfur, pitch and ash assaulted my nose as I neared the demon. His looks were so deceptive that I could understand how Leitha had been so easily tricked. His hair, now drying, was black, wavy and thick. The thought of running my fingers through his luscious locks slipped into my mind before I could dismiss it. Amon hissed behind me as he read my thoughts. There was no time now to deal with a jealous vampire. I leveled my eyes to Arioch's and held his gaze as he moved around me, studying me, sniffing the air around me. His nostrils flared and he pulled back from me in alarm.

"You are human," he cried, "How is this possible? A human witch with power such as this? Master Vampire, do you know what you have here? Are you aware of her power?"

"I am, demon," Amon smiled at the demon's confusion, "and you are on your own."

Turning his eyes back to me, Arioch leered, "Let's see," he hissed, "How shall I take the little witch? Shall I rip out your heart, slit your throat, tear out your entrails, or just kiss the air out of your lungs till you suffocate."

"And how shall I destroy you, Arioch?" I smiled as I paced a circle around his perfect form, "Shall I slit your throat or tear out your heart? Kissing you until you suffocate is out of the question because, demon boy, you smell."

With that Arioch bolted forward and grabbed me by the throat, lifting me with one hand. My feet dangled helplessly above the ground but I was calm and determined. I sensed Amon move up behind me and put my hand out, stopping him where he was. The demon rubbed his right hand down my breast and ribs atop Amon's shirt and murmured, "Almost a pity. We could have some fun before I kill you." He half-turned me and smoothed his hand over my bottom. I felt Amon's fury rising and prayed for his patience. When Arioch turned me back to face him, he lowered me just enough and I raised my knee quickly between his legs and slammed it into his privates, naked and vulnerable as they were. He let out a howl and hurled me across the room, where I landed hard against the tile wall. Dazed from the impact, I staggered to my feet as he came at me with a wicked roundhouse to my jaw. Stars bloomed behind my closed eyelids and I felt blood trickle down my chin from a split lip. Ignoring the pain, I put on a burst of speed and launched myself into a kick, landing my right foot squarely on his chest. He exhaled roughly as he flew backwards. I made the mistake of stopping to wipe the blood from my lips and Arioch was back and upon me, his eyes flashing, lips drawn back in an evil snarl. Clutching me once more by the throat, he pulled me up close to his body, this time locking one sharply taloned claw into the tender flesh of my rump. Hot little lances of pain shot into the meat of my left flank. His huge throbbing penis jutted and moved against my abdomen, causing me involuntarily to cringe.

"What do you think, Master Vampire?" he taunted, "Shall I take her here in front of you before I kill her? She is but a small thing. When I am done with her she will beg for death." I smiled and whispered, "You wish," as my power, born of rage and fear, rushed down my arms and a dagger of energy and of icy steel materialized in my right hand. Leaning closer to the demon I whispered, "Check Mate," as I drove the knife of power smoothly between his ribs and into his heart. His reptilian eyes widened in surprise then narrowed in anger. With a deafening howl Arioch disappeared and I dropped to the concrete, landing on my hip.

"Damn," I hissed as the rough surface of the concrete floor bit into my skin. Amon rushed to me, the relief clearly written on his face.

"What were you thinking?" he yelled, " You have no idea what powers demons have, he could have skinned you alive and walked off with your still beating heart in his hand. Your foolishness is unbelievable! You are under my protection. It is not your place to fight. He had no right to accost you here in my home. The honor of dispatching him should have been mine. You will not behave so again!"

I smiled as I got up, rubbing my jaw, my hip and my throat. "Are you done ranting?" I asked quietly, secretly delighting in his alarm. "I'm sorry I didn't take the time to consider that I might be insulting you or stepping on your toes, but it was my fight."

Just then Winter and Chimaera ran in. looking like storm troopers.

"What's going on?" Winter demanded, "There was a disturbance in the air, something has been here."

"The creatures outside were very much alarmed," Chimaera agreed.

"Just dealing with a demon," I answered, "that seems to be a fairly common occurrence around here."

Chapter 26

Pulling Amon's shirt around me to cover my nakedness, I went down on my knees at the edge of the pool for a moment to catch my breath. Exhaustion landed on me and the adrenaline must have worn off because my jaw throbbed and my throat burned. My back had also started to ache where I had landed on it when Arioch tossed me. Admittedly, I wasn't really in shape for demon fighting. I had no idea when I freed Leitha that her demon would come looking for payback.

"Paybacks are always a bitch," I moaned miserably. Hanging my head, I breathed deeply and tried to concentrate on calming myself. At length, wobbling to my feet, I made my way to Amon and he supported me as we started from the room. Winter and Chimaera followed behind us.

"So Little Sister fought a demon?" Winter asked as we moved slowly down the corridor.

"Fought and destroyed," Amon answered with a touch of annoyance in his voice.

"Leitha's demon?" Chimaera interjected.

"Yes, it was," I replied.

"I had thought that he might desire some retribution." Chimaera added nonchalantly.

"Man, Chimaera," I turned to give him my most disgusted look, "You could have maybe, oh I don't know, WARNED ME!" If I'd had the energy right at that moment, I probably would have broken his nose. Lucky for him, I was wiped out.

"Ah," I whined, gingerly touching my chin and lip, " I'm famished. I really wanted to eat and I think my jaw may be broken."

"If your jaw was broken you would be unable to move it to speak," Chimaera offered matter of factly.

I just shot him a venomous look and kept moving.

"Tell me, Pet," Amon began and I knew immediately what he was going to ask.

"Yes," I answered before he could continue, "I knew I could take the demon."

"Then why did you let him hit you?"

"I don't know how to explain it," I shrugged, "Just think of it as foreplay." I don't know if my answer satisfied Amon or just piqued his curiosity, as he raised one eyebrow at me, but he made no further comment.

"Cat," Winter started again and I raised my hand to shush him.

"Winter," I shook my head, "Unless my hair is on fire, can't it wait?"

A low menacing growl sounded from somewhere behind me and I froze as Winter answered, "No Cat, I don't think it can wait."

"Then what the devil is it?" I turned and gasped to see both vampires, their eyes glowing and their teeth exposed, staring at me as if I was dinner. "What's the deal, you guys?" I followed their gazes down to the back of my left thigh. Three thin ribbons of blood converged behind my knee and were streaming down my calf.

"I don't get it," I turned to Amon, "why are they acting like this? Surely they've seen my blood before."

Amon stepped behind me and looked as the other vampires had done. "The location of your wounds and your attire," he explained, "They have stirred Winter and Chimaera's bloodlust, and mine for that matter. I need to stop the bleeding, to seal your wounds. I hope this won't embarrass you."

"What do you mean?" my breath caught in my throat as Amon knelt behind me and lifted the tail of my shirt. He wrapped his arms around my thighs, probably so I couldn't run away, and began to lick the claw punctures on my bottom. I blushed furiously as both Winter and Chimaera watched with lascivious grins on their faces. From out of my memory the image of the little Coppertone Girl ads rose unbidden.

"The wounds are not sealing," Amon stated momentarily.

"What does that mean?" I tried to turn to see his face but he held me firmly and would not let me move, "Why won't they seal? Why can't you seal them?"

"The demon must have had poison or some type of venom on his claws," he nodded and stood, "We need to deal with this immediately." Swooping me into his arms we half-ran, half-flew down the hall to the parlor. Winter and Chimaera had both charged down another corridor without being told. All this alarm was starting to scare me.

When we arrived at the parlor, Amon seated me on the sofa gently on my right hip, then disappeared without comment. Chimaera returned instantly, poured a glass of red wine, and handed it to me. I sniffed the dark thick liquid suspiciously.

"You didn't put anything in this did you?" I hissed at Chimaera, "Like blood or something?"

"No blood," he replied earnestly, "Just some toads' eyes, lizard's teeth and strychnine."

"Oh, well," I nodded, "If that's all." I took a mouthful and knocked it back, "See you in Hell," I boasted, then broke into laughter as Chimaera stood uncomprehendingly before me. I was developing a twisted taste for teasing the vampires. They were just so easy.

Winter soon came back with Bishop in tow. Chimaera stepped out of the way to allow Bishop to examine me, then disappeared from my line of sight.

"His Lordship tells me that a demon has infected you with poison or venom," he grimaced as he pulled my shirttail up and looked at the claw marks, " these marks, they are already turning black."

"What does that mean?" I cried, "Is my ass going to fall off or am I going to die from this?"

"We must remove the venom," he said calmly, "His Lordship will see to it," Bishop then moved up closer, as he cleaned the blood from my lip and checked my jaw, moving it one way then the other. It was very disconcerting to have him so close when I was naked beneath Amon's silk shirt. When he looked up from my lip, I saw that his brilliant blue eyes too were glowing and his teeth were shining.

"Relax Bishop," I smiled and took the wet cloth from him and scooted a little farther away, "Just give me an aspirin and a cold compress and I'll be ready for the next round."

"The next round?" he recovered himself and shook his head in confusion.

"Just a joke, Bishop," I patted his hand as he pressed a cold compress to my lip. "I was hungry, but I don't know how easy eating is going to be with my jaw so tender."

"She should have red meat," Amon commanded. He had silently returned wearing black jeans and having donned a fresh white shirt. Again, he wore those sexy black leather boots. It dawned on me that I would likely never adjust to how silently vampires could come and go. It was creepy.

"Yeah," I fumed, "Put it in a blender and I'll drink it."

Bishop looked at me with alarm, "Really?"

"No, Bishop," I shook my head, "I was being sarcastic, obviously with little success. Just bring me something easy to eat. I don't care if it's red meat or not." The impulse to stick my tongue out at Amon was strong, pushy vampire, but I managed to ignore it and sat back on the sofa with the cold compress against my lower lip.

Amon, Chimaera, and Winter drew close together across the room, speaking in hushed tones. After some apparent debate, Chimaera and Winter disappeared and Amon returned and sat beside me on the sofa. Pulling me into his embrace, he picked up my wine-glass from the table and put it to my lips.

"Drink, Little One," he whispered, his voice heavy and mesmerizing, "The wine will strengthen your blood, make you stronger."

Though I was suspicious of him, I drank the wine. Soon I was warm, relaxed and calm. The lights in the room grew dimmer, or my vision was failing. Bishop came in and silently placed a tray of food on the table before me. He smiled enigmatically, then disappeared.

"We should remove the venom before you eat," Amon nodded, "And you probably aren't going to like it. Perhaps we should get it over with?"

"What exactly are you going to do?" I asked as he rolled me onto my right side, lifted my legs onto the sofa and propped a pillow beneath my head. He then lifted my legs and sat down behind me, his right arm draped over my hip.

"Just close your eyes and try not to think about it, Cat," he smiled mysteriously. "I shall try to be quick." He waved his hand across my bottom and the pain was gone. I felt pressure on my flesh but couldn't tell what was happening. Curiosity got the better of me and I lifted my head to see what he was doing. My stomach did a little lurch when I realized that he was sucking the venom out with his mouth, like you would with snakebite. In his left hand he held a small pewter cup and was spitting the poison, mixed with my blood, into it. Lying back down, I closed my eyes and considered that there

225

were worse things than having a vampire's mouth on your ass. He must have read my thoughts because he rewarded me with a gentle caress along my spine.

When his work was complete, he patted my hip and I swung my legs off of his lap. He stood and strode to the fireplace, where he dumped the bloody venom. A fire leapt up from the logs lying on the grate and a foul odor wafted from the flames. He then poured himself a glass of red wine, drank it, and returned the empty glass to its tray. Returning to sit beside me, he slid his left arm across my shoulders and embraced me.

"Eat, Cat," Amon insisted as he brought a fork full of food to my mouth. The room was so dark that I could not see what I was eating and I almost turned my head like a two-year-old. "Trust me," he encouraged.

I opened my mouth and tasted the salty sweet food. It was tender, easy to eat, and unrecognizable. I swallowed and it settled easily on my stomach. Opening my mouth again, I felt like a baby bird waiting for its mother to shove worms into its beak. Amon fed me with incredible patience, food then wine, more food then more wine. When the plate was empty Amon put down the fork then rose to refill my wineglass. As he sat down beside me, I rested my head on his shoulder and played with the buttons on his shirt.

"So," I sighed, "Are you angry with me?"

"Angry?" he traced his fingertips down my arm, "No. Just concerned. Your power has surpassed mine. We cannot let anyone know that you still live. The Council would destroy you if they learned of what you have done, the force you are now."

"Wait a minute," I struggled to sit more upright to look him in the eye, "Your power and mine are two totally different things. You wield your power, it serves you. Though I told you, I don't think this power could make me do something I don't agree with, my power seems to have its own agenda. I had an inkling of an idea about releasing Leitha before I asked you about her, but it was my magic that directed me to do it. Tonight, it was my power that wanted to fight that demon, although I did secretly delight in toying with him. This power is using me, not the other way around. I hate feeling like a puppet, but I seem to be powerless except to go along with it and try to understand as much of it as I can. You are the master of your power, I'm just a pawn."

He pulled me to him and kissed me on the mouth, his tongue parting my lips, brushing over my teeth and circling my tongue. "Don't ever say again that you are not mine," he warned, "You are mine, and one day you will believe it." His hand brushed up and down my arm, then caressed my neck. "You should feed," he whispered.

"I just ate," I insisted, "What more do you want?"

"I want you to feed," he answered as he unbuttoned his shirt. I was getting a very uneasy feeling, my mind was spinning but the urge for his blood had returned. He slid a finger across the skin above his heart and a thin line of thick, rich blood appeared. Wrapping his hand around the nape of my neck, he kissed me briefly, then forced me down to his chest. "Feed, Cat," he demanded and pressed my mouth against his wound. As strong as the urge was, I fought to keep my mouth closed, to refuse his command.

"No, Amon," I whimpered, "I cannot. Not now, not yet. Please don't make me do this."

He sighed, released me, and ran his finger along the wound, catching a few drops of blood while sealing the wound. Pressing his finger to my lips, he whispered, "Then at least take this. It will fortify you, and strengthen our bond."

Opening my mouth, I licked the precious drops of blood from his finger and felt them go down my throat like fire or acid. The burning was intense, but the energy that accompanied it was incredible. My nerve endings tingled and electricity rode along my skin, shimmering and rippling in waves. I drew his finger into my mouth and wrapped my tongue around it, sucking it firmly with all the strength I could muster. Amon's eyes lit with lust as I moved my mouth from his finger, across his palm and wrist, then finally to his chest. Catching a nipple with my teeth, I flicked my tongue across it causing him to draw a sudden breath and stiffen beneath my touch. He dug his hands into my hair and roughly pulled me up to his mouth. Breathing deeply, he kissed me forcefully, demandingly exploring my mouth. His hands began a gentle assault up my arms then down the front of my shirt, well, his shirt. Still kissing me, he caressed my naked thighs. He slid one smooth hand beneath my shirt and rubbed his fingertips gently over my skin, squeezing and massaging my breasts. In one fluid movement, he had me on my knees before the couch and he was behind me, his body pinning my torso to the cushions. His soft, silky hair spilled out across my back as he kissed my spine. His hands moved slowly and tenderly across the backs of my thighs, glided smoothly over my bottom, then returned to the sensitive flesh between my legs. Flipping up the back of my shirt, he bent and kissed my bottom, his breath hot on my skin. I couldn't keep from wriggling in anticipation, but he continued to stroke, pet, and caress me. My heart had started hammering in my chest and I was panting. The sweet, slow, frustrating torture he was putting me through was mindbending. Every muscle, every nerve, every fiber in my body was singing and thrumming. Perspiration was trickling down between my breasts and beading on my forehead. I was going to start screaming or whining if he didn't enter me soon. Though his mouth never left my skin, still kissing my flanks, I finally heard his zipper being opened and smiled with delight when he pushed his hard length up against me. He held his tip just at the mouth of my sheath, intentionally teasing me, making me squirm and push myself back against him.

"Ah, ah, ah," he whispered and held my hips away from him, "I think I should now teach you a lesson about obedience." He slipped one hand between my legs and brushed his fingers over my mound. Intentionally administering feather light touches. He knew that I was aching for firmness and force, I sought to drive myself against him, anything for release. Pulling his hand from me, he slapped me lightly on the right cheek of my rump.

"No no, Pet," he murmured, "I am your Master and you belong to me now, don't you?"

I looked over my shoulder and saw him smiling wickedly, "You are a cruel bastard," I snarled.

Sliding his smooth hands over my bottom, he smiled. "Say it, Cat, I am your Master and you belong to me."

"No," I whimpered in anger and frustration as he removed his hands from my flesh. "I belong to no man, vampire or otherwise."

"Are you sure you can't say it?" he taunted me, barely containing his amusement, "I am your Master and you belong to me."

"I am so going to pay you back for this someday," I hissed.

"You belong to me," he chanted and slid his palms up my flanks and back. He then slid his fingers gently into my center, moving them slowly in circles, stretching and opening me.

"Fine, fine," I cried tears of agony as he had kept me so excited for so long, my need was a painful thing. "I belong to you," I whimpered, "I belong to you."

At last he moved my knees apart and shoved his throbbing penis deeply into me. Long, firm, forceful strokes had me clutching handfuls of couch cushion. Having been at the peak of ecstasy for so long, I thought I would tumble over the edge in no time but I didn't. My body was rebelling at having been so tightly strung and having been denied satisfaction. Blood roared in my ears, my heart rattled inside my chest, my lungs pulled in ragged breaths as I sought relief. Amon thrust time and time again into me, my muscles clenching tightly around him, his abdomen slapping my backside noisily. Colors started swirling in my vision as he bent over my back and brought his hands up beneath my shirt. Roughly he grabbed my nipples and pulled and tugged on my breasts. His movements quickened and I finally felt the approach of release. One, two, three more forceful ramming strokes into me and I came, screaming and crying. At that same moment he threw his head back and howled. He leaned over then cupped my breasts tenderly and laid his head heavily on my back, his member still throbbing deep within me.

"Now do you believe that you are mine?" he asked, his voice still deep and thick with lust.

"I hate you," I seethed.

"No you don't, my Precious," he pushed the shirt all the way up my back and began rubbing me, "You love me."

"Yeah, well, that may be true," I admitted, "But I hate you too. And you?"

"How can you ask, Catherine? I have loved you from the moment you were born," he lay his chest down on my back and stretched his arms out on the couch, taking my arms with him. "I never hoped to have you like this, now or ever," he added. We lay there, spread-eagle, slowing our breathing and our heartbeats together, his body covering and mirroring mine. I felt him kiss my shoulder blades and lick lazy circles on my spine. Slowly, he began rubbing his smooth cool hands up my arms.

"What are you doing?" I asked gruffly, "Don't even think about what you're thinking about." Already sore from our exertions, the thought of his powerful, supernatural strength going through me, within me, caused a panic in my gut.

"Too late, Cat," he began moving inside me again, "Remember? You admitted that you are mine, that you belong to me. As this is so, I may do with you as I please." With slow rhythmic thrusts he slid his length into then out of me again and again. His hands once more found my nipples and he roughly pinched them. I gasped at the pain and the rush of moisture that issued from between my legs. On and on he rode me, my breasts achy and heavy, swinging gently with our movements, our juices sliding down my thighs. Just as I was about to climax, Amon shoved the total length of his shaft brutally into me, harder than he ever had, and I screamed and bucked as wave after wave of orgasm took me. Though part of me was furious with him, I had to admit that he was one hell of a lover, and I realized that I could resent that too. Lying exhausted and mindless for what seemed like an eternity, I was content to withdraw from my dimmed reality and simply be. At last coherent thought returned, along with aches and soreness heretofore unknown.

"I know this isn't the time because now I'm too tired to think let alone talk, but you and I are overdue for a long serious conversation," I stated, struggling to lift his weight from my body.

"We are?" he asked innocently.

"Oh yeah, big time," I nodded and pulled down my shirt as he withdrew his still firm member from between my legs. " *What is it with vampires,*" I thought, " *don't they ever go soft?*"

"Not with you around," Amon smiled as he pulled up his jeans.

"Stay out of my thoughts," I warned, "You'll find something you don't like one of these days."

"My apologies," He grinned guiltily, "Occupational hazard."

"Isn't that dangerous?" I nodded at his zipper, as he drew it up, "You wear no underwear."

"Why would I?" he genuinely smiled.

I started to answer, then thought better of it. Why men wore underwear was not my area of expertise. I had assumed it was so they wouldn't get caught in their zippers, but what did I know?

"Never mind," I moved over to the bar and used a bar towel to wipe the moisture from between my thighs.

"Oh," he looked disappointed, "I was going to lick that off."

"No you don't. Don't you get any more bright ideas," I warned and flicked the towel at him, "I plan on living to see tomorrow. I don't know if anyone has ever died from too much sex, but I don't want to test the theory right now"

"We could go again," he leered and reached for me, "and again and again."

"Down boy, now you're just bragging," I swatted his chest as he grabbed me and pulled me into his arms, "Besides, surely the sun will be up soon. I don't know about you but I am spent."

"The thought of you naked beneath me has me incredibly energized just now," he smiled, "but you are correct, the sun will be up soon. We shall sleep together."

"You're getting very pushy," I complained, "couldn't you just ask me to sleep with you?"

"Why would I?" he grumbled, "You are mine."

"Oh," I sighed, "this is going to get old real fast."

He hoisted me over his shoulder again, rubbing my thigh with one hand and my bottom with the other. The trip to the coffin room was wickedly slow as he caressed and tickled me all the way. I was squirming and laughing helplessly by the time we arrived.

"There is fresh sleepwear for you over there on the shelf on the wall," he offered as he put me down on the dirt floor.

Going to the shelf, really more of a stone ledge, I discovered that he had thoughtfully supplied me with a pair of crisp, soft pink cotton sleep pants and white cotton knit muscle shirt. I rolled the waistband on the pants down to my hips and knotted the shirt above my navel. "Now *give me a bowl of popcorn and a TV and I'd be my old self,*" I thought as I climbed into the coffin. Amon wore a beautiful dark blue billowy shirt over black satin pajama pants and he wrapped his arms around me and closed the coffin lid. His heart beat steady and strong beneath my ear.

Chapter 27

The scene that unfolded in my mind as I slept was more of a vision than a dream. I felt a rush of speed and motion then I slowed and stopped beneath a canopy of cedar trees. Gray clouds moved sluggishly across the late afternoon sky and soft drizzle pattered down on the leaves and the grass. A dove cooed peacefully from a branch above my head. Older headstones near my booted feet tilted and canted at uncomfortable angles, looking like rotten teeth in the mouth of the old cemetery. Mourners stood in the distance beneath a somber burgundy awning or huddled beneath black umbrellas. She was there, I could feel her. Her sadness was almost unbearable and I longed to take her in my arms and comfort her. I knew that I would not, could not, approach her now, or ever.

As the crowd began to disperse, I could just make out the shape of two coffins, sitting side by side beneath the awning. She appeared as the mourners separated and headed for their respective vehicles. Her blonde hair shimmered in the gray of the day and her eyes, which I knew were normally bright and the color of the forest, were swollen and red-rimmed. She moved slowly, though with the elegance of a dancer. She was tall and willowy, yet strong and proud. Everything in me cried out to rush to her, to claim her and make her my own, but I would not. Though I knew that she was the fulfillment of my dreams, the answer to my prayers, I could not take her life. Though she was suffering greatly now, she would recover and live on, as all mortals do. Lifting her head, she turned and looked straight at me, though I knew that she could not see me under the cover of the shade trees and through the rain. Her eyes scanned the horizon as if searching, looking for me, though she did not know of my existence. I felt her, perhaps she felt me.

The flickering image of a hospital room, lights dimmed, monitors beeping and humming replaced the vision. In the bed stirred my blonde beauty, wrists wrapped in white bandages and surrounded

232

by padded restraints. She slept fitfully, her sorrow palpable, tears escaping her closed eyes. I stepped out of the shadows and stood before her, touching her hand with the tip of my finger. Her movements stopped and she calmed beneath my touch. She would survive this attempt to destroy herself, it was not yet my time. Let the years pass for her, let her have a normal life until I would be forced to introduce myself and turn her world upside down.

Standing beside the open window of the quaint little bungalow, I was comfortably cloaked in the darkness of the pre-dawn hours. The heat of the late spring night had forced her to throw her windows open wide in search of a refreshing breeze. Within she lay weeping amidst the wadded and crumpled bedclothes. Though she was unaware of it, she slept, only oh so lightly, her anguish denying her the deep restorative sleep she craved. Invite me in, I demanded and heard her softly murmur, "Please do come in." Standing instantly over her, I smelled her sickness. It radiated from her pores, fouled her breath, and rushed through her veins. Her tears were not due to her illness. She wept from a deep feeling of abandonment. Her man, weak and useless, had left her. Though she felt little love or affection for him, she still missed his presence in their home, his sound, and his smell. She missed the comfort of sharing her space with another human being. Leaning over, I kissed her fevered brow and she stilled as I took her pain. She slept, deathly pale and now motionless and I worried that my time might be upon us, that her days might be numbered.

My eyes fluttered open to find Amon watching me, his eyes filled with calm satisfaction. My sleep had once again been his memories, I realized. The first image had been my parents' funeral and the second after I had slit my wrists and was recovering in the hospital. The third scene was when I had just been diagnosed with leukemia and Michael had left me. I had been privy to Amon's thoughts, his feelings, and even his intentions. He did love me, I marveled, in such a manner as I might never fully comprehend. To love me enough to stay away from me for thirty-seven years was quite a testament to his willpower and his determination. I knew that had the situation not left him with no other course of action, he would not have entered my world until I was on my death bed.

I stretched my arms and reached up to plant a kiss on his beautiful, imperious smile. He clutched my arms and held me to his mouth a moment longer, then released me.

"You have touched me," I smiled mysteriously.

"I have?" he asked uncomprehendingly, as I guarded against him entering my mind.

I just nodded and smiled, silently staring into those dark, fathomless eyes.

"Throughout my life there have been moments when you've been with me, haven't there?" I went on, "You were at my parents' burial, at the hospital after my suicide attempt, and I even invited you into my home in my sleep. Were there other times as well?"

Looking pointedly away from me he grinned sardonically then nodded silently.

"Tell me," I insisted, not willing to let him off the hook.

"The first time you performed as Hunter's Moon in that little honky-tonk bar in Morgan City?" he murmured, lost in the memory, "I was there."

"You were at Pete's?" I laughed, "How is that possible? There couldn't have been more than forty or fifty people in the bar all night. Surely I would have seen you."

"I did not enter until you had begun playing and the house lights had been lowered," He explained, "And I managed to step outside before you took your breaks."

"So," I smiled, "you were there at Pete's Imperial Palace? Unbelievable! There's probably no better example of a dive in all of Louisiana." I suddenly had a thought, "So that means that you saw me play back then. Surely, there was no magic visible when I played Pete's."

"No," he agreed, "At that time there was no magic that I could see, but that means nothing of course."

"Of course," I nodded, having no idea what he meant, "Were there any other times that you were near me?"

"I danced with you at Mardi Gras," he smiled broadly.

"You did?" I gasped, "What, when I was twenty or twenty-one years old?"

He nodded.

Recalling the spring break that my best friend from college, Jodie, and I had driven to New Orleans for the festivities, I chuckled. We had such fun but we couldn't really afford it so we slept in the car. Back then I had an ancient Oldsmobile Delta 88 and it was certainly big enough to sleep in. I stretched out across the front seat and Jodie got the back. These days it would be so dangerous to do such a thing but back then we were young, daring, and short on funds and it seemed like the thing to do at the time. Guys hoping to get into our pants kept us fed and drinks in our hands for the three days and nights we were there. They all went home disappointed, as I recalled. The street dances were loud and frenzied and I couldn't recall dancing with anyone in particular. Suddenly, I remembered being pushed roughly by the crowd into an open doorway, where Jodie and I found ourselves in Tante Etienne's Palmistry Parlor. We were rather tipsy, exhausted, and able, by coincidence, to come up with the funds to have our palms read so we settled comfortably and waited our turn behind an elderly couple from Arkansas. When the couple had departed, happily chatting about how intuitive Tante Etienne was, Jodie hopped up and presented her palm, asking the reader about possible love interests or success in her chosen occupation. Tante Etienne's reading was predictable, as far as I was concerned, Jodie would meet the man of her dreams soon, she would marry and have many children, and would be a success at all she turned her hand to in this world. Jodie giggled and hauled me up off the sofa when it was my turn, "Come on, Cat," she gushed, "You gotta find out what's gonna happen with you!"

I reluctantly sat across the table from Tante¢ Etienne and offered her my hand. She was not as old as I had first thought and was, in fact, quite striking. Her dark eyes were piercing and her hands were long and graceful as she took my hand in hers. She studied my palm silently. I expected to hear that I would marry my high school sweetheart, or I would meet a tall dark handsome man, or something of that sort. Instead, she just stared at my palm. At last she cleared her throat and released my hand.

"You are watched," she announced mysteriously. "Great powers will play a part in your future. You will be both blessed and cursed. Now, be gone. I can tell you no more!" She practically herded us out of her shop and did not let either of us pay her for her services. At the time I just thought she must have been tired and overworked by the influx of Mardis Gras revelers. Looking back now, perhaps she wasn't so far off the mark.

"Who were you dressed as?" I returned to the matter at hand and tried to plumb the depths of my memories.

"Lucifer, of course," he smiled wickedly, "I believe I just wore a black suit with a harlequin's half-mask painted red with horns."

"And we danced?" I marveled.

"Indeed," he nodded, "And I watched over you all the time that you were there. It was perhaps less than wise to have slept in your car."

"Yeah well," I shrugged, "One of the pitfalls of youth, you think you're impervious to everything and that nothing will ever happen to you. Pity I can't remember our dance."

"I did not intend for you to ever know about it," he added "so why would you remember? I intentionally did not make an impression on you."

"Wow," I considered all that I had learned and was astounded at the complexity of Amon's existence.

"So," he murmured, "what would my Lady wish to do this evening?" His fingers brushed little trails of fire up my exposed arms and my breath quickened at his touch.

"Has the sun set?" I asked as I considered how best to approach the subject of the prophesy and Arathia's possible deceit.

"Any moment now," he nodded and got up.

"Something of a question has occurred to me," I murmured as I stirred and stretched lazily, then rose from the coffin to join him

"Yes?" he paused to regard me seriously.

"Your beast?" I hesitated, then ploughed on, "Do all vampires have one? I mean, do you get a beast and a member's card when you're brought across?"

"Brought across?" he looked at me curiously.

"That's what Anne Rice called it when a person was turned into a vampire. You know, like brought across into the darkness?"

"I see," he nodded and smiled, "And yes we all have an animal side, though there are no member's cards that I'm aware of. The beast is a primal and, for the most part, mindless force. It's what allows us to hunt, to become predator and to recognize prey. We Master Vampires have more power so our beasts have more power, so to speak. We are more dangerous than most vampires both because of our powers and because of our animals. So, do you fear me now?"

"No," I grinned, "I was just curious."

"Do you know the saying about curiosity and the cat?" he chuckled.

"Oh, yes," I stepped nearer to him and traced a finger along his jaw, "And satisfaction brought her back."

He smiled a broad and genuine grin and wrapped me in his arms, obviously proud of my reference to satisfaction. The man's ego was unbelievable.

"So what shall we do to fill our evening?" he murmured into my neck.

"I think a shower, some food, then," I stepped up in front of him and wrapped my arms around his neck, "I wish you to take me flying. Away from here, someplace where we won't be disturbed. We need to talk."

"So you have said," he replied. "And I am most interested to hear what you have to say. Very well, a shower, meal, and then we shall go elsewhere and you will tell me what you must."

As we stood naked beneath the pelting water of the shower, we held each other and clung together really more than washed. He was beside me, his arms enfolding me, and I felt the ghost of his memories in my heart and my mind. I had no desire to move, as any movement brought me inevitably closer to confronting our truths and our destiny. The weight of my approaching task lay heavy on me and my mind worked feverishly to consider every possible outcome. How would he take my revelations? I knew that he would believe me, he would feel my truth. His reaction to my knowledge of the prophecy, of my conviction of Arathia's involvement in a greater plan, was impossible to foresee. I had no choice but to confess all that I knew and hope that he might have a greater understanding of the situation.

"You are uncharacteristically quiet this evening," he noted as he smoothed the wet hair back from my forehead.

"Lots to think about, I guess," I kissed the beads of water from his chest, "and I really don't want to think about any of it. It makes me weary."

"This is the matter we will be discussing far from here later?" he kissed my closed eyelids and lifted me gently in his embrace, hugging me tightly.

Dropping my head, I nodded into his chest and he wiped the water from my face and looked intently into my eyes.

"I do not like how much pain this is causing you," he slid his hand along my cheek and cupped the side of my head in his palm. Setting me down beneath the spray, he moved his other hand to the other side of my face, trapping me between his hands. "Perhaps you should tell me now, as the weight of this matter seems to be eating at you and my curiosity has turned to extreme concern."

"No," I frowned, "Not yet. I'm still stewing, turning it over in my mind and I'm not done. In a while, after I've eaten."

Releasing me, he nodded, "And I should feed tonight."

As we stepped out of the shower, I tossed Amon a towel, which he wrapped around his waist. Then I draped a towel over my shoulders, rubbing vigorously to dry myself. He left the room as I began to dry my hair. When my hair was dry I brushed it and threw up my hands. There was nothing I could do at the moment to improve its wild appearance. Its length, weight and thickness had increased dramatically in the time I had been in Amon's company, to the point where I now considered it a mane. Never in my life had I expected to have such thick, wild, long hair. The notion that I was changing under his influence moved uncomfortably into my mind… another issue.

Chapter 28

Amon sat dressed and relaxed by the fireplace as I stepped out of his bathroom, still wrapped in my towel. He wore a black shadow-striped satin shirt with a mandarin collar and black pleated trousers. Tall black leather boots covered his calves up to his knees. The silver dragon's head belt buckle and his silver hair were the only points of light in his darkness, until he smiled at me and his teeth shown white, dangerous and alluring.

"You know, a woman hates it when her man is more beautiful than she is," I teased as I let my eyes drink in the whole sight of his magnificence. "Are you using your glamour on me?" I teased as I leaned down to kiss him and run my hand over his luscious hair.

"I would never use a glamour on you," he answered, "And it pleases me to hear you call me your man." He then indicated the clothes laid across the bed, "This is for you to wear tonight. I will let you dress while I go feed, then I will return for you. Bishop is fixing a meal so you can eat while I am gone."

"No, wait," I demanded, as I picked up the beautifully designed long black dress that he had chosen for me. "You will take me with you. I want to see you feed."

The look of surprise, no shock, on his face was priceless. He stammered, "But, but feeding is, well... it is very private, very intimate."

"More intimate than what we did last night?" I challenged, as I slipped the dress over my head and pulled its long sleeves up my arms. Already, I had become accustomed to wearing no undergarments and lightly tossed away the bra and panties he had brought me. Moaning with delight, I spied the exquisite black leather, midcalf boots that stood beside the bed and smiled at his thoughtfulness when I found the soft short socks tucked inside. Though I could easily wear a long dress like this without panties or bra, I could not wear leather boots without socks. Jumping on the edge of the bed, I pulled on the socks and laced up the leather boots. They were perfect with the ballet-length full skirt of the dress and the long sleeves and fitted bodice made me feel feminine and sexy, both rather unusual sensations for me.

When I looked up from dressing, Amon was still staring at me, his face a mask of disbelief. He shook his head, "You really want to witness my feeding?"

"You don't kill anyone do you?" I suddenly thought.

"No, of course not," he replied hastily "I would spare you this sight, though, as you may see my beast."

"As you may recall," I reasoned, "I have already seen and felt your beast."

"If you insist, Cat," he sighed, "I will allow this, though it goes against my better judgment."

"Then yes," I nodded, "I insist." I walked over and took his hand, pulling him up out of the chair. "What do you think?" I asked as I spun, the hem of the full skirt lifting, "Does it suit me?"

He grabbed me roughly around the waist and, digging one hand into my hair, pulled me to his lips. "It suits you, indeed," he breathed as he claimed me with his mouth. For an instant my heart soared with joy that such a man as this would want me, then reality smacked me again with a reminder of what he wanted from me. Perhaps brief moments of joy would be all I would ever know in this world. I reluctantly pulled away from him.

"Just give me a minute," I held up my index finger and grabbed my wet towel to toss into the bathroom. Normally, I wasn't a neat freak but the thing looked so out of place wadded up on the expensive looking rugs.

As I glanced through the bathroom door I spied Winter standing against the far wall with his finger before his lips, indicating the need for silence. His blonde mane and golden eyes glowed softly in the darkened room making him look like a phantom. The effect was startling, but I managed to not cry out in surprise.

"Just let me, uh, see to something before we go," I stammered as I stepped into the bathroom and closed the door behind me, making sure it latched. I flipped on the light switch and Winter's eyes returned to normal.

"What are you doing here?" I whispered as quietly as I could. Turning on the faucets to cover our voices, I stepped close to Winter.

"There is something afoot tonight," he whispered conspiratorially, "the wolves are restless and Chimaera and I both feel a threat. If everyone believes that you are dead, the danger must be aimed directly at His Lordship. He does not believe himself at risk but I do, and so does Chimaera." He handed me a small pistol nestled in a leather strap holster and a short, silver, throwing knife also in a sheath. "This goes on your calf," he instructed, showing me the straps of the gun's holster, "and this on your forearm. You're right handed aren't you?"

"Yeah," I nodded, still turning the pistol over in my hands, "I am." The gun was a Baretta 3032 Tomcat, a 32 caliber automatic that fit snugly into my palm. I had trained with a full-size pistol and the little subcompact felt more like a toy than a weapon to me.

"Gun on your right calf," He took the holster and, going down on one knee, began securing it on my leg just above my beautiful boot. His hands were smooth and strong, his movements sure. "Knife on your left forearm." I pulled up my left sleeve and tried to fasten the sheath to my arm. Though its holster was designed to be put on single handedly, I had no real experience with such things and mostly fumbled with the straps until Winter came to my rescue. Finished fastening the thing, he patted my sleeve back into place and looked at me pointedly.

"The gun is loaded, seven shots, one in the pipe, safety on," he smiled reassuringly, "The knife is razor sharp. These things will only buy you a little time if the attack comes from a vampire, but its something. Watch your back and His Lordships, 'tite soeur."

"Gotta go," I nodded, checking to make sure that neither the knife nor the gun showed beneath my dress. Though it was probably a false assumption, for the first time since being dragged into this world, I felt like I had some control now just being armed. I stepped out of the bathroom and joined Amon, who stood waiting patiently near the bed.

"You should eat before we leave," he suggested as he took my hand, luckily my right one, and we started for the door.

"Am I going to want to see you feed on a full stomach?" I teased.

"Remember, it is you who desire this," he warned.

"I know, I was just kidding," I agreed, "Fine, I'll eat first."

When we arrived at the parlor, I found that Bishop had prepared a lovely steak with a baked potato and a salad. Rich red wine filled my glass and I ate and drank with unfamiliar zeal. Amon sat reading an antique-looking book, mostly ignoring me as I chewed the tender, succulent, rare steak. Cleaning my plate of the last of the potato, I downed my wine and smiled, wiping my mouth with my napkin. "No room for the salad," I smiled, "But I think I'll survive on what I did manage to eat."

"Very well," he smiled and stood, closing the book with a snap. He offered me his hand, "Are we ready to go?"

"We are," I nodded with a sense of fear and anticipation, taking his hand. "Where do you go to feed?"

"Anywhere there is nightlife is acceptable," he replied, "Lake Charles is good on the weekend, but New Orleans or Houston is preferable during the week. Bars, nightclubs, restaurants, all are open later in the bigger cities."

We stepped through the French doors onto the veranda. The cool night air lifted the ends of my hair and the hem of my skirt. Amon took me into his embrace and I wrapped my arms around his neck, anticipating the rush of adrenaline that accompanied flight. His power stirred and moved around him and mine could not help but answer. Our magics wove together as we lifted into the night, free of the bonds of gravity and weight. The cold of altitude tore through me, lashing my face and tugging at my dress. Burrowing into Amon's neck, I kissed the warm flesh there and marveled that he could make himself warm for me, make his heart beat for my comfort. He growled deep in his throat and held me tighter as we flew through the night sky, the lights and colors of the real world screaming past us in a blur.

A light rain was falling and the cobblestone streets of New Orleans reflected the flashing neon signs that announced the bars and jazz joints of the French Quarter. Revelers and musicians alike gathered beneath porches and overhangs before the establishments' open doors. Loud music and the smell of Cajun food and liquor wafted out to the street. Amon moved me into the doorway of a closed bank and leaned down to kiss me.

"Stay here, Cat," he whispered, "this won't take long." He pushed away from me and strode elegantly down a wide alley, circles of gold from overhead lamps glowing in puddles down its length. I watched as a young musician, cased guitar in hand, stepped out of the back door of a club and Amon spoke to him. From my vantagepoint it looked as if they were exchanging pleasantries, smiling and laughing comfortably. Amon bent over the young man and a mist rose from the ground, obscuring my sight. Moments ticked by silently before the mist disappeared and Amon and the musician spoke again then took leave of each other.

"That was rather disappointing," I smiled and slid my arms around his waist when he returned.

"It doesn't always go that smoothly," he admitted, licking his lips.

"Is that it?" I added, "Is one enough for you?" Though it might have been a rude question, I had to ask, after all what did I know about vampire feeding?

"He was young and healthy," he murmured, "his blood was rich and strong, but I should perhaps have a bit more while I am here. I do not feed every night and sometimes my feedings have to sustain me for several days."

We strolled arm in arm through the mist, heading past Jackson Square and toward the riverfront beyond. A beautiful blonde-haired young woman wearing the uniform of a croupier rushed past us and I was surprised and relieved that Amon let her walk by without incident. Though I hated it, I was secretly jealous and did not like the idea of him feeding on another woman. A young black man selling maps walked back and forth in front of a kiosk near the wrought iron fence surrounding the square and Amon stopped and feigned interest in a map to engage him in conversation. I stood perhaps three feet away as Amon spoke low and deeply and the young man's eyes glazed over. A look of anticipation and rapture lit the man's face and he smiled and turned his head, exposing his neck. Amon dug his teeth into the young man's throat and held him in a shadowy embrace while he fed. Though I should have been frightened, alarmed, even disgusted at the scene, I was strangely fascinated and intrigued. Did the young man feel the same lust and erotic sensations I did when Amon drank from me? When he was done, Amon released the man and turned to me, his black eyes glowed green and his expression was feral and vicious. I gasped and took a step back as his eyes returned to normal and his facial muscles relaxed. The young man smiled and shook Amon's hand, bowed and said "Good Evening, Ma'am," to me as he pocketed the twenty dollar bill Amon had slipped him.

Amon put his arm around me as we continued our walk along the riverfront.

"So you always feed on young men?" I asked.

"Whenever possible," he replied, "I prefer their blood."

"Why?" I stopped and faced him, the answer already stirring uneasily in the back of my mind.

"A young man's blood is stronger, more nourishing than that of a woman," he answered matter of factly.

"If I ask you why," I struggled with a hunch, "are you going to say something sexist?"

"No," he shook his head. We walked on.

"Okay, why is a man's blood stronger and more nourishing?"

"A woman loses blood monthly," he nodded, and an elephant walked into the conversation. Should I leave it standing, towering over me or should I confront it and force it to leave? Without another moment's hesitation I began, "Amon?"

He stopped and stiffened beside me.

"I used to be regular as clockwork," I explained, "and I haven't had a period since I've been with you. At first, I assumed it was because I was so weak and so ill. But I've been growing stronger and getting better. My seizures are less frequent and yet, still no period. Have you been doing something disgusting to me?"

He turned to me, horrified, his mouth opening and closing like a fish out of water, "Of course not, why would you even think of something so, so wicked?"

I shrugged, "I was just trying to account for the situation." I looked at him again and he lowered his gaze as if suddenly investigating his boots. "Is there something you should tell me?"

He escorted me gallantly across a wide plaza to a wood and iron bench and seated me on the damp wood. Rather than sit beside me, as I had expected, Amon began pacing before me and my unease became palpable.

"When you were mugged," he paused and glanced down at me, "you suffered much internal damage."

"Yes?" I murmured uneasily.

"Your liver was bruised, Cat, and the doctors had to remove your spleen," he finally sat on the edge of the bench beside me, "and your uterus."

There it was, those three words I had dreaded made a reality by their utterance. The world swam for a moment and tilted a bit before righting. I had never really considered having a child, wasn't totally sure I even liked children, but to have the possibility ripped away in one breath. I had to sit silently and work my mind around this news. It should have been a relief not to have to deal with the monthly inconvenience, but I felt strangely bereft. Tears rose unbidden and shimmered red in my eyes. I fought not to release them. Amon held me close and kissed first one eye then the other and I finally laughed as I realized that he was licking my tears of blood. The pity party had been broken up for now and I would revisit this situation at some later time.

Amon started to stand as another horrible thought occurred to me. I grabbed his hand, looking up into his eyes, I whispered, "Was I raped?"

His silence said it all as he looked down at me sorrowfully. He pulled me up and wrapped his arms around me. "I am so sorry I was not there to protect you," he murmured.

"Why don't I have any memory of it?" I begged, "Why don't I have any scars?"

"I took your memories when I took your pain," he spoke softly, lovingly, "The few drops of my blood that you were given healed your scars and any undetected damage. You know that your attackers were dealt with."

"Attackers?" I moaned, inwardly cringing, "there was more than one rapist?"

"That was uncertain according to the medical tests and police reports, though it appeared so," he replied, "but they all paid."

Taking his arm, I started walking again, hoping I looked much more brave and heroic than I felt. I was not sure if I should be angry with Amon for taking my memories or thankful that I would not have to suffer the long term psychological trauma of being a victim. What possible good could come of harboring painful, possibly debilitating memories? I would just be grateful and think only of the future, what little I suspected I had left. Walking in silence, he drew me to him and lowered his lips to my ear, "Are you ready to fly, Little One?"

I nodded silently and once more turned to face him, slipping my arms around his neck, careful to keep my left forearm resting on my right hand. He leaned down and kissed me with so much tenderness, so much affection, I rose on my tiptoes and slipped my tongue and my power into his mouth. His eyes flew open as he felt my magic

245

and he accepted it and dominated it. We rose toward the sky, a misty cloud covering our departure. I closed my eyes for a moment as my body adjusted to the change in atmosphere, then opened them and looked at the stars suddenly streaking by. We left the clouds and the gentle rain behind as we flew into a moonlit sky, though the moon was surrounded by a ring of light. Winter was right, it was a bad moon. Other dark forms moved past us and I moved uneasily against Amon. "Relax, Little One," he murmured, "They are only nighthawks out for the hunt."

As we slowed and shifted vertically, I realized that we were landing on the horizontal branch of a Live Oak tree. My boots were a bit high heeled and I teetered for a moment before Amon steadied me and helped me to sit down, my feet dangling in the air. Looking around at the darker shadows of the night beneath the huge tree, I marveled at the beauty, the stillness, and the movement. All manner of living creatures crept, and flew around us. The night was alive.

"You are silent, Cat," Amon spoke quietly as if reluctant to disturb me.

"Where are we?" I asked, still unsure how to start the conversation.

"We are back on my estate, behind the house, though on the edge of the property so we won't be disturbed," he nodded almost imperceptibly in the darkness. "You have much to tell me?"

"I don't know where to begin," I smiled weakly, unsure if he could see my expression. Seeking diversionary tactics, I changed the direction of my thinking when an obvious question, not yet asked, came to me. "Do you do anything besides drink blood, govern your vampires and have incredible sex with unwitting mortals?" I asked lightly.

"This is what you wished to ask me?" He looked doubtful. "And I would hardly consider you unwitting."

"Touché, and no it just occurred to me," I shrugged, though I wasn't sure if he could see me in the darkness. "What do you do for money? Your human guards must insist on being paid and you can't keep a stable full of thoroughbreds without money for feed and things. Surely, you must pay taxes on the estate even if you own it outright. I was just wondering where you get your money." And I secretly wondered if it was in unending supply, though I shielded my thoughts from him.

"I run a bit of a financial empire, if you will," he answered at length, "Several investments that I have made over the centuries have accrued sizeable gains and interest. Much of my time is spent overseeing those investments, rearranging capital and dispersing interest. I guess you could say that I'm a financier, in that I back several rather large business concerns. Is that what you wanted to know?"

"Yes, and I'm sorry if I insulted you," I admitted, "Its really none of my business but it does perhaps give me a clearer picture of who you are. And I confess that I'm having trouble coming up with a graceful way to broach this topic that now faces me."

"Take your time, Beloved," he answered, "We have time before the sun rises."

"I like it when you call me Beloved," I murmured, "It means a lot to me."

"You have no idea how much you mean to me," he replied as he slipped his arm around my shoulder.

The silence between us spun out before me. He had given me the perfect segue and here I sat, terrified to utter the next word. At last I lowered my gaze to the ground and answered, "I know exactly what I mean to you."

"What are you saying?" he turned those black-silver eyes on me.

"I know about the prophecy," I admitted, "I know what you need from me."

Amon was dead silent for the longest time. My heart was beating wildly, anticipating his reaction. Fury finally rose in his eyes, "Who told you of the prophecy?" he hissed.

"No one told me," my voice rose to answer his anger, "I saw it. I saw it."

"You saw it?" he cried, "What do you mean, you saw it?"

"I know you don't want to believe it," I swallowed, "But I've been dreaming your memories since I woke up in your care. I have relived the memories of your battles, your wounds, even when you were made Vampire. And I saw the Oracle give you the prophecy. I know that my Life's Blood is what you need to make you impervious to the weaknesses of being a vampire."

"This is not possible," Amon shook his head. "This is incredible. This has never happened before." He leaped off the branch and landed gracefully on the ground beneath me, his silver hair shimmering in the moonlight. He began pacing, striding back and forth like a panther in a cage.

"Be that as it may, it is true," I breathed a sigh of relief at just getting this much of the issue out. "And there is more and this I don't know what to make of."

"What is it?" he demanded, looking up at me.

"I know the identity of the Oracle," I admitted.

"You cannot," he croaked, his voice thick with emotion. "No one, not even the priests who served them, knew the identities of the Oracles."

"I do," I insisted soberly, "and it was Arathia."

He stopped still in his tracks and stared at me, his eyes two white-hot disks in the darkness. "I sense the truth in your words, but I do not know what this means either," he finally spoke. "I have no idea why Arathia would have been the Oracle then and my advisor and friend now."

"She may be many things," I warned, "but she is not your friend."

"How long have you known of these things?" he put his hands on his hips then motioned for me to join him. I literally took a leap of faith, launching myself feet first from the limb, and Amon caught me in his arms, lowering me gently the rest of the way to the ground. I was relieved that the pistol on my calf had not discharged on impact.

"Some time," I admitted, "I wasn't sure how or when to bring this up to you but after Kasimir's assassination attempt, hell, attempt nothing. After Kasimir killed me, I realized that someone else must know about the prophecy and they don't want you to succeed at fulfilling it. Someone doesn't want you to have the power that will come with fulfillment of your destiny." I paced in counterpoint to his steps, the two of us meeting side by side in the middle of our circuit.

Amon said nothing so I continued, "I know that you had planned to keep me alive and safe here with you until I grew to old age, but let's face it, we don't have the luxury of that time anymore. You must fulfill the prophecy and soon, or the next assassin will take even the possibility of success out of your hands."

We paced like toy soldiers, meeting each other, unable to meet each other's eyes. Neither of us spoke. The silence was a swelling, breathing thing that threatened to explode, taking us with it.

Finally, as I marched past Amon he grabbed me by the waist and pulled me into his embrace, my back fitting snugly against his chest, his lips brushing against my ear.

"I feel like I only just touched you for the first time," he breathed. "I am not willing to lose you so soon." He kissed my neck and ran the tip of his tongue down my jugular to my collarbone. Fire burned on my skin where he touched me and I held his arms so he would not release me.

"Don't get me wrong," I sighed, "I don't want to die. I'm not being selfless or, God forbid, even noble, I'm just trying to be practical. If or when someone discovers that I'm still alive, the assassins will be back until they succeed. As much as I trust you to protect me, things happen inevitably and a determined killer will do the job. I just think that if I'm going to die, you should at least be the one to kill me, to harvest my Life's Blood. At least that way I won't die in vain."

"How can you speak of this so lightly?" Amon gasped, "I will not take your life and there will be no further discussion on the matter."

I turned in his arms and touched his face lightly with my hands, "I am your possession, remember," I whispered as I kissed his chin, his cheeks, and the corners of his mouth. "Yours to do with as you please." Kissing him hard on the mouth, I abruptly released him and bolted from beneath the Live Oak, giggling as I scurried through the forest. He gave chase. There was little underbrush but I had no doubt that Amon's sensitive ears could detect my movements. I considered removing my boots, but decided it would take too long and expose my somewhat tender feet to sharp sticks, stones, and all manner of living creatures. Deciding silence was my best cover, I put my back to a tree and slowed my breathing, struggling to keep from giggling like a schoolgirl.

"Here Kitty, Kitty, Kitty," Amon called softly from a distance, his voice mimicking a night bird. Knowing that he was toying with me, I held my breath and froze. "Kitty Cat," he sang, his voice softer, more distant. I held my ground, waiting for him to move a more comfortable distance from me. I had been concentrating on Amon so I was thoroughly startled when I noticed a pack of wolves sitting silently between the trees not twenty feet from me. A large gray-brown wolf with eyes shining yellow moved away from the others and began slowly stalking toward me. Luckily I was already standing still, for the wolf's menacing movements would surely have frozen me otherwise. I opened my mind and my first truly telepathic conversation with my vampire.

Amon, there is a wolf about to eat me!

Relax, Love, these are my animals, they will not harm you. The wolf approaching you now is the Alpha Female. She is mate to the Alpha Male, his first lieutenant, and protectress of the pack. She is determining if you are a threat before allowing her mate to scent you. If you are armed, now would be a good time to remove your weapons.

You've known all this time that I was carrying? You're just taunting me!

It is she who needs to know that you mean them no harm.

Moving smoothly and slowly, I held my hands out before me then reached down and pulled out my pistol, making sure the safety was still on. "See," I whispered, never letting my eyes leave the wolf's, "just a little gun, nothing to worry about. Oh, and this little tiny knife." I slid the blade from my sleeve and held it up for her to see. Putting both the weapons on the ground before my feet I leaned back against the tree.

If these are your animals why don't you call them off? Tell them I'm basically a nice person, wouldn't hurt a flea, and I even donate to the World Wildlife Fund.

The Alpha Male wishes to meet you. If he accepts you, you will have the entire pack's devotion and protection.

And if he doesn't accept me, it's Little Red Riding Hood all over again, huh?

The female had returned to the others and the huge gray Alpha Male now strode forward. I swear that he almost swaggered as he neared me. His eyes were golden-green and reflected non-existent light. Picking up his pace, he padded toward me and leapt upright, pinning me against the tree with one paw on my chest. My heart was hammering as he lowered his muzzle toward my neck and sniffed. Warm breath tickled my ear, as he smelled my hair. Panic was threatening to undo me.

Please call off your dog, Amon. He weighs a ton.

He is not done scenting you, Beloved.

He isn't going to pee on me or anything is he?

He will memorize your smell and you will be pack.

The great beast finally pushed off my chest and dropped down on all fours. He nuzzled my waist, sniffed my hands, licked my fingers then dropped his head to my skirt. Moving lower, his warm moist breath bellowed against my bare leg as he moved his nose beneath my hem then started lifting his head.

Amon, he's sniffing me!

I told you that he would.

No, you don't understand. He's sniffing under the skirt of my dress.

And?

And I'm not wearing any panties!

Hearty laughter echoed through the trees and it was laughter rife with lust.

Lucky wolf!

Locking my knees together, I squirmed a step back further against the tree. I tried to smooth the skirt of my dress down, but the wolf just growled and continued his upward-moving investigation.

"Nice wolf," I murmured, "um, your wife over there isn't going to like you getting so friendly with me. And between you and me, she's much better looking than I am. Probably smells much better, too. Me? I run like a girl, couldn't kill a rabbit to save my life, and my howling is really pathetic. So, I think we should end things here and just stay, you know, friends.

His nose had reached my pubis and he inhaled deeply two or three times, then seemed satisfied and pulled his head from beneath my dress. Amon materialized silently at the back side of the tree and moved his hands to rest on my shoulders, the tree trunk between us.

You did well! You have been accepted.

Great, I wasn't sure whether he was going to ravish me or eat me. Either way, he wins!

The wolves all lifted their noses and howled into the night, the younger ones yipping and barking, unable to emit the mournful ululation of their elders. Abruptly, the Alphas turned and silently disappeared into the darkness, the pack following magically. Amon released my shoulders and came around the tree, favoring me with his most lecherous smile.

"I should be jealous," he moaned as he leaned up against me, his breath hot and moist. "I do not like another male smelling you, your heat, your sweat, your musk." He handed me back my weapons.

"Hey, big boy," I chuckled, "you could have called him off anytime."

"I wanted him to know you, to accept you so you would have the pack's protection," he whispered as he moved his body against mine.

"Just let me know the next time you plan to bring me out here and I'll be sure to wear underwear," I breathed, my lips brushing the tender area beneath his ear, my tongue touching the pulse in his neck.

Silence filled the forest as Amon pressed his mouth to mine, his tongue prying my lips open, running along the edges of my teeth. His hands slid around me and smoothed and cupped my bottom, feeling that I was indeed pantiless. My breasts firmed and tingled, pressed against his chest. In the distance a wolf let out a low mournful howl then abruptly stopped. A twig snapped somewhere.

"Do not move!" Amon commanded, "We are not alone." He stood silently listening, his head raised in alarm. "Stay here and get low to the ground," he demanded as he turned and disappeared into the darkness.

Chapter 29

I heard nothing as I crouched against the tree, slipping the knife back into its sheath. Clicking off the safety once more, I held the gun at arm's length, bracing myself and scanning the distance down the sight. No one stirred near me. The wind suddenly picked up and the leaves rustled both in the trees and on the ground. My hair flew across my face and whipped about me. Grabbing my hem, I tugged my skirt down over my knees as the gale increased. Lightning flashed in the sky and a few drops of rain spattered around me. My anxiety had me frozen with indecision. Should I obey Amon, I even hated the sound of that word "obey," or should I follow him in case I could help, could guard his back?

Stepping as lightly and moving as quietly as I could, I followed what I thought was the path of Amon's flight. The level ground soon gave way to a steep slope and I was forced to slowly pick my way down through rocks and brambles. A small stream ran along the floor of the hollow and I cursed softly when I stepped into the chill water, soaking my boot. Sensing motion on the rise above me, I came to a halt and tried to listen above the roar of the wind. Sharp and heavy, unidentifiable sounds came to me and quickened my pulse. I tore up the side of the hill, unconsciously rubbing my thumb over the end of the Tomcat and wishing I were ambidextrous so I could have the knife ready too. Shadows moved quickly up the hill on either side of me, matching then exceeding my speed and I realized that wolves were running with me. Above me, two shots rang out in the wind. As I looked up toward the top of the hill, lightning flashed and froze the image of Amon holding a person up by the throat, roaring his rage into the night sky. Wind whipped his silver mane and light bounced off of his belt buckle. The left leg of Amon's pants, I could see, bore two ragged holes and a dark stain was spreading on his thigh. His eyes burned like nothing I had ever seen. I watched mesmerized as he started to lift his left hand to his enemy's face, then abruptly Amon twisted his wrist, snapping the man's neck. He tossed him away like a loathsome bag of garbage before collapsing to the ground. The roar of the Master Vampire's rage and pain filled the forest and the wolves took up the call and screamed with him.

"You're hurt," I panted as I reached Amon and threw myself down beside him. Quickly I slid the Tomcat into its holster. "I can heal you."

"There is no time, Cat," he shook his head. "The sun is coming up and I must get to cover."

"You can't fly with that injury," I warned, "at least not and carry me."

"I won't leave you here alone," he promised.

"Look, I'm not a vampire so I don't care if I'm out here after the sun comes up. You get back to the house and let Bishop take care of you till I get there. I'll walk back and then I'll heal you as soon as I can."

"You are not Vampire," he winced at the pain of his injury, "But my blood has touched you. You may feel pain if you are forced out into full sunlight."

"Fine, I'll make my way back to the house keeping to the trees, I'll stick to the shade. Do these woods go all the way back to the house?"

"Except for maybe the last four or five hundreds yards," he nodded, "The house lies perhaps two miles toward the east so you can just head toward the sunrise until you reach it. Lily usually has the veranda doors open to the breeze during the daytime so you can sneak in unnoticed and make your way down to me. You must be careful that no one sees you, other than my men. Remember Arathia, Lily and Lucius think you are dead."

"Don't worry about me," I smiled, "I'll be fine."

"This wound is but an inconvenience," he stated, "I will heal. I am in no danger so you are not to take any unnecessary risks to reach me. Is that clear?"

"For Heaven's sake," I fumed, "Let's just get you to safety."

"There were three assailants," he drew in a deep breath, "Two of them will stay down until the sun hits them, the third I'm afraid you will have to see to."

"See to?" I turned my eyes to his, a sense of dread washing over me. "And what is that a euphemism for?"

He ignored my sarcasm, "Your blade, did Winter give it to you?"

"Yes, he did," I answered.

"Good, then it is silver," he nodded, "You must run it through the vampire's heart and drive the tip into the ground."

"It's not long enough, it's just a little throwing blade," I protested.

" You will have to find a way to get enough force to drive the knife through to the hilt. As long as some heart tissue is pinned between it and the ground, he will be unable to regenerate before the sun comes up," he shot me a look of impatience. "Now, can you do this thing I ask of you?"

My stomach did a little somersault as I considered the possibility, "What do you suggest?"

"If you can't summon your power, use your foot or a sturdy piece of wood to hammer it through," he replied.

I stood and surveyed the area. My concern for Amon had been so intense and so all-consuming that I hadn't given a thought to his attackers. The scene that now greeted me was gruesome, something out of a horror movie. Two partial bodies littered the ground behind us and the one assailant with the broken neck lay quivering maybe fifteen feet from where I stood. Blood, or I assumed it was blood as it only appeared as dark staining, was streaked and splattered across the ground. The wounded vampire mewled and writhed piteously. He was clearly trying to reanimate. I groaned inwardly as I pulled the too short throwing blade from beneath my sleeve, wishing it were a rapier. Self-doubt and the reality of what I was about to do kept me rooted to the spot where I stood.

"I don't know if I can do this," I whispered.

"Are you squeamish?" he looked up at me, obviously in pain.

"No, damn it," I put my hands on my hips and almost stamped my little foot, "I am not squeamish!"

Forcing one foot in front of the other, I moved toward the vampire that lay struggling on the ground. Refusing to look at his face, I dropped to my knees and held the knife over his chest. Drawing on every ounce of courage I possessed, I drove the blade down in one vicious swipe. The creature screamed and bucked as I pushed the hilt in using the weight of my upper body for force. After some resistance, his ribs gave way and the blade went through his heart and into the ground beneath him. My hands were covered in thick black goo but the knife disappeared, leaving only the butt of the hilt barely visible in his flesh. The creature ceased all movement.

My knees were shaking as I got to my feet and returned to Amon. I wiped my hands on the ground beside him.

"It's done," I remarked, "He's pinned to the ground."

"Good," he smiled weakly and started to rise. I put my arms beneath his and helped him to stand.

"Now, time for you to go," I nodded, "I'll be back to the house as soon as I wash my hands and throw up."

"Please be careful," he added, "I feel no others in the woods now, but you must keep your eyes open. Be aware of your surroundings. My wolves will go with you and protect you."

"Okay," I pushed at him, "Just go please, and let me get going." He pulled me into his arms and kissed me.

"I can't stand to leave you like this," he murmured, "don't you dare think to leave me. You know I would always find you."

"Go, for God's sake," I yelled and tore myself away from him, running full tilt back down the hill toward the stream below. Only after I felt his departure did I slow my run to a walk, then stop to catch my breath. Bending at the waist, I rested my hands on my knees and struggled to steady my breathing. Around me I could sense furtive motion and knew that the wolves were waiting for me. Crouching beside the little stream, I rubbed my hands together in the cool water, rinsing as much of the black blood from them as I could. Using the skirt of my dress to dry my hands, I stood and looked at my surroundings. The forest was still silent in the predawn and I summoned my energy to start up and out of the hollow.

Reaching the top of the next rise, I stood silently looking around, trying to pick out the direction of the growing daylight. After a few moments, my patience was rewarded as sunlight began to creep across the forest floor. Moving into the shade as deeply as I dared, I began following the sun, the wind still rifling my hair and raising my skirt. At least if I was forced into the sun, the wind was high and the air was cool.

At first the walk and being alone in the forest was invigorating. I listened to the birds singing their morning song, small creatures stirring in the leaves, and insects buzzing past my ears. Through bushes and brush, high weeds and brambles I walked, picking my way around fallen trees and over downed rotting branches. As cool as the air was, I soon grew warm in my black dress and yanked the sleeves up my arms and pulled the shoulders down as far as I dared.

Perspiration was ringing my waist and trickled between my breasts and my shoulder blades. My feet, in the leather boots, were soaked. I wadded the fullness of the skirt into a ball in front of me and pulled it up to let the air reach my legs. Lifting my hair from the back of my neck, I grinned ruefully at the thought that I must look like some French harlot walking through the woods on her way to work, anticipating the touch of all those men with rotting and missing teeth, dirty fingernails and filthy bodies.

Realizing that my mind was wandering, I shook my head briskly and took a deep breath. Lethargy was stealing over me and all I really wanted to do was lie down and go to sleep. I had no idea how far I had come or how long I had been walking, but it felt like both a great distance and a long time. My legs gave out a few minutes later, luckily as I stepped into the deep shade of a cedar tree. Needles poked and scratched my skin, but I didn't care, I had to close my eyes for a minute. Leaning my head against the trunk of the tree, I murmured, "I'll just rest here for a few minutes, just long enough to catch my breath."

When I woke whimpering in pain, I first thought it was the onset of a seizure and panicked that Amon was not with me. Then I realized when I moved, that the pain was just my stiffened muscles protesting the running and walking I had done. I stretched and yawned and looked around at the darkening woods. "Darkening woods," I whispered, "oh my god I've slept the day out here."

Staggering to my feet I turned away from the sunset and took off through the woods at a panicked pace. The huge Alpha Male wolf ran up beside me and paced me, though I was sure he longed to run flat out. Stumbling over a tree root, I threw out my hands to catch myself but never reached the ground. Chimaera appeared from out of nowhere again and caught me around the waist. I squealed as he hauled me up and set me on my feet. Panting, I tried to catch my breath and recover from the shock. When my breathing had slowed a little I looked up at Chimaera. He stood motionless, looking at me with those icy blue eyes. His black hair lay thick and long on his shoulders, nearly covering his black duster. Beneath the coat, he wore a black silk tee shirt and black pleated trousers. Like Amon, Chimaera evidently favored black leather boots.

"Great," I moaned dramatically, "it would be you." Looking at his attire, I asked, "And who dresses you guys?"

"We wear black to blend into the night," he shrugged.

"I see," I nodded. "Does Dior have an "After Sunset" line?" He ignored my attempt at humor, weak though it was.

"You slept here all day?" the dark haired vampire eyed me suspiciously.

"Of course not," I snapped, "I snuck off to a Howard Johnson's for a bed and a shower. Had some food too. Don't I look clean and refreshed and well fed?" I ignored his look of dismay and pulled a few twigs out of my hair.

"His Lordship is most anxious to see you, but Arathia is with him now," he sidestepped my sarcasm.

"How is he?" I asked as I pulled my sleeves down and the shoulders of my dress up.

"The bullets he took were silver," Chimaera replied, "so he heals, but slowly."

Looking at him quizzically, I smiled, "You mean you guys really are affected by silver, like the werewolves?"

"It only slows us down," he explained, "unless it's a blade that pierces the heart and pins us to the ground. A bullet through the heart will only delay a vampire."

Nodding, I grimaced, "Yeah, well, I guess I know about that little factoid."

"Arathia is seeing to Sin's care, but your Healing Hand will be faster," he admitted, "I think she is annoying him more than anything."

"Well, why the hell can't you or winter or Bishop distract her, get her away from him?"

He raised an eyebrow and his nose, sniffing at the air. "Is that jealousy I smell?"

"No," I snarled, "It's sweat and dirt and probably wolf."

"How tantalizing," he purred as he moved toward me, "ready to fly, Witch?"

"With you?" I gasped as he slid his arm around my waist.

"Of course," he smiled wickedly, "do you not trust me?"

"No, of course not," I replied, "You would be just as likely to dump me into Lake Pontchartrain."

"If our flight path went that way I might be tempted," he admitted, "But that's miles in the other direction and His Lordship wants you back now. I understand that you have done this before."

I nodded, "But not with you."

He lifted my arms and placed them around his neck, leaning toward me with his mouth very near my ear. As he embraced me he whispered, "It is all the same," and I kissed his cold lips and let my power dance along his skin. Laughing, probably at my audacity, he launched us skyward and I hid my eyes in the hollow of his neck, the softness of his hair. Unlike Amon, Chimaera had little thought for my comfort and made no effort to have his heart beat or to exude heat. The chill that went through me was profound. Though his power was nowhere near as strong as Amon's he was still a formidable creature and my respect for him grew ever so slightly. Most likely just to frighten me, Chimaera rolled us as we flew and I fought not to scream or hit him.

When he landed his feet firmly on the ground, Chimaera set me down and abruptly released me. I staggered two steps back then landed clumsily on my rear end.

"You did that on purpose," I gaped at him accusingly.

Giving me that "Who Me?" innocent smile, he reached his hand down and took my wrist. Hauling me briskly to my feet, he pulled me near and murmured, "Whatever do you mean?"

"Okay, first you do that aerial acrobatics stuff with me holding on for dear life," I began, "and you are so lucky I didn't throw up on you. Then you intentionally put me down so fast that I'd land on my ass."

He did not reply but slipped one arm around my shoulder and leaned his head down to me, his hair obscuring my view. "You must remain close to me, touching me, as we approach the house. I will cloud the minds of anyone who might see us, but you must not speak or break contact with me or the magic will fail."

"You're just loving this aren't you?" I growled, chilled in his cold embrace.

He chuckled low, "Indeed, the smell of the forest on your skin and in your hair, and the tantalizing pulse throbbing in your neck has given me all manner of ideas. I feel the need to feed."

"Well, I'd like to help you out," I teased, "but I don't think your master would appreciate it."

With that, we moved smoothly from the cover of the trees and approached the back of the house. Warm lights glowed in the tall windows and spilled through the French doors across the Veranda.

Chimaera pushed me into some bushes near the foundation of the house and warned me to be quiet and stay hidden.

"I will speak with Winter and find out where Arathia is and if anyone else is about. When it is safe to do so, I will open the door and you will steal in, quickly and quietly. Make your way downstairs and hide in the hallway until we make sure His Lordship is alone."

I nodded silently as he turned and disappeared. Crickets chirruped near my feet and a mosquito whizzed past my ear. The longer I waited, the more uneasy I became. The need to see Amon, to touch him and heal him, was overwhelming and I was about to blow my cover and go in on my own when the door on the veranda swung open.

Rising from my place of cover, I ducked and ran up the veranda steps and through the open door, pausing when I entered only long enough to put my back to the wall. Inching my way quietly, I scampered past the parlor, ignoring the murmur of voices within. Gaining the corridor, I turned left and headed toward the stairs, keeping close to the wall. Down the stairs and around a few corners, I encountered no one, but neither Chimaera nor Winter were there to give me the "all clear" so I moved furtively. The door to Amon's coffin room stood wide and soft light spilled across the corridor. I heard nothing but crept past the room and stepped around the corner, finding a safe place to hide and observe. Standing silently in the hallway, I could feel Amon's pain radiating to me and I yearned to race in there and end his suffering. Suddenly voices within the room rose in heated discussion, though I could not make out the words.

So intent was I on watching Amon's doorway that I was startled nearly to death when Winter slipped his hand over my mouth and pulled me away from the corner. He smiled and put his finger before his mouth, signaling silence. I nodded my head and he released me. I smacked him lightly on the chest.

"Did you have to sneak up on me like that?" I whispered, "You nearly scared me to death. Where is Chimaera?"

"He is in the parlor with Arathia, and Thammuz has just arrived. They will be here soon," he nodded and handed me a gown, "Slip this on."

"Why, what is this?" I gaped.

"It's the gown we buried you in," he answered. "Put it on and I'll sneak you in and put you in your coffin. As soon as Arathia and

Thammuz have come and gone for the night, I'll close the door to the room behind them. Then you can climb out and see to His Lordship."

"Why do I suddenly feel like I'm in an Abbott and Costello movie?" I remarked as I lifted the skirt of my dress and yanked it off over my head. Winter looked taken aback as he lowered his gaze over my naked body. I grabbed the gown from him and slipped it over my head, smoothing its length down my thighs.

"Get a grip, Winter," I smiled, "I'm way past modesty at this point. Besides, I don't think there's anyone in this house who hasn't seen me naked."

"Well," he cleared his throat, "until a moment ago there was me."

"Hope I didn't embarrass you," I pecked him on the cheek.

"Oh," he grinned, "It's not embarrassment. Are you ready?"

I took two steps forward then stopped, "Wait a minute," I grumbled as I stooped to unlace and remove my boots and socks. Unfastening the Tomcat's holster took me a moment, but I managed to remove it with the pistol inside and slipped it into one boot. "I don't suppose they would show but it's just tacky to wear boots to bed, or coffin," I explained. Standing the boots together neatly beside the pile of wadded dress, I tucked the socks in the top and shoved the whole mess up against the wall.

"Help me?" I whispered, offering him my left forearm. He quickly removed the empty knife sheath and handed it to me. It went into the boots with the gun and holster.

"I'll see to that in a moment," Winter nodded at my attempt at neatness, "Come, let's get you back in your casket before Arathia and her guest return. Sin is resting, healing himself, but they will disturb him shortly." He took my hand and pulled me around the corner and into Amon's room. His coffin stood closed, gleaming dully in the soft lights. Winter opened my coffin and bid me enter with a flourish and a bow. Climbing in as gracefully as possible, I smoothed my hair and Winter helped me smooth my gown. He laid me back and crossed my hands on my chest.

"I think that is how we buried you," he sighed, "Even if you aren't dead, you should not have moved. I think this is right. We'll hope that no one disturbs you so it won't matter, but just in case."

"Is Sin okay?" I whispered just before Winter closed the coffin lid.

"He is weak and in pain," he smiled sadly. "But he is healing. Slowly."

"Any word on who attacked him?"

"Not yet, but an investigation has begun," he replied. "Now you, lay down and be quiet."

Before I could comment, he lowered the lid and I lay in repose.

Amon, I am here with you.

I felt your approach the moment you landed in Chimaera's arms.

Yeah, well, traveling with him is not the most pleasant experience, but I am here, and that's what's important. How is your pain? I can feel twinges of it.

The pain is nothing, but I miss your touch and the smell of you. As soon as Arathia and the Council head have gone, I want you here with me.

The minute they are gone.

The sound of approaching voices stopped further mental conversation. I recognized Arathia's husky sound and Thammuz's deep baritone. Inside my coffin I strained to make out what they were saying, though I did recognize the sound of Amon's coffin opening. They were speaking with him about the attack. I caught only snatches of conversation until I lifted my lid just enough to let in a crack of light and their words. Amon was saying something about strangers paying him respect and I immediately conjured the vision of him in a black suit, his hair slicked back and his cheeks stuffed with cotton. Smoking a cigar, he offered his hand for some lackey to kiss his ring. Of course, The Godfather would come to mind at a time like this.

Shaking the image from my mind, I listened more intently as Arathia began speaking.

"And what of your little witch?" she asked almost snarling.

"Her heart beats and she resumed breathing," Amon answered, "but she has not returned. I have tried to call her back, but she wanders beyond my reach."

"Perhaps she is trapped beyond. Maybe someone is holding her there?" Thammuz suggested.

"No, I would feel her alarm, her distress, if she were being held against her will. When I try to reach her all I sense is darkness and peaceful silence," Amon reasoned.

"If she cannot return," Arathia purred smoothly, "you will take her Life's Blood?"

"When I am convinced that she cannot or will not return, yes," Amon replied.

"I know that you have said that the Oracle needs to bless this precious gift," she added slyly, "but as a Seer and a Sorceress, I offer my services to do this for you. It would be my pleasure to bless the human witch's Life's Blood."

Suddenly the lid of my coffin was lifted and I felt light touch my closed eyelids.

"I appreciate your offer of assistance, Arathia," Amon spoke and the sound of his voice washed over me and calmed me. Imagining lying in his arms, I hid my mind with him.

"You are right," Arathia said over me, "She breathes but she is not here. Don't wait too long, Sin. You wouldn't want to let her slip away and die. Her Life's Blood would be wasted." Her cool smooth fingertips stroked down the side of my face and it took every ounce of will power I had to remain with Amon and not to fly back to my body and flinch or cringe. Finally the lid closed and darkness returned. Slipping away from Amon, I returned to my body. I was more than willing to skip listening to any further conversation from Arathia and focused my attention on the silence and resting.

Chapter 30

A soft rap on the lid of my coffin and I woke startled that I had been sleeping. The lid opened and Winter offered a smile and his hand to help me out.

"Thammuz left the house a few minutes ago and Arathia just retired to her room. You still have some time before the sunrise," he nodded as he escorted me to Amon. The vampire lay calm and beautiful in his stillness until he opened his dark eyes and sat up and smiled at me.

"Cat," he murmured, "I am relieved to see you well."

"I'm fine, Sin," I kneeled beside his coffin and examined his thigh. The wounds were drying but still open and ragged looking.

"I will be outside guarding the door," Winter stated, then turned and left, closing the door firmly behind him.

"I thought he'd never leave," I grinned, "my hand has been tingling and itching to heal you since I got back. I really need to do this and now." I laid my left hand on his thigh and it started to glow and thrum. The flesh beneath my touch began to stitch and mend, the muscles rethreaded and vessels reconnected. Concentrating on the silver and its toxins, I drew the foreign matter from his wound and, as the glowing subsided, caught the metal in my grasp. Two irregularly shaped drops of silver, covered with black crystalline matter lay in my palm.

"Here's your offending substance," I smiled and offered the metal for his inspection.

"Your power is remarkable," he nodded and, curling my fingers into a fist, kissed my knuckles. Pulling my hand from his touch, I hurled the silver blobs across the room and heard them plunk dully into the dirt.

"Come," Amon invited, "lie beside me. I need to touch you."

Moving into the coffin beside him, I reveled in his embrace, the feel of his warm skin and the sound of his heart beating softly in his chest. He nuzzled my hair, the top of my head.

"Your hair smells of cedar," he murmured, his soft breath seeking and finding my ear, "your skin smells of earth and green growing things." He kissed my forehead. "You taste of salt, sweat, and the heat of the sun." Pulling me up to his level, he pressed his mouth to mine and breathed deeply. "I haven't tasted the sun in ages," he whispered as he gathered my gown into his hands and lifted it off over my head. "I want it all." And because I could not bear to hurt him, I bit off remarking that he might soon be enjoying walking and tasting the sun again.

Starting at my mouth, he kissed, nuzzled then licked my skin, down my chin, my neck, chest and breasts. Moving downward he continued to taste me, my ribs, my tummy and abdomen. Parting my thighs, he tasted my rising heat and I squirmed beneath him, his tongue and lips tantalizing and exciting me mercilessly. Flipping me over, he began again at my hair, breathing deeply, absorbing the scent of the sun on me. He moved methodically down my body, shoulders, back, waist, lower back, and bottom. Kissing the backs of my thighs, my knees and my calves, he drew me in, piece by piece. I rolled over and kissed him, digging my fingers into his thick mane, pulling him impossibly closer. "You slept the day in the woods, I understand," he whispered with an odd tone to his voice.

"Well, it isn't like I planned it," I smiled, unsure, "I got so hot and tired then my legs gave out. I just stopped to rest for a few moments. The next thing I knew I woke up and it was getting dark."

"You were alone?" he asked pointedly.

"Except for your wolves, yeah, I was alone," I insisted, unease stirring deep within me.

"The pack stayed with you?" he grinned.

"Yeah," I grumbled indignantly, "Wasn't that the whole point of our little trip to the woods? So the pack would accept and protect me? Well, they did."

For some reason, that seemed to satisfy him and he resumed kissing my mouth and my throat. His hands found my naked breasts and I moaned as he rubbed and kneaded them. They were swollen, heavy and tight feeling in his hands and I ached for his mouth to suckle them. My nipples rose hard and erect, excited for him. I pulled his shirt open and kissed his hard, smooth chest. Running my tongue up his abs, around his navel, and across his ribs, I claimed his nipple with my teeth and gently bit it, flicking my tongue over its tip. He gasped as I exerted slight pressure with my teeth, nipping and teasing him. Slipping his hands into my hair, he roughly pulled me up to his face and past it, lowering my breast into his mouth. I straddled his chest as he kissed first one breast then the other. With slight effort, he loosed his throbbing member and guided my wet, pulsing center down over it. The sensation of lightning went straight from between my legs, up through my core, and into my brain. Gently lifting then lowering my hips, he commanded the rhythm, shoving himself into me in long, smooth, sure, strokes. I rode him, sure and steady, pace increasing as my need grew. His hands were like fire on my breasts and every nerve was touched with electricity. Smoothly, he rolled me over so he was on top of me. Pulling my legs around his waist, he thrust short intense strokes into my wetness, then withdrew and drove long and deep strokes. Varying his movements thusly, he had me crazed and crying out for release. When I knew the next long stroke would roll me over the edge, he delivered two or three short strokes, and my excitement would continue to increase. Shoving myself up at his pelvis and holding on as tightly as I could I moaned and snarled, "Finish it, damn you, finish it now!" He smiled and withdrew almost to the tip of his throbbing hardness, then shoved hard and deep and continued to drive until the pressure touched off a climax of incredible proportions. My whole body quivered and trembled, my silken sheath spasmed and contracted around his rock-hard sword, drinking in and drawing up his fluids. Relief washed over me and I started to laugh with the release, until my laughter gave way to bitter tears. He lay softly resting on my chest, and the thought that I might soon have to give this up, give him up, saddened me to my soul.

"This soon comes to an end," I sobbed softly into his glorious hair.

"Why do you say that?" he raised his head and looked into my eyes.

"You heard Arathia," I nodded, "She's ready to do me in today. And if not her, an assassin will. Anyone who is brave enough or desperate enough to attack you directly, is not worried about surviving it. They want you gone. You are too powerful, they don't trust you, especially after your association with me."

"Why do you worry about such things?" he sighed, rubbing his hand up and down my body.

"I don't know," I admitted, "as twisted as this whole situation is, I have never felt so connected to anyone, never been so close to anyone as I am to you. When you are away from me I physically ache to touch you. The sound of your voice is enough to calm my soul, the look in your eyes enough to stir me to arousal. As fantastic and unbelievable as this is, it's too perfect. I know it won't last. Nothing in my life that I have ever loved has lasted and then once more I am alone."

"You are not leaving me, Cat," he demanded, his voice thick with emotion, "I have spent centuries alone and lonely. You are the first woman I have found who knows me, who feels what I feel, and with whom I can share power. I do not know what all this means, but I know that I am not willing to let it go yet. I feel the importance of our connection. There must be more."

"Perhaps," I smiled through my tears, "Perhaps there is a purpose to all this. I don't know." I lay my head against his and stroked his hair, touching his face lightly, tracing the lines of his mouth with my fingertips.

"Tell me," I whispered, "What does Amon mean?"

"It means "dangerous enemy"," he replied.

"And did you give yourself this name?" I teased.

"No," he shook his head softly, "I just grew to fulfill it."

"Chimaera told me that vampires bear the names their sires give them, is that true?" I asked.

"It is," he kissed my fingertips.

"Why did your sire call you Sin?" I mused, "Was it because he knew you would be such a temptation?"

"That, Beloved," he looked up into my eyes, "Is a story for another time."

"Oh," I smiled as he rose and kissed me again and again. His movements became insistent, demanding and he parted me and took me again. Through the night we made love time after time, never tiring, never sating our desire. We both soared through wave after wave of orgasm as outside the thunder and lightning built then crashed through the night sky. Rain fell relentlessly from the clouds and wind scoured the air clean.

Sometime before sunrise Amon must have left me because I found myself in the grips of the most vivid and disturbing dream.

This dream was mine, not a memory of Amon's. In a glade of green surrounded by tall graceful trees, a crowd gathered around me. We all moved and surged reluctantly forward. Peasants, farmers, and craftsmen alike shuffled on as if being drawn or pulled with no will to resist. At last ahead I could see Arathia seated on a throne made of a growing tree, it's trunk having grown and bent backward creating a wide and deep seat, limbs like fingers surrounding her on both sides and the split center forming a backrest. She wore robes of shining silver like finely woven chainmail and tiny shoes created from leaves and vines covered her feet. Glistening crystals adorned her black hair and on her head she wore a crown made of bones or antlers. Before and below her stood a huge stone altar stained brown and worn smooth. In its center ran a narrow trench that terminated at one end in a narrow downward tilted slit. In my mind a goddess had always been a thing of mythology, a beauty that wore an outfit like a genie and went around plaguing mortals with love spells and inspiring poetry and music. Evidently, Arathia had not been that type of goddess as first one then another peasant kneeled before her offering her a life for sacrifice. She was much involved in her prey but suddenly she turned her eyes to me and froze. She recognized me and I knew her. The dream dissolved and blissful darkness returned.

The familiar pain of a seizure woke me, wracking my spine and legs with agonizing muscle spasms. Blinding white lights blossomed behind my closed eyelids. I drew my body into a ball to steel myself against the onslaught. Even as Amon woke and realized my situation, I rose out of my body and floated just below the ceiling. From here the pain could not reach me and it wasn't until Amon drove his teeth into my neck and sucked toxic blood from me that I slammed back into myself. I gasped as I returned and the sensation of Amon drinking from my veins caused my toes to curl and my loins to stir.

"I felt you leave," he whispered, obviously upset, "your spirit fled."

"I didn't go far," I smiled weakly, "just above us. Tell me, Amon, how is it that I am able to leave my body? Is this another manifestation of my power or is it something else?"

"It is a side effect of my blood," he replied, "Just as I can fly, you, as a mortal, can fly only without your body. The down side is that while you are away, your body is vulnerable. You should not attempt to project your spirit if you are not certain of your body's safety."

"Is that why you were so concerned that I slept alone in the woods?" I guessed, "You were afraid that I might have left my body and that it was unattended there in the forest?"

"Yes, I was concerned until you assured me that the wolves were with you," he explained, "The pack would have alerted me if there was trouble, so I know that you were undisturbed."

"Care to tell me what might have happened to my body while I was gone?" I asked.

"I would not," he shook his head, "the possibilities are endless."

"Someday," I murmured and twirled his hair in my fingers, "you will tell me a few of the possibilities?"

"Perhaps. Do you feel better now?" he succinctly changed the subject, stroking my hair and running his fingers down my neck.

"Thanks to you," I nodded and kissed his forehead, sliding my fingers into his silky hair, "but I would feel a thousand times better if I could soak in a hot tub. After last night's workout, I have aches in places I didn't know I had places."

He looked into my eyes and passed his hand over my body. My pain was gone.

"I can see to a hot bath," he added as he kissed me chastely.

We rose, I slipped my gown on, and he led me quietly from the room. Up the stairs, along the hallways and up a second flight of stairs we moved. Finally reaching the sapphire room, he directed me to be seated in one of the occasional chairs while he disappeared into the bath. I lay my head back against the back of the chair and, closing my eyes, thought, "You gotta love a man willing to draw you a bath."

At last, Amon touched my hand and drew me up out of the chair. He led me into the bathroom, which he had set aglow with flickering candles. The moist air was redolent with the fragrance of orange blossoms. Steam rose from the foam-covered water and I paused only long enough to drop my gown and step into the tub. I sat then sank beneath the bubbles, leaning back and relaxing in the moist heat. Amon, I noticed, began unbuttoning his shirt, then sat on the edge of the tub behind me.

"And what exactly are your intentions, sir?" I smiled as I admired the smooth taut planes of his muscular chest.

"I thought, my lady," he bowed and began to run his fingers through my hair, "to shampoo your hair, if you so desire."

269

"Well," I smiled broadly, "if you insist."

Just then a knock sounded at the door and Winter called softly for Sin.

"Come on in, Winter," I called through the closed door, "I am decent."

Winter silently opened the door and stepped into the room, closing the door behind him. He wore a pale chambray shirt tucked into his blue jeans and snakeskin boots. His wild blonde hair lay thick on his shoulders and he looked more like an ad for Stetson cologne than a vampire bodyguard.

"I am sorry to disturb you, My Lord, My Lady," he nodded awkwardly, "But the Council have arrived and seek a word with you."

"Indeed?" Amon looked at him pointedly.

"Evidently Thammuz informed the other members that Cat still lives, even though, as far as they know, she has not recovered. They wish to discuss the matter with you," he smiled sympathetically at Amon.

"Very well," Amon rose, "I will see them. You will stay with Cat until she has finished her bath then escort her back to her coffin. If she wishes food, you will see to it but you will at no time leave her unattended. Either you or Chimaera must be with her at all times."

"As you will it," Winter murmured as Amon stood and buttoned his shirt.

"I will return to you as soon as possible," Amon smiled at me, "You know what to do should Arathia open your coffin?"

"I will hide my mind," I nodded, "if I can't get to you, I'll construct a wall in my mind and hide behind it."

"Good," he touched my hair, "Arathia must not know of your recovery, at least until I can determine the Council's intentions." He turned and strode from the room, nodding silently to Winter.

"I will wait outside," Winter offered.

"No, wait, Winter," I smiled, "stay here and talk to me. Keep me company."

"If you wish," he grinned and leaned against the far wall.

"Yes," I murmured as I leaned back and closed my eyes again, "that is what I wish." Stirring the bubbles around me I sighed deeply.

Silence settled between us and I finally opened my eyes and looked at Winter. I raised my eyebrows at him, it was so obvious he had something on his mind. Cocking my head in question, I smiled, "Yes?"

"You kissed Chimaera," he said with a touch of disbelief.

"What's this," I laughed, "a little vampire boy gossip at recess?"

He looked at me uncomprehendingly.

"A joke, winter," I shook my head.

"You did it on purpose didn't you?" He grinned boyishly, "You wanted him to feel your power."

"I may be guilty of a little showing off," I admitted, "Why?"

"I shouldn't say," he looked down sheepishly.

"Come on Winter," I coaxed," what?"

"He said that you blew him away, though he didn't use those exact words," he chuckled, "that his lips burned for hours afterwards."

"Good," I smiled self-indulgently, then looked at Winter who was watching me expectantly. "What is it Winter? Do you want to touch my power?"

"Yes," he smiled genuinely, "and no."

"Meaning?" I asked.

"I would love to touch your power but you might destroy me." He admitted reluctantly.

"What do you mean?" I cried, amazed. "You know I would never hurt you." The thought that I might be capable of destroying anyone had never occurred to me. It shocked me that anyone would think I might.

"You destroyed a demon," he reasoned, "your blood scared off two other demons and you released Leitha. You could destroy any one of us at any time."

"Just because I could," I fumed indignantly, "doesn't mean that I would. Those demons were all threatening me, I would not of my own volition destroy a being simply because I could. Wait a minute Winter, are you afraid of me?"

"Of you, no, 'tite soeur," he swallowed, " but of your power, oh yeah."

"Hold on, Winter," I marveled, "Is this why the Council are so concerned? Not because I am likely to destroy them but because I am capable of doing so? Surely there are other beings capable of destroying vampires."

"There are others," he agreed, 'but those who are considered a threat are bargained with and they sign a treaty agreeing not to wage war with us."

"So what if I offered to sign a treaty?" I suggested.

"Being an individual, the Council would not consider a treaty with you binding, as there would be no collective will to force you to honor your agreement."

"Let me get this straight," I struggled for understanding, "If the threat is one from a community of the enemy, you reason with them, come to an agreement, and sign a treaty. If, however, the threat is from a single entity, you remove it, destroy it. Is that a fair assessment?"

"It is," he nodded soberly.

"Damn," I hissed, "So I can't win. What if my powers disappeared?"

"Do you expect them to?" he asked hopefully.

"Hell, I didn't expect them in the first place, as easily as they appeared, they could disappear." I chuckled despairingly.

"Wishful thinking?" he grinned.

"Oh, yeah," I nodded.

At last I stood and dried myself on a towel while Winter turned gallantly to face the wall. I pulled my gown back down over my head then stepped forward, touching Winter on the arm. He turned and I looked into those gorgeously wild golden eyes. Rising up on my toes, I touched the side of his face and placed my lips softly on his sweetly bowed mouth. Gently opening his mouth, I released a little of my power and let it enter him as well as play along his lips. Winter's eyes widened in surprise then relaxed in amusement as he realized what I was doing. He leaned into me, wrapping one arm around my waist and pulling me to him, then kissed me back. Admittedly, a part of me wanted to melt into him.

"Just because I can," I breathed huskily, "doesn't mean I ever would."

"Ooh, la,la, Cher," he growled, "part of me wishes you would. Your power is quite an aphrodisiac, Little Sister, best keep this under cover."

"Promise," I crossed my heart, "you're the last. And you've been hanging out with Bear too long, you're beginning to sound like him."

"May be," he straightened himself, " now, we'd best get you back to your coffin in case the Council members wish to assure themselves of you current, uh, inaccessibility."

"Fine," I agreed, "But you're going to have to sneak me some food. I don't care what it is, cheese and crackers, peanut butter sandwich, don't even think about adding jelly, or a bag of chips. I crave sustenance."

"As soon as you are relaxing in your coffin," he nodded, "I will have Chimaera watch you while I petition Bishop for some food for you, okay?"

"Deal." I smiled as we stole silently down the hallways and down the stairs to the coffin room.

Crawling back into my coffin, I straightened myself, then assumed the position, finally crossing my arms on my chest. Winter smiled down at me and whispered, "I'll close the lid for a little while. Chimaera will be outside the door until I come back with some food. I'll check on the meeting while I'm upstairs, see how things are going for His Lordship."

Chapter 31

Alone in the dark silent coffin, I thought of Amon and his discussion with The Council of Five. Before really becoming aware of my will to do so, I left my body and floated out of the room to the library where the meeting was going on. Amon stood relaxed, his silver hair gleaming in the soft lights, his white shirt a stark contrast to the darkness of his eyes. He was leaning against the fireplace mantle, arms folded across his chest. Long legs extended and crossed at the ankles, he exuded quiet authority and the confidence of one who had wielded power for a very long time. A fire burned low behind him, mostly red embers in the grate, and candles softly lit the elegant room. Chesmne and Nephthele were seated in the two leather armchairs while Mastiphal leaned against a bookcase. Thammuz stood before Amon, evidently speaking for the Council.

"We are pleased to see that you are healing so quickly," Thammuz smiled, indicating Amon's leg.

"Yes, it heals," Amon nodded, "but slowly. Damned silver."

"We would not disturb your rest if this was not important," Mastiphal offered from across the room.

"Very well, what is it?" Amon replied tersely.

"We are concerned that the witch may recover," Chesmne spoke up, "your witch."

"And since when is my life the object of speculation and discussion for the Council?" Amon stiffened.

"The magnitude of the witch's power has us greatly concerned," Thammuz said reasonably. "We would not dare to dictate to you any part of your life, we only seek to understand and perhaps to recommend."

"Go on," Amon smiled grimly.

"Arathia has informed us that she believes the witch released Leitha," Nephthele answered, "She could not sense her presence and did a reading of the area. She saw the witch touch Leitha and believes that she now has a Healing Hand."

"Perhaps she does," Amon agreed, "But it is a moot point since she has not returned to her body, and may never do so. Do you feel she is a threat in her current condition?"

"No, of course not," Thammuz added quickly, "but she may recover at any time. The Healing Hand, while it poses no threat in itself, does imply a much greater power than we have known in centuries. If she is capable of dispatching Leitha to her Gods, who knows what other abilities her magic has given her."

"You are correct," Amon nodded and I could feel his anger growing, "She did indeed wield the Healing Hand and what's more, she used it to remove your Mark of Penitence. I too believe she released Leitha, because she knew the creature to be miserable and suffering. She is a power to be reckoned with and her magic may have just gotten her killed. She may never be able to return and we may never know what glorious powers she could have offered us and the world, but please, if The Council has a recommendation, I am happy to hear it."

Everyone remained silent apparently surprised by Amon's revelations. I sensed Winter outside in the hall, pausing to check on the meeting's progress, then he moved on.

At last, Mastiphal spoke, "Her power is great and she is a great threat to you and to your subjects. You should deal with her immediately. Remove the threat."

"Are you such cowards, is your fear so great that you would destroy her because you assume she is your enemy?" Amon roared, "She has harmed no one and has in fact been attacked repeatedly by humans and vampires alike. The fact that you wish to see her dead because you do not understand the source or intent of her power makes you as bad if not worse than the humans that seek to destroy us blindly. We now live in secrecy because man's fear would have him annihilate our species, though our threat to him is slight. You would do the same to the witch?"

"She is an unknown element," Thammuz offered, "if we knew that you controlled her, we could perhaps rest more easily."

"I would like to tell you that I do," Amon smiled ruefully, "but the truth is, no one controls her. She is like the wind or the storm, wild and untamable. I can assure you, however, that she poses no threat to our people. Whatever her magic's purpose, it is not aimed at us."

"You know this to be true?" Chesmne stood and touched Amon's arm, looking deeply into his eyes.

"I do," he said succinctly.

"I trust your word, Your Lordship," she nodded and turned to the other Council members, "what say you all?"

"I agree with Chesmne," Thammuz smiled, turning to Amon, "Your word is good enough for me."

Nephthele and Mastiphal looked at one another then Mastiphal spoke. "I do not know that Nephthele and I accept your word as fact, however since the witch has not yet recovered, it does no good to concern ourselves with this matter right now. If she recovers, we can address the issue, and if she does not, our worry is unnecessary."

Amon's dark eyes burned with barely contained fury and I wondered if Mastiphal and Nephthele knew just how close to danger they danced. At length he growled, "Be aware, I am your leader and only suffer your suggestions at my indulgence. My word and my will are law, and it would be wise to remember that. I will deal with the witch when and how I see fit and you will either take my word or not. Be advised, however, that you do not want me for an enemy. And tell me, Council members, what of the witch's attacker? Has Kasimir confessed or admitted why he tried to kill her? "

Thammuz shook his head, "He has not."

"I allowed you to take custody of him, but if you do not punish him soon I will take it upon myself to do so. As your leader and as the offended party, it is both my right and my duty to see that he is dealt with. This creature, this member of the Council, attacked and tried to kill a human, and not just any human but one in my home and under my protection. He will be punished." Amon's voice was dripping with venom and his words were heavy with anger.

With that Amon paused to regard each member of the Council then turned and walked out of the room. I flew past him and back downstairs, rushing back to my body. Pausing a moment, I saw Chimaera hurry to Amon's side and speak with him in low, urgent tones. Suddenly, I was forcefully drawn into the coffin room and was horrified to find Arathia standing over my open casket. She was murmuring something powerful and it was pulling me back into my body. As Amon and Chimaera stepped into the room, I raced into

Amon's mind, thankful to have a safe place to anchor my spirit. Arathia's chanting stopped and the pull ceased.

"Arathia," Amon smiled concealing his annoyance with her.

"I sought to bring you back your witch," she nodded graciously, " and I thought I felt her spirit for a moment. I really thought I was going to be successful, but she slipped away again. I am so sorry."

"Thank you for trying," he replied soberly, "perhaps she is not strong enough yet to return to us."

"I don't think she wants to come back," she shook her head, "I think she intentionally fled my spell."

"You may be right," Amon agreed, "but I will give her more time just in case she strengthens or changes her mind." He leaned down and took my hand and I fought to stay in his mind, as his touch drew my desire. "Chimaera, please escort Arathia from this place. I will stay with Cat for a time."

"As you wish," Chimaera nodded, and took Arathia by the elbow, leading her from the room.

The sensation of returning to my body was like ramming into a wall. I gasped at the blunt force, then opened my eyes and looked up at my beautiful vampire.

"Welcome back, you little spy," he grinned and kissed my forehead as I sat up.

"You knew I was there in the library?" I marveled.

"Yes," he nodded, "I felt you the moment you floated in, then I saw you near the ceiling. What did you think of our little meeting?"

"It was very illuminating," I shrugged, "You made a very good point when you brought up their unfounded fears. Very eloquent."

"At least we now have some idea of the Council's thinking," he shook his head, "though I am shocked at the depth of their fear of you."

"I guess it's understandable," I added, "even Winter admitted to being somewhat fearful of my powers. I couldn't believe that anyone would be afraid of me, or would think me capable of destruction."

I climbed out of my coffin and stood before Amon, encircling his waist and snuggling against his chest.

"So," he murmured, stroking my hair and kissing the top of my head, "you are a fearsome thing." He dropped his hands to my back, then stroked down my gown across my lower back. Cupping my bottom in his hands, he squeezed and lifted me gently. I wrapped my arms around his neck and pulled him down into a kiss. He moaned and moved himself suggestively against me.

"Rats," I sighed, "Winter is bringing me food. As much as the thought of having wild vampire sex with you right now excites me, I really am famished. And after your injury you should probably feed, shouldn't you?"

"I don't require blood, but it would serve to strengthen me," he admitted.

"Great," I pushed him away, "you go feed, I'll eat and we'll meet back here before sunrise. Deal?"

"You're getting pushy," he observed, "Don't let your power go to your head, Little One."

"Why?" I moved forward again and touched his chest with one finger, "Afraid I might be able to take you?"

"Oh, you can take me," he caught my hand in his and kissed my fingertips, "anytime." Bending down, he kissed my neck and I brushed him off. He smiled wickedly, then turned to go. "Feed well, Beloved, as will I."

As Amon left, I turned around and surveyed my surroundings. As sadly appropriate as this room was for sleeping, resting, whatever, it was most definitely not a room for dining. I determined that as soon as Winter arrived we would leave for a place more conducive to eating. Padding around the dirt floor barefooted, I looked down at my gown and silently vowed that as soon as possible I would see it burned. I was developing a rather healthy hatred for the garment.

At last Winter came in bearing a tray and smiled at me.

"Before you get all happy with yourself over your accomplishment," I warned, "I do not want to eat in here. Sin left to feed so we're on our own. Let's go somewhere else."

He gave me that put-upon expression and sighed, "Where do you wish to go?"

"To the pool." I suggested brightly, "I noticed a table and chairs at one end of the room. It would be the perfect place to eat."

"Okay," he nodded, "I don't think Arathia even knows the room exists so you should be safe there."

"Let's go," I took the tray and let Winter lead the way, making sure the corridors were clear and that we were unobserved.

Once we arrived, I took the tray to the table and busied myself putting out the place setting. I was really looking for a way to get rid of Winter for a little bit so I could take a dip in the pool before eating. Luck was with me as I noticed he had forgotten to bring anything to drink.

"Winter," I turned and smiled sweetly at him, "would you be so good as to bring me a drink?"

"Of course," he bowed dramatically, "what would My Lady prefer? Wine? A beer?"

"I feel like going all out tonight," I grinned, "how about a gin and tonic?"

"As you wish," he turned to go then turned back to me, "you will, of course stay here and hide if you hear anyone but me coming?"

"Of course," I nodded exuberantly.

The minute he was gone I pulled the gown off over my head and took a running dive into the deep, clear pool. The water was cool and invigorating and I felt my whole body coming awake. I dove deep and knifed smoothly through the water, my muscles straining and stretching. It felt wonderful to be moving and getting exercise again. My nerves relaxed and my lungs pushed gentle breath out through my nose. As I surfaced and set a steady rhythm, arm over arm, legs pumping and kicking, it was as if a fog lifted from my mind. Softly glowing lights in the pool floor created gently rippling cones of luminescence and I counted them as I swam from one to the next. I opened my mind and let random thoughts tumble through. Soon the visions of my empty hospital room returned and I noted the I.V. stand with its empty bags, tubing, and needles. Winter's words about the drops of Life's Blood popped into my head, "*We vampires can see them, to us they glow almost like liquid neon, they glow amber.*" Transfusion! Suddenly everything connected. In my head bells rang, coins clinked into slots, lights flashed and sirens screamed. Of course, it had been in front of me all the time! I almost drown in my excitement, taking in a startled lungfull of water. Gaining the shallow end of the pool I stood in total amazement. I wiped the water from my eyes and slicked my hair back from my face, then just stood in shock and surprise.

By the time Winter returned I had dried off and wrapped a fresh towel around myself. Sitting at the table, I was chewing on a piece of shrimp when he came in and placed my drink on the table before me. I couldn't help myself, I beamed at him. He took the seat beside me.

"What?" he smiled suspiciously, "what's happened, besides your taking a swim?"

Jumping up from my seat I bounded into his lap and put my arms around his neck.

"I'm so excited," I squealed, "I figured it all out." I kissed his forehead.

"Figured what out?" he cocked his head, almost comically.

"How Sin can fulfill the prophecy without causing my death. It was right there in front of me all the time. I have to find him, oh and I need to see Bishop. Could you find Bishop for me?" I pecked him on the cheek and returned to my seat, picking up another piece of shrimp and washing it down with the gin and tonic.

"Are you alright?" he murmured, "should I get Bishop to give you something?"

"I am better than alright," I smiled, "don't you see? I know how Sin can fulfill his prophecy without me dying. He gets my Life's Blood and I get to live!"

"Does His Lordship even know that you know about the prophecy?" he asked, looking stricken.

"Yes, of course, we've discussed it," I took another drink, "now, will you go get Bishop for me? I really need to talk to him."

"Will you be okay here by yourself?" he asked as he reluctantly stood to leave.

"I'm great," I replied, "I'm just gonna finish my meal"

"Promise you won't go anywhere?" he regarded me doubtfully.

"I promise," I crossed my fingers over my heart, telling perhaps my first bold-faced lie.

Feigning calm and relaxed interest in my meal, I forced myself to stay seated until Winter was gone, then bolted for the far wall. There had to be a door somewhere behind the drapes, I knew it. Pulling first one panel then another aside, I finally found a glass sliding door that led out to a small patio. There were no lights on this side of the house, deep shadows stirred in a gentle breeze. Stepping out into the night air I let my mind soar and knew that Amon was close. I called to him with my thoughts but he did not answer. Moving out into the grass, I walked far enough onto the lawn to be able to see the roofline. The severe peak stood out darkly against the starlit sky. Moving around the corner of the house I came into view of the widow's walk, the railing barely visible in the dark. There, knees bent up against his chest and head bowed, crouched Amon, looking much like a gargoyle. His silver hair covered his head and shoulders like a shroud and he silently brooded.

"Amon," I called softly, "Amon, please hear me. It's important."

I detected no movement, but in the space of a single breath he swooped down from the dizzying height and stood before me, eyes simmering with anger.

"Are you daft, woman?" he snarled as he grabbed me around the waist and started to carry me back to the house. I squirmed out of his grasp and jumped away from him.

"Wait a minute," I demanded, "this is really important. I have to talk to you."

"What could be so important as to cause you to run around outside nearly naked? You realize that you are at risk of being discovered, fully functioning and recovered, when you are supposed to be nearly dead?" he pointed out with obvious impatience.

"Please, please listen to me," I grabbed his hands in mine, "this is the best possible information. Please, I need to speak to you alone."

Looking at me, standing wet-headed wearing a towel, he sighed and shook his head, "Witch, you are impossible," he murmured as he took me into his arms and led me back into the pool area, closing and locking the sliding doors then closing the drapes. He led me back to the table and bade me sit down while he grabbed another towel and draped it over my shoulders.

"At least dry your hair and warm yourself for a moment," he suggested as he took the seat Winter had occupied.

"Okay, please, just listen to me," I begged, "Let me get it all out and then you can ask me anything you want, okay?" Pulling the towel up over my head, I rubbed my hair and dried it as best I could.

He nodded silently and smiled, obviously indulging a lunatic.

Chapter 32

"**I** know how you can fulfill the prophecy without taking my life!" I began, "Just listen, please don't say anything. I'll get distracted. Anyway, I was swimming, just thinking, and I remembered that when I first came here Arathia told me that with all things magic the devil is in the details. I didn't know what she was talking about at the time. But when you told me about Leitha's deal with the demon, how she assumed her husband would return to her instead of her going to hell to see him, I started to get the idea. I relived your memory so I heard the prophecy and the Oracle never said that you had to take my life, only my Life's Blood." I quoted, "You will find this mortal, touched by magic, and obtain her Life's Blood. Bring it to me that I may bless it to fulfill the prophecy."

"But taking your Life's Blood means that you are dead," Amon insisted.

"Maybe back then it did," I smiled, "but that was before modern science, technology, and modern medicine. When I was first treated for leukemia I was transfused, infused, and every other type of "fused". Don't you see? Bishop can give me a transfusion, assuming you can get enough type B, Rh-positive blood. As soon as you see those glowing drops of Life's Blood run through the tubing, you remove the needle and put the stuff into a tube or a vial. Top off my supply, clean me up and there you are, half way home to fulfilling the prophecy."

Silence fell between us as Amon wrestled with doubt and I waited breathlessly for his reaction.

At last he looked up. "This will work?" he questioned hopefully.

"There's no reason it shouldn't," I grinned.

"That is not exactly the same as saying 'of course it will work'," he grumbled.

Taking his hands, I pulled him to his feet and slid into his arms, looking up into those unbelievably beautiful eyes. "Of course it will work," I assured him.

"This is incredible," he smiled at last. "You are sure?"

"I'm sure, I've had it done innumerable times" I laughed, "and I have another idea as well."

"Yes?" he asked, moving me slowly in his embrace, dancing to silent music.

"After sunset, you will go to Arathia and tell her that you've been trying all evening to reach me without success," I explained, touching the buttons on his shirt. "Tell her that you've decided that it's futile to put off taking my Life's Blood any longer, but that you wish her to try one last time to bring me back. She will do that voodoo she does and viola', I will be miraculously returned. My subsequent weakness and disorientation should keep her at bay long enough to get things set up for the transfusion. She will not know about our plans until we actually put them into action. I'm not sure why, but I know she will be needed there during the transfusion."

"She has offered to bless the Life's Blood, as the Oracle directed," he nodded, "without admitting, of course, that she was the Oracle."

"Yes, well," I shrugged, "that was to be expected, but I think that her presence will be needed for something other than a blessing. I just don't know what."

Amon bent and kissed me tenderly on the lips then pulled me tighter against his body. His kiss became more demanding and I melted into him, happy to abandon all thoughts and considerations. We slowly turned around and around, rocking and moving to our own secret rhythm as we touched and explored each other with our hands. He stroked the length of my hair, down my back, and up my arms. I touched his back then slid my hands along his ribs and up his chest. It was sweetly fulfilling and comforting just to be together and touching one another.

Winter cleared his throat as he, Bishop and Chimaera entered the room. I noticed that Bishop carried his little leather medication kit, winter must have told him that I was having a fit of some sort.

Pointing at the kit I smiled, "That will not be necessary, Bishop, I am quite fine, really."

"I'm glad you are all here," Amon released me and turned to address his men, "I have news of some importance, though I'm sure Cat would say that it's her news."

"No," I sat down in my chair and crossed my legs, "this is all yours."

"Very well," he bowed slightly to me, "you are all aware of the prophecy and of my hopes for the future. Though Cat, Catherine, was supposed to give her life, her Life's Blood, to fulfill that prophecy she has discovered an alternative. Bishop, your medical training is excellent so I shall leave the decision of this scheme with you. Cat believes that you can transfuse her blood, until we can obtain her Life's Blood, with donor blood of her type. Once we see the glowing liquid flow into the tubing, we transfer it into a vial, see to her health, and are ready to proceed to fulfill the prophecy. Do you think this is possible?"

"Though we have never had cause to test this theory in the time since medical technology has blossomed, I see no reason that this would not work. Perhaps Cat, more than anyone, knows the importance of blood transfusions and I'm sure she underwent many in the early stages of her leukemia treatments. I will need to type and cross match her blood and it may take me a few days to secure a sufficient amount for a complete transfusion. I can't just go to the bloodbank and withdraw nine or ten units of whole blood without raising some eyebrows so I'll have to procure a few here and a few there. Yes, however, I think it will work. I believe Cat, Catherine, is correct."

"Arathia will reawaken our sleeping beauty," he beamed at me, "after sunset tomorrow, and we will proceed with the plan from there. No one must know of this until the last possible moment, and I'm hoping that the Council will not hear of Cat's recovery until we have tended to our business."

"So," Chimaera smiled, "we are to witness the fulfillment of a prophecy and this far from the time of the Gods."

"Hopefully," Amon agreed, "and if all goes as planned, our beautiful witch stays with us forever."

"Forever?" I gulped my drink, "that's a long time."

"Not long enough," he shook his head.

"I will see to the details," Bishop stood, then turned to me, "I will need to draw a small amount of blood from you, Cat, to verify the blood group and Rh factor, then I can see about obtaining the proper amount for a full transfusion"

"I'll come with you," I stood and began to follow him out of the room. "I'll be right back," I called over my shoulder

"I will wait here," Amon nodded, then turned to speak to Chimaera and Winter.

As I followed Bishop down an unfamiliar hallway he turned and gave me a curious smile.

"What is it Bishop?" I sighed, "What am I missing?"

"I don't know that you are missing anything, Cat," he stopped and waited for me to catch up to him then linked his arm through mine. "I'm just not sure you understand everything, all the risks." His expression was solemn, his blue eyes regarding me with concern.

"All what risks?" I stopped our forward movement and looked at him pointedly.

"Cat," he explained, "Life's Blood, by its very nature is difficult to obtain and will not flow from you veins unless you are at risk of dying. If I transfuse you, that is, replace the blood I take as I take it, you will be in no danger of dying and your Life's Blood will not move from your body. I will have to drain you to the point of death, maybe beyond, then use a rapid infuser to replace your blood supply. In order to reduce the risk of brain damage, we'll reduce your body temperature with a cooling blanket. I may have to use a defibrillator if your heart stops. This will be tricky." He looked at me solemnly, his black curls framing his cherubic face. It was difficult taking sobering news from such an angel, but I found myself trusting him implicitly.

"Why is it that nothing is ever as simple or as easy as I think it should be? You cannot tell Sin this," I begged, "He will not even try this if he thinks it's dangerous. The Council and Arathia are already questioning his judgement where I am concerned. He won't be able to put off fulfillment of the prophecy indefinitely and at least this way I have a chance of surviving. If Arathia has anything to say about it, I won't survive the next attempt."

"Very well," he agreed, "I will not lie to him, but there's no reason to inform him of all the details of this operation. If he doesn't specifically ask, I won't volunteer the information, how's that?"

"It will do," I nodded as we resumed our walk. We ended up in the kitchen, a room that I had never seen before. It was warm and welcoming with deep, rich cherry cabinets and black marble countertops. The center island matched the cabinets and sported a grill as well as four burners in its cooktop. A copper exhaust hood hung suspended above the stove. Cherry panels covered the doublewide refrigerator and terra cotta tiles covered the floor.

"Wow," I marveled, "this is great! What a beautiful kitchen, it almost makes me think I could cook something edible in here."

"Are you not a good cook?" Bishop grinned as he readied an empty hypodermic, alcohol and cotton swab, and tourniquet.

"I haven't starved to death," I shrugged and offered him my left arm, "but I'm not very creative and my attempts at exotic cuisine have been, well, miserable failures."

Wrapping the rubber tourniquet around my arm, he found a vein and deftly slid the needle into it. Removing the tourniquet, he pulled back on the plunger and watched my blood fill the hypo. He withdrew the needle, placed a cotton ball on the injection site, and then pushed my arm up to put pressure on the wound.

"Very smooth," I smiled, "You're very good at this."

"Thank you," he nodded graciously, "and you are done."

"Great," I turned to leave the kitchen, "how do I get back to the pool?"

Pointing at the door he offered, "Left out the door, then right, then left at the second hall to the left, then right. Third door on your left."

"Sure," I rolled my eyes, "Left, then right, then second left, then right, then third door. Can I send up a flare when I get lost?"

"Open your mind," he grinned, "His Lordship will guide you back, I'm sure."

"Yeah," I added brightly, "that should work." Stepping through the kitchen's swinging door, I turned left then stopped to concentrate on Amon's location. He was like a beacon in the dark and I relaxed when I realized that I could easily find him.

When I returned to the pool, Amon was alone and sitting at the table, his fingers steepled and his eyes closed. He appeared as a tormented angel, angst and turmoil clearly etched on face.

"You look, um well," I struggled for the proper word, "torn I guess." He scooted his chair back and I sat on his lap. "Something wrong?" I slipped one arm around his neck and leaned over to kiss his forehead.

"Just worried about you," he smiled weakly, "I worry that this scheme of yours will not work, that I will not be able to keep you safe from harm, that The Council will challenge my decisions about you and force me to act against them. Perhaps I borrow trouble."

"I'd say so," I rubbed the back of his neck and kneaded the tense muscles in his shoulders. He closed his eyes and breathed deeply, then released his breath and seemed to relax. "So, this is my last night as a member of the nearly departed," I observed. "What shall we do with these last hours before sunrise?"

Leaning his head on my chest he murmured, "I could spend the time making incredibly slow, soft, passionate love to you."

"Mmm," I purred, "that sounds wonderful." I stroked his hair and lifted his chin, searching those ebony eyes for a hint of what would remove their pain.

"Or, if you would like a change of scenery," he brightened, "we could ride out to the forest and make love amidst the trees, under the stars."

"That sounds perfect," I nodded, already anticipating the sight of Amon sitting astride Abraxis, "just give me a few moments to go back to the room and get dressed."

"I will escort you back to the blue room, then I'll ready the horses," he replied as he lifted my hips and placed me on my feet, then stood. Leaning down, he slipped his fingers over the edge of my towel and pulled my body up against his. His mouth found mine and his kiss was tender, passionate, and full of promise. When he released me, we both gasped for a moment, then Amon led me by the hand from the pool room and back upstairs to the sapphire room. As he opened the door for me, I turned to kiss him and he was gone. Vampire speed was so unsettling.

Though I would likely never understand how it was possible, Amon had chosen an outfit for me, for riding, and had it laid neatly out across the bed. I smiled broadly at his thoughtfulness and his impeccable taste as I inspected the black jeans and matching black leather calfskin boots. A pair of white fuzzy socks peaked out from the knee-high shafts. The white blouse was dramatically detailed with vines of black velvet flocking and the black leather belt bore a silver dragon's head buckle, similar to the one Amon regularly wore. Silver lace bra and panties were, upon closer inspection, made of some impossibly fine material, which may have been silk but felt more like gossamer. I ripped off my towel, anxious to feel the lingerie against my skin, and slipped them on, luxuriating in the smooth, water-like sensation. Leaving the remaining garments behind, I ran into the bathroom and hurriedly plugged in the blow dryer. Tossing my hair, I dried it as quickly as possible then, after a perfunctory brushing, wove it into one long braid falling down my back. I wasn't generally much of a braid-wearing person, but knew that it would keep my hair from whipping across my face and getting in my eyes as we rode. Quickly washing my face and brushing my teeth, I turned off the bathroom light and stepped out into the bedroom, relieved to find it still empty. I donned the beautiful blouse, buttoned it and tucked it into the snug fitting jeans. The leather boots were butter soft and, I was pleased to see, nearly without heels and felt as natural as a second skin over the fuzzy soft socks. Sliding the belt around my waist and through the belt loops, I wrestled for a moment or two with securing the dragon's head buckle. It was more complicated than it looked but I finally figured it out and was waiting at the door when Amon returned. He strode silently down the hall, his black satin shirt shimmering, and his black boot length cloak stirring with his movement. He smiled approvingly as he noticed my attire. "Two things are you missing," he murmured softly and produced a long cape of black velvet from out of thin air. Its generous hood lay atop a double-layer capelet that draped gracefully from the shoulders, making it look a cross between something out of Sherlock Holmes and Robin Hood. It was exquisite and I wrapped it lovingly around myself. He smiled and bent down to kiss me, his cloak encircling me within his arms.

"And this completes the ensemble," He whispered as he took my hand and slipped a large malachite ring up the index finger of my right hand. The stone was dark, mysteriously shaped, and made me feel a little uncomfortable. Power emanated from it and made my skin prickle.

"Amon," I whimpered, "I don't like this." I tried to remove the ring to return it to him, but it would not move.

"Please," He took my hand and held it in his, "the ring is for protection, it has a power all its own. If we run into danger tonight, the ring will act as a lightning rod for your powers. I will not take any chances with your safety, so please wear this ring. For me?"

Kissing me again, he moved my arms down to my sides then drew my hands behind my back, leaning me backwards in his embrace. He drove his tongue into my mouth and kissed me as thoroughly as he was able. The ring on my finger hummed and tingled, then settled comfortably on my hand.

"I am not sure that I can wait until we get to the forest," Amon breathed as he released me and drew me down the hallway, my cape swishing softly against my boots.

Stealing out the veranda door, past the parlor, we ran quietly to the darkened stables. Abraxis and Bella stood patiently waiting, saddles gleaming and bridles jangling gently as they nuzzled each other. I drew up short when I saw that Amon had readied Bella for me.

"Amon," I gaped, "I can't ride Bella. I don't have that much experience. She's way too much for me to handle."

"Nonsense," he smiled, his white teeth shining in the darkness, "Bella is Abraxis' mate, she will follow him anywhere and he needs her with him."

"What is that, some kind of allegory?" I quipped, "am I to see a parallel between us and the horses, 'cause if you think I'm going to follow you anywhere…"

"Just use your will and Bella will obey," He nodded as he lifted me up into the saddle and spread my cape across Bella's rump, "if you have any trouble with her, just give her her head and she'll go with Abraxis."

"Where have I heard that before?" I murmured as I remembered the overheard conversation between Amon and Bishop where Bishop had said something very similar of me.

My eyes were adjusting to the darkness and I smiled with lustful appreciation as I watched Amon smoothly swing himself into Abraxis' saddle. Sitting there astride the massive steed, Amon looked perfectly natural, like he was born to ride. For an instant, he looked like an ancient warrior, then he clucked to Abraxis, snapped the reins, and we were off at a brisk trot. Trying not to panic, I intentionally loosened my grip on Bella's reins and let her drop her head to pick up speed. Lowering myself in the saddle, I held onto the horn and let the mare race by Abraxis. Behind me, I heard Amon summon his mount to speed and the race was on. It occurred to me that I was unsure of our destination, so I opened my mind and willed Bella to the forest. She must have heard me because she suddenly veered to the left and we flew smoothly over the open field of grass. Realizing that we were riding recklessly, I gently tugged Bella's reins and gave her plenty of room to slow her speed. Just as I willed it, we slowed to a comfortable gait, then turned to view the approach of Amon on Abraxis. He looked a little testy.

"You may think that Bella is Abraxis' mate," I smiled, "and he may think so too, but the fact is Bella knows that Abraxis is her stallion. Just thought you men should know that." Bella snorted and shook her mane.

"Welcome to the world of male and female equality," Amon sighed dramatically and patted Abraxis' mighty neck, "or should I say more correctly, the world of female superiority?"

"As you like it," I laughed and turned Bella, trotting ahead toward the dark shadows of the trees. Amon rode abreast of us and leaned over to grab Bella's reins. He drew both steeds up and swung out of his saddle. Dropping their tethers, he came and reached up to catch me as I dismounted.

Not letting my feet touch the ground, Amon embraced me and kissed me on the lips, spinning us around and around. "Come," he whispered, "let's go into the woods."

Releasing me, he led me by the hand through the trees and into the deepening shadows. As we walked I began sensing motion high in the trees. Sinewy movements on the ground heralded the arrival of the pack, though none approached us directly. Flapping sounds broke the silence of the forest and Amon brought me to a halt, stepping behind me. His hands rested comfortably on my shoulders and he leaned his head next to mine and whispered, "Look in the trees, Beloved."

I stood silently for a moment then began to pick out the shapes of numerous birds, large birds, perching along the branches of the surrounding trees. Golden eyes glowed from the shadows as the birds sat placidly regarding us, unmoving, only occasionally blinking.

"Amon," I whispered as quietly as I could, not wishing to disturb our visitors, "are these more of your creatures? Are they like your wolves? Did you call them?"

"No, Precious," he answered as his hands moved down my arms and crossed protectively, or possessively, around my waist, "The owls are yours."

"What do you mean, the owls are mine?" I hissed, "They aren't mine, I didn't call them."

"They are yours," he assured me, "and they have come to pay their respects and to curry your favor."

"Amon," I turned in his embrace and looked into his shimmering black eyes, "I don't even know what that means. What do I do with them?"

"Well," he bent down and began to nuzzle my neck, "I had plans to make love to you here in these woods, so unless you fancy an audience, I would dismiss them." His breath was warm on my neck and his kisses were stinging my throat. Other parts of my anatomy were beginning to stir.

"What do I do, run screaming and waving my arms in the air to scatter them?" I squirmed, my mind barely able to construct a coherent thought as his mouth moved slowly over tender, sensitive areas.

"You could," he pulled away and looked me in the eye, "or you could just thank them for their noble gesture, let them know you appreciate their loyalty and offer of their services, and send them away. Promise that you will call them should their aid ever be necessary."

"Oh, I just go speak to them?" I marveled at the simplicity, "Or do I use my mind?"

"You could use your thoughts to address them," he replied, "but the lesser members of the flock will think more kindly of you if you speak to them. They are not all that accustomed to communicating silently."

"Okay," I sighed, "Wish me luck." I rose to my tiptoes and kissed his cheek.

"They are your creatures, Cat," he added. "You need no luck. They adore and worship you."

I moved quietly to stand before the largest single congregation of owls, perhaps twenty or so in the nearest tree. Their perfectly round eyes blinked and stared at me and at first I felt a little silly when I began speaking to them.

"Great winged owls of the forest," I called, "I thank you for your show of respect and loyalty. I appreciate your dedication and your affection. I bid you go about your lives and I promise that, should the need arise, I will call you for assistance. Thank you, my beautiful and noble creatures, please be gone." With that, the largest owl flapped its wings and disappeared into the night. After that, one after another of the great birds lifted gracefully from its perch and sailed skyward. Suddenly a deafening roar of wings echoed through the forest then grew more distant and quieter as the remainder of the flock took wing. Silence returned as I turned and walked back to where Amon was spreading his cloak out on the ground. Taking my face in his hands, he kissed me and smiled, "Your natural magic, your power, is a thing to behold. I stand in awe of you."

"Come on," I grinned, not really understanding what all the fuss was about, "You're making me blush."

He took my hands and unbuttoned my sleeves, then wrapped my arms around his waist and murmured, "Oh how I love to make her blush." I pulled gently away from him and began to unbutton his shirt, at last pausing to pull the tail of the garment from inside his jeans. Stretching up to reach, I slid the shirt from his broad shoulders and pulled it down his arms, tossing it away into the leaves. Moving my hands across his smooth muscular abdomen, I kissed his skin and tasted his flesh. Marveling at the strength and softness of him, I laid a line of kisses from his belt to his collarbone, pausing to tease first one nipple then the other. He gasped as I sank me teeth, ever so gently, into the skin at the base of his throat. Stepping away reluctantly, I slipped off my boots then stood to look at Amon as I slowly unbuttoned then removed my shirt. Sliding down my jeans and stripping off my socks, I stood wearing the shimmering silver bra and panties beneath my beautiful black cape. Amon's eyes burned in the darkness, desire coming off of him in waves. My anticipation had me breathing heavily, waiting for his approach. A low guttural growl rumbled from his throat.

"Take that off," he demanded, looking pointedly at my bra, "I want to see you."

I hesitated, almost fearful at the force and the lust in his voice. Finally I reached around and unhooked the bra, dropping it slowly to land on Amon's cape. The night air was mild, only slightly cool but a chill touched my skin. Even from the four or five feet that separated us, I could see Amon's body reacting to the sight of my naked breasts and I longed for him to take me into his arms. Locking his gaze on me, he began removing his boots then his pants. As he stood, his manhood bobbed huge and swollen and I found myself moving toward him as if hypnotized. Our eyes met and my gaze never faltered as I approached and kneeled before him, taking his length in my hand, then my mouth. He moaned and gently touched my hair, rocking forward and back on the balls of his feet. He untied my cape and tossed it away. When I gently squeezed his sac, he uttered something explosive in some unidentifiable language, then stiffened before me. Lifting me from my knees, he growled and carried me forward by the elbows. Shoving my back against the trunk of a tree, he tore away my panties and pushed my knees apart, driving his length all the way into me. The force drove the air from my lungs and I gasped as he withdrew then moved into me again. I slipped my legs around his waist and he set a slow but steady rhythm. He kissed me tenderly and rubbed one hand over my painfully erect nipples, as his movements became more demanding, more forceful. My breathing became ragged and loud as my passion mounted and our pace quickened. Though I was helpless against the tide of physical stimuli, I realized that I was not seeking release. I didn't want this to end. Then as the orgasm shook me, the muscles of my womb clamped down hard on Amon's member and he growled and released his juices deep within me. We stood motionless, panting and enjoying the rippling sensations of our pleasure. The pain was exquisite as he moved within me, slowly, after our climax. He seemed to know that after release, my body needed to go still before relaxing. By moving, he was able to keep sensations tearing along my nerves, tingling along my skin, and ripping through my mind. Slowly, he pulled himself out of me then he lowered us to the ground and began his assault anew.

"No," I whimpered, "please, no more. Let me rest, everything's too sensitive, I can't bear it."

"Yes," he whispered warm breath into my ear, making me writhe beneath him, "you can bear it. More than that, you want it." He raised himself up on his hands, then slowly, excruciatingly, slid himself back into me, every part of me still quivering and throbbing. Propping himself on his elbows, he slid his mouth over my right nipple. Flicking it gently with his tongue, he then locked his lips around it and suckled, pulling hard, making me whimper with pain and delight. Sucking, then kissing, then licking and sucking again, he drove me almost to madness with desire before moving his attention to my left breast. By the time he was finished with that nipple I was squirming and bucking beneath him again, my breath catching and my heart slamming against my ribs. Blood rushed in my ears and my vision swam as he pounded his massive member into me again and again. At that last moment, he grabbed my waist and yanked me off the ground onto his lap. The forceful change of position allowed deeper penetration than ever before and it scared and surprised me. I screamed when the next orgasm tore through me and Amon once more released himself into me.

At length, we collapsed on his cloak and relaxed in each other's embrace. My head resting on his naked chest, I played my fingers along his muscles and traced his ribs. In the distance an owl hooted and a wolf howled mournfully. I snorted at the thought that both Amon and I had creatures around us whom we called our own. Life among vampires was, at least, not boring. As he touched my chin and lifted my face to his Amon smiled, "What do you find amusing, Kitty Cat?"

"The sounds of both your wolves and my owls," I shrugged, "did I just say my owls? Wow! This is just, unbelievable. It's extraordinary. I have my own animals. And they're birds. Why would they be birds? Why not bunny rabbits or kangaroos? Do you know?"

"An owl is a creature of great strength and wisdom," he explained, brushing one finger idly across my lips " they are swift, excellent hunters and will serve you well. You should be honored to hold dominion over such creatures."

"I am," I rose to meet his eyes, "don't get me wrong, I'm honored. I just wondered why not the bunnies, why not the kangaroos?"

"First," he took my hand in his, "kangaroos are not indigenous to Louisiana so I think that would be a problem. Perhaps they are your creatures but since there are none here, they can't very well serve you, right? Secondly, a bunny, as you call it, is prey. They eat, hide, and reproduce. How would such a creature serve you?"

Not truly being sure of how an owl would serve me either, I nodded, looked thoughtful, and rested my head again on his chest. "I just wish we could stay out here forever," I sighed wistfully, "without you turning into a charcoal briquette at sunrise."

Sitting bolt upright, he pulled me roughly against him. "I will not tell you again, I am Master Vampire and I do not combust and I do not turn into a charcoal briquette, whatever that is," he snarled, "The only reason I had to leave you alone in the forest at sunrise was because I was wounded by silver. I feel discomfort in full sunlight, that's all. You deride me and your words are disrespectful! Do you wish to be taught a lesson? "

"No, no," I tried to pull away from him, "I was only joking, lighten up. No lessons in respect required here, no sir. My point was that this is perfect here with you like this, and I hate that it has to end." His grasp on my wrist was like iron and I knew that it was futile to struggle.

"That is all?" he asked, his eyes searching my expression for any sign of deceit. He looked me in the eye and captured me in his gaze. I think I stopped breathing as he regarded me suspiciously. My heart hammered in my chest as fear gripped me. I so did not want a lesson in respect, as the possibilities of punishment were terrifyingly infinite.

"You know I speak the truth," I dared at last to breathe, "you can feel the honesty of my words."

Relaxing again, he nodded, "You are right, you meant no disrespect."

We shared a lengthy silence as I was too hurt and too frightened to speak. At last, I drew a deep breath and observed, "You know, you are very touchy. One minute you're all kisses and sweet talk and the next minute you're threatening to eviscerate me. Are all vampires like that or is it just you?" Hey, I had to know.

Moments ticked by heavily before he finally answered.

"You are incorrigible," he sighed, "No one in their right mind would have the nerve to ask such a thing of a Master Vampire."

"Why not?" I replied before even considering the wisdom of such a question.

"It is obvious you do not understand my position, or have little respect for it," he shook his head, "but I will answer. I am now feeling emotions that have not stirred within my breast for centuries, have had no reason to stir. One minute my heart is overflowing with tender feelings for you and the next I am determined to keep you safe by forcing you to submit to my will. In my world everyone submits to my will, for to do otherwise is to risk incurring my wrath. My authority is absolute. I am unused to dealing kindly with someone who does not obey me. I care for you deeply, but I do not know if I can adjust to your modern, mortal values, your need for independence, and your desire for control."

"So is a Master Vampire like a governor or a mayor or something?" I plunged ahead, having already insulted him I thought I might as well get it all out of my system. "You have referred to the other vampires as your subjects?"

He sighed and shook his head, probably in disbelief, "Closer to a Prince or a King, and yes, they are my subjects. They have my protection and I have their loyalty."

"So you are royalty?" I gasped, "And I just made a huge social faux pas by asking these questions, right?"

"Though I am not of royal lineage in the mortal world, yet indeed I was a knight," he added, "In my world I am royalty I guess you would say. And I rule absolute."

Recognizing a heightened sense of self-preservation, I bit back the next comment and closed my mouth with a snap. After a few moments my heartbeat finally slowed and steadied. I resumed breathing normally, then stretched out on Amon's cape. Lying on my back, arms spread eagle, I muttered under my breath, "Once again, stupid, do NOT piss off the vampire! When will you learn? Vampires are very touchy, and touchy about being touchy!" Staring up into the dark canopy of the trees, I sighed and reluctantly sat up.

"I suppose we should get dressed," I suggested, "then we can take our time getting back to the house." I stood and began scouring the area for my clothes. The cape, my jeans, shirt and boots I found with little problem, but it took a little rifling through the leaves to find my socks, bra, and panties. The panties were of no further use, having been ripped to shreds, and I tucked them into my pocket. I dressed as gracefully as possible, balancing on first one foot then the other, and finally relaxed when I slipped my boots on my feet. Pulling leaves and twigs from my braid, I smiled in the dark, watching Amon slip his shirt over his rippling biceps, then bend to retrieve his boots and belt. Moving smoothly through the shadows and moonlight, as majestically as a jaguar, he was the picture of an erotic dream.

Pausing in his dressing, he looked up at me and smiled lewdly, "Thank you, Cat. Only you thinking of me as your man could please me more."

"Damn," I snapped my fingers, "I have to remember to guard my thoughts when I'm appreciating your form or its going to go right to your head." Smiling ruefully, I did guard my thoughts as I revisited the fear I had felt only moments ago and the knowledge that he was capable of great violence, violence from which I had previously believed myself immune.

"It is just a good thing that you do not often go wandering in my thoughts of you," he murmured as he bent and kissed my cheek and nuzzled my ear. "You would blush from your head to your toes."

Pulling his cloak up from the ground, I shook it as well as I could, but its length made it a little unwieldy so I handed it to Amon and suggested he shake it out. He did so and slipped it around his shoulders, shaking out his silver mane. He wrapped me in my cape and I secured it at the throat, fighting the urge to withdraw from his touch. I refused to allow myself to fear him, he had become too important to me and if my actions caused an occasional butting of heads, so be it.

Sudden silence stopped us in our tracks as we walked back to our mounts. The crickets, cicadas, nighthawks and other unseen creatures stopped all sound simultaneously. Amon stood and took my hand, then motioned toward the horses. I sprinted to Bella and threw my leg over her saddle, grabbing up her reins as quietly as possible. Amon had silently mounted Abraxis with that uncanny vampire speed and stealth. We stayed our mounts and eventually the night sounds of the forest resumed. Relaxing a little, I nudged Bella forward and began following Amon on Abraxis. Moving along the edge of the woods, Amon led us back toward the house as clouds began obscuring the stars. Out of the darkness came an unusual sound and I was startled when a small owl landed on my shoulder, its talons digging gently into my clothes and just touching the skin beneath. I gasped at the creature's appearance.

"Amon," I called gently, "It would seem that I have a visitor."

He turned and looked at the owl. Nodding, he explained, "She is here as a warning to you, Cat. There is danger near. She offers her protection."

"Hey," I glanced at the owl out of the corner of my eye, "you are welcome to stay and protect me. I appreciate what help I can get."

Chapter 33

Amon and I rode silently, straining to hear the sounds of the night beyond the soft jingling of our horses' bridles and the soft reassuring clomping of their hooves. Occasionally I would spy a wolf slinking through the trees, accompanying us and matching our speed, but the pack was keeping its watch from a distance tonight. Coming to a dirt road, we stepped out of the cover of the trees and jumped our mounts across a shallow ditch. Turning, Amon urged Abraxis forward and I let Bella have her head to follow. I was admiring the way even the partially starlit sky shimmered in Amon's silver hair and how straight and proudly he rode, his cape draped romantically across Abraxis' rump. Admittedly, he resembled the cover of a paperback novel, I mused as weariness stole over me.

Suddenly Bella reared up on her hind legs and whinnied in alarm as two men stepped out of the shadows, stopping and standing before us. I struggled to stay in the saddle. The owl flapped her wings and screeched her alarm but held tightly to me. Opening my mind to Bella, I willed her calm and reigned her in. She danced and snuffled her displeasure but at last she did settle down. Amon did not seem alarmed, sitting calmly in the saddle, and Abraxis seemed indifferent to the newcomers.

"Hail, Your Lordship," the first man stepped forward, bending low at the waist, "I am Darien, late from upstate New England, mostly Maine, here to taste of your southern hospitality, by your leave." His face was round and pleasant and when he smiled dimples appeared, lending him a deceptive youthfulness. His dark hair was cut and styled short and sleek and his clothes were expensive looking and stylish. Though he addressed Amon, his blue eyes kept coming to rest on me. He seemed neither surprised nor alarmed at the sight of the owl on my shoulder.

"Darien," Amon nodded, "I am Sin, Master of the southeast. Abide by my laws and you are welcome here for a time. Am I to understand that you are here for what, vacation, a change of scenery? Or do you run from your sire or your previous Lord?" Behind him, I saw the shadows of his wolves moving restlessly and my alarm grew.

"No, Your Lordship," he beamed a toothy smile and I realized that both men were vampires, "I flee neither my sire nor my previous Lord."

"And your friend, Darien, what is his story?" Amon nodded at the other silent vampire.

At last Darien's companion stepped forward and presented himself.

"I am Rowan, Your Lordship. I hail from Ireland, originally, though I've been here in your United States for a few years. I come from New York and I too seek the hospitality of the south," he spoke evenly with a trace of Irish brogue. His long, wavy red hair and freckles told the truth of his origins and his attire spoke of a less than elaborate lifestyle. He wore jeans and a dark long coat, tee shirt and broken-down boots.

"It is a coincidence that you two arrive in my territory now?" Amon asked, showing no signs of dismounting.

"Coincidence?" Darien turned to regard me, "No, Your Lordship, no coincidence." Approaching me alongside Bella, Darien offered his hand, "My Lady?"

I looked uncomfortably at Amon. He nodded silently as if I should know what was expected of me. The owl stiffened and dug her claws more deeply into my shoulder. Opening my mind to Amon, I put my hand in Darien's and nodded silently. He lightly kissed my fingers and my stomach suddenly rolled.

"Your name, Lady?" Darien insisted, looking up curiously into my eyes, "For to behold your beauty is to behold the Lady Rhiannon, she of the wild horses." His voice was smooth, almost purring, but I could not see his expression clearly in the gathering shadows, and the tiny hairs on the back of my neck stood up. I did not trust these two and was, for some reason, loath to admit my identity.

"Surely Rhiannon was a myth and I assure you I am not," I murmured softly, "And my name would mean nothing to you, for I am not of your world." I withdrew my hand from his and was instantly calmer.

"You are not of my," he stuttered, "you are not.., you mean." Stepping back, he tried to recover his composure.

Rowan stepped forward and bowing, took my hand. At his touch, my heart began hammering in my chest and I could not breathe. I gasped as the ring Amon had given me began to draw my power up from the pit of my stomach. Never had I experienced such blackness, such absolute evil and I yelped and pulled my hand from his. The owl let out a scream and flew into Rowan's face, her talons slashing and blinding him with his own blood. He swatted blindly at her, but she deftly avoided his attack and returned to perch calmly on my shoulder as if nothing had happened.

"You are she, whom we seek," he seethed, his voice dripping with venom, "the witch! You live, you're mortal and you wield a Hand of Power!"

Darien exclaimed, "She is human, damn it. She's human!"

With imperceptible speed Amon dismounted and grabbed first Darien in one hand, then Rowan in the other. He lifted them both into the air and roared his anger as his beast fought to emerge. My power boiled and rolled inside me and I knew that the threat was real. Amon lowered Darien to his feet then touched the right side of the vampire's face with his left hand, almost a caress. Amon's hand began to glow and burn then light flashed around us and Darien screamed and disappeared in the blinding fire. Amon then turned his fury on Rowan, who had crumpled to the ground holding his hands over his bleeding eyes, and dispatched him in the same manner as Darien. One quick caress and the blackguard was no more. In the span of a heartbeat, the whole incident was over and Amon turned to me with a look of surprise, shock, and dismay on his face.

When the vampires were gone I suddenly drew a ragged breath and threw myself from Bella's saddle, the owl screeching and taking flight. Tears rolled down my cheeks as I drew painful breath after painful breath. My eyes were useless as blackness swirled, obscuring my vision. It was as if Rowan's black heart had infected me the moment he touched my hand and I shook my head as if to clear it. Sitting awkwardly on the ground I cried and hugged my knees and tried to calm myself. Seeing the vampires destroyed like that was stupefying, but the feeling of danger, of absolute terror when they touched me was what had frozen the blood in my veins, what had left me unable to breathe. They had come here intent on my destruction. They had been dispatched to destroy the witch, to destroy me.

I had sensed that mortal death would have been merely one among the number of experiences awaiting me at their hands.

Amon came to me and took me into his arms. I buried my face in his chest, crying and staining his black shirt even darker with my tears.

"They were so evil," I sobbed, "I have never in my life felt such wickedness, such blackness. Amon they came here to destroy me. Why? Why does everyone want me dead? I don't understand any of this." Hugging him tightly to me, I struggled to make sense of everything then a thought occurred to me. Looking up into his eyes, I whispered, "That thing you did with your hand, what was that? "

"Shh," he murmured, "do not concern yourself with such matters. It is a power that I thought long dead within me and it would be prudent to not speak of it. Perhaps someday I will tell you the whole story, but for now, please do not speak or even think of it." He said soberly, and I felt the importance of his words. Once again, a notion danced around the periphery of my mind but would not present itself, leaving me feeling oddly disconcerted.

"I will not think or speak of it," I said softly, "I promise." I held onto him tightly until he pulled me up and kissed me and my power swirled around us and snapped in the air. My returning vision swam red as anger colored my emotions and adrenaline rushed through me. Gusts of warm air whipped our hair and rustled our cloaks as my rage peaked then dissipated.

"Amon," I realized, "they came here to kill me. Don't you see? They knew that I wasn't dead, or assumed that I wasn't. I'm not safe in my own coffin. Whoever sent these goons is taking no chances that I might recover. And I am not the ultimate goal. Getting rid of me is just one step toward taking your power and your role as leader of this area. Someone must know that if you are successful at fulfilling the prophecy you will be an unstoppable power. You are the ultimate target!"

He smiled sweetly at my tirade, obviously amused at my tantrum. Running his finger along the tracks of my tears, his slipped the drops of blood into his mouth, then kissed and licked my cheek.

"Though I suspect a plot to take my position and my power, I have no proof, and though you believe it also, we do not know this for sure. Admittedly, it is likely. You need not, however, concern yourself for me," he smiled.

"What do you mean, I need not concern myself?" I gaped, "Why would I not? Are you suddenly invincible? Amon, you were recently shot or have you conveniently forgotten that?"

"I forget nothing," he nodded patiently, "but that power of which you will not speak or think? Its return is a monumental thing and indicates that our futures have just brightened, our chances of success have greatly improved." Cupping the back of my head in his hand he forced his mouth down on mine and parted my lips with his tongue. When he released me I looked into his eyes and saw, for the first time, a light burning deeply within him. Perhaps it was just my imagination, maybe it was hope or a newfound purpose to his existence, but the sight of that fire steeled my resolve and bolstered my courage. At that one moment, forever frozen in time, I knew that I was indeed his and that there was no going back. The tide of my anger and fear had risen and ebbed, leaving me suddenly weak and weary feeling.

"I am so tired," I moaned as Amon swept me up into his arms and carried me over to Abraxis where he easily hoisted me into the saddle then slid up behind me. "I'm tired of being scared, of thinking, of trying to figure things out." My chin rested on my chest as Amon urged Abraxis forward and whistled for Bella to follow. The jangling of her bridle assured me that she was behind us. "Your wolves," I wondered aloud, "they didn't attack. Why not?"

"You were the one under attack, Cat," he explained, his mouth reassuringly close to my ear, "Your owls had the right to first defense, and your young friend did herself proud when she blinded Rowan. I told you that your creatures were powerful allies, didn't I?"

"You did," I agreed, "So if my owl had failed or if you had been under attack?"

"My wolves would have been the ones in the fray. Now, hush," he murmured, "you're exhausted. Rest in my arms until I can get you back into your casket." He kissed the top of my head, then laid his chin beside my ear as Abraxis carried us steadily home. "We'll rest the day away then later tonight, I will petition Arathia to try once more to awaken you."

"That's right," I whispered as the steady movement of Abraxis' powerful haunches lulled me into a stupor and Amon leaned me back into the crook of his arm. I rested securely, feeling safe if a little uncomfortable.

When we arrived back at the stables, Amon dismounted then caught me in his arms and carried me across his shoulders, taking huge and incredibly fast strides, into the house. The sun had not yet begun to rise and Winter and Chimaera were waiting for us in the foyer. Closing my eyes, I ignored their questions and words of concern and pretended to be sleeping. Amon did not break stride but took me directly to the coffin room and put me down on the lid of my casket. Closing the door behind him, he turned to me and nodded, "Your gown is in your coffin, you should change right away and try to get a little rest. I must inform the guards of these new developments then I will gather you to rest with me when I am ready. I know you don't want to think about it but you should feed before we attempt this deceit on Arathia."

"I'm not hungry," I grumbled as I yawned and stretched. Struggling to get out of my clothes, I was half falling and stumbling in my urgency to get some rest.

"Here, let me help," Amon steadied me, "Just hold still and let me do this before you hurt yourself." With that he deftly undressed me and slipped my gown over my head. At last, he propped me on my coffin and pulled off my boots and socks, then unbraided my hair and smoothed it out as well as he could. "And I did not mean food when I said you should feed," he added as I clambered into my coffin.

"Oh," I smiled sheepishly, realizing his meaning, "I get it. We'll discuss the matter when you return." I lay back against the satin pillow and laid my arms across my chest. "Strange how easily I have adjusted to lying in repose," I murmured as I slipped into sleep.

Blissfully unaware of anything, I was startled when Amon woke me and bid me join him in his coffin. Grumbling beneath my breath about how he never joined me in my coffin, I padded across the dirt floor and crawled in beside him. Embracing me, he kissed the top of my head and held me silently. Though I expected him to draw down the lid to his coffin, he did not and I wondered why he would choose to leave it open. Once I had decided it didn't matter, I slid my hand across his chest and closed my eyes leaning my head on his shoulder.

"Cat," at last he murmured, "you should feed."

There it was, the reason he left the lid open and the topic I had successfully wiped from my mind. I opened my eyes and looked at him, his beautiful face in profile.

"I don't understand," I sighed, "why do you think it's necessary that I drink your blood? Won't that make my seizures worse?"

"As I understand it, your seizures are caused by toxins produced by your body trying to fight the effects of my blood in your system. You're already infected so any additional amount of my blood will be of no consequence and will only serve to strengthen our connection. I will be better able to help you hide your mind from Arathia until she brings you back. She must not sense your presence until then. You know she is a very powerful sorceress and she may read our deceit in your mind when you return. Your taking my blood will lend you some of my strength and perhaps my power to aid us."

"To help us pull this off?" I smiled at his frustration in making me understand. Old World English left something to be desired in getting to the point.

"Yes," he looked relieved, "exactly, to help us pull this off." Stroking his fingers softly down the side of my face, he leaned over and kissed me.

"I want to know the truth first," I drew back and looked him straight in the eye, "if I take your blood, will you be able to control me?"

His laughter was surprising and genuine, his smile reaching the depths of those dark eyes. "Oh, Cat," he chuckled, "no power on this earth could control you, let alone give me control over you. You are a wildly erratic, unpredictable, incredibly passionate, powerful force. I am an eight-hundred year old vampire, I am powerful, feared and even reviled by my people, yet you come into my world with no fear of me, little regard for tradition or respect, and yet concern yourself with my welfare and the politics of my station. If I had thought for a moment that my blood would give me control over you, I would have taken you when you first arrived."

"Hmm," I nodded, "that all sounds very logical. Why am I still hesitant?" I slid one knee across his thighs and rested my chin on his sternum, my hands moving smoothly over his cool skin.

"Perhaps you are reluctant because you find feeding as we do repulsive," he suggested, his hand smoothing my hair down the side of his chest.

"I don't know," I answered honestly, "what if I can't swallow it? What if it makes me gag or throw up? That would be humiliating. I could never look you in the face again." The realization that we could be speaking of another type of bodily fluid rushed blood up my neck and face. I could feel my cheeks burning as I clamped a mental guard down on my thoughts.

He smiled, "I guarantee you will not gag or throw up. You can swallow it and nothing you could ever do would be so humiliating that you could not look at me again."

After considering the situation for a moment I finally sighed, "How does this work?"

"I open a small wound beneath my heart and you drink from it," he said simply, as if it was the most obvious thing in the world.

"No," I shook my head, "if I'm going to do this thing you ask, I want to do it as you do. I want to drink from your neck." Locking my eyes on his, I challenged him. He met my gaze without flinching. Silence settled between us and I waited to see which of us would weaken first.

At last his chest rose and then he exhaled loudly. "Very well," he nodded, "if that's what it takes to get you to take my blood, you may take it from my neck. You should however know that in my world, this would be considered an act of subservience. For me to bare my throat to you would be tantamount to submitting to you."

"I like that idea," I grinned, "I think I'd make a great Alpha Female."

"You would at that," he agreed then fixed me with his eyes, "you agree to this? Are you ready for this?"

"As ready as I'll ever be," I nodded and watched transfixed as he drew a fingernail across the left side of his neck. Blood blossomed along a thin line then ran into one gathering drop moving toward the lower edge of the cut. I slid myself forward along his chest and kept my eyes on that crimson drop. It did not run, but seemed to wait for me. Amon turned his head sharply to the right and the cut opened, beckoning me. I ran my tongue up his neck from the lowest edge of the wound to the top. His blood tasted neither salty nor coppery like human blood, it was sweet and, somehow, rich. I could taste the power and the strength on my tongue. Pressing my lips to the cut, I sucked gently and drew his blood in to fill my mouth. The whole emotional image of this action was very erotic, very stimulating and satisfying. Amon was right, I swallowed it easily and craved more, though it burned through me. He drew my left arm up to his mouth and bit into the skin just above the scar on my wrist. As his teeth dug into my vein and my tongue touched his wound, the blood circuit between us was complete and electricity jumped through us. When at last I was able to pull my mouth away from Amon's throat, I gasped at the sensations and emotions that ran through me.

"Oh my God," I gaped, "Suddenly I want you so bad. This hunger, this need is, wow, it's incredible. I feel like I could almost cry. What is this I'm feeling?"

Running his tongue over my wrist to seal the wound, he turned and regarded me sympathetically. "What you are now feeling is my hunger, though since it is new to you it likely feels more like bloodlust. It is a side effect of drinking my blood and will disappear momentarily."

"And you?" I touched the side of his face and made him meet my eyes, "what about you?"

"My hunger is constant," he smiled bitterly, "and is only sated when I feed or when I am making love to you. For those precious moments when I'm drinking of my prey or moving within your body my hunger, my need, disappears. To be Vampire is to be in constant hunger, constant need. After our initial bloodlust, we learn to live with it, to control it. Those of us who are Master Vampires have greater control over ourselves and need to feed less often than those weaker and younger."

"Oh, holy cow," I moaned and writhed on his chest, "no wonder you want my Life's Blood. If it works you won't feel this will you, you won't need to feed at all, right?"

"That is what the Oracle prophesied," he nodded and licked his finger, sliding it up the wound on his neck to seal it.

"I had no idea that being a vampire was so," I shrugged dramatically, "painful, so full of suffering. To know that for the rest of your life, your very long life, you would feel this need, this incredible unsatisfiable hunger, it would be devastating. When you lost control and I saw your creature? You released control over the hunger didn't you? That's your beast isn't it, it's like the animal manifestation of your hunger, your need."

"Yes, it is. Your pity is unnecessary and unwelcome though," he hissed, looking away from me, "I am…"

"Yeah, I know," I interrupted sarcastically, " I am an eight-hundred year old Master Vampire and I don't need pity or concern from the likes of a lowly mortal right? Well, here's a news flash for you Master Vampire, I don't pity you, okay? I might feel a little empathetic, because that's what I do, it's who I am. You are what you are and you've had plenty of time to practice. If you want to be all noble and broody, that's fine, but I'll still feel the same way. That's just me, deal with it."

Turning to look at me, he smiled broadly and hugged me tightly. Laughing, he kissed my lips, my eyes, and my forehead. "Very well, you little minx," he chuckled, "as you wish. Now, the sun is about to rise on the last night of your demise. You should rest, as will I."

As he pulled down the lid to the coffin I interjected, "I really liked that baring your throat to me concept. It gave me quite a primal rush."

"It would," he grumbled as the lid dropped securely into its track and all light was extinguished.

Chapter 34

Whether it was because I was exhausted both physically and emotionally, or because I was sleeping in the arms of a vampire, I did not dream and was grateful for it. When Amon opened the lid to his coffin and carried me, still half-asleep to my own casket, I did not complain or even bother to rouse myself. He arranged and posed me as I had been buried then leaned down to whisper in my ear.

"I am going now to fetch Arathia. Make yourself absent from your body and when I return come to me. I will hide you with the will of my mind. When Arathia works her magic you will feel the pull of her words, tarry a bit if you can then return to your body. Remember that you've been gone since Kasimir strangled you so you should be a bit confused, weak and disoriented. I will keep my mind open to you so if Arathia tries to upset you or trap you in a lie, I will warn you. Are you ready for this?" He stroked my cheek and kissed me tenderly on the lips. I batted my eyelids in acknowledgement. "I will go now," he added. Lowering the lid to my coffin, he turned and left the room. I felt his absence as soon as he moved across the threshold.

Slipping out of my body, I floated up to the ceiling, lingering for a bit to adjust to the sensations of weightlessness. After a moment I moved down the hallway. I saw Winter and Chimaera standing outside the parlor and Amon and Arathia chatting amicably together on the sofa inside. Jealousy reared its ugly head when I saw Arathia smile and lean over to lay her hand on Amon's knee. I wanted to slap her silly. Moving up behind Chimaera, I made the hair on the back of his neck move and he turned to glare at me.

Feeling frisky are we, Witch?

Come on, Chimaera, I'm bored. It's tedious hanging around here waiting for Sin and the wicked witch of the west. By the way, can you see me or can you just hear me?

I sensed you and felt your presence when you touched my neck but I can't actually see you. And don't worry, Cat, I'm sure Sin and Arathia will be with your body shortly, then we can be done with this whole charade.

It can't be too soon for me.

Moving up to Winter, I blew softly, then laid a kiss on his cheek. He smiled and looked at Chimaera.

"'*tite soeur*?" he whispered.

"Oui," Chimaera nodded, "she's bored, she says."

"Remarkable," he murmured and touched his cheek where my lips had been.

As Amon and Arathia stood to leave the parlor, I moved behind Chimaera just in case Arathia, like Amon, could actually see me, then stayed with him until they disappeared down the hallway.

You may stay here with me until Sin calls you.

Thanks, Chimaera. I don't want to be caught out in the open before Arathia can call me back.

I can shield my thoughts so you are safe.

You know, this is twice we've been together in my mind, or with me in yours. One of these days you and I are going to have to talk.

Indeed? Must we?

Oh, yeah, you wiseass vampire, we simply must.

I await this discussion with bated breath.

Worms on your tongue? I laughed at my own tired little joke and Chimaera winced at the sound echoing through his head. *Sorry about that.*

Worms on my tongue?

It's an old joke, bated breath, get it? Baited breath? Worms? Bait? You vampires have got to get a sense of humor and a TV. Humor is so much easier to understand through the use of a television.

I'll let His Lordship know and I'm sure he'll take it under advisement.

Sin's in the coffin room, I sensed, gotta go Chimaera, thanks.

Much luck, Witch. Be careful.

At Amon's call I drifted back toward the coffin room and slipped unnoticed into his mind. His strength and his will were powerful tethers and I knew that I was safe there until I was willing to leave. I watched from a distance as Amon lifted the lid to my coffin and Arathia regarded my pale, still body. She began the spell by closing her eyes and chanting a soft, beckoning song. Moving her hands rhythmically, she began swaying slightly and her voice became louder. I began to feel the pull of her words, but Amon held me in his thoughts, not yet willing to release me. Arathia's chant increased in both volume and intensity and her will became clear. The tugging of her words became stronger and my hold on Amon slowly weakened. At last he released me and I slammed once more into my body, gasping at the pain and the force. I drew a deep breath and fluttered my eyes open. Arathia beamed down at me, glorying in her accomplishment.

"You are back with us, Cat," she gushed as she touched my cheek. I fought the urge to swat her hand away.

Looking confusedly from her to Amon, then back, I mouthed a few words but made no sound. Coughing, I clutched my throat and tried to sit up, but feigned weakness and dropped back against the satin pillow of my coffin.

"Sin, she needs water," Arathia demanded and Amon produced a glass of water out of thin air. He came to me and lifted my head, then pressed the glass to my lips, directing me to sip it slowly so I wouldn't choke. Taking two or three small sips, I sighed and closed my eyes and Amon laid my head back down on the pillow.

"She is back but she is weak," Amon regarded me soberly, "she has been gone long. I expect she must be a bit disoriented. Bishop should look at her right away."

"I will go get him," Arathia offered with a sly smile, "so you may have a moment alone with your little witch." With a flourish of her purple silk gown, she turned and left the room.

Amon leaned over my coffin and kissed me on the lips. "You were very convincing," he whispered.

"Convincing, hell," I coughed a little, "It hurts to be yanked back into your body. It didn't take a lot of acting ability to pull this off. So what's next?"

"We will have Bishop examine you, diagnose you on the mend, and move you back into the sapphire room," he replied. "And do not forget, you have been dead for a while so you should act bewildered." He rested one hip on the edge of my casket and smoothed my hair back from my forehead. I touched the silver dragon's head belt buckle and looked up questioningly.

"Silver?" I whispered noting how beautiful he was in the black paisley shirt and black jeans he wore.

"White gold," he smiled and took my hand in his. He lifted it gently to his lips and kissed my fingers, pausing to slide his tongue over my fingertips

"And Chimaera's earring?" I asked.

"Platinum, I believe," he frowned, "or titanium. You would have to ask him to be sure."

I grinned then dropped the smile when I heard Arathia and Bishop arriving. Amon stood up and moved away so Bishop could get to me. Winter and Chimaera stepped just inside the room, moving to stand guard on either side of the door.

"How are you feeling?" Bishop smiled as he wrapped a blood pressure cuff around my arm and began to pump it up.

"A little tired," I admitted, my voice weak and raspy, "but don't even think of suggesting a nap. I feel like I've been asleep for a year. So, what's happening? Where am I?"

"You are in Sin's coffin room," he answered, his blue eyes twinkling, "we brought you here after the attack so you would be safe."

Finally managing to sit up, I looked around then down at the coffin I was in. "Oh, God," I whined, " was I dead or did you just not expect me to survive? Am I a vampire now? Did Sin have to make me a vampire?"

"Calm down, Cat," Bishop patted my arm before he took my wrist to check my pulse, "You are not a vampire, His Lordship did not make you one of us. As for the coffin, it seemed wise to let everyone think you were dead, that way you were no longer in danger. We were all hopeful that you would recover and return to us."

"And the explosion? And my attacker?" I gasped, "It was that guy on The Council, I can't remember his name." I put my fingers to my temples and rubbed as if my head was aching.

"Kasimir," Bishop nodded, "and the explosion was a minor disturbance apparently intended to do just what it did, draw your protection away from you." He placed a stethoscope on my chest and held up a finger, indicating the need for a moment of silence.

"Did he confess?" I asked when he was done listening to my heart, "did he say why he attacked me?"

"He has neither confessed nor explained his motive for attacking you," Amon offered.

Laying my hand on my forehead, I murmured, "I remember I asked him why while he was strangling me and he said it was none

311

of my business, no, wait, it was no concern of mine. Now I ask you how could my death be no concern of mine? I don't think I'll ever forget that. How long have I been out of it?"

Arathia stepped near me and touched my hair. "Poor Cat," she cooed, "Sin tried to call you back and I cast a spell to bring you back but nothing worked. You've been gone for several days and we were afraid you were gone for good. I'm so glad Sin suggested I try one more time."

"You brought me back, Arathia?" I smiled, "I don't know how to thank you. I'm so grateful." I reached out and squeezed her hand.

"You can thank me, Cat," she purred as she bent down beside me, " by telling me how you released Leitha."

"I released Leitha, the, what did Sin call her, the ringwraith?" I feigned surprise, "I did? Are you sure?"

She nodded, "I did a reading of the room after your attack and I saw you touch Leitha. After that, nothing, no one has seen her and I believe she has been released from her torment."

"I would really like to help you, Arathia," I gushed, "considering all you've done for me, but I don't remember even seeing Leitha. And if I released her, I truly do not remember doing it, let alone how I might have done it. I'm so sorry. Maybe it will come back to me once my head stops spinning."

"Yes," Bishop offered, "though she doesn't want to sleep, she should take it easy, some things may come back to her in time. And she should feed, Sin, she needs the strength."

"Wait a minute," I cried, "you said that I'm not a vampire so why should I feed. People don't feed, they eat. What are you saying?"

"It was Sin's blood that made it possible for us to save you, its strength, its power was what kept you from crossing over permanently. You should feed, accept more of his blood to make you stronger," Bishop explained as he packed up his medical instruments.

"I don't like the idea," I shook my head, "it seems, I don't know, unnatural. People don't drink blood, vampire or otherwise."

"Don't worry, Bishop," Amon replied, "I'll see to it that she feeds."

"Whoa there, hello," I huffed, "I'm right here. You needn't talk about me like I'm somewhere else or incapable of making a decision."

"Fine," he turned and glared at me, "we'll discuss this privately in a moment."

"You are not making me do anything I don't want to do," I insisted as I sat up again and started to crawl out of the coffin.

"Winter, help her out of there," Amon snapped his fingers and Winter rushed to me, lifting me out. "As you all can see, it appears that I will be spending this night catching our little witch up on what's been happening and convincing her of what is in her own best interests. Winter, Chimaera, Bishop, feel free to go feed if you wish, I will see to Cat. Arathia, you may stay or if you have other matters to attend to?"

"I do, Sin," Arathia beamed and swirled out of the room, her silk gown fluttering behind her. Bishop followed her out then Chimaera turned to smile at me. Winter leaned me against the now closed lid of my coffin then he flashed me a quick grin, his golden eyes shining. He turned, then he and Chimaera left together.

Once we were alone, I got up and moved into Amon's arms. "Well," I noted, "that's the first step. Now we just have to keep our heads down and stay away from The Council until Bishop can get the necessary amount of blood, then we're good to go."

"Good to go," he echoed, as he kissed my neck, my ear, my cheek. "Bishop was not kidding, you know. You do need to feed again. He told me that to go through with this transfusion, this extraction of your Life's Blood, you need to be as strong as possible to survive. And you will survive, Cat."

"Of course," I whispered as he continued to nuzzle and kiss me, "and we'll discuss my feeding later."

Wrapping his arms around my waist his hands traveled lower and gently squeezed my bottom. He pulled me into his muscular body and I could feel the hardness of his manhood beneath his jeans. "You'll feed, Cat," he breathed into my mouth as he kissed me.

"We'll see," I insisted, "later, I don't want to think about it or talk about it now."

"Kitty Cat," his voice pulsed with warning, "would you refuse me? Would you disobey?"

"You have a choice," I smiled brightly, ignoring his questions altogether, "You can either wait for me while I bathe, or you can join me either in the tub or in the shower."

"Actually," he sighed, "I have some rather unpleasant business to attend to this evening. It won't take long but perhaps it would be best if you bathe while I am gone and I will return to you as soon as I am able."

"Fine," I agreed, "I'll take a long hot bath then I want to go out to the garden tonight, before the rest of the world finds out that I'm alive and the target on my forehead returns."

"You will have a guard with you or you will not step one foot out the door, it that clear?" he commanded, his expression stern and fixed.

"Crystal, sir," I threw him a mock salute, "I promise, no foots out the door unless a guard is with me, okay?" I stretched up on my tiptoes and kissed his mouth, softening his expression and melting his resolve.

Lifting me into his arms, Amon hugged me tightly then carried me from the coffin room.

"This feels silly when I'm completely capable of walking by myself," I laughed, "Oh, and I get to burn this hated gown at the first possible opportunity. Maybe if there's a fire in the fireplace later I can chuck it in. I want this thing to be reduced to nothing but a pile of ashes." "Fine," he replied, "as soon as you get in the tub, I'll take the gown and burn it." We had moved up the stairs and proceeded along the hall until we had reached the door to the sapphire room.

"Oh no you don't," I shook my head, "I want to see this burning for myself. I'll do it."

Amon put me down and opened the bedroom door. Soft lights threw shadows across the room and the fragrance of flowers wafted to meet us. The bed had been turned down and a red rose was laid on the pristine pillowcase. Picking up the rose, I raised it to my nose and breathed in the deliciously sweet and spicy fragrance. I turned to Amon and smiled.

"You can go take care of your business," I suggested, "I'm quite capable of drawing my own bath. Arathia is busy elsewhere so she won't be checking in on how debilitated I am. I'll be fine."

"I will make sure there's a guard on your door before I leave," he nodded as he took me in his arms and kissed me tenderly.

"You gave the boys a night on the town," I reminded him, "You told them to feel free to go feed."

"If they did so, they most likely will have returned by the time you finish your bath," he explained, "They were not offered a night on the town, just the opportunity to feed. They will be gone for no more than an hour or so and I doubt that all three of them went, anyway. Besides, Bear and Dodge are in their quarters so I could call one or both of them should the need arise." He leaned down and nuzzled my neck and stroked my hair.

"Bear and Dodge have quarters here on the estate?" I marveled, "apparently there's a lot more to this place than I've seen."

"Their bunkhouse, if you will, is on the far side of the stables and a bit north. They have been living there since I brought you here," he smiled and brushed the side of my face with his palm.

I leaned my cheek on his hand and closed my eyes, enjoying the sensation of being cradled. He brought his other hand up and held my face between his palms then lifted it and kissed me. His mouth was warm and forceful and I realized that I could go on kissing him forever.

"I would like nothing better than to go on kissing you forever," he nodded, "but, alas, duty calls."

"Stay out of my mind unless you're invited," I grinned and pushed him away. "You vampires already have egos as big as all outdoors. You keep monitoring my lustful thoughts of you and I'm not going to be able to stand you."

"My apologies," he bowed gallantly, "I will try to fight the temptation, but even your thoughts feed my hunger. I will now take my leave so that I may return to you as soon as possible. Enjoy your bath and perhaps get some rest?" He raised his eyebrows in question.

"We'll see," I nodded and headed for the bathroom. Once I got there I had even decided to shower instead of taking a bath, but, for some reason, I reached for the faucets above the big garden tub and closed the drain for the water to collect. While the bath was filling, I went back into the bedroom and rummaged through the dresser drawers for something to wear. Not sure of the weather outside, I decided to just take a pair of panties and matching bra back into the bathroom. The remainder of my clothes I would decide on after my bath. Turning down the lights in the bathroom, I lit the fifteen or twenty white column candles surrounding the tub. Stripping off my funerary gown, hopefully for the last time, I stepped into the water and leaned back against the back of the tub. I squeezed excess water from my washcloth and folded it and laid it across my eyes. Just relaxing, letting my mind wander, I was startled when a vision appeared in my mind's eye. The background of a huge granite block came into focus first, then the chains set into the wall solidified.

At last, the figure of a vampire, Amon, appeared shackled to the stone and the light in the sky told me the sun was rising. I knew he had told me that he would only feel discomfort if moving about in the full light of day, still I sat up in alarm and tossed the washcloth across the room. Water sloshed wildly against the side of the tub and splashed over the edge where it slapped sharply on the marble tile floor. Pulling the drain plug, I stood and grabbed a towel to dry myself. Mostly still damp, I struggled into the panties and bra and threw open the bathroom door. I ransacked the dresser for a pair of jeans and a tee shirt, tugged them on, then bolted across the room and yanked open the door. Startling Winter, I grabbed his arm and pulled him into the room, braiding my hair as I spoke to him.

"Winter, where's the Tomcat?" I rushed from one thing to another, finishing my hair, pulling out a pair of socks, rummaging under the bed for my boots.

"The Tomcat?" he stammered, "you mean the pistol? What do you want it for?"

"I don't have time to go into a lot of detail, Winter," I fumed as I wrestled into my footwear, "Sin is in danger and I'm going to go get him. I need the Tomcat. Oh, and I can't use the calf holster with jeans, how can I carry it?"

"Wait a minute!" He shook his head, "Sin is in danger? Are you sure? How do you know this?"

"I just told you, Winter," I answered, exasperated, "I don't have time to explain everything. Trust me, I know he's in danger. Now about the Tomcat?"

"It should be in the dresser, top drawer under some clothes," he nodded, "There's a loop on the back of the holster that you can slip your belt through. You can wear it at your side if you want, but if you're not used to it I'd recommend you wear it behind you, against the small of your back."

"Thanks Winter," I smiled with relief as I tore through the drawer and found the gun and holster. "Help me with this?" I slid my black leather belt through the loops of my jeans until I reached the halfway point at my back. "I'm not sure I can get it turned the right direction."

He moved up behind me and slid the belt through the holster, then through the next belt loop on my jeans. While Winter held the pistol in place, I slid the belt the rest of the way around and fastened it with the dragon's head buckle. I felt the reassuring weight of the gun lying heavy against the small of my back and reached around to practice draw it from the holster. It came smoothly and easily out of the holster and I returned it and smiled at Winter. "Okay," I remarked, "this is the deal. I had a vision that Sin is chained to a boulder or a huge chunk of granite somewhere. The sun is coming up and he's helpless. I know it won't kill him but it will be torture for him to have to endure the pain. I'm not going to let that happen. I'm going to go get him."

"You know he's meeting with the Council?" Winter reasoned, "I'm sure he's safe."

"Maybe he is right now," I replied, "but he won't be for long. I know what I saw." Banging open the closet door, I grabbed my black velvet cape and threw it over my shoulders.

"Cat, you can't do this," he pleaded, "Sin will kill me if I let you go off like this. And if he is in this situation that you've seen, what then? What can you do?"

"I don't know what I can do, Winter," I insisted, "but I sure as hell am going to do something. And if Sin is tortured or, somehow killed, it won't matter if he's angry at you or at me will it?"

"Cat, you can't do this," he grabbed my arm as I started past him.

"Are you going to stop me?" I snarled, "Are you going to physically restrain me? Because that's what it'll take for you to keep me here. Either come with me or step out of the way." I grabbed his hand and pulled it off my forearm.

"Cat, you're putting me in an impossible situation," he sighed, "I'll go with you. I just hope when he kills me for letting you do this, he'll be quick."

"Come on, I'll saddle Bella and you can saddle your own mount," I took his hand and pulled him down the hallway.

"Wait a minute," he tried to pull away from me, "why are we riding? Why can't we fly?"

"First of all, I've never flown with you and I have a tendency to fly with my eyes closed, at least part of the time," I explained, " and secondly, my vision was from ground level. I'd never recognize the area we're looking for from the air."

"Oh," he nodded, "that makes sense. Why don't I get Chimaera to help us?"

"There's no time," I shook my head and resumed tugging Winter down the hall. By the time we made it down the stairs to the French doors at the back of the house, I was running.

My sense of urgency was almost blinding me as I tore through the doors and across the veranda. Sprinting through the garden, I jumped a couple of low bushes and pounded across the open ground to the stables. Lights burned inside but the stables were empty. I grabbed a saddle and hoisted it into Bella's stall. She snorted and pawed at the ground, probably sensing my unease. Tossing a saddle blanket across her back, I jerked the saddle into place and went around for the strap. Once the saddle was snug and secured, I took her bridle from a nail on the wall and pushed the bit into her mouth then fastened the leather straps and adjusted her ears and bangs. Abraxis was snorting and moving about restlessly in his stall, apparently anxious that Bella was leaving without him. Leading the mare from the stall I called to Winter.

"Are you ready, Winter?" I asked. "The night's a'wastin'."

"Just a minute," his voice came from the stall at the far end of the stable, "I'm coming." He finally led Avalon out of his stall and met up with me at the stable doors. I threw my leg over the saddle and clucked for Bella to go. Once we cleared the corral, I urged the mare through the gate and kicked her flanks for speed. She picked up her feet and raced over the open field with Winter, on Avalon, struggling to keep up.

"How do you know where to go?" Winter yelled after a few moments of hard riding.

"Whoa," I reigned Bella in and slowed her to a stop, "I have a general idea where it might be, but I could use some expert help."

"Expert help?" Winter panted as Avalon danced to a halt.

"Shh," I held up my hand for silence and closed my eyes to concentrate. "Just give me a minute." I opened my mind and called my owls. Lifting my arm to a horizontal position as I had seen falconers do on television and in movies, I waited patiently. My patience was rewarded when a large gray-blue owl landed gracefully on my forearm, his razor sharp talons only gently piercing my sleeve. I stroked his snowy white chest with my right hand and murmured softly, "Thank you for answering my call. I seek your aid in finding an area with a huge granite rock or boulder. It doesn't really look natural, so it may have been quarried here, as it's almost square. You know this land, great owl, do you know of this place I seek?"

The great bird screeched loudly and leapt skyward, its mighty wings gracefully lifting it higher and higher.

"Come on, Winter," I smiled, "I think we have our guide." I urged Bella onward, trying to keep the owl in my sight. As fast as Bella was, we were losing the owl and I was beginning to lose hope when it careened back in a lazy circle then sailed on. Apparently the owl knew we could not possibly keep up with him on the wing.

Chapter 35

Chasing the bird for perhaps another twenty minutes, we finally neared him as he circled and seemed content to go no farther. He finally screeched and disappeared into the trees and Winter and I followed the sound of his calls. At last reaching a clearing, I spied the wall of granite and jumped from Bella's back. Racing to the shackled figure, I stopped and gasped as Chimaera raised his head and looked at me.

"Chimaera!" I gaped.

"Winter," he hissed, looking past me, "what are you doing letting her come out here?" His black hair was matted and mussed and his clothes were streaked with dirt and grime.

"Have you ever tried to stop her from doing something?" Winter answered as he swung down from Avalon's saddle.

"Had I been guarding her, she would not be out here, Winter, I am disappointed," Chimaera shook his head slowly.

"I thought you were Sin," I explained as I neared Chimaera and examined his situation. "I had a vision and I guess I assumed it was him, because we're so telepathically linked. I didn't even think that it might be you I was connected to, although I guess I should have."

"I'm sorry if I unintentionally linked my mind with yours," Chimaera smiled weakly. "I would never knowingly lead you into this trap. And you do know that this is a trap don't you, Witch?"

"Oh, yeah," Chimaera," I smiled ruefully, "I know it's a trap and I know that the trap was for you, not me."

"What do you mean?" he glanced at me questioningly. "How can you know this?"

"How did you come to be here, Chimaera?" I asked straight out.

"I was on my way back from feeding," he sighed and pulled against his chains. "I heard you calling for help and even though I couldn't conceive of how you would come to be out here, I had to check it out. I couldn't very well have returned to the estate only to find you gone. Anyway, when I followed your call to this place, I saw what I thought was you lying on the ground. When I went to your aid, I realized that it wasn't you, though the demon had taken on your likeness. The next thing I know, I'm chained to this rock and you two are riding up like the cavalry."

"Exactly, the trap was for you, Chimaera," I explained, "and whoever called up the demon probably intended to leave Sin more vulnerable to attack by pulling away one of his lieutenants."

"How do you know it was for me?" he asked.

"First of all," I smiled, "the demon didn't send me the vision, you did. And secondly, if the trap were for me the demon would still be here and would have attacked by now. My scout tells me that the area is clear so the demon is gone."

"Your scout?" he raised his eyebrows.

"Never mind," I brushed his questions aside, "first things first, you've been injured." I leaned down before him and inspected the deep ragged gash in his left thigh. Blood had painted his pant leg a solid black in the darkness.

"Is this life threatening?" I asked as I pulled the torn fabric away from the wound.

"The blade was silver," he nodded, looking down at me, "but it should heal once it bleeds enough for the silver to be washed from the wound. I will not perish from this wound or from being exposed to the sun. You should return to the estate. Winter, take her back."

"I'm not leaving you, Chimaera," I replied, "So when did you realize the demon wasn't me?" I made small talk as I exposed the injury. It was tricky tearing the fabric around the stab wound without causing further damage or pain.

"Let me think," he sighed. "I noticed that her hair was a little darker blonde than yours, her eyes were slightly deeper green, and, oh yeah, when she leaned into me to fasten the shackles I noticed her breasts were bigger than yours."

Laughing, I stood and slapped my left hand hard against his wound. He stifled a cry of pain, his eyes wide.

"One thing I may have overlooked in educating you about humor?" I smiled as my hand began to glow and tingle. "Timing is crucial."

Grimacing through the pain and half-laughing, he squirmed beneath my hand. "I see your point," he murmured, "and in the future I will remember your words."

"Very wise of you," I purred as his flesh knitted beneath my hand. At last the healing was complete and Chimaera breathed a sigh of relief. I removed my grip on his thigh and tossed away tiny shards of silver. Stepping between his feet, I slapped my right hand hard against his crotch. "You never want to make a joke and possibly insult the woman who literally or figuratively has your jewels in her hand."

"I understand," he breathed sharply as I leaned into him, "and Cat?"

"Yes Chimaera?" I smiled sweetly.

"I may have been mistaken," he grinned down at me, "your breasts may be bigger."

"Nice try at a save, buddy boy," I laughed.

"All right, you two," Winter interrupted, "before I have to step in to stop something neither one of you will live to regret, let's see about getting out of here."

Stepping back from Chimaera, I nodded and looked around. "I don't suppose you can get yourself out of those chains?" I asked pointedly.

"Alas, they are silver alloy," he shrugged. He bowed his head in embarrassment, his long black hair hiding his face, "I can't believe I allowed this to happen, and now His Lordship is going to have all our heads for allowing you to put yourself in danger."

"I don't suppose you saw where the demon hid the keys?" I remarked sarcastically.

"No keys, Witch," he spread his hands, looking up at me from beneath a fringe of long lashes, "the chains are bolted into the rock."

"Okay," I concentrated as I paced back and forth on the uneven ground before him. "You can't do it yourself, we can't use a key, we don't have tools or time to get them before sunrise..."

"Should we get His Lordship to help?" Winter offered.

"If he's still with the Council," I shook my head, "there won't be time to summon him and get Chimaera back to the estate before sunrise. What about my power?"

"Can you draw and maintain enough energy long enough to melt silver?" Chimaera asked doubtfully.

"Probably not," I admitted, "my power has a tendency to show up out of the blue in the form of a ball of energy. It's very intense and very quick. I'm just learning how to call it and control it."

"Leave me," Chimaera insisted harshly. "Get back to the safety of the estate. Leave me here. I will not perish. You can send help back with the necessary tools this evening when the sun sets."

"I am not leaving you, so hush and let me think," I snapped back at him, "Okay, so I've ruled out all the obvious answers to the problem."

"That leaves us with?" Chimaera shrugged.

I smiled and pulled the Tomcat from its holster. At the sound, his head came up abruptly and he tried to move away from the barrel of the gun. Aiming at the bolt at Chimaera's left hand I grinned, "Do you trust me?"

"Of course not," Chimaera shook his head, his eyes wide, "you're just as likely to shoot me in the head as not. How is your aim?"

"You've seen Winter shoot," I replied, "how's his aim?"

"Not bad," Chimaera answered, "he shoots fairly well."

"He's not as good as I am," I assured him, "but the choice is yours."

Sighing deeply he dropped his head, "Very well, just make it quick before I change my mind."

"Winter," I called, "take Bella and Avalon away from here. I can hit the target but I can't guarantee where the ricochets will go. I'm shooting at metal and rock, I can promise you there will be ricocheting."

Pausing a moment until Winter disappeared with the horses, I turned back to Chimaera and whispered, "Are you ready?"

"Go ahead," he nodded briskly.

"Oh," I teased, "I'm told that when the hammer hits the firing pin, there's a flash of light. You might want to close your eyes. Or I could be wrong."

"You're enjoying this too much. For Goddess' sake, woman, just do it!" he yelled.

With that, I took careful aim and evenly pulled the trigger. The silver bolt in the rock shattered into pieces as the bullet rang off of at least three separate surfaces.

Chimaera winced and yanked his left hand free. "Rather close wasn't it?"

"Don't complain, Chimaera," I smiled, "you're a quarter of the way free."

"Finish it, quickly," he pleaded and I took mercy on him and without hesitation, aimed at and destroyed the other three bolts. His chains fell away and he sank to the rock strewn ground before the wall.

"You're weak," I noticed as I kneeled before him, "you've probably lost all you gained from tonight's feeding. You need blood."

"It would help," he admitted, "but I don't see any humans around here and I can't feed from Winter." Chimaera struggled to stand, then gave up and sat back down with his back against the stone wall.

"What am I, chopped liver?" I huffed.

"You've completely lost your mind, Catherine," Chimaera cried, "I can't feed from you. His Lordship would have me drawn and quartered. A Master Vampire does not share."

"Hey," I smiled, "I've already got one vampire coursing through my veins and the last thing in the world I need is another one. You can't feed from me but you can take my blood." I stood and called to Winter. He returned to the clearing, the horses following him.

"Winter, do you have your blade?" I called.

"Why do you ask, *'tite soeur*?"

"Never mind why," I snapped, "do you have it?"

"What are you thinking, Cat?" Chimaera asked with worry in his voice.

"Hush," I demanded, "Winter, your knife. Give it to me." I impatiently tapped my toe against the rocky ground, hand held outstretched.

"Cat," Winter whispered, "this is a really bad idea. You're going to get us all in trouble. His Lordship is going to be angry."

"He'll just have to get over it," I replied as I took the knife and moved up beside the still resting Chimaera. "If Chimaera can't at least protect himself on the way home, he's of no use to us. He needs his strength."

Steeling myself against the pain, I slid the sharp edge across my right wrist and hissed as blood oozed into the wound. I turned my wrist over and let the blood drop as Chimaera opened his mouth. A little of the liquid dripped down his chin and splattered down the front of his shirt, but with a slight adjustment, I moved the flow so Chimaera could drink.

"I know this is not the most efficient way to do this, and certainly not the most pleasurable, but it will work," I smiled as my blood flowed in a steady stream into the weakened vampire's mouth. After a few moments I started to feel light headed and had to steady myself by resting my left hand against the stone wall.

"Winter," Chimaera commanded as my knees began to weaken, "take care of her." He licked his lips and wiped his mouth on the back of his hand.

Winter caught me as I started to sit down rather ungracefully. I had intended to heal myself with my left hand but when I put my palm against the wound nothing happened. I held pressure on the cut.

"Oops," I smiled weakly, "guess I didn't plan that as well as I thought. I thought I could heal this myself, but I can't seem to stop the bleeding." Blood still oozed between my fingers and dropped to the ground, splattering on the rocks. I was losing my grip on the wound as my hand filled with liquid.

"Chimaera," Winter gasped, "She's still losing a lot of blood, should I seal her wrist?"

"No," Chimaera commanded, "she did this foolishness for me. If one of us is to risk incurring His Lordship's anger, it should be me." With that Chimaera pulled my right wrist out of my grasp and lifted it to his mouth. "I'm sorry about this, Cat." He licked the blood from my wrist then licked it again and sealed the wound. My hands were both covered in blood and it was becoming sticky and tacky. I wiped the gooey stuff on my pantlegs and tried to stand, untangling my feet as I moved. Winter came up behind me and helped me up. I was a little wobbly on my feet but managed to steady myself and whistled for Bella.

When the horse jangled up beside me, I leaned against her saddle and tried to lift my foot into the stirrup. After missing twice, Chimaera got up into Bella's saddle and reached down for me. Taking his arm, I hoisted myself onto the saddle behind him and he urged the mount forward. Winter jumped on Avalon and we left the clearing. In the skies above I could just make out the shape of an owl and held out my left arm an instant before a small brown owl landed gently on it.

"What the devil?" Chimaera gaped, turning to see the bird on my arm.

"Relax, Chimaera," I murmured into his back, "she's just one of mine. She's here to protect me." I moved my elbow slowly and she walked up my arm and perched on my shoulder, her claws gaining purchase on my cape.

"Since when do you have your own creatures, Witch?" Chimaera asked, his voice full of dismay.

"I don't know," I sighed, "for a while."

"Owls, those were the scouts you mentioned?" he smiled and shook his head, his hair brushing against my face as I wrapped my arms around him and rested my cheek on his back.

"Yeah," I moaned, as profound weariness overtook me. "She'll alert us if there's any danger."

As we rode on I leaned against Chimaera's back and rested as the rhythm of Bella's gait calmed and relaxed me. I was beginning to feel better, the lightheadedness was letting up and the weakness was diminishing. As we approached the estate, I actually thought I had even regained my wits until Chimaera drew Bella to a halt and gasped in surprise.

"Cat," he said warily, moving his shoulder to rouse me from my rest. His voice imparted warning by just saying my name, as he seldom used it. I peered around him see what had drawn his attention. The skies ahead, above the house, were roiling with black and gray clouds and for an instant I thought of the Addams Family, or was it the Munsters? One of those creepy families always had a storm cloud churning over their house and that's what the estate resembled at that moment. Lightning burst from the clouds and showered sparks where it hit the ground below and I realized that this was no naturally occurring storm.

"Oh, man," I moaned as my stomach did a little somersault, "somewhere on this property there is one hugely angry Master Vampire and I think one of his boots has my butt's name on it."

"I fear his other boot may bear my name," Chimaera sympathized.

When we reached the gate to the corral, I slid down from Bella's back and bid my owl farewell as she took wing. "You and Winter take care of the horses," I nodded at Chimaera as I turned to face the house, "this is my mess to clean up."

"Are you sure?" Chimaera queried as he dismounted, "He may be dangerous."

"Nothing personal, Chimaera," I turned to give him a coy smile, "but I think I have a better chance of surviving his anger than you do. I'm cuter."

He smiled and nodded, "You may be right at that."

As I started walking toward the garden, a sudden crack of lightning lit the skies and I recognized a familiar form on the sheer peak of the roof. This time, however, the shape was not that of a crouching gargoyle but of a towering menace. Amon's cloak blew up behind him and the wind whipped his silver hair. Even from this great distance I could see the fury burning in his eyes, that canine gold of a wolf's eyes. My heart was suddenly pounding in my chest and my mouth went dry. Preparing myself for the worst, I stepped quietly through some shrubs and into the garden. Instantly Amon swooped down and stood before me, his anger pulsing and moving around me like static. Keeping my eyes down, I held up my hands and cleared my throat.

"If you'll just give me a minute," I looked up at just that moment when Amon raised his hand and suddenly I was hurled several feet through the air, landing hard in the bushes. It all happened so quickly that I could not even tell if he had physically touched me or just used his power to attack me. A wicked rosebush tore its thorns across my cheek as I crumbled into the foliage. My vision swam with blinding light and the side of my face was first numb then began to sting. As I struggled to get out of the hedge, Amon was upon me again and lifted me with one hand then tossed me down at his feet. This was so not going as I had planned.

"What in the name of the Goddess were you thinking?" he snarled and paced around me, his hands on his hips, "Why must you insist on defying me?"

"Amon," I whimpered through the pain of my rapidly swelling cheek, "It wasn't like that. If you'd just let me explain."

Suddenly he spun and drove me onto my stomach on the grass. Straddling my legs, he pinned me with his weight and I stiffened and stilled when I realized that it was his beast that had taken over. A very deep, low, menacing growl was building in him as he sniffed the air around me.

"I smell blood," the creature snarled and I struggled to turn over beneath him. His weight remained, anchoring me to the ground and I kicked my legs and jerked my hips until I finally gave up and lay quietly beneath him. The long, incredibly strong, fingers that held my wrists to the ground took on a claw-like appearance and as Amon's mouth neared my ear, I could sense that it had grown longer and more canine.

"Please, Amon," I whined, "I know you're still in there somewhere. I didn't mean to anger you. I didn't try to leave you, I thought I was going to rescue you."

The creature moved over me and one claw ripped through the leg of my jeans as it swatted me. Feeling fortunate not to be bleeding, I struggled once more and managed to turn over onto my back. As I lay there beneath him, I could see the battle between Amon's control and the beast that was his hunger and his fury. Myriad emotions rippled across his face. Panic was driving the air from my lungs and I couldn't draw enough breath to speak. I was like a rabbit before a hawk, afraid to move because he might notice me and afraid to stay still and perhaps miss my only opportunity of escape and survival. Opening my mind to his was like opening the door on a tornado. His emotions, anger, fear, worry and relief, swirled like a maelstrom and I withdrew from his mind, quickly putting up my mental shields. Suddenly the beast howled a wild, ferocious cry and launched itself from me. As Amon disappeared into the night, I stood and brushed myself off, sobbing quietly, then gingerly touched the side of my face. The skin there was hot and I felt the blood trickling down my cheek. Unsure of what to do, I finally started toward the house as the lightning ripped through the sky and a pelting rain began. I was soaked to the skin within moments and was relieved when Winter and Chimaera ran up behind me and hustled me across the veranda and through the French doors.

As I wiped the water and bloody tears from my eyes I turned to the vampires, "Is this storm a vampire's temper tantrum?"

"This storm is a Master Vampire's rage," Chimaera answered, "Are you hurt?" Taking my chin in his hand, he turned my face and looked at my cheek.

Pulling away from his touch, I covered the deep scratch with my hand and shook my head, "It's nothing, I just fell into some bushes." Even as the words left my mouth I wondered why I hadn't told them about Amon attacking me. "So, Sin, His Lordship, came home and found us all gone and assumed the worst, is that what you're thinking?"

"I think that's safe to assume," Chimaera agreed, "And now it's going to take a while for his anger to dissipate."

"You might want to go back to the blue room and get some rest, Cat," Winter suggested, "I'm sure he will come back to you when his fury is spent."

"I feel horrible," I nodded as I started up the stairs, "I didn't even consider him getting back here before us. And now I realize that I was so focused, so concerned with you, Chimaera, that I had my mind closed. If he tried to touch my thoughts, there was nothing there. Oh, God, he must have thought I was dead, or worse."

"He has a right to be upset, '*tite soeur*," Winter murmured, "You should not have raced out there without thinking, although I'm sure Chimaera is grateful."

"Don't you dare say I told you so, Winter," I spun on him, "I will not be reprimanded by you and I will not apologize for trying to save and protect someone I care about. Granted, I thought it was Sin, but I would have gone if I had known it was Chimaera and I would have gone for you."

Winter stopped on the landing and looked back at me, his expression one of disbelief or exasperation.

"Do you realize that you're talking about you, a mortal, putting yourself in danger to go to the aid of an immortal? Do you know how crazy that is?" he grinned and spread his hands.

"Granted, you're immortal," I nodded, "but you're not impervious to pain or suffering. And any friend of mine is welcome to what aid and protection I can offer."

"I pity His Lordship," Chimaera shook his head slowly.

"Oh?" I sneered, involuntarily landing my hands on my hips, "And just why is that?"

"I fear he has no idea what a handful you are," he laughed as we turned the corner and approached the door to the sapphire room. "No offense intended, Witch, but you are something else," he smiled as he opened the door for me, "and I'm grateful that you are."

"See you guys," I sighed as I stripped the wet and muddied velvet cape off and took it into the bathroom. "You know," I said out loud to myself, "I am getting so tired of people being amused at me, no, at vampires being amused at me." I took off my wet clothes and dried myself on a warm towel, noticing gratefully that Amon had apparently had a towel warmer put in my bathroom. "You do what you think is right," I continued my soliloquy, "No, what you know in your heart is right, and you get that infuriating bemused look. Man, I hate that!" After donning the black satin robe, I dried my hair and brushed out the tangles. Having no idea what to do with the sodden cape, I finally laid it out in the tub so that it could dry, but I had little hope for its salvation.

Turning off the bathroom light, I went into the bedroom and sat down on the bed. I was feeling eighteen different degrees of terrible thinking about what I had put Amon through, while at the same time wondering at my concern for his feelings. It wasn't that I was normally unfeeling or even oblivious to other peoples' feelings, but I had been living on my own for so long, that I seldom felt such remorse for what was clearly a misunderstanding. Although I knew that Amon would get over it, I really hated that I was the cause for his pain and suspected that it was because I had shared his blood and was so closely connected to him emotionally as well as physically.

Restlessly I paced around the room, sitting in first one chair, then the other, then the bed, then walking again. I opened my mind to Amon but found only a wall there. Either he was shielding his thoughts or his beast was still in control. Finally deciding that relaxation was out of the question, I stole downstairs into the parlor and poured myself a glass of white wine. Pulling a cigarette out of my pocket, I stepped out onto the veranda and lit it, deeply inhaling the smoke. The storm had played itself out and I hoped that meant some of Amon's anger had gone with it. As I stood there sipping my wine and smoking my cigarette, Bishop stepped out and moved up beside me.

"I have good news, Cat," he said softly, "I have been able to obtain all the necessary blood and equipment for the transfusion. We can do it tomorrow after sunset." He gently took my elbow and turned me to face him. "Has something happened? Is there something wrong?"

His soft black curls stirred around his face, the breeze bobbing them gently. His preternaturally blue eyes glowed softly in the darkness and his white teeth gleamed when he spoke. His gaze fell then settled on my scratched cheek.

"It's nothing, Bishop," I smiled weakly, "Just a misunderstanding between His Lordship and me, and between some rosebushes and I."

"Is there anything I can do to help?" he asked with such concern that I almost started to cry again.

"No, Bishop," I sighed, "I guess this just has to run its course. But thanks for asking,"

We stood together silently watching the night sky. He was probably enjoying the sight of the breaking clouds and the returning stars, though I was scanning the heavens for some sign of Amon. And though I realized the foolishness of this, as I knew that he flew so swiftly as to be undetectable to anyone standing on the ground, I still dared to hope that I might catch sight of him.

"You know, Cat," Bishop startled me out of my reverie, "If you're having second thoughts about going through with this trans-fusion, this extraction, I'm sure that His Lordship would not mind. If he had any idea how potentially dangerous this could be, I'm sure he would insist that you not go through with it."

"I have no intentions of changing my mind or backing out of this," I assured him, "and you promised that you would not tell Sin of the risks. Bishop, you promised."

"I know," he nodded thoughtfully, "and now I'm having second thoughts about that. Maybe he should know the truth, maybe we have no right to keep this information from him. What if something happens to you?"

"Either way, you will get my Life's Blood for him, right, Bishop?" I fixed him with my stare, "whether something happens to me or not, Sin will have his prophecy fulfilled. We'll just do our best to see that I make it through, and I have no plans to die tomorrow."

"Knowing your will," he grinned, "you'll come through it just fine. I guess I shouldn't be worried."

"That's right, Bishop," I returned his smile, "just relax."

"You have fed, right?" he asked brightly, "You have taken more of His Lordship's blood, his strength? That should act as insurance against your crossing over."

"Yes," I lied easily, "All taken care of. Well, I think I'll turn in now, big night tomorrow, I probably need some rest. See you tomor-row, Bishop." With that I turned and went back into the house, feel-ing only slight guilt for having lied to him. I could not, no I would not, risk him refusing to go through with this scheme if he thought that I hadn't fed. Faint hope still remained that Amon would return and we could clear the air before the sun rose in the eastern sky.

Though I had first headed toward the sapphire room, halfway there I realized that I would be unable to rest anywhere until I spoke to Amon. So I turned around and went downstairs and into his coffin room. The two coffins, his and mine, stood closed and empty, their finishes gleaming in the soft light of the wall sconces. Though it was probably poor etiquette, or even rudely unacceptable, I opened Amon's coffin and climbed in uninvited. Just the feel of the fabric that had touched his skin and the almost undetectable fragrance of pine needles, green grass, and warm rich earth that was Amon's scent were enough to calm me and my soul grew peaceful and quiet. Leaving the lid open, I closed my eyes and curled up to sleep in the satin.

Chapter 36

Cold seeped into my bones and the wind whipped my hair across my face. Coming fully awake, I found myself in Amon's embrace, his arms and his cloak wrapped around me. We were flying across the night sky. I slid my arms around his waist and laid my head against his chest, touching my bare feet on the tops of his boots.

"Amon," I breathed, "I am so sorry for what I put you through. It was all my fault and I promise it will never happen again. I'm just so sorry." Trembling partly from the cold and partly from fear, I tightened my hold on him

"Cat," he returned my tightening embrace, "It is I who am sorry. I never meant to attack you or to hurt you. I lost control of my beast again and I shall never forgive myself for that."

"No, Amon, please," I begged, "Can we just let this go, forget it ever happened?"

"I want you to understand, Little One," he pressed his mouth close to my ear, "so we are going to my secret aerie, my most favorite place in this world, and I will explain matters to you, yes?"

"Fine," I agreed, "anything you say." I closed my eyes and burrowed my face into his neck, content to be in his arms and back in his good graces.

When Amon set us down on the ground, I turned from his embrace to survey my surroundings, pausing momentarily to regain my balance. We were on a rocky outcropping, presumably part of some mountain range, and the forest and hills spread out in all directions below us. The night sky had mostly cleared of clouds and the stars twinkled brightly as if freshened by the earlier storm.

"We're not in Louisiana anymore are we?" I marveled as I turned to appreciate the view from every direction. Each sight was breathtakingly beautiful. "I never thought to ask," I added, "just how fast can you fly?"

He turned and looked into the distance, cutting a powerful and dramatic figure against the darkness.

"I fly almost as swiftly as I can think," he spoke into the distance, "And you are correct, we are not in Louisiana nor in any state or area of which you have heard. This spot is virtually inaccessible to humans, so we will not be disturbed here."

Rubbing my hands up and down my arms, I leaned my hip on a rocky ledge and struggled to get comfortable. My satin gown was little protection against the night air at this altitude and my bare feet were chilled from the cool stone. Amon, seeing my discomfort, came over and wrapped his cloak around my shoulders and lifted me up on a level piece of rock so my feet no longer touched the ground. I drew my knees up beneath the cape and tightened the fabric around me, the warmth relaxing my chills. For a moment I just sat and admired Amon, his powerful arms and shoulders, his slim hips and legs. A soft breeze stirred his long silver tresses and billowed the sleeves of his dark gray silk shirt. The angles and planes of his face stood out against the shadows of his eyes and chin.

"I think, Dear Cat, that you deserve an explanation as to where my anger came from tonight," he brushed my hair out of my face. "Rest assured that it was not entirely your fault." He turned and rubbed his hands together, apparently deciding on where to begin. "You know that I have not cared about someone in many centuries. To be without that emotional investment is to live without risk, I now see. When I thought that I had lost you it brought back memories that I had denied for several hundred years. My rage and pain roared back to life and my beast took control."

"Who was she?" I whispered tenderly.

"She was a young woman from my village. Anna." he smiled fondly, "a beautiful, bright, giving soul, she was the local midwife. Having great knowledge of herbs and plants, she successfully saw hundreds of women through difficult births. I thought to marry her and build a home, till the earth and raise children but she was smarter than I. She saw me for what I really was, a fighter, and a warrior. Knowing that I would never be content in a normal existence, she sent me off to the crusades with a pouch full of herbal ointments and her scarf, its blue the color of a Friesian sky at morning. Of course, when I was made a vampire I could not possibly return to her, as she was a deeply religious and God fearing woman. I knew that she would never be able to accept what I had become and vowed to never let her see me again. Perhaps a year or two after I had been changed, I was travelling with my sire through Germany and happened to spy her rushing into a cottage in a small village. I recognized her immediately. Inquiring of the locals, I found that she had traveled from Friesland to attend to the birth of a relative's baby. Standing hidden in a nearby copse of trees, I watched the little cottage all night, hoping to catch sight of my Anna once more. Just before sunrise I heard the screaming of someone in unbelievable pain, then weeping and cursing. Though I knew something was wrong, my sire bid me remain hidden and let the lives of humans play out as they were intended. The plaintive cry of the newborn babe should have brought cheers of happiness and celebration but instead it brought harsh yelling and the sound of furniture crashing and things breaking, then silence. Moments before the sun was about to breech the horizon, I stole out from cover and looked through the cottage window. My Anna lay dead in a pool of blood, her body beaten and bruised, and her face barely recognizable. The mother had apparently died in childbirth and though the baby survived, the father's rage at the loss of his wife had caused him to lash out at the only person available. Though I am sure she had done all she could for the woman, Anna could not save her and her husband killed Anna for it. My pain, my feeling of loss was so intense it was like a dagger in my heart. The rage I felt at the man who had murdered Anna was blinding."

"Did you kill him?" I asked quietly, not sure that I wouldn't have done the same thing.

"I wanted to," he nodded, "but seeing that beautiful infant, lying there in her cradle and knowing that she had already lost a mother, I could not deprive her of a father, however unworthy he was to raise a child. Anyway, as soon as the man collapsed, I stepped into the cottage and gathered my Anna's remains, taking her body back to the woods. Having nowhere for my anger to go, I called down the storms for the first time that night. Suffice it to say that after that child's birth, the village suffered several days of unrelenting violent storms. Once I had seen to Anna's burial the following evening, I released my beast and tore through the countryside for hours, night after night, for nearly a week. Thinking back on it now, I believe that was when my sire realized that he had brought across a Master Vampire, for he left me to my own devices shortly after that."

"And you haven't cared about anyone since then?" I murmured thoughtfully, realizing the depths of pain that my recklessness had caused him. "You haven't loved anyone since Anna?"

"There were women, of course," he smiled ruefully, "one or two I even thought I cared about, maybe even loved, but when fate or whatever force controlled the situation took them out of my life, there was no sorrow, no sense of profound loss. My beast had not reared its head for love since Anna's death."

"And when you thought I was dead?" I moaned miserably.

"Pain and anger more blinding even than that I had felt after her loss," he nodded. "Cat, we have become part of each other and I cannot lose you."

"You do know that I'm mortal, Amon," I scooted forward and jumped off the ledge landing before him. "I will die someday, you know. You will have to accept that at some point."

"Maybe after fifty or sixty years of living with your stubbornness, your willful recklessness, I may tire of you and be happy to see you go," he grinned as he took me into his arms.

"Fifty or sixty years?" I laughed, "Amon I'm already thirty-seven. Just how old do you expect me to get?"

"A hundred or a hundred, fifty," he nuzzled my neck and lifted me in his embrace.

"Oh, speaking of living," I added, "Bishop told me that he has everything ready for the transfusion and we can do it tomorrow after sunset."

"I know, but only if you are sure about this, Cat," Amon smiled and looked deeply into my eyes. "Only if it is something you really wish to do. The prophecy no longer holds the interest for me that it once did." He stroked one graceful hand down the back of my hair and lifted my chin to kiss me. That feeling of completion, of total serenity and profound peace settled over me as his lips touched mine and I knew that I would never yearn to be anywhere else but in his arms.

"I really want to do this, Amon," I whispered, "I know that this is important and that it is right that I do this." Knowing that I had no words to explain the feeling of fate rushing up to meet me, I let the matter drop.

Pulling back from me, he drew his hair from his shoulder, exposing his neck. "You must feed once more, Beloved," he offered his throat. "Please, take my strength."

"No, Amon," I shook my head, "I no longer require some sign of your submission, your willingness to bend to my will. I now yield to you and will feed as you wish. However, don't confuse my acceptance with submission, or even worse, subservience."

"Never," he whispered. His smile beaming anticipation, he opened his shirt and drew a thin cut with his fingernail below his breast, just over his heart. Cupping my head in his hands, he whispered, "Drink of me, Beloved. Drink of my heart."

I leaned into him and placed my tongue at the edge of the wound, catching the first drop of Amon's blood. As I sealed my lips around the opening, I drew in his strength, his power, and his blood. The taste was stronger, richer, and more tantalizing than before and I found myself swallowing one mouthful in eagerness for the next. He hissed in pain or rapture, I wasn't sure which, but he did not command me to stop so I continued to drink. I rubbed my hands up his back and worked my mouth rhythmically along his wound. The electricity, the heat, the energy I was receiving from his blood was starting to make me feel intoxicated and Amon finally pulled me away and steadied me as he sealed the wound with his saliva. He kissed me quickly and buttoned his shirt.

As the sensation of his vampire hunger, his constant need, swept over me and through me, I was surprised to find that it was no less intense, no less painful for having experienced it before. I clinched my fists and squeezed my eyes shut, my knees drawing up to my chest involuntarily.

"I could never get used to this hunger, this feeling," I gasped, waiting for the sensations to subside.

Silence spun out between us as Amon waited for my body to relax and my mind to calm down.

"So tell me of your adventure, earlier this evening," he finally broached the subject when I opened my eyes and dropped my hands, stretching out my legs.

"It really wasn't anything," I shook my head, "I had a vision that you were in jeopardy and I forced Winter to ride out with me to save you. Only when my owl led us to the rock wall I had seen in my mind, it was Chimaera that was shackled there. He was wounded in the thigh and I know that he said he wouldn't perish either from the wound or from being exposed to the daylight, but I had to heal him and see to his release. It was a demon who had taken my likeness to ensnare Chimaera and I guess I felt a little guilty about that."

"How did you release him?" he smiled and rubbed his hands across my shoulders.

"I shot the bolts out of the wall," I grinned, looking down at my hands.

"You shot the bolts out of the wall?" He gaped, "With what?"

"Winter had given me that little Tomcat pistol," I admitted, "remember the one I had carried when we were out in the woods the first time, when the Alpha male wolf had to check me out? It was that pistol."

"And you shoot?" He shook his head, "You really shoot?"

"I'll have you know that I am an expert marksman, you male chauvinist vampire," I pouted.

"The more I learn about you, and I thought I knew it all," he added, "the more I am impressed and intrigued. You are something else."

"Please, I'm getting tired of hearing that," I swatted him away, again there was that bemused look, "although I am gratified to hear you admit that you don't know everything there is to know about me. No woman ever wants to hear that." Moving forward, I hugged him and stood on tiptoe to kiss him on the chin. "Anyway, Chimaera's wound had caused him to lose a lot of blood, so I cut myself and bled into his mouth, no teeth or biting involved. I don't understand vampire etiquette when it comes to feeding, but Chimaera was adamant that he would not feed from me, so I had to be creative. When I was unable to heal myself, he did seal the wound, but that's all. Then we rode back and that's when I met you in the garden."

"I really dislike the idea of you sharing your precious blood with anyone other than me, but I am grateful that you were resourceful enough to save Chimaera" he shook his head in amazement, "You really thought to rescue me? I have never in all my years come across someone with such loyalty, such selflessness, and such blind reckless need to protect. You are very much like the Alpha female of the pack, she will sacrifice herself with no hesitation to save her offspring."

"I'm not sure if that comparison is a compliment, but as I'm getting sleepy, I'll take it as such," I smiled and yawned, leaning against his chest.

"The sun will be up shortly and you should rest," he nodded as he took the cape from me and wrapped it around his shoulders.

Taking me once more into his arms, he placed his lips on mine and then whispered, "We must fly."

When we returned to the estate, Amon set us down in the garden. Pink was seeping into the eastern sky and the birds were just beginning their morning songs. We stood embracing each other, listening to the sounds of daybreak and breathing in the fresh morning air. When we went inside Amon informed me that Bishop would be setting up the equipment for the transfusion and suggested I sleep with him in his coffin once more.

As we stepped into the coffin room, I noticed that he had supplied me with a lovely royal blue peignoir embellished with black lace and ribbons. Okay, it looked like something you'd see on the cover of a Harlequin romance novel, but I didn't mind dressing "girlie" every once in a while. Watching him undress, I noticed the pale red mark over his heart and felt a touch of relief that, as it turned out by my feeding, I hadn't lied to Bishop after all. Amon donned a white poet's shirt and black satin pajama pants and he looked absolutely delicious. I sighed a breath of regret that the sun was rising and there was no time for lovemaking.

Later, as I lay surprisingly awake in Amon's arms, I replayed in my mind the memories of my life, fully understanding the need to be reflective. Guarding my thoughts, I reminisced through the years of my childhood, blissfully spent in the love and comfort of my parents' home. I tiptoed through the teen years, not really wanting to look too closely at that time of awkward beginnings and emotional roller coasters. Part of me would always love and miss Michael, my ex-husband, as we had some wonderfully romantic and new experiences together and the other part would always feel the sting of betrayal and broken trust. It dawned on me how I hadn't really struggled with who I was or what I had become until after we divorced and I lost all sense of myself. When my health crisis hit, my leukemia, I had rallied and had become strong and determined but I had never really recovered the image of myself. Now, since being with Amon, this incredibly impossible Master Vampire, I felt like I had returned to where I had started. Knowing for the first time in a long time exactly who and what I was, and knowing that I could lose it all tomorrow was a freeing notion. I realized that it didn't matter whether I survived the transfusion or not, I was where and what I was always meant to be and anything that happened after this moment was gravy.

"Why are your thoughts concealed, Cat?" Amon asked softly, his fingertips lightly stroking down my upper arm.

"Why are you trying to read my mind, Vampire?" I grinned and leaned closer to his body. As most always, he had his heart beating for me and had made his flesh warm. Only his unnatural beauty gave him away as anything other than a normal human male.

"I am only curious if you are thinking about me, of course," he murmured as he drew my hand up to his mouth and kissed my palm.

"Wow," I breathed, "we have got to do something about your ego."

"Were you thinking about me?" he smiled, his teeth shining in the dark. His fingers stroked trails of fire up my arms.

"How could I possibly be thinking about anything else?" I replied as I moved up to kiss his warm, tender lips. Melancholy tore through me momentarily as I thought of how I would miss kissing Amon if something were to go wrong tomorrow and I slammed my mental shields down hard before he could taste my sadness.

"I know you are anxious about tomorrow, Little One," he said soberly. "Shall I will you to sleep?"

"You can do that?" I marveled at yet another of his magical abilities.

"I can," he nodded almost imperceptibly. "But you must release your mind shields, open up to me, Cat."

Closing my eyes, I visualized the wall around my thoughts crumbling, dissolving into dust.

Sleep Cat. Rest safely and securely in my arms and heed my will. Sleep!

Chapter 37

I found myself walking along a dyke, the water below was wind-swept, gray-brown, and choppy. The sky above was clear and dazzlingly bright blue. In the distance brown and white cattle grazed on impossibly green grass. Windmills on the other side of the water turned slowly, their white sails blinding in the sun. Everywhere I turned the colors were intensely vibrant and I stood dumbstruck at the beauty that surrounded me. From the far end of the polder I could see a shape moving toward me and waited patiently as the distance between us closed. I could at last make out the shape of a woman. Her dress was pale blue and her apron and bonnet were the same blinding white as the sails of the windmills. As she neared I could see wisps of coppery blonde hair sneaking out from beneath her cap and the blush of health and vigor blooming on her cheeks. Her clear eyes were as blue as the sky and her smile was broad and open, as genuine and honest as she was. When she recognized me, she dropped her pail and the bundles she carried and ran to me laughing, launching herself into my arms. I hugged her, laughing with delight, and danced around in a circle with her in my arms.

"Anna," I whispered as my eyelids fluttered open.

Amon still held me in his arms, though the lid to the coffin was now open, and was watching me closely.

"What are you doing?" I stretched and yawned a little.

"I was watching you sleep," he answered softly, "You were dreaming."

"It wasn't a dream," I shook my head, "It was a memory of yours. I was seeing it as if it were happening to me. You were meeting Anna on a dyke somewhere, on a, was it called a polder?"

"Yes," he smiled brightly, "those are the manmade fields created after a dyke is built and the windmills have pumped out all the water."

"See, you know it was a memory of yours," I reasoned, "because I had no idea even what that was when it came to my mind, or your mind in your memory. It's kind of confusing."

"I believe you, Cat," he grinned, "though I think I shall always be both surprised and amazed at this."

"Has the sun gone down?" I changed the subject, "Is it time for the transfusion?"

"Winter was in a few moments ago," he replied, "he said that Bishop was making the final preparations and that we could go to the room he has prepared any time we wish."

"If needs be done, would twere it done quickly," I misquoted as I untangled myself from Amon's arms and legs and made my way out of the coffin.

"Shakespeare?" Amon queried.

"I think so," I nodded as I began looking around the room for clothes, then realized that they probably weren't necessary as I would be effectively "playing patient" in a while.

Amon got out of his coffin and offered me his arm. As we strode from the room he leaned down and whispered conspiratorially, "I am having Lily prepare you a meal, oh and she is waiting to see you again. Winter explained to her that we had been forced to pretend that you were dead to protect you from a crazed fan that had followed you here from Club Psyche. As far as she knows, that is the reason I brought you here in the first place, for your own protection."

"That's clever and a little devious," I observed as we began the climb up the stairs.

"You may bathe or shower before or after you eat," he added.

"Whoa," I chuckled, "you're making me feel like a condemned prisoner before her execution."

He drew up short and gaped at me. "I did not intend to make you feel like that," he exclaimed, "I only wanted to do something nice for you, though anything I could do would pale in comparison."

"It's not a contest," I pressed my hand against his chest and stretched up to kiss his cheek, "and thank you. Maybe a quick shower and a cup of coffee, and perhaps a beignet?"

"I'm sure that we can do better than that," he smiled and took my hand, drawing me into his arms. He scooped me up and carried me into his bedroom, which had been lit with candles and scented with fresh flowers. A vase of long stemmed red roses stood on the table before the occasional chairs and another vase of creamy white calla lilies stood gracefully on the dresser. Yet another small vase of red miniature roses adorned the nightstand. Smiling at his thoughtfulness, I stepped into the bathroom while Amon turned on the shower.

"What would you like to wear this evening?" he asked politely.

"I will leave that decision," I smiled and bowed, "in your impeccably capable hands." With that I stripped off the peignoir and stepped into the shower, adjusting the temperature to as warm as I could stand.

I adjusted the spray to as hard as possible and stood, eyes closed, beneath the beating torrent. After washing my hair, I lathered and rinsed my skin then adjusted the water temperature to a brisk, invigorating cool. I squeezed the water from my hair and stepped out of the stall, taking up a bath towel and drying myself vigorously. Stepping in front of the vanity, I wiped the steam from the mirror (*when had he installed a mirror?*) and peered at my own image, barely recognizable now. My hair, though wet and partially plastered to my head, was uncharacteristically long and the shades of blonde had blended into streaks, giving it the look of freshly pulled saltwater taffy. My skin, normally rather ruddy, was unusually pale and gave me

an almost frail appearance. My green eyes looked disproportionately large and doelike with dark rings beneath them. Deciding that living among the vampires was taking a toll on my perception of beauty, as well as other things, I dismissed my visage and set about drying my hair. Plaiting the now below-the-shoulder blade length into a smooth braid, I secured it with a piece of black ribbon that I took from the sleeve of the peignoir. Wrapping a towel around myself, I opened the bathroom door a crack and peered out into the bedroom. Amon sat silently, head bowed, on the edge of the bed, a silver-gray garment lying across his lap. Though I couldn't see his face, he appeared sad, somehow bereft and a sob escaped my lips before I could cut it off. He looked up and smiled at me.

"Cat, you look lovely," he stood and offered me the dress he had chosen. It was a silvery-gray satin sleeveless sheath, very simple and very elegant. A part of me recognized meaning in its color and was delighted and honored by it, though most of me had no idea from where that notion came.

"I'm sure I will in this," I smiled as I accepted his gift. "You look incredibly masculine and sexy, as always." I stretched up and kissed his beautiful face. He was breathtaking in a crisp white dress shirt and black brocade vest. At his throat was a lace jabot secured with an onyx stone. His black pants were skintight and disappeared smoothly into his impeccably polished black leather boots. A black satin ribbon, similar to the one I wore, secured his long thick silver hair at the nape of his neck and its length hung softly down his back. He sat back down on the edge of the bed. "Though I could never compare with you, you rat," I sighed and draped the dress across one of the chairs then turned and stepped in front of Amon, moving to stand between his knees. He watched with a curious expression as I slipped my hands behind him and untied the ribbon that held his hair.

"Witch," he murmured hesitantly, "what are you doing?"

His eyes followed my hands as I carefully removed the onyx pin at his collar and began unbuttoning his shirt.

"I want you to do something for me, Amon," I whispered as I continued down the line of buttons.

"Yes?" he answered automatically, more interested in what I was doing than what I was saying.

"Though I fully intend to be around for fifty or sixty more years, as you say," I remarked, "I know in my heart and in my mind that nothing will go amiss tonight and that everything will turn out as we plan. However, just in case, will you make love to me now?" I pulled his vest and shirt off and stroked my fingertips along his smooth, muscular shoulders, then bent down and placed my mouth on his.

"Dear Cat," he moaned as he stood and wrapped his arms around me, "I will not make love to you "just in case." I will however happily make love to you just because."

"You are becoming a witty vampire," I grinned and stepped away from him. "Wait a minute," I added, moving quickly to the bedroom door. I stood silently and concentrated then wove a ward of protection before the door. The complicated and intricately designed ward appeared as a neon red cord, twisted and knotted and curled back upon itself. It glowed and softly hummed then became invisible.

"You know that either Chimaera or Winter is on the other side of that door, don't you?" Amon asked uncertainly.

"Why do you think I cast a spell on it?" I laughed as I dropped the towel and walked seductively into his arms. I touched the cool silky skin of his broad chest and planted kisses along his collarbone.

Moving my lips steadily upward, I licked and kissed his throat, his neck and the tender hollow just below his ear.

"Cat, you are bewitching me," he gasped as I scraped my teeth along the rough edge of his jaw.

"Only as a woman bewitches a man," I answered as I finally reached his mouth and took it forcefully, driving my tongue deeply between his sharp fangs. Sucking in his juices, I pulled his lower lip into my mouth and gently, playfully nibbled it until he pulled away and stepped back. Reaching around me, he drew my braid along my shoulder until it lay upon my breast. Then he took pains to untie the ribbon slowly, methodically, intentionally brushing his fingers across my nipple time after time. My abdominal muscles clinched and my nipples hardened and became erect. My heart was beating rapidly and my breath came in tight little gasps. Using both hands, he carefully unwound my braid and shook out my hair, bunching it in his fists. He drew my tresses to his nose and breathed deeply.

"I love your scent," he breathed again, as if hypnotized.

"And I yours," I answered as I drew my tongue up his breast. He hissed softly as I nipped at his skin and it occurred to me that being in his company was giving me an oral fixation. I could not remember ever being a biter before and figured that it was another side effect of the vampire blood running through me. As he leaned his long hard body against me I felt his desire, his need and pressed my palm against the zipper of his jeans. He moaned and ground his hips beneath my hand. Delighting in taking my time, I rubbed my hands around his waist and up and down his back. He bent down and kissed my ear, then my neck, his lips and tongue pausing to pay attention to the pulse beating hard and fast beneath the tender skin.

"You stir so many hungers in me," he whispered into my neck.

"Help yourself," I nodded, referring to my blood, "It will just be that much less that Bishop will have to take."

With that, Amon lifted me by the elbows, turned, and tossed me softly onto the massive bed. Pausing to remove his boots and tight black pants, he joined me on top of the comforter. Rising on his knees above me, he looked down at me hungrily and my heart did a little quickstep at the desire and emotion in his eyes. His swollen member drew my attention and he slowly wrapped his hand around its base and stroked it invitingly. The picture he made kneeling beside me, muscles hard and taut, shining hair loose and wild, his eyes shimmering, made my insides turn to molten liquid. He was so sensual, so sexual and so completely without inhibitions. Here was the epitome of animal magnetism, lust, hunger, and desire. And he was in bed with me!

Moving up my thighs, he drew his fingertips along my skin, lighting my nerves on fire and causing ripples of tickles. I squirmed uncomfortably until his touch reached my breasts, then I stilled and closed my eyes. Reveling in the sensation of his touch, I moaned as he gently lowered his weight, forcing my legs open with his knees. His tongue softly circled my nipple, then his lips locked onto it and he suckled eagerly. Deep within me, muscles clinched and relaxed, and juices began flowing. I wrapped my long legs around his pelvis, eager for his entry. Tonight, he did not tease me or withhold himself from me, but smoothly slid his length into my wetness. My breath caught in my throat as the sensation of connection and completion accompanied his invasion. He moved gently and rhythmically, working himself deeply within me then withdrawing smoothly. The tender and languorous movement was delicious and when he kissed me I slowly drove my tongue into his mouth to match his thrusts between my legs. As the need began to rise and my breath began to quicken, I thrust my hips up to meet Amon's,

wanting him forcefully inside me as deeply as he could go. Understanding my desire, he obliged me and forced himself deeper, causing me to gasp in painful delight.

I smiled at his look of concern. "Yes, feed," I hissed and moved my hair off of my neck.

Pulling me off of my back and into his lap, he drew me into his embrace. As he drove his razor sharp teeth into my jugular vein, the sudden pain caused a surge of fire through my body and the intensity of my orgasm shook through me. The sensation remained and repeated as he sucked demandingly on my neck. His member throbbed deeply within me and I writhed and clutched fistfuls of his hair. Power and electricity flowed through us, from my veins to his mouth, from his sword into my sheath. I was exhilarated, invigorated, completed and yet undone. As the physical wave calmed, I relaxed and willed my racing heartbeat to slow. He lowered me back onto the bed, careful to not break our connection.

"What have you done to me?" I sighed, "You've ruined me. No mere mortal could ever touch me the way you do. No man could ever look at me the way you do. The way your eyes move over my body with such passion, such desire. I will never be satisfied with another man."

"Good," Amon released my neck, and rising, smiled through bloodstained lips, "For if another man were to ever touch you, I would be forced to kill him." He bent over my neck and sent chills up my spine when he licked and sealed his bite marks.

"Oh, please," I swatted his arm for teasing me. Subtly, I fortified my mental shields, not wanting to upset him with my thoughts. That little voice of mine had been berating me, screaming sarcasm when Amon waxed romantic with promises of a life together. "He's feeding you what he thinks you want to hear, AND YOU DO, you sap!" After this night, and the fulfillment of the prophecy, I expected that a Master Vampire, soon to be an Uber Vampire, would have no further use for a mere mortal witch like me. His beauty and his power already put him way out of my league and I was sure that once he had my Life's Blood, I would be sent home with my tail between my legs.

A cracking sound shot through the room, followed by a muffled "Damn" and Amon and I froze staring at each other. For an instant I thought it had been gunfire. Another weaker crackle echoed followed by a hissed "oof." Amon and I smiled and broke into gales of laughter when we realized that someone had run up against my ward on the door and was paying for it painfully.

"Your Lordship?" Chimaera called through the closed door, "There seems to be some sort of force field surrounding the door."

"Indeed?" Amon managed to answer with a straight face, his voice strong and forceful.

"Please, Sire?" Chimaera sighed loudly, "Instruct your witch to remove her ward."

At that, both Amon and I dissolved into laughter and silliness. The mental picture of Chimaera being zapped by the ward as he unknowingly tried to knock on the door, then having the nerve to try it yet once more, was too rich, too funny for words. Only Chimaera could be pompous enough to think that he could get around my spell. As soon as I could regain my composure, I waved my hand at the ward and let it dissolve. Instantly Chimaera knocked and Amon called out for him to wait a moment. I disappeared into the bath-room, grabbing my towel off the floor as Amon quickly dressed and answered the door. Though it was rude, I eavesdropped, peaking through the partially opened bathroom door.

"Lily is waiting outside with a cart full of food," Chimaera remarked, "Shall I have her bring it in?"

"Yes, please do," Amon nodded as he picked up the gray dress from the chair where I had left it. "I'm sure Cat will be dressed soon and will want to eat." He rapped lightly on the door and when I opened it he handed me the dress and a pair of matching silver pumps.

I was touched to find that Amon had supplied me with a lovely white lace bra and panty set which he had secreted in a velvet pouch draped over the hanger, and put them on with pleasure. I slipped the dress over my head, put the shoes on, ran a brush through my hair, and was braiding it once more as I stepped out of the bathroom. Lily squealed and ran at me, her arms outstretched, as she laughed and hugged me, gushing about how glad she was to see me and how it was great that I wasn't dead. When at last she released me, she stepped back and took a look at me. Shaking her head, she clucked, "Lord, Miss Cat you have got to eat something before a breeze picks you up and carries you away. Hasn't anyone been feeding you?"

"Yes, Lily," I assured her, "I've been fed, but the food was no where near as good as yours."

"I didn't know what you'd want so I just brought a little of everything," she smiled as she wheeled the cart over to the occa-sional chairs. "Come sit down and see what I've brought you."

As Lily began lifting the silver domed lids off of the trays, I noticed that she had made scrambled eggs, buttered toast and sausage. On another platter she offered some strange looking reddish stuff with a similar colored gravy and a salad. The third platter held a small thick steak with deep fried onion rings and stuffed mushrooms.

"It all looks delicious, Lily," I shook my head, "I don't know what to eat."

"Lily," Amon came up behind me and encircled me in his arms, "Miss Cat needs some red meat."

"I have Steak Tartar," she pointed at the reddish stuff, "or a bacon wrapped filet."

"Steak Tartar?" I wrinkled my nose, "As in raw meat? I gotta say no."

"Cat," Amon chided, "Please?" His embrace tightened ever so slightly and I fought him.

"I would do almost anything to please you," I turned and gave him my sweetest smile, "But I cannot take raw meat. I will have the filet mignon, okay?" I pecked him quickly on the cheek.

"Fine," he agreed, "If that's the best you can do." He stepped behind me and offered to seat me as a gentleman.

"Thank you, Sir," I nodded and took the seat. Lily brought the steak, onion rings and mushrooms and placed them on the table before me. She placed a linen napkin and silverware beside the plate.

"Miss Cat will have some Merlot, Lily," Amon directed and I shot him a look of exasperation. He returned my glare, "You will!"

"Fine, the Merlot," I acquiesced as Lily placed a wine-filled crystal goblet on the table. "Don't you have somewhere else to be?" I beamed broadly up at Amon.

"I do," Amon admitted, "Take your time and eat at your leisure. I will return for you directly." He turned and left, leaving Lily nearly open-mouthed. She turned to me with her eyes wide in surprise.

"You and Mr. Montjean?" she gaped, "You and Sin? You two are an item?" Wringing her hands on a towel, she grinned as she covered the unwanted platters and started to wheel the cart away.

Smiling at the sweetly nostalgic phrase, I shook my head, "I don't know that I would say that, Lily. I probably won't be around here that much longer, surely not long enough to be considered an item." I made invisible quotation marks in the air with my fingers. Though I should have been feeling relief at the prospect of leaving this strange existence to return to a life of normalcy, I felt somewhat sad and empty inside.

"I understand that the weirdo that was stalking you was caught," she added as she pushed the cart to the door then returned to take a seat in the chair beside mine. "Lord, Miss Cat, when I saw you lying there in that coffin, oh, I was horrified. What happened to you? How did you do that, you sure did look dead."

"When I was attacked I lost consciousness. I guess I was in a coma or something and they decided that it would be the perfect cover to bury me. By letting the world think that I was dead, Sin thought he could protect me.

"So now that you're safe, will you be returning to Lake Charles?" she asked sweetly, "I surely will miss you."

"Yes," I sighed, "I guess I'll be returning to Lake Charles and I'll miss you, too." Though my thoughts had not taken me down the road that far into the future, I found myself accepting this even as the words left my mouth.

She stood and nodded at the plate, "Best eat now, I'll pick up the dishes later. Nice to have you back among the living, Miss Cat." She pushed the food cart through the door, then smiled when she turned to close it behind her.

Though I picked up the knife and fork and cut into the juicy pink steak, the thought of leaving had taken my appetite away. I shoved one piece of meat into my mouth as Lily called goodnight, then spat it out in my napkin as soon as she left. Picking up the goblet, I sniffed the bouquet of the rich looking red wine then took a small sip. It didn't taste like it used to, but I took a drink and sat back to close my eyes and think. My mind was whirling with all sorts of thoughts and feelings, I couldn't focus on anything. I realized when I opened my eyes that Lily had taken the domed platter cover with her when she left and that when Amon returned he would certainly notice that I had not eaten. Doing the only thing I could think of, I wadded up my napkin and tossed it on top of the plate, nonchalantly covering the food as if it had been eaten. Taking the glass with me, I went to the bed and sat down, idly tracing the carved dragon on the headboard with my index finger. Smiling, I decided that I would remember the dragon as Dave. Dave the Dragon, it had a nice ring to it. Restlessly standing, I walked around the room committing everything to memory, the furniture, the colors, and the fragrances. I was making a mental inventory when Amon returned. He looked startled when he stepped into the room and nearly ran into me.

"Cat," he smiled, "Are you finished eating already? My errand didn't take me as long as I had expected and I was afraid that I would interrupt your meal. I considered staying away for a while, but decided that I would rather be with you."

"That's sweet," I murmured and reached out and touched his chest, the crisp white shirt and the beautiful black vest. He had once more tied his hair back at the nape and I touched it where it drew back over his ear.

"Are you alright?" he asked seriously, "You seem, I don't know, sad." He stepped before me and rubbed his hands down my bare arms then stepped back and looked at me. "You look exquisite in that dress, Cat, you're beautiful."

"Please don't tease me, Amon," I sighed, "You don't need to flatter me. I won't change my mind about going through with the transfusion."

"What are you saying?" he gasped, "Do you really think me so shallow that I would try to flatter you into doing this thing? I don't care if we go through with the transfusion or not, I've told you this. I'm telling you that you are beautiful because you are." He took me into his arms and took my wineglass, sipping deeply from it. "You are the most exquisitely tall, blonde, green-eyed beauty of a witch that I have ever seen in my life. Your mind is quick and sharp, your wit is beguiling. I love to see you smile and your laughter is like bells in my ears. Your voice, when you speak, soothes me and when you sing, it enchants me. How can I make you understand how much you mean to me?" He smoothed his hand along the side of my face and I looked down, unable to meet his eyes. I was ashamed that I had thought so little of him, that I thought him capable of such obse- quiousness. He lifted my chin and forced me to look at him. Tears were clouding my vision as I looked into those beautiful ebony eyes, thinking how I was going to miss him.

"Cat, you're crying," he spoke softly, touching one tear with his fingertip, "tell me what's wrong. I know there is something bother- ing you. You've been hiding your thoughts from me all night."

"Oh, it's nothing," I sobbed weakly, "Just stupid human stuff, merely a pity party. Nothing for you to worry about." I shook my head as if to clear it and pasted a smile on my face. "I'm ready to do this thing now if you are and if Bishop is ready to go."

"I'm sure he is," he offered, still regarding me doubtfully. "Are you sure you want to do this? It's not necessary, you know." He leaned over and kissed my cheekbones below my eyes, softly tasting my bloody tears.

"No," I brightened, squaring my shoulders and inhaling deeply, "I'm sure. I want to do this."

"Very well," he turned, "Just let me put this down." Stepping over to the table, he placed the near empty glass down and lifted the napkin from my plate. Standing silently, he said nothing but joined me across the room and opened the door. Chimaera stood sentry beside the door and he straightened and nodded at me as we stepped into the hallway.

"Catherine," he smiled, formally offering his hand, "You look lovely tonight." As I put my hand out to touch his, he took it and kissed it demurely.

"Thank you, Chimaera," I croaked as my voice choked with emotion. Screwing up my determination, I decided that I had to get a grip on my feelings or I was going to end up a puddle on the floor. "I trust your hand is not permanently injured," I nodded, referring to the ward.

"Very nice work, Witch," he grinned wickedly and showed me his right hand. The knuckles were red with angry white welts across them. "I'll heal, eventually."

"Sorry," I lied and then chuckled as Amon moved me down the hall. We walked silently for a little while then Amon cleared his throat and slowed our steps.

"Cat," he stopped and turned me to face him, "why did you not eat? You took one bite of your food and I think you spit that out. What's wrong?"

"Nothing's wrong," I cooed as Chimaera came up behind us, "I just found that I had no appetite. Maybe I'm too excited about tonight, I just couldn't eat. I'll eat later."

"You promise?" he looked pointedly at me, "That's all it is?"

Lowering my mental shields a bit I nodded, "I promise."

You feel the truth of my words?

Yes, there is truth there, Cat, but there is something else, too. It is something that I cannot quite grasp.

Probably just nerves, I am kind of jumbled tonight.

If you insist, Cat.

Yes, Amon, I insist.

As we went downstairs, I realized that Bishop must have set up a room near Amon's coffin room. I thought to myself how it would at least be convenient if something went wrong tonight, they could just drag my carcass down the hall, chuck me into my coffin, take me out back and bury me. The instant I completed my little sick fantasy Amon drew me up short and spun me around to look at him. Realizing that I had left my mental shields down and Amon had been privy to my twisted little joke, I covered my face with my hands and shook my head.

"Cat," Amon spoke in alarm, "We should not attempt this tonight. You really do not want to go through with this. This distresses me greatly that you could even entertains such thoughts, that you would put my foolish desires before your own welfare"

Lowering my hands, I smiled broadly and sympathetically at Amon. "Don't worry about me," I chuckled, "that little scenario is just my very human way of dealing with stress. I always imagine the worst possible thing that can happen to steel myself, mentally fortify myself.

Generally, something much less dramatic, something much more mundane happens and I'm relieved."

"You really do not expect us to drag your carcass down the hall, chuck you into your coffin, take you out back and bury you?" he quoted my thoughts verbatim.

"No," I grinned at his concern, "the way I see it, if anything less than what my sick mind can imagine happens, the night will be considered a success." I leaned up and kissed his cheek, hoping to relax the furrows on his brow. "I should have hidden my thoughts again, I'm sorry. It's hard to explain just how my mind works and why I think the way I do."

"Your mind works very," he struggled for the correct word, "disturbingly."

Laughing at the irony of being told such a thing by a vampire, I nodded, "You are not the first person to have told me that." I slipped my arms around his neck and kissed him very earnestly and very deeply. "I want to do this, it's right and it's meant to be. Now, come on, the night's a wasting'."

Light spilled from the doorway two doors down the hall from the coffin room. As I stepped inside I saw Bishop had spared nothing in setting up the room for the procedure. Against the far wall stood the much hated and much dreaded hospital bed, the protective railing standing up on one side, dropped down on the other. A chrome I.V. stand stood on the railing side of the bed, a length of clear empty tubing looped around its horizontal arm. On the open side of the bed an empty collection bag hung from a hook below a portable procedure tray stand. The soft flashing lights of the defibrillator indicated that it was juiced up and ready to go, standing near the wall just waiting with paddles charged. Beyond the I.V. stand was an odd looking piece of equipment that could only be the rapid infuser. Drawing in a deep breath, I found myself thrown back in time to when I was being treated in the hospital, when my leukemia was beating me. At least in this situation, I had a choice and I had control.

Bishop came in behind us pulling a cart with what looked like a temperature-controlled chest. It resembled a dorm room sized refrigerator, except it did not have the faux wood finish most tiny refrigerators do. Surely it was the supply of blood to replenish me.

"Cat," Bishop greeted me, "You look beautiful tonight." His deep blue eyes regarded me seriously, as if he was searching for something in my demeanor, in my expression, to convince him of my resolve.

I looked at Amon. "Did you tell him to say that?" I glanced at him suspiciously.

"Of course not," he held up his hands defensively, "he said it because it's true."

Shaking my head, I grumbled, "I wish you guys would knock it off, you're making me paranoid. No more comments about how I look okay? Good or bad."

"Very well," Amon agreed, "No more comments, period."

"Are you ready to begin, Cat?" Bishop turned to me, a rubber tourniquet dangling from his hand. That beseeching expression had returned to his face.

"Yeah," I sighed, "Let's do this." I stepped forward and perched on the edge of the bed. Bishop slipped a pillow behind me and I scooted over and stretched out "Remember, if anything happens, you promised to get the Life's Blood for His Lordship no matter what," I spoke under my breath.

He nodded silent assent. "Okay," he explained briskly, "I will begin to drain your blood first. As your volume depletes I will cover you with a cooling blanket to protect your brain function and your heart. As soon as your Life's Blood is extracted, I'll use the rapid infuser to bring up your blood volume, then warm you up. This really shouldn't take too long, but you may experience some light-headedness, dizziness, even a feeling of euphoria."

"Oh yippy skippy," I quipped, "I could use some euphoria. So, I just lie here and bleed, huh?" Instantly I regretted my attempt at levity when I saw Amon wince at my use of the word 'bleed'.

"That's pretty much it," Bishop nodded as he slid the needle into my vein and connected the tubing.

I looked at Amon, "Are you getting squeamish on me?"

"I do not like to see you suffering," he ignored my jibe. Shaking his head, he paced uneasily.

"You don't have to stay, you know," I remarked, intentionally baiting him.

"How could I be elsewhere?" he answered as he moved up beside the bed and took my hand in his. His brow was so knitted and his eyes were so creased with concern that it made me feel bad for thinking that he was using me, that this was his only reason for having anything to do with the likes of me.

I smiled, "I appreciate the fact that you are refraining from salivating like Pavlov's dog." I lifted the clear tubing, now deep red and full of blood. There were moments that I simply had to jest.

"You go too far, Kitty Cat," he warned soberly.

"Humor, sweetie, a joke?" I smiled, then added, "I think this would have been easier for you if I had hated you and forced you to violently take my Life's Blood, wouldn't it?"

He nodded, "It would be the more expected reaction. I am unaccustomed to such generosity, such selflessness." Bending over, he kissed my forehead and smoothed some errant hairs from my face.

"Yeah," I grinned, "I'm just a regular Mother Theresa. I'll be expecting canonization shortly," My eyes began to feel heavy and I leaned over to see the bag beside the bed was filling rapidly. "Doesn't look like this will take long."

Bishop moved up beside the bed and checked both the tubing and the bag. He smiled at me and patted my shoulder reassuringly. "You're doing fine, Cat. Try to stay with us as long as possible and I'll try to make you as comfortable as I can."

The world began to take on a softened look, sharp lines blurring at the edges, colors blending into one another. I closed my eyes for a moment and squeezed Amon's hand. When I opened my eyes I found that the room had tilted awkwardly and my stomach lurched a little. Panic hit me momentarily and I sought the comfort of Amon's eyes and a reminder of why I was going through this. He was looking at me with such love, such warmth, I immediately felt strengthened in my determination and offered him a little smile.

"When this night is over," he leaned over and whispered gently to me, "we shall greet the sunrise walking down the cobblestone streets of the Vieux Carrè. Would you like that?"

"You are such a romantic," I nodded, "I can think of nothing I'd like more than to see the sunrise on New Orleans with you. Of course, you know the only people alive and moving there at that hour are street sweeper operators and drunken partygoers with huge hangovers."

"Hmm," he considered, "It does sound romantic doesn't it?" Holding my left hand, he traced the edge of my jaw with the pads of his fingertips, pausing to stroke lightly across my bottom lip. "You are so…"

"No," I held up my right hand, eyes closing heavily, "no comment, remember?"

"I'm sorry," he murmured, "You're right. Cat, what's happening, can you still hear me? Stay with me."

"I'm still here," I groaned heavily, "but I'm not sure how much longer I can hold on." I felt Bishop move up beside the bed again and figured he must be switching collection bags. After a few moments I felt a gentle cooling sensation as he laid the chilling blanket over me.

Amon, have I ever told you that I love you?

No, you have not, and I would not have chosen these circumstances to hear it for the first time.

Sorry, I just thought you should know. I take a chapter from the 'better late than never' files."

Surely, it is not that late?

I'm beginning to feel strange, kind of distant, like I'm being pulled away.

Cat, please stay with me. I beg of you, do not go.

Don't worry Amon. I won't go far, at least I don't think I will.

Darkness took me into the depths and the weight of my body disappeared. I felt as if I was floating, though the sensation was different than when I had left my body using magic. Moving deeper into the darkness, I was neither frightened nor even concerned. I felt as if I was following a path I knew from childhood and knew it so well I could walk it blindfolded. Somehow, I was retracing steps I had taken before, and was startled at the realization. Surrounded securely, buoyed by the absolute darkness, I curled up feeling safe and complete, as if I was home. There was in the true sense, no sight, no sound, and no real sensation. I simply was. Then slowly I noticed that a small light had appeared in the distance.

Chapter 38

"Catherine," a powerful and comforting voice called. I was so comfortable, so totally relaxed and secure that I fought to ignore the call.

"Catherine," the voice repeated more insistently.

"Yes?" I finally answered, not really understanding what was happening. For a moment I thought it might be Amon who was calling me, then I realized that the voice, though husky, was definitely female.

"Catherine, come to me," the voice commanded and I found myself uncurling, standing, and moving toward the light without even considering the matter. Walking, yet not really walking like I normally would, I moved steadily toward the light in the distance. Striding patiently, I moved on and on. It seemed as if I had walked for hours and yet the light was getting no nearer.

"Who are you?" I called into the void, "What do you want with me?"

Only silence answered and I kept moving doggedly onward. I was unable to reckon time in this place but it seemed as if I had been here for a very, very long time. Plodding onward, I grew weary of trying to reach the light and then the thought that I might be going into The Light passed through my mind.

"No Cat," the voice reassured me, "You will not cross over into eternity. The light you are heading toward is not the One Light, nor is it your time to go into it. Come, do not give up, you will reach me."

Amon, can you hear me? Can I reach you?

You are faint, Little One, but I can hear you. Hold on, Beloved.

Its okay, Amon. I'm not going anywhere.

Breaking the mental connection with Amon was easy, it had become too much of a strain to maintain it. Once free of his mind, I began running toward the light, wondering what my heartbeat and blood pressure would look like on a monitor. As I ran, shapes of gray ephemeral matter passed by me, some trying to touch me, some unaware of my passing. Moving through the spirits, I picked up speed and determination when I realized that at last the light was growing larger and I was finally drawing nearer its source. Though it was probably only minutes it felt like another hour before I actually stepped into the light and came to a halt, bending over and panting at my exertions.

"I don't know who you are," I gasped for breath, "but I hope you appreciate this. I haven't run like this in years."

"If you had only thought," the voice replied, "you could have flown."

"Now you tell me," I complained. "Nobody likes a wiseass," I grumbled beneath my breath, "but then nobody likes a dumbass, either." I stood, holding onto my side, the sharp pain from running causing a hitch in my breathing. You'd think in the spiritual realms that you'd be immune to the inconveniences of physical discomfort, but no, at least not me. "Now, who are you and what do you want with me?" I called.

"I am she who bestowed your powers upon you," the voice echoed around me. "I am the powers of many, but you may call me Nemesis."

"Nemesis," I murmured, struggling to recall my high school mythology. All that really came to mind was an episode of Hercules with Nemesis and something about the Golden Hind, and I really couldn't remember what the point of that story was. "Goddess of what, retribution? Justice?"

"In this case, both," the voice agreed, growing louder.

"What can I do for you, Nemesis?" I stood, looking around in the bright light that encircled me, "How can I help you?" There was nothing surrounding me, only the light.

"It is the very nature of your being, the essence of your spirit that would cause you to ask these questions," the voice explained, still growing in volume. "Your willingness to give of yourself, your need to help, these traits are admirable and noble. Who and what you are is what has drawn me to you. It is for these reasons that I seek your assistance."

From what appeared to be my right, though nothing in this place was as substantial and solidly linear as the world I had left, the light appeared to dim, then a darkened shape came into view. The shadowed shape continued to grow as the light behind it threw it into silhouette. At last I could recognize the outline of a woman, tall, stately, robust and shapely. As she neared I saw that her hair was frosty white and fell in waves down her shoulders and almost to her hips. She was resplendent in a garment of crystalline silver, and at her throat a pendant of the crescent moon gleamed gently. Her bright clear blue eyes shone with power and knowledge and her skin was flawless and translucent. In her hair trembled flickers of light and I smiled when I realized that they were stars. On her right upper arm she wore a band of softly glowing metal, seemingly lit from within. Quicksilver, I thought from out of nowhere. A snowy white owl was perched on her left shoulder and its golden eyes regarded me evenly, familiarly.

"I would have a word with you, Little Witch," she stated as she lifted the owl from her shoulder and settled it on her left hand. She stroked its breast and murmured softly words of comfort to it, then turned to me. "I require the use of your human form for a short time."

Unable to even consider what that meant, I smiled and spread my hands, "Of course, anything you wish."

"That is kind of you, Cat," she nodded serenely, "I will only need it for a short space of time and will return it in excellent condition to you."

"I doubt that it's ever been in excellent condition," I quipped sarcastically.

"Very well, then," Nemesis replied, a smile playing along her perfectly shaped lips, "I will return it in the same condition that I took it, fair enough?"

"Sure, hey," I smiled, "whatever I can do." This had to be a dream, what did I care?

"I seek to right a wrong, to settle a score, if you will," she spoke soberly, "Your Master Vampire is in the middle of an intrigue that is not of his making and I wish to dispel it."

"Wow," I breathed, "He has dealings with the Gods?" And why would that not surprise me?

"Something like that," she smiled cryptically, "He has been deceived and manipulated in defiance of the collective will of the Gods. I seek to rectify this." She moved toward me and touched my cheek gently with her hand, "I thank you, Little Witch."

I stood mutely, unable to think so near an actual Goddess. Waves of her power washed over me and I struggled to stand still as she carefully handed the white owl to me.

359

"This is Agamemnon," she smiled as she rested the bird on my forearm, "He is Athene's creature here to help. Please keep him company while I am gone."

The owl was huge and perfectly snow-white and it was nearly weightless as it settled comfortably on my arm. Its talons gently grasped my flesh but I felt no pain or discomfort. It felt like I was wearing a bracelet, nothing more.

"What is he?" I smiled as I brushed the back of my hand down the owl's snowy chest, "backup?"

"Backup?" she looked at me curiously, "Oh, humor. No, Athene's owl is witness to tonight's events, as you shall also be. Though you will remain here, you will see and hear all that transpires with your Master Vampire in your world."

I turned to her, smiling sardonically, "I would hardly call his world my world." The owl flapped its graceful wings restlessly then settled once more.

"His world is indeed your world now, Cat," Nemesis remarked, "I must not tarry for you cannot remain here too long." With that her form began to shimmer and become insubstantial. Agamemnon screamed a poignant call as Nemesis disappeared and the floor beneath my feet opened up to reveal the transfusion room below. Indifferently, I looked at my prone form, still and pale against the white sheets of the hospital bed. Strangely, I felt no sadness or desire to return to that form, but I did feel the pain of being separated from Amon. With his silver hair shining softly in the light, his head was bowed as if in prayer and his hands were cradling my left hand. Bishop was moving methodically from one piece of equipment to another and I watched as the tubing that was carrying my blood began to shine a bright amber color. As he collected my Life's Blood in a glass vial, Bishop was startled by a sound behind him. He turned, almost spilling the precious fluid, and gasped as Arathia and Thammuz entered the room. Turning back to his work, he remarked, "You two startled me. I almost spilled Cat's Life's Blood."

"I am sorry, Bishop," Thammuz bowed then turned to Amon, "Your Lordship. Arathia informed me of the witch's recovery and I just came to pay my respects. I had no idea that I would be interrupting such a monumental happening as this."

"You finally decided to take her Life's Blood?" Arathia smiled like a Cheshire cat at Amon. She was practically drooling. Resplendent, as usual, she wore a viciously purple silk gown, snug in just the right places, billowing in the rest. Her jet-black hair was combed straight back from her forehead and her makeup was dramatic, though tasteful. A choker of what had to be real diamonds highlighted her gracefully long neck and delicate earrings completed the look. Arathia, seemingly, was always the picture of perfection.

Amon stood and turned to face the newcomers, never letting go of my hand.

"I am not taking it," he said sternly, "She is giving it. She insisted and I am beginning to regret that I allowed her to do it." The weight of tonight's actions were clearly heavy on his shoulders and I felt a pang of regret that I had insisted on doing this, seeing how it was affecting him.

"She insisted that you take her life?" Arathia gaped dramatically, her hand going to her throat. Her delight was obviously difficult for her to disguise.

"I do not believe she intends to lose her life, Arathia," Thammuz pointed to the equipment, "I believe that these modern medical devices are intended to extract her Life's Blood without taking her life. Am I correct?"

Amon nodded and sighed deeply, "You are, and her Life's Blood has been taken. Now we must attend to her recovery."

I watched from above as Bishop put the amber glowing vial into Amon's hand.

"You do realize that if you bring her back," Arathia exclaimed excitedly, "you may not be fulfilling all the requirements stated in the prophecy?"

"The prophecy never explicitly states that the witch must lose her life," Amon answered calmly, "Just her Life's Blood. Though when the prophecy was first uttered to take Life's Blood meant death, it need not be so now. And in any case, she has technically died." He indicated the softly glowing monitor with its bright green line running straight across the screen. "You can see that her heart no longer beats and she does not breathe."

"Leave her this way," Arathia stepped forward and touched his arm, "This chance to be free of the constraints of your curse will never come again. You may be risking everything to save this mere slip of a human. Is her life worth the possibility of never again being able to move about comfortably in sunlight, of being forced to continue feeding as you now do? Is anyone worth that?"

"I will hear no more of this," Amon tore his arm from her grasp. "She will live, at whatever cost." In his hand he tightly concealed the glowing vial, and moving it behind his back he unwittingly put himself between Arathia and the precious fluid.

As I watched from above, I noticed Winter step into the room below, moving quietly with a look of worry on his face. He closed the door gently then took a chair against the wall and sat down. Suddenly he looked up at the ceiling and I got the odd sensation that he could see me, but surely that was my imagination.

Looking at the owl, I spoke softly, "Well, Agamemnon, if we're to be treated to theater, we might as well be comfortable. As there are no lounging couches like they're supposed to have on Olympus, I guess we'll just have to sit on the floor." Holding the bird carefully aloft, I crossed my legs at the ankles and sat down slowly. I lowered Agamemnon to rest my arm on my knee and he seemed to accept the change. A ripple suddenly rolled through the air and the owl screeched and flapped its wings. Agamemnon's golden eyes glowed suddenly with a warm familiar light. Thinking whatever had passed was gone, I once more turned my attention to what was happening in the room below.

"Cat," Winter whispered.

I looked around but could see nothing but the light and the drama unfolding through the floor. The owl looked at me pointedly.

"Winter where are you?" I called, beginning to think I had imagined it. Looking down, I saw that Winter was still seated in the chair against the wall, his head resting on his chest. He appeared to be sleeping.

Agamemnon squeezed my arm with one claw as if to get my attention.

"Cat, it's me," Winter answered and the bird stepped up my arm to look me in the eye.

I think my other hand flew to my mouth in surprise.

"Winter," I exclaimed, "You're an owl?"

"Actually in this case Agamemnon is allowing me to use his body," the owl answered, "Much like you are allowing Nemesis to use your body."

"So, in the real world, I mean the world down there," I pointed to the floor, "can you turn into an owl?"

The birds golden eyes slowly blinked, then his oval face tilted to look at me, "Where do you think I got the name Winter?"

"Oh man," I smiled then laughed, "You can turn into a Snowy Owl, can't you? Why didn't you say something when you learned that I was given dominion over the owls?"

The bird lifted its wings slightly as if to shrug, "I think I knew on some level the moment I met you that I belonged to you. When I learned that I was one of your creatures, I figured that eventually you would know it too."

"I guess I did feel some connection to you," I admitted, "though I thought it was just because you're a nice guy." Running my hand down the bird's back, I realized how soft yet how powerful the creature was.

Winter laughed, his voice recognizable yet somewhat reedier than normal, "I am a nice guy, 'tite souer, and I am your nice guy."

"You mean that I can summon you as an owl?" I marveled.

The bird nodded its head, "And as a man, of course," it answered, as it sidestepped on my arm for better purchase or a more comfortable position.

"This is cool," I remarked, "So, that's your special vampire ability, turning into an owl?

"Among others," he answered succinctly.

"And what about Chimaera?" I wondered, "What's his specialty?"

"Chimaera is a psychopomp," the bird preened contentedly.

"Psychopomp," I murmured, plowing through my memory, "I should know what that is. What is it exactly?"

"A psychopomp escorts souls between worlds," he answered as if it were obvious.

"So," I reasoned, "that's why he could bring me back after I was strangled?"

"That's right," the bird stretched then settled.

"Amazing," I breathed. "I don't think I'll ever get used to this world. Everything is so surreal, so unreal, and so fantastic. Anyway, Winter, why are you here?"

"Just to check in on you," Winter explained, his golden eyes glowing. "I will have to leave so Agamemnon can return when the drama below really gets going."

"Do you know what's happening? Or what will happen?" I asked excitedly.

Once more the owl closed its eyes wisely, "I know what Agamemnon knows and that is a lot. I can guarantee quite a performance below this night, and not everyone will live to tell about it. But have no fear, Little Sister, you and His Lordship will endure."

"Well," I smiled weakly, "That at least is good to know." Winter flapped his wings gracefully and screeched, "I must return now," he called as the ripple of air slipped past me again. "Agamemnon must have his body to witness the happenings below. And they commence." Agamemnon settled once more and his eyes winked at me then he turned his moon-shaped face to the floor.

Though the monitor below still glowed with the green horizontal flatline, the body on the bed stirred and all conversation stopped suddenly. My normally dark green eyes opened and glowed turquoise, presumably the mixture of Nemesis' crystal blue eyes superimposed over my own. She lifted her arms and pushed the cooling blanket aside then gracefully sat up. No one said a word as she swung her legs over the side of the bed and took in her surroundings. One at a time, she looked at each person in the room as if sizing them up, then she smiled as her eyes came to rest on Amon.

He took two hesitant steps back and gasped, "Who are you and where is Cat?"

"Be calm," Nemesis purred, her voice rich and smoky, "Your witch is safe. She generously offered me the use of her body. She is unusually selfless for a mortal."

"She is," Amon agreed, "Now who are you and what do you want?"

Nemesis raised her arms and stretched cat-like, then stood and removed the needle and tubing from her arm. "You have replaced the witch's blood supply?" she asked Bishop and he nodded mutely. "Good, well, Master Vampire, to answer your first question, I am an emissary, if you will. Certain occurrences have come to the attention of certain deities and they have dispatched me to rectify the situation. I bear the powers of these deities so I am actually many, but for the sake of simplicity, you may call me Nemesis."

"You are an Elder?" Amon raised an eyebrow.

"Indeed," she nodded and turned to Arathia, "Do you not recognize me, Mi Hermanna?"

Arathia's eyes widened and she slowly shook her head, "I am not your sister and you have no right to interfere in the business of man, or of vampire."

"What an interesting statement coming from you," Nemesis smiled wickedly, "I could say the same thing to you, could I not?" Moving fluidly across the room, Nemesis stepped in front of the stricken sorceress and hissed, "You have displeased us greatly."

"I don't know what you're talking about," Arathia stepped backwards and almost bumped into Thammuz.

"Would you like to confess your crimes, Sister?" the Goddess touched Arathia's chin with one finger and the sorceress froze. "No? Then perhaps I should explain, yes? What do you think? Should I tell it as of old, a story perhaps?"

"Be gone, Nemesis," Arathia snarled, "You have no business here. We are about to fulfill a prophecy handed down centuries ago by an Oracle."

"Oh yes," Nemesis said soberly, "An Oracle. I know, but I think an explanation is necessary, don't you?"

"No," Arathia shook her head adamantly, "No, not now." She began chewing on her lower lip, an obvious sign of nervousness.

"Oh, yes," Nemesis smiled and returned to the bed where she perched on the edge, gracefully crossing her legs. She clapped her hands as if calling for attention then added, "Please, everyone, especially you, Warrior, get comfortable for it is time for a tale."

Winter remained in his chair but everyone else moved as if hypnotized to find comfortable seating. Amon moved to sit at the foot of the bed a few feet from Nemesis. Bishop leaned comfortably against the far wall, his hip resting on the cart that had carried the blood. Both Thammuz and Chimaera took seats on a small sofa at the other end of the room, where they were still within earshot but out of the line of fire. Arathia stood frozen to the spot, her face twisted in anger.

Chapter 39

"Should I begin with once upon a time?" Nemesis chuckled, "No, perhaps not, for those tales were fictional fantasies and this story is true. Very well, long, long ago, before even the time of the Druids, we Gods walked among mortals here in this world. We could sometimes be cruel but I like to think that we were mostly benevolent. Mi Hermana, Arathia, was very powerful and was worshipped as a Goddess. Her worshippers offered her grains and flowers to assure good crops and many children. One year a storm destroyed the crops just before harvest and in desperation, her people offered her stones filled with lamb's blood after the autumn slaughter. She approved. So, though originally a fertility goddess, Arathia developed a taste for blood and to win her favor her subjects were forced, after that, to make blood sacrifices. In natural progression, her hunger grew and she soon demanded not just blood, but human blood."

"Stop these lies now," Arathia screamed and threw herself at Nemesis, who calmly raised her hand, sending the angry sorceress tumbling backwards. She landed in a heap near the door and Winter stood and placed himself between her and any means of escape.

"Thank you, Winter," Nemesis nodded at the gesture. "To continue, Arathia's taste for blood became more exotic, if you will, when she first tasted Life's Blood and became intoxicated by its power. After that, her demands were always for Life's Blood and she would not be satisfied by anything less. I believe she nearly destroyed whole villages with her hunger and her cruelty."

Beside Winter, Arathia collected herself, smoothing her black hair and straightening her purple silk gown. Clearly, she was trying to retain what dignity was left to her, so she remained on the floor as if she had intended to take a seat there all along.

Nemesis stood and looked down at her dress and feet then smiled, "This is a nice body, but it's too thin. You should see that your witch eats more, Master Vampire." She ran her hands down her hips, smoothing the silvery satin, " The dress is not as flowing and feminine as what I once wore, but it is flattering for a figure such as this. And I do appreciate the color, as I am quite fond of the moon."

Amon nodded, his eyes alone giving away his unease. It was clear that he thought Nemesis was becoming too comfortable in my body.

"Do not worry, Warrior," Nemesis smiled sympathetically and touched his face, causing me a touch of jealousy, "Your Little Witch will return to you shortly, and she is seeing and hearing all that happens here." She moved away and walked about the room. When she picked up the thread of her story, she paced back and forth, looking much like a college professor addressing a class.

"So," she began again, "When we Gods saw that our time among men was drawing to an end, we decided to leave this world, but Arathia came pleading to us to be allowed to remain. Though some of us disagreed with the decision, it was determined that she should be allowed to stay." Nemesis cleared her throat softly coughing, "But, we took most of her powers with us when we left. She was also forced to agree to one absolute rule. It was decreed that she would not be allowed to take or accept the Life's Blood of any mortal, even if it was offered freely by the donor or another mortal. Of course, words being what they are, Arathia enjoyed the loophole that she could not take Life's Blood but that did not stop her from spilling it and killing and torturing mortals. She just had to waste the precious fluid, but she still got some perverse pleasure from that act. Eventually, she learned that if she could obtain the Life's Blood of a mortal touched by magic, without breaking our rule, she would regain her godhead. Can you imagine? Arathia, here in this world alone with all her powers and no one to stop her? She would have wreaked havoc on the entire human race." Nemesis moved to stand before Amon, her hips touching his knees. She put out her hand, "Cat's fluid, please, Warrior."

Amon hesitantly placed the vial in Nemesis palm and Arathia screamed her disappointment and anger to the heavens. Touching the glass to her forehead, then to her lips, Nemesis whispered, "Blessed be this Life's Blood," then smiled and returned it to Amon. "Keep that safe, Master Vampire."

Continuing her speech, Nemesis spread her hands, "Having retained her ability to see into the future, Arathia foresaw Catherine's birth and that her blood would hold magic. She saw what the mortal

367

could possibly mean to you, Warrior. She realized that the witch's blood could be the key to regaining her powers and she could use you to aid her. By posing as the Oracle, she was able to feed you the prophecy which would put her in the position of receiving Life's Blood touched by magic, without breaking our rule. As a vampire, you are not mortal and can therefore offer the fluid, ostensibly for her to bless," Nemesis explained. Moving to stand before the trembling sorceress who still cowered on the floor, Nemesis crouched and laughed, her laughter melodic and bell-like. "Of course, once she had it in her hand she would have drank it and returned to her former state, that of Goddess, wouldn't you Arathia? Your impatience undid you, Mi Hermana, for when you began your machinations to bring these two together, you thwarted your own plans."

"What do you mean, machinations?" Amon stood and regarded Nemesis, his impatience beginning to show.

"After centuries of waiting for Cat's arrival," Nemesis stood and addressed Amon, "She could not stand for you to wait a normal human lifespan to take Cat's Life's Blood. Being forced to endure another seventy or eighty years for the witch to reach the end of her natural life for you to go to her was more than Arathia could bear. To that end, several years ago, she took a hand in the witch's life when she planned the deaths of Cat's mother and father. Oh, of course, she arranged it to look like an automobile accident, but it was all part of her grand scheme. She wanted the witch separated from friends and family, cut off and left vulnerable, both emotionally and physically. Also, the mugging outside the club? That too was of Arathia's design. She hired those thugs to attack and beat Cat to force you into action. She knew that you would be compelled to step in to protect her and your hopes for the future."

Amon stood stock still, his hands clinching into fists and his eyes burning red. Nemesis stepped before him, shielding Arathia from his look. "Don't worry, Master Vampire, she will pay," she promised. Though the room below was on the basement level of the house, it was clear that everyone there heard the thunder rumbling and the wind screaming outside. Amon, in his anger, was calling down the storm and it was violent.

"So," Nemesis continued, "When you took Cat in, Arathia first sought to insinuate herself between the two of you. Then when she realized the scope of the witch's magic her jealousy gave her tunnel vision for a time and nothing but determining the source of Cat's power mattered. When her attempts failed, she had to admit defeat or risk raising your suspicions. When she realized that you were growing fond of each other, she sought to again control the situation by orchestrating the attempted kidnappings and the assassination attempts. She promised Kasimir your power and your position in payment for his attack on the witch, though she likely would have just destroyed him rather than pay. She fed Sabre, Master Vampire of the Northeast, misinformation, telling him of your increasing power and desire to widen your territories so that he would dispatch his men, Darien and Rowan, to kill Cat. In her desperation, she had convinced herself that she or you would be able to reach the witch in time to retrieve her precious fluid. All along she has been working quietly and under the guise of friend and counsel. Ironically, by forcing you into Cat's life while she is still of a desirable age, Arathia unwittingly planted the seeds of romance. When that attraction was consummated, when Cat's power rose to meet yours, Warrior, the impact was so strong and so loud that it stirred us. We Elders were wakened from our slumber when your powers merged and I was sent to discover the cause of the disturbance. Imagine my surprise when I found Arathia in the middle of all this deceit and manipulation? Still after all these many ages, working and scheming to get what she wanted."

"Long ago Arathia told me that she had once been worshipped as a Goddess," Amon murmured, "She neglected to say what type of Goddess, and she seemed so genuine that I never thought to ask. I've been such a fool!"

"This is all a lie," Arathia whined pathetically, then she turned, her expression full of anger, "I have been nothing but a friend to Sin and the witch, and a willing advisor to his Council of the Five."

"Please, Arathia," Nemesis begged sarcastically, "would you like to try that denial again, with a little more conviction? I'm sure they will all believe you the second time."

"You gave the witch her powers didn't you?" Arathia snapped, "You bestowed your gifts on her and caused her power to challenge Sin's."

"I did," Nemesis agreed, "Or rather, we did. If you had any idea of the deities that willingly donated their powers to see your work undone, you would tremble in fear and hold your tongue. We

Elders knew that she would likely need these powers to survive your schemes. And we needed to quicken the warrior's powers."

"What does that mean?" Amon asked quickly.

"And why do you keep referring to Sin as the warrior?" Arathia added.

"Soon," Nemesis cooed mysteriously, "All in good time. So, Mi Hermana, your plans have come undone and your deceit brought into the light. Your time draws to an end, as does mine." With that Nemesis touched Amon's face and looked at him fondly, "Your witch will return momentarily. Her powers, our gifts, are hers and will remain so until her time is finished unless she chooses to deny or return them. As you of all people should know, once the Gods gift you, they do not rescind their gifts. I would ask one thing of you, Warrior."

"What is it?" Amon breathed uneasily.

Leaning very close to him, Nemesis whispered just loud enough for all to hear, "Do our bidding."

With that Nemesis returned to the bed and resumed a prone position. "The prophecy still stands," she announced, "though you may wish to ask yourself if the conditions have indeed been met. As Arathia is so fond of saying, the devil is in the details." She closed her eyes and suddenly the room grew still. No one breathed for a moment then everyone looked at each other in disbelief.

Bishop raced to the bedside and hooked up the monitors again, checking my body for a pulse or any sign of respiration. When he found no movement, he slammed his fist sharply on my sternum and began CPR. Though still watching from above, I felt the impact of the blow but still had no desire to return to my body.

"Will she be alright?" Amon asked brusquely as he approached the bedside.

"I don't know," Bishop answered between breaths, "She's still artificially cold, but she's been dead a long time."

"I believe that time ceases when one in among the Gods," Thammuz offered as he stood and moved from the sofa, "Or in this case, in the presence of a Goddess."

"I hope you're right," Bishop shook his head and flipped a switch on the defibrillator. A high pitched whine announced its powering and finally a series of short beeps signaled its readiness. Bishop lifted the paddles and squeezed clear goo on them then directed

Amon to tear the front of the dress. When my chest was bared, my white lacey bra shining in the light, Bishop placed the paddles on either side of my heart and pressed the buttons. Though I saw my body jump under the jolt I was not drawn back into it.

"Nothing," Bishop exclaimed then added, "We have to bring her body temperature back up. Your Lordship, flip that blanket over and turn the switch to warm. She needs a moment to heat up."

I felt a rush of warm air surrounding me as the blanket began to glow a soft red. Agamemnon stirred uneasily on my arm until Nemesis returned then he leapt into the air and circled the light, coming to rest once more on the Goddess' shoulder.

"I thank you for your generosity, witch," Nemesis smiled. "Now your warrior awaits you."

"May I ask you a question, Nemesis?" I dared.

"Ask what you will," she regarded me wisely as she stroked Agamemnon's breast.

"Why is this happening to me?" I struggled for understanding, "I mean why me specifically? Why is my blood magic? Why am I so important that a Master Vampire would know of my birth and subsequent life?"

"You do not know your heritage?" She raised an eyebrow. "You were not informed of your birthright?"

"My parents only alluded to some catastrophe whenever I asked about our family. Their sadness, when I brought the subject up, caused me to stop asking for a time, then they were gone and it was too late."

"I see," She drew herself up and nodded wisely, "very well, in payment for your generosity, I will tell you what you wish to know. Your mother, like your grandmother and her mother and grandmother before her, was a natural born witch. Your two aunts were both witches as well, though perhaps not as powerful as your mother would have been. For some reason, your mother chose not to embrace her magic, as was her right, and your aunts and your grandmother resented her decision greatly. They accused her of being a traitor to the family and eventually disavowed her. When your grandmother passed from her earthly life to the next, your aunts contacted your mother, but since the funeral was one of, let us say unorthodox ritual, your mother would not attend. Your aunts disowned your mother and struck her name from the family tree."

"That's horrible," I gasped, realizing that there had existed a totally unknown and complicated side to my mother. She had always seemed so simple and so sweet.

"Your father, on the other hand, had the opposite situation," She shook her head. "Born the seventh son of a seventh son, with a caul on his head yet, he was blessed with the ability to see and communicate with the spirits of the dead. He could predict when a person would pass on, and he could speak to and understand wild creatures. His family, being simple and extremely religious people, made fun of him, then vilified him when his sight was recognized as psychic power. They believed he had dealings with the devil and kicked him out of the family. So you see, coming from where your parents did, they could not help but infuse their offspring with their considerable gifts."

"But I've never spoken to animals or the dead, I had no idea that real witches existed until Amon came into my life," I exclaimed.

"A witch's power comes to her when she is ripe and when it is ready. Your time is now, Cat." Nemesis smiled sagely.

"I don't understand," I added before Nemesis could disappear. "Would the magic of my Life's Blood have worked on any vampire or was it specifically meant for Amon?"

"Your Life's Blood would have brought about certain freedoms in any vampire," she nodded as she continued to stroke Agamemnon's breast. "However, only Amon had the psychic connection with you to feel it when you were born and to find and protect you during your life. Ironically, had Arathia not given Amon the prophecy, he might never have known to look for you. He might have felt something at your birth and during your lifetime, but he would not have known what those feelings were. Arathia unwittingly brought you two together, in spite of her intentions. Now, your warrior awaits."

"Are you sure I'm to go back?" I asked, "I don't feel drawn back, maybe I don't know how."

"You know the way," she nodded and then shimmered into nothing.

Suddenly I was alone and panic hit me for a moment before I could think to open my mind and call for Chimaera. He responded instantly.

Catherine, follow my voice. I will lead you back.

I can't see you, Chimaera.

Just follow the sound of my voice, you have done this before. Trust me, Cat.

His words drew me from the light and into the darkness. My feet carried me without conscious thought and I hurried to keep up with Chimaera's voice. Below, I could hear Bishop ask Amon why Nemesis referred to him as the warrior and Amon answered that everyone knew he had been a soldier.

"I felt she meant more than just that," Bishop remarked, then I heard him say," Let's try again."

After a moment Bishop called, "Clear," and I felt a tremendous force on my chest and had to stop and catch my breath. Chimaera's voice grew distant and I rushed forward as soon as I could move again.

I heard nothing but moments later the force slammed into my chest again and everything stopped. Silence and stillness surrounded me and I was enveloped in darkness. Suddenly, I thought to breathe and gasped a ragged breath through the pain in my chest. My lungs burned back to life as I struggled to fill them with fresh air. A mask came down over my nose and mouth and air was forced into me. After a moment I could hear my heart beating, a little fast at first then settling into a comfortable rhythm. I opened my eyes and the room swam back into my vision. Amon stood beside my bed looking quite sober and ragged. His head was bowed. I was too weak to keep my eyes open, they closed heavily, but I could speak.

"Amon, you look like Hell," I murmured as I struggled to move the mask off of my face.

"Catherine," he exclaimed, the relief obvious in his voice, "Thank the goddess you are back."

"I'll tell her if I see her again," I smiled weakly, pleased that I could still joke.

"Did you say Amon?" I heard Thammuz ask with an odd edge to his voice.

Somewhere in the room I recognized Arathia's voice as she hissed and snarled, chanting, "No, no, no. It can't be, it can't be."

"I'm sorry," I whispered, "I didn't mean to. It just slipped out, I'm so sorry."

"It is all right," Amon reassured me, holding my hand. "My days of denying my identity are over."

"You mean that you are Amon?" Thammuz gasped, "THE Amon?"

"No, no, no," Arathia cried again, "he cannot be Amon, Amon is dead, long gone if he ever even existed. He cannot be Amon, no, he cannot. I do not believe it."

I heard murmuring and gasps as I strained to open my eyes. They simply would not obey me.

"What am I missing?" I whined, "What did he mean by THE Amon? And why is Arathia so frightened that I can hear it in her voice?"

"Little Witch," Chimaera explained, "Amon is the stuff of history, and many believed him a myth like King Arthur. Legend had it that a knight, a mighty warrior, fought with such skill and such passion that when he was wounded and lay bleeding on the field of battle Apollo himself, impressed by the man's prowess, descended and touched him, bestowing on the warrior many wondrous powers. I don't remember all of them, but the most important, I believe was the Hand of Destruction."

"Meaning what, exactly?" I murmured, eyes still not responding.

"It is said that Amon could destroy an enemy, not merely kill but literally destroy, by simply touching him with his left hand. And only the Hand of Destruction could destroy a deity in human form." There was a moment's silence then Chimaera gasped, "Oh God and Goddess, it is you! You are Amon! In your left hand you wield the Hand of Destruction and in Catherine's left hand she wields the Healing Hand. Oh, I see it now, don't you? The two of you complete each other. Together you are balance and equanimity. Her light balances your darkness."

Silence echoed in my ears as no one dared speak.

Arathia began whimpering again and her words were becoming panicked and choked. "No, no, no. This cannot be, they would not do this to me. They have no right, no,no,no."

"Amon?" I clutched blindly at his hand, "What did Nemesis mean when she told you to do their bidding?"

He sighed loudly, "I will see to it, Beloved. You rest." He released my hand and I found I held the vial of Life's Blood in my grasp, at least that's what it felt like it was. I heard his footsteps move away from the bed and fought to open my eyes. I managed a brief glimpse to see Amon approaching Arathia. Her eyes were the size of dinner plates and she kept moving backwards until her back was against the wall. Anger replaced her fear and she suddenly became still, her head held up proudly and her shoulders straightened. Her gaze penetrating, she held her ground as Amon moved up and placed his left palm on the side of her face almost tenderly. He whispered, "Time to go home," then I could hold my eyelids open no longer. Shrinking from the terror and despair I felt in Arathia's final shriek, I was grateful that I could not see her demise. I felt power prickling along my skin and recognized the movement of Bishop covering me with a soft sheet. Apparently, Amon had dispatched Arathia back to her Elders as they had commanded. I now understood why he had silenced me when I had witnessed his use of the Hand of Destruction.

When he returned, he took my hand and kissed my forehead.

"So if you're THE Amon," I smiled. "What happened to you? Why were you hiding your identity?"

I felt him lean closer and heard his heart beating for me, "When I was made a vampire," he said softly, "my powers disappeared, or at least I thought they had, because I was unworthy to wield them. All these centuries I thought Apollo must have taken his gifts back. It was not until you came into my life and your power challenged mine, that I felt those powers stirring, returning to life. I now realize that I had denied my powers because I felt unworthy to use them. I suppose I was judging myself and of course I found myself wanting."

He brushed his fingers down my face and touched my lips gently.

"How do you feel, Kitty Cat?" he breathed.

"Tired," I murmured, and drew in a ragged breath, "and a little sore. Arathia is gone?"

"Yes, you're safe, Little Sister," Winter stepped near the bed. "Nice to see you again."

"My owl," I sighed, "I wish I could see your golden eyes, but my eyes are too heavy to open. Come." I held out my palm and felt the familiar curve of Winter's cheek in my hand. I smiled and touched his hair. "Thank you for keeping me company."

"Anything for My Lady," he nodded gently. "Being here in Louisiana, I don't often shapeshift into my species of bird, since this is not my natural territory, but I am at your beckon call and will do so at your bidding."

"It's okay, Winter," I breathed, "I understand. I wouldn't want someone to shoot you as a rare bird and Louisiana is full of rednecks with rifles."

"Thank you, My Lady," Winter bowed and stepped away.

Chimaera took his place and took my hand in his.

"Chimaera," I smiled, "I have got to stop following you around."

"You have got to stop dying, Little Witch," he chuckled, "I'm not sure any of us could go through this again."

"I can't disagree with you," I chuckled, "But thank you for leading me back, I'd have been lost without you."

"It was my pleasure," he bent forward and placed a soft kiss on my forehead. "I am at your service."

"What creature do you shift into?" I asked, refusing to release his hand. Realizing that I had never seen him in animal form, I tried imagining what he most closely resembled. With my fingertips I traced the curves of his face, trying to discern his creature beneath the smooth flesh.

"Would you care to guess?" he challenged lightly, stroking his hand down my wrist.

"Hmm," I thought aloud, "let's see, with your pretty boy looks and personality? My first guess would be a peacock, but no, maybe a panther or a tiger?"

"Not a bad guess," I could hear the smile in Chimaera's voice, "but no, I am pack."

"You are one of Amon's wolves?" I marveled, "There is some symmetry in that, and heaven knows you are a wolf." I couldn't help but chuckle as I finally released his hand. Lying back on the bed, I sighed deeply, the weariness suddenly washing over me again.

"Wow," I exclaimed softly, "this is just like the end of The Wizard of Oz, when Dorothy comes back and everyone is surrounding her bed and telling her how they missed her. Considering how nice he's been, I guess now I'll have to change Chimaera from the Captain of the flying monkeys."

"Excuse me?" he hissed.

"Never mind, Chimaera," I dismissed him with a wave of my hand, "You can keep the monkeys."

"You need rest, Little One, you're not making sense," Amon spoke tenderly, soothingly. "I would suggest you feed but I know you would fight me on the matter."

"I'm too tired to feed," I answered weakly, my breath already becoming deeper and more regular, "and too tired to fight. Just let me sleep for a little while then we'll go strolling down the cobblestone streets of the Vieux Carré. And I am making perfect sense about the Wizard of Oz. You've just never seen the movie."

"Sleep," Amon commanded and I could not resist his power. "Rest now, you are safe and I am here."

Chapter 40

As I gave up the struggle and let sleep take me, my last waking thought was that I was so exhausted, surely I would sleep dreamlessly, needing the comfort of deep and blissfully mindless sleep. Unfortunately, once more that was not to be the case, for almost the moment I fell asleep the scene I had witnessed from above began replaying itself in my mind. So far removed from everything while I watched, I had apparently been protected from the painful emotions that I would have normally experienced had I actually been there. Now these emotions, like demons, came tearing back through my mind, shredding my heart into little pieces when I went over Nemesis's words. Arathia had my parents killed to get to me. It was my fault that my parents had died! My anguish was like a chain wrapped around me and I fought and struggled to break free. Though I could not fully waken, I did surface enough to overhear Amon talking with Bishop.

"See how she tosses and turns," Amon spoke with worry in his voice, "She is not resting when she fights like that. Can you not give her something to make her sleep more soundly?"

"In her weakened state, it would be risky to give her a drugs," Bishop replied, "There is no way to determine what effect the medication will have on her when she is so depleted. Perhaps you could take her pain?"

"I can try," I heard Amon answer, "but this may not be the type of pain that I can take away."

He must have passed his hand over me because for a few moments I felt calmer, more settled. Then the horror of what Arathia had done to me, how she had ripped the fabric of my life, drove over me like a freight train and I cried at the waste and cruelty. My emotions were so raw that I had no control over them. My grief, my despair, was as intense as it had been when my parents were killed. It was as if I was reliving my parents' deaths all over again. I struggled to wake myself, to escape the nightmare.

378

"Cat," Amon's calm voice sliced through the anguish, "You must not blame yourself for what has happened. You are not responsible for the deaths of your parents."

"Don't you see?" I cried, "I am! I am responsible! It was because of this stuff, my Life's Blood, that Arathia had them killed. If I didn't have this they would still be alive."

"You cannot shoulder this burden, Little One," he murmured to me like you would to a panicked horse. "It is not yours to bear. Arathia alone is responsible for your parents' deaths. Put the blame where it belongs, Beloved."

I sobbed, "If only I had known what Arathia wanted, I would have gladly given my Life's Blood if she would have let my parents live. Hell, I'd have given it daily."

"The Gods knew this," Amon's voice soothed me, "That is why they forbade Arathia from taking or even accepting it from a willing donor. They knew that you would do anything to protect those you loved and that it would make you vulnerable to Arathia's wiles."

"But if I could have found a way," I argued, "they would still be alive, don't you see? I failed them."

"Cat, listen to me carefully," he commanded, "Arathia was never meant to possess your Life's Blood. You remember what Nemesis said about how wicked and cruel she was when she was a Goddess? And how she would have wreaked havoc on humanity if she had regained her powers while she was here alone? Cat, it was right how things worked out, although if I could I might bring Arathia back and destroy her all over again for the attacks she orchestrated on you, especially the first one that put you in the hospital."

For a moment, I recalled Nemesis's words about how Arathia had hired the men to attack and beat me, I guess maybe the rape was their idea. A part of my soul mourned, feeling that if my blood had been normal my parents would still be alive and probably bouncing my children, their grandchildren, on their knees. The ghosts of my parents, wailing their disappointment at me, scampered about in my dreamscape. Wispy forms of infants, toddlers, children and teenagers shimmered around me weeping, their voices like reeds rustling in the wind. The whole family of my regret, the lives that would never be, haunted my soul.

"Amon," I breathed sadly, "Please wake me up. I've had enough of this torment and wish to waken, but I cannot by myself. Please rouse me, Amon,"

"I cannot, pet," he replied, his voice growing fainter, "You must rest, your body is weak and sleep is the best medicine. Sleep, Cat."

"Amon, no!" I panicked, "I can't rest with all these emotions and all these ghosts, swirling around me! Please, please, wake me up." Tossing and turning on the bed I struggled to wake myself, without success.

"Go deeper," Amon demanded, "Go past the pain and slip into the peaceful void. Sleep, now, Cat."

"But the prophecy," I complained even as I felt myself tumble deeper into the darkness, "I wanted to see it fulfilled. Please, I want to wake up."

"Later, Little One, now sleep," His voice disappeared as I finally reached the restful, calm waters of dreamless slumber.

His words must have worked for the next thing I knew I was waking up alone in his coffin and I was furious. The anger I felt was like a living thing and I knew just where to direct it. My body felt leaden and slow and I struggled to clear my mind of the cobwebs of my dreams. My hand still clutched the glass vial and I slid it into the satin lining of the coffin. Peering up from under heavy lids, I saw Amon standing beside the coffin looking down at me, that mask of concern firmly pasted on his face. I raised my hand, beckoning, and he crouched down beside me. Sliding my fingers along his jaw, I whispered, "Amon."

"Yes, Cat," he answered innocently.

"Don't you EVER do that to me again!" I snarled and slapped him hard across the face, sobbing, "When I pleaded, I begged you to wake me that's what I expected you to do." His eyes watered and his expression was one of utter shock. He idly touched the side of his face with his hand. Tears sprang to my eyes as I recalled the painful dreams.

His face grew granite and he forcefully grabbed my wrist, "You dare to strike me, witch?" he growled. "Have you lost your mind?"

"I don't know, but I am so angry with you right now that I can't see straight," I pulled my hand away from him and started to get up, still sobbing. He threw an arm across my chest and pinned me down in the satin. "These feelings, they're ripping me apart," I cried.

"Your body needed rest," he spoke angrily, "I would not have you risk your health and push yourself beyond safe limits just to see the prophecy fulfilled."

"It wasn't your decision to make," I exclaimed indignantly.

"Indeed, it was my decision," he answered, "And it was in your best interest to rest."

"You don't understand," I stilled weakly beneath his arm, "I was powerless against the demons of my dreams! The ghosts of my parents, of the children I'll never have were torturing me. You could have saved me. If you had roused me from my sleep like I asked, they would have disappeared."

"I am sorry for whatever you had to go through, what anguish you had to endure," he replied softly, "But you had to sleep, your body was demanding it."

"Well," I remarked as I pushed his arm off of my chest and sat up, "From now on, be advised. I don't take orders from my body, or anyone else for that matter!" Using the edges of my hands, I wiped the tears of blood from my cheeks.

"Cat, I," Amon stopped in mid-sentence, looking me in the eye, "I, oh." His eyes were wide in amazement and I could read confusion in his expression.

"What is it?" I snapped, for he was looking at me like I had sprouted a second head.

"Cat, your eyes," he murmured, slowly shaking his head.

"What about my eyes?" I demanded, looking at my blood-streaked hands, "Are they bloodshot or something? I know I look horrible when they're bloodshot, they look like a couple of pimento-stuffed olives in a martini, all red and green."

"No, it's not that," he answered carefully, "they're white."

"Good, I'm glad they aren't bloodshot!" I considered for a moment, "Then what's wrong?"

"Your eyes are white, Cat," he repeated softly, almost reverently, "You no longer have green eyes. They are now white."

Shaking my head in disbelief, I chuckled, "People don't have white eyes, Amon. Don't tease me."

Before I could say another word, he scooped me up in his arms and carried me quickly from the room. The torn fabric of the ruined gray dress flapped in the rush of air that surrounded us as he nearly flew up the stairs and into his bedroom. Not stopping in the outer room, he carried me straight through to the bathroom and gently deposited me on the floor before the mirror.

"Oh, no," I whispered at the sight of my image there before me. Amon was not teasing, my irises were now silvery-white, seemingly filled with what looked like tiny frosted white branches. Though my vision was normal, my pupils had gone from the normal black to frosted gray. If I had thought once that Chimaera's pale blue eyes made him appear blind, I now knew that I had him beat. The effect of frosty white irises in my pale face with my blonde hair was shocking. "I look like something out of The Omega Man," I moaned, "Do you think its permanent?" I turned to Amon and he startled a little when my eyes met his.

"I do not know," he shook his head, "but I'm guessing that something as dramatic as this is a mark of the Gods, probably from Nemesis using your body. I would expect it to be permanent and it may also mean that you now wield another power, yet unknown."

"Amon," I recognized the silvery-white color of Nemesis in my eyes, "I'm the only one that actually saw Nemesis as she truly appears. Could this be a side effect from that? My eyes are now the color of her hair, her skin, and of Athene's owl, Agamemnon."

"It is possible that seeing her as she is, in all her divine glory as it were, affected you physically," he reasoned. "Only time will tell, I suppose."

I sighed and bowed my head, "One thing's certain, I can't very well be seen looking like this. People will think I'm a circus freak, and at this point I'm not sure I'd disagree."

"Cat," Amon lifted my chin with his hand and still visibly shied when he looked into my eyes, "If anything you are more beautiful than ever. And of course you are safe to be seen by anyone in my household, though we may have to construct a cover story for Lily and Lucius."

I chuckled at the thought of how Lily would react to seeing me like this. "Maybe I should stay away from them for a while until I adjust to this new development," I suggested, "And let's face it, you can't even look at me without blinking in surprise, I don't think your choir singing Baptists are ready to see this. Let's wait and see how long it takes you to adjust, Master Vampire."

He moved up behind me and turned me by the shoulders. Though he did not flinch this time when he looked at my eyes, I could still see an involuntary amazement pass across his face like a fleeting shadow. Pressing his lips to mine, he kissed me solidly, then pulled away. He looked me in the eyes once more and the surprise was gone.

"I am sorry that I forced you to sleep," he murmured as he ran his hands down my arms and moved his body closer to mine, "There was nothing else to do to help you. Sleep was the only thing to restore your strength. I did not realize that you were not alone in your dreams"

"Well," I nodded and pressed my body to the length of his, "I will forgive you this one time, Warrior. But don't let it happen again. It's pretty safe to assume when I ask for help, I need it. Please don't deny me, if you care for me at all."

He moved aside the length of my hair, lifting it from my shoulder and exposing my neck. Gently he lowered his mouth to my throat where he laid fiery kisses on my skin. Moving up my neck, he nibbled the skin just beneath my ear, then whispered, "Care for you, Precious? I worship you."

Feeling deliciously wicked, I borrowed a line from a movie. "Worshipping is best done on your knees," I decreed in a haughty tone.

Amon's head flew up at my words and his eyes twinkled with desire when he realized my intent. He kneeled reverently before me and I pushed one high-heeled foot onto his chest. Taking my foot into his hands, he slipped off my shoe and bowed to kiss my instep then my ankle, his hand sliding up my calf.

"How do I get into My Lady's good graces?" he smiled wickedly as his hands moved up my legs, sliding up my outer thighs.

"Is that what you seek, Warrior?" I writhed beneath his touch, "To find your way into my good graces?"

"It is, Lady," he nodded as his fingers slipped into the waistband of my panties. "Perhaps they might be here." He added as he slowly drew the lace down my legs then lifted one foot after the other to remove the lingerie. He brought them to his nose and breathed deeply, smiling up at me from beneath long dark lashes.

I was speechless as my heart began pounding and my body began its sensual stirrings.

"Alas, not here," Amon looked sadly down at the crush of lace in his hand, "I should have to continue my search." He tossed the panties over his shoulder and returned his hands to my thighs. Bunching up the fabric of my dress, he drew it up, exposing my naked heat.

Gently nudging my legs apart, he lowered his mouth to my most intimate parts and my knees began to quiver with excitement. His tongue darted into my depths and I gasped as the pressure of his teeth touched my mound. After a few moments of his mouth nuzzling and devouring my velvet folds, he pulled away and shook his head,

"I think I was close," he grinned, "But I did not quite reach them."

"You were very close," I gasped at the burning need to fill the void he left when he moved his mouth.

"Perhaps they are hidden deeper," He purred as he slid first one finger then two into me, "Maybe I can find them with my fingers."

I moaned and rested my hands behind me, leaning my weight on the vanity.

"Perhaps you can," I murmured. He slid his fingers in and out of me, my juices coating his hand and smearing the inside of my thighs. My need was quickly turning into a demand. My pulse was racing and my legs were threatening to turn to Jell-O beneath me. "Or perhaps my good graces can't be reached by mere fingers," I added as I gently pulled him up, then ripped open his jeans. "Perhaps something longer is required," I teased. His stiff member bounced free as I pushed his pants down his hips. Taking in the beautiful sight of his turgid length, I cupped his balls in my hand and squeezed gently. His eyes rolled back in his head then he suddenly lifted my hips and drove himself between my legs. My heat tightened around him and he thrust his smooth hard length into me again and again. Driving me back against the bathroom wall he shoved his pelvis forward then pulled his member nearly out of me. I wanted him so badly that it hurt everywhere. My nerves burned, my muscles clinched and my mind went spinning with desire for him. He held my bottom with one hand and opened the front of my ripped dress with the other. Tearing off my lace bra, he tossed it away and locked his mouth on my nipple, sucking and circling it with his tongue. Coming up from beneath the swell of my breast, he ran his tongue over my flesh then paused to look up at me. The desire, the hunger was evident in those black eyes and I silently nodded my assent. Pausing for one brief, delicious moment, he smiled then slid his teeth into the tender flesh of my breast. The pain toppled me over the edge and the orgasm clamped my muscles down hard on his length. He thrust in time with his sucking and I went crazy with the sensations that bombarded my mind. Amon drank briefly from my breast then raised his head to howl at the heavens. As he thrust once more, then twice, he shoved hard against my womb then emptied himself into my clutching velvet folds. I bucked shamelessly beneath him as a second wave rushed over me. Panting, he leaned his weight into me, his hair falling across my shoulder.

"I believe sir," I breathed with my sultriest voice, "that you are, even at this moment, in my good graces again."

"What a joy to find them," he smiled into my bare breast, idly licking my skin and flicking my nipple with the tip of his tongue. His member throbbed and moved within me. "And what a delight to search for them."

"Don't you think we should," I smiled, "Oh I don't know, maybe go fulfill a prophecy or something?"

"I am not done with you yet, witch," Amon said sternly, moving his pelvis gently against my abdomen.

"Amon," I shrugged, "I am spent, everything about me has turned to liquid. I am completely undone."

He lowered my feet to the floor, sliding out of me, then turned me in his arms. Placing my hands on the vanity, he lowered his torso across my back and slid his hands down my ribs, wadding the length of my dress up as far as my waist. Catching my aching breasts with his fingers, he lifted their weight and pinched my nipples. My blood roared in my ears and the aching muscles of my womb throbbed in anticipation as his length gently stirred against the inside of my thigh. I was surprised that I could stand. Pushing me down on the sink, he spread my legs and shoved himself painfully inside me. My insides thrummed and sang and a raw need returned with a vengeance. As he bent over me, doggie style, he touched my breasts again, setting off a rush of erotic fireworks. I drove myself backward against him and he pushed me forward, demanding control. Putting his hands on my hips, he purposely slowed his movements and denied me his touch. Only his length slid in and out of my wetness, his hands directing the motion. My whole world spiraled into the sensations at my center and everything else vanished. He was intentionally keeping me teetering on the edge of satisfaction and I was growing frantic in my need. Every time he slid smoothly into me, I expected more of a force, more demanding, but he refrained, teasing and titillating me. Amon was driving me wild.

"Now, Witch," he purred as he leaned over my back, "Will you ever again dare to strike me?"

"If I say maybe or yes," I practically wept and laughed simultaneously, "you'll just walk away won't you?"

"Oh, I can almost guarantee it," he hissed and slid one hand up my ribs where he stopped and rested it just below my breast.

My swollen, aching breasts physically yearned for his touch. The heat in my abdomen and between my legs was threatening to incinerate me. "Fine, then" I whispered, "I'm sorry I did it and I'll never dare to strike you again."

"I cannot feel the truth of your words, Little One," he moaned, "Open your mind to me."

As I envisioned the walls surrounding my thoughts crumbling, Amon grabbed me hard and pistoled into my throbbing center. I screamed in delicious pain. He pulled roughly down on my shoulders and snarled in anger as he came and I climaxed again and again around his length. Holding me tightly against him, he touched my lower back, near my left hip and I felt a sharp burning sensation.

"What the hell is that?" I gasped in pain and tried to move away from him.

His grip was vice-like and he refused to release me. "I read your mind, Kitty Cat, and you lied." He hissed, "You are not sorry for your behavior."

"Alright, damn it," I complained, "I told you what you wanted to hear. I'm not sorry, and I'd do it again. You pissed me off!"

"You temper will be a problem," he spoke with venom in his voice.

"What have you done to me?" I tried to touch my lower back and he held my hand away.

"I have marked you," he boasted and my fury rose.

"What the devil?" I scrambled beneath his weight, "another Mark of Penitence? You know how well the first one worked on me."

"No, no, Kitty," he ran a finger down my spine, "this is a mark of obedience. You now bear one side of a triangle and you have two more chances. When the triangle is complete it will cause you physical pain to displease me."

"What?" I cried, "How dare you? You're going to send me back to my world branded like a horse? I am not chattel, you know. I'm going to have a hard enough time passing for normal, looking like this. Heaven knows I'm going to need contact lenses."

Finally releasing his hold, he eased out of me then he turned me to face him. I still caught a slight flinching when he looked at my eyes. "What's this about sending you back to your world?" he demanded.

"Come on," I sighed, "Don't deny that you've been deciding what's to become of me. You have what you needed from me, now what do you do with me? I've certainly been thinking about it."

"You're right," he nodded, "I have thought long and hard on the matter. I was going to give you the option of returning to your former life. I believe that I could wipe the memories of the time spent here in my world from your mind. I could return you to the hospital, unconscious, and you would recover from your coma in due time. Any stray memories or thoughts of this world would be attributed to your head injury."

"And what about my power?" I asked, barely daring to hope how this conversation might end, "what would become of my magic?"

"Since you would have no conscious knowledge of it, I believe it would sleep," he explained softly, "I think it would go dormant. You might have a few psychic inklings, maybe catch a friend's errant thought, but even that could be written off as a result of your brain damage."

"And this is what you want me to do?" I looked down at my hands and held my breath.

"Of course not," he exclaimed, "I don't want to lose you, but I am willing to let you make the decision."

The enormity of his offer lay heavily on me momentarily. That I might return to my previous existence, that I could resume my old life, the possibility was tantalizing. The decision rose to the surface quickly, even as I opened my mouth to speak.

"I cannot "unknow" what I know now," I shook my head, " the life I once had has been ripped away from me and I'm thinking now that that is for the best. Anyway, it's done and it can't be undone."

He wrapped me in his arms and hugged me tightly.

"So what happens to me now?" I nearly cried, bloody tears likely looking hideous now in my white eyes.

Amon burst out laughing and pulled me into his arms. "You will remain here with me. You will be mine always." He kissed my eyes one at a time, gently licking the tears from beneath them.

"I don't understand," I choked on emotion, "why would you want me here? I'm nothing but a mortal, an inconvenience in your world. Let's face it, I'm not the easiest person to get along with. Now that you're going to be a super vampire, if the prophecy works out, why would you want me around? I'm a pain in the ass!"

He laughed again, this time the happiness reaching fully into his black eyes. "You are right, Witch," he smiled ruefully. "You are indeed a pain in the ass, and you have much to learn about living in my world, but I would walk through fire for you, Cat. I love you, and your spirit, your force, intrigues me. You are unlike any mortal I have ever known and I do not want to ever lose you."

"You're going to have to make some adjustments in your archaic thinking, Vampire," I moaned and touched the mark on the small of my back. "In my world, a gentleman does not brand a lady to gain her obedience. They live as equals, a team. Both are entitled to their opinions and their emotions. And a gentleman does not use sex as a weapon to punish a lady for a slight transgression."

"Only during sex, when I may have you at my mercy, do I have your complete attention, Cat," he remarked. "I am sorry, but I am accustomed to a certain amount of respect and obedience. No one has ever dared do what you did to me. Perhaps I overreacted, but you have to remember that I am a ruler, a leader, and my word has always been law. I am not comfortable with anyone challenging me, in any way."

"Yeah," I exhaled slowly as I slipped my arms around his neck, "like I need to make a mental note of that!"

He kissed me and brushed my hair back off my forehead, looking deeply into my eyes.

"Witch," he smiled and slowly shook his head, "you take my breath away."

"I'll never in this world compete with you, you wickedly handsome man," I laid my head on his chest. "Now I think a shower would be in order, and maybe some fresh clothes before we see to your, uh, transformation?"

"If you will allow me," he bowed slightly, "I shall choose some appropriate attire, something that will look fetching when we walk down Bourbon Street."

"I could definitely get used to you choosing my wardrobe," I smiled as I peeled the tattered gray dress off, recalling what a dismal chore I had always found choosing the day's attire to be.

Stepping into the shower stall, I turned on the water and let the heat soak my sore muscles and trembling limbs. I washed my hair and lathered my skin then just stood and relaxed beneath the spray. Turning Amon's words over in my mind, I considered. Had I made the right choice, could I have returned to my previous, normal life? At length I decided that this world, as terrifying as it sometimes was, had become too important to me. Knowing now of the reality of these fantastic creatures, I could not go back to not knowing. This world held too much fascination, too much possibility and I had to admit it, I found that the idea of living without Amon bothered me more than I could bear. Besides, Arathia had so effectively minimized my family and circle of friends and acquaintances, that I had very little to go back to. Had there been a memorial service for me after my disappearance, I'm sure I would have been horrified at the few people in attendance. Most attending, I'm sure, would have been simply curious or religious do-gooders who felt a need to see me on my way.

Chapter 41

As I stepped out of the shower, I realized that I had left my Life's Blood downstairs in Amon's coffin and panic that it was unprotected hit me. I hurriedly wrapped a towel around myself and rubbed another towel through my hair. As I stepped out of the bathroom I saw that Amon stood, dressed impeccably as always, bearing clothes for me. He wore a black satin shirt with soft billowy sleeves and banded collar. His gray brocade vest was highlighted by pearl buttons and a white gold Celtic dragon rested at his throat. His thick silver hair was woven into a braid and secured by a strip of black leather. His black leather boots were knee high and accented with silvered roses hand-tooled into the shafts. He was gorgeous and my breath caught in my throat, my heart doing a little somersault at the sight of him.

"My Lady," he smiled and offered me the hanger he held.

"I'll be right back," I held up my index finger and grumbled as I ran past him.

"Cat, what is it?" he called after me.

"Just a minute," I answered as I flew bare-footed down the hall, down the stairs and burst into the coffin room. Relief washed over me when I saw that the room was empty and I rushed to shove my hand down the satin lining of Amon's coffin. As my fingers touched the glass vial, I started breathing again and brought the precious fluid up to my lips and kissed it.

"Thank the Goddess that you're still here," I whispered to the faintly glowing tube. It seemed only fitting to thank her, instead of uttering my traditional sigh of "thank God".

When I returned to the bedroom, Amon still stood there, regarding me quizzically. "Cat, what's happened?"

"Nothing," I smiled while trying to catch my breath. I showed him the vial. "I forgot that I had left this alone. Since we went through Hell to get it, I didn't want anything to happen to it." I handed the tube to him and he passed me a garment on a hanger.

"I agree," Amon nodded," but I hardly think the footrace was necessary."

"Hey, I wasn't taking any chances," I turned and headed once more for the bathroom.

Looking at his choice for my attire, I found that he had brought me a romantic looking dress of black crushed velvet and lace. The sweetheart neckline was edged in black lace and dropped elegantly into a boned and fitted bodice of velvet. The billowing sleeves were sheer black lace gathered snuggly at the wrists then continuing in thick folds over the hands. Panels of lace covered the velvet skirt, which dropped to a ballet-length hemline. A small satin-covered hanger behind the dress bore a set of matching black lace panties and bra, garter belt and stockings. I had to laugh, as I had never in my life worn a garter belt and stockings.

"Wow," I breathed as I turned the dress and lingerie, "you are expecting a lot out of me. I don't know if I even know how to put on a garter and stockings." I grinned as I looked back over my shoulder.

"If you need help," he nodded and moved up behind me, nudging his front against my back, "I would be pleased to be of assistance."

"You," I brushed him away, "Back off, Master Vampire. Give me a chance to pull myself together." Stepping inside, I closed the bathroom door soundly behind me and hung the dress out of the way. First, I dried my hair and braided it, for if we were flying before dawn it was the best way to keep it out of my eyes. I had nothing to tie it off with, so I tore a strip of my gray dress and knotted it at the tail. With a little concentration and some patience, I managed to slip into the lingerie and did a fairly decent job of donning the stockings. They felt strangely disconcerting and looked even stranger when I discovered that the panties were actually thongs. I slid the dress over my head and hissed a little as the weight hit the burn on my lower back.

"F---ing vampires," I swore softly under my breath. Glancing at myself in the mirror once more, I startled myself with my eyes of frosty white, made more dramatic looking by the contrast of the black dress. Amon knew how to dress for effect, I had to admit. I stepped out into the bedroom and Amon stood and smiled at me.

"You are breathtaking," he beamed and swept me into his embrace. "And we have guests downstairs."

"Guests," I shook my head. "That usually does not bode well for me."

"Here," he held a white gold dragon barrette in his hand, "you need this."

"I do indeed," I smiled as I swept my braid around and removed the scrap of gray fabric. Securing the barrette, I flipped my hair back. "Now if I just had some shoes," I remarked, offering him my stocking clad feet.

"Perhaps these," he pulled a pair of black leather boots that laced up the front from behind his back. Like his boots, these had silver roses climbing up the shafts and I had to refrain from squealing like a girl when I saw them. Grabbing them from his hands, I flounced down on the edge of the bed to put them on. The mark on my back stretched and smarted a little with my exertions and I sighed heavily in frustration.

"When I reach forward, this burn or brand or whatever rubs against my clothes. It hurts," I pouted, "Will you put them on me?" Almost adding that it was his fault that I couldn't do it, I caught myself likely just in time to avoid adding a second arm to the triangle. Already I was dreading walking the razor's edge of his discipline and vowed to keep my mental shields up for protection. He might be able to forcibly alter my behavior, but I would not allow him to alter my thinking.

"Of course, Cat," he took my foot in his hands and slid the boot on. "And I am sorry for your mark. I now regret that I did so, but once started it cannot be undone." He spoke gently as he laced up the boot. "I will try to be more circumspect if the issue of another piece of the triangle should come up."

"Why don't you just say what you're thinking?" I chuckled, "You mean when the issue comes up. And you fully expect it to, don't you?"

"We do come from completely different worlds," he nodded as he placed the other boot on my other foot. "I believe we see things diametrically different and we will likely clash wills again."

"The difference being," I dared, "I can't physically force my will on you. I can't hex you with magical marks to control you."

He smiled weakly as he looked up from beneath those gorgeous lashes, "You think not?" As he tied the last lace up he shook his head, "It scares me already how much power you have over me. We do not even know the scope of your abilities. You may be surprised."

"Pretty words, Warrior," I remarked as I stood and looked down at my boots. They were beautiful. When I looked up at Amon, he flinched again as he saw my eyes. "That's it," I threw up my hands and sat back down. "I'm not going anywhere. No one will see me looking like this. You can't even look at me without flinching and you've been beside me since it happened. Not to mention the fact that you say you love me so you probably have more reason to try to adjust than anyone else does. I cannot go downstairs and have your guests gaping at me all night. You go ahead, I'll stay here."

"I will not go without you," he turned and went to the bedside table. Opening the small drawer, he drew out a pair of small hexagonal-lensed black glasses. The frames were silver wire and the lenses were so dark as to appear opaque. Of course if they were his glasses the frames were likely titanium or some other metal. "And I do love you," he added as he returned and handed the glasses to me.

"Cool," I muttered to myself, "I'll look like a cross between Stevie Nicks and John Lennon." I slid them on and peered through them at Amon. As dark as they were, they were strangely comforting to my eyes, though I had not realized before that my eyes were now more sensitive to light. It made sense though, I thought, who had ever heard of gray pupils?

Amon actually looked more at ease when I covered my eyes, and he seemed to relax as he took my arm.

"Shall we go My Lady?" he purred.

"So," I looked at him sideways, "Who are tonight's guests?"

"The remaining members of the Council," he answered matter-of-factly. "They are here both to witness the prophecy and to petition Chimaera to join them, at least temporarily, to fill the vacancy caused by Kasimir's betrayal. I do not know, Chimaera's personality is rather volatile. I am not sure he has the temperament for the job."

"Oh I disagree," I smiled broadly. A light bulb of an idea flashed on in my mind, and it would not have been a surprise to find it visible above my head.

"Indeed?" he stopped and looked at me.

"Sure," I nodded, "And since I'm likely to get hauled up in front of them for one infraction or another, it wouldn't hurt to have someone whose ass I saved on the Council."

"So that's it?" He shook his head grinning, "Seeding the Council with allies?"

"Hey, wouldn't you?" I hugged his arm tightly, "I'm just looking to cover my butt."

"Surely, that is my job now," he growled and wriggled his eyebrows.

"Let's don't go there," I warned as we stepped into the parlor. The room seemed unnaturally crowded with the remaining four members of the Council, and Amon's men. Bishop stood before the bar and he poured me a glass of red wine, bringing it to me as Amon and I came in. Winter stood looking out the window, his golden waves shining in the light from the wall sconces as well as the candles that were scattered here and there throughout the room. Chesmne and Mastiphal stood speaking together in hushed voices. Chesmne was outrageously attired in an orange and black sheath, spikes of orange standing out of her multicolored hair. Mastiphal wore a simple russet colored shirt left loose over a pair of black breeches with black boots. He looked very much the swashbuckler with his reddish blond hair pulled back from his face, secured at the back with a leather braid and his goatee neatly trimmed. Nephthele and Thammuz both sat on the sofa, Nephthele in a gown of pale pink silk and Thammuz in a dignified black Nehru jacket and trousers.

"Cat," Bishop smiled and bowed as he handed me the drink, "how do you feel now?" He looked curiously at the sunglasses perched on my face.

"I feel fine, Bishop," I accepted the wine and smiled. "I just look a little ragged." Touching the glasses I nodded as if in explanation.

"I see," he murmured. "I am glad you feel well, anyway. And that you can be with us tonight."

"Yes," Thammuz approached with his hands outstretched and for a moment I thought he was going to hug me. "You have proven yourself no enemy and have risen in our estimation of you. We do not even know how to address you now."

I started to say just call me Cat, when Amon spoke up, "You may address her as My Lady, as she will soon be my mate."

I think my mouth actually fell open when I heard those words and I turned to look up into those twinkling black eyes. Speechless, I found I could not even form a cohesive thought. I was suddenly emotionally swamped into the depths of his eyes, though I was vaguely aware of murmurs of surprise and words of congratulations being uttered in the distance.

Your mate?

Yes, Beloved, my mate.

What exactly does that mean?

It means that we become one.

Did I agree to this without knowing it?

Would you refuse?

Closing my mind soundly, I stood silently for a moment just to let him taste how it felt to be powerless. I let the moments tick by. Then I grinned.

No, Warrior, I would not refuse you. But it might have been polite if you had asked.

Touché', Mi Amour, touché.

Winter stepped up and bowed deeply before me. I touched his golden hair and he raised his eyes inquiringly. "Is there something wrong with your eyes, My Lady?" he whispered, the furrows in his forehead evidence of his concern.

"No, Winter," I whispered back, "I'm fine."

Chimaera moved away from where he was leaning on the fireplace mantle and sauntered before me.

"I trust that when you become His Lordship's mate," he remarked, glancing at Amon, "You will not go stubbornly galloping off across the countryside."

"Why Chimaera," I gushed, "Are you verbally chastising me? After I pulled your cajones out of the fire?"

"A thousand pardons, Cat," he bowed slightly. "I only meant that you should be more careful and put your own welfare first."

"Down boy," I shook my head. "I know very well what you meant. And you should know by now that I do as I please."

Amon pulled me close and I looked up into his ebony eyes. They were smoldering. "And as he pleases, I guess," I grumbled. I was never going to get used to that.

"So we're here to finish this thing," I changed the subject. "Time to fulfill a prophecy."

Amon pulled the small glass vial out of his pants pocket. The blood within pulsed with a soft amber light as he held it up between his thumb and index finger. Looking down at me with love in his eyes, he murmured, "Are you sure?"

"After all we went through to get it?" I grinned, "Having endured the theater in the round? Oh, yeah, I'm sure."

"Nemesis warned that all the conditions might not be met," Thammuz reminded us.

"Yes, but after all," I reasoned, "what would be the worst that could happen? As long as Amon doesn't turn into a frog or grow a tail, we know that the blood won't harm him. I say it's worth the risk." There were mutters of agreement and dissension fluttering about the room. Good thing we weren't voting on this, I thought.

"How will we know if it's worked?" I thought out loud as Amon removed the stopper in the vial.

"I have no idea," he replied as he lifted the tube to his lips, threw back his head and drank the glowing liquid. He closed his eyes and bowed his head, hands held together on the vial as if in prayer.

"Anything?" I asked pensively.

"I feel a stirring," Amon breathed, "but that may just be because I am so near to you."

"Very clever, Warrior," I smiled then let out a gasp as evidence of the magic made itself known. From his scalp, moving from the roots then crisscrossing down his braid to the ends of his hair, jet black crept like a curtain until all that was left of his gorgeous silver hair was one shock at his left temple.

"Wow, that's better than Grecian Formula," I marveled and everyone else in the room looked at me as if I was insane. "It's a man's hair coloring," I explained to the vampires, they were so sadly educated in television commercials.

"What are you saying?" Amon lifted his head and looked at me. I gaped at him.

"Well," I breathed unevenly, "first of all, your hair has returned to its original black." I moved forward and fingered the streak of silver left at his temple, "Except for this one lock. It's very chic, very stylish so don't worry about that. However, if you are able to walk in the daylight without pain? I don't think you're going to have such an easy time passing for human."

"What do you mean, Cat?" He looked at me suspiciously, "What is wrong?"

"Amon," I smiled at the coincidence, "Your eyes are now blood red with a little halo of amber around your pupils. I can't even describe what it resembles, but no one will mistake you for a normal man."

"If the prophecy has been fulfilled," Nephthele suggested, "won't you be able to see your reflection in a mirror? Oh, how I miss seeing myself."

"That is right," Amon nodded quickly, then grabbed my hand and pulled me from the room. "Excuse us!"

Racing down the hallways and up the stairs, I got tickled at the situation and began laughing as I ran. When we reached his bedroom, Amon bolted into the bathroom and flipped on the lights. There was silence spilling from the room as I finally caught up with him and reached the open bathroom door. Leaning against the frame, I watched as Amon reverently touched his image in the mirror, then touched his own face and hair.

"I have not seen myself in over eight hundred years," he marveled, "I cannot believe what I am seeing. And I have never seen eyes this color." He turned to look at me, his face full of emotion and confusion. "Can you accept this?"

Though those blood red and amber eyes, now accented by his long jet-black hair should have startled me, they didn't. The effect was dramatic even disturbing, but on him it worked. His new appearance made it clear that he was a creature of power and yes, of danger. I stepped into the room and he took me into his arms, sliding the glasses from my face. His expression still faltered when he looked at my eyes.

"Accept it? I love it. We make a fine pair o' two," I remarked as he lowered his mouth to mine.

"I suppose we will know no more about our success until the sun rises," he replied, his hands smoothing up and down my back.

I hissed and pulled from his embrace when he brushed over the mark, stirring the pain in my lower back. "You still have guests downstairs, remember? And New Orleans awaits us." I added as I stepped out of the bathroom, replacing the glasses on the bridge of my nose, "And I suggest that if you have another pair of these, you get them. New Orleans may be a wild and rowdy party town, but we won't be able to blend into the crowd looking like this, at least not until Halloween or Mardi Gras."

When we returned to the parlor, Thammuz stood and bowed before Amon. He smiled, "I believe we have some proof of the success of this evening. The full measure of your abilities will be made manifest in time, I assume. Chimaera has graciously agreed to sit on the Council until such a time as a permanent replacement can be chosen. We have all shared in the joyous news of your future union. It has been a momentous evening."

"Cat?" Amon turned to me, his eyebrows raised. I knew what he was suggesting and shook my head. I had no intention of revealing my eyes to anyone, especially not the whole Council.

"No," I took his arm and turned him to face me. Speaking in hushed tones I added, "They don't trust me or even especially like me. I'm not one of you. Please, let's just go." I moved forward and retrieved my wineglass, tossing back its contents. I set it back down and nodded at Winter and Chimaera.

"Ladies and Gentlemen," I smiled graciously bowing to the other Council members, "it has indeed been a momentous night and congratulations Chimaera. Now, Amon and I are going to greet the sunrise elsewhere. We bid you good night, or good day, or whatever you guys say."

Taking Amon's hand, I laughed and pulled him through the French doors and out into the garden.

"Here," Amon smiled and pulled a black velvet cape out of the air, "wrap yourself in this, Beloved." He repeated the gesture and his own cape appeared. He threw it over his shoulders. "You know that you should have revealed this new development," he nodded and touched the glasses on the bridge of my nose.

"Why bother?" I shrugged, "I think it will be easier if I just fly below their radar. They will probably never accept me, whether I'm your mate or not. And the white eyes are certainly not going to help."

"Ready to fly, Little One?" He slid his arms around me beneath my cape and I wrapped my arms around his neck.

"Yes," I breathed as he leaned down to kiss me. As my love for him stirred deep within me, my power rose and smacked loudly against his. Lightning exploded in the sky and I laughed as we rose into the night air. Snuggling my face into his neck, I licked his throat and felt him growl in pleasure.

"You are a formidable power, Witch," he leaned down and murmured in my ear.

Lifting my eyes to the sky, I watched the lightning dance on the horizon, the stars streaked by in the night, and the neon and vapor lights below became a ribbon of radiance. The cold wind blew wisps of my hair around my face and loosed a few hairs from Amon's braid as well. When he felt me shiver, Amon pulled me closer against his chest and I felt the heat radiate from him.

Chapter 42

When we touched down on the riverfront in New Orleans, Amon kissed me briefly before releasing me. The smell of the Mississippi, the flat odor of dead fish, rich mud, and diesel from the barges, assaulted my nose and I wrinkled it in distaste.

"I don't think I would ever get used to that smell," I sighed and drew Amon away from the river's edge toward the noise and lights of the Vieux Carré. Amon slipped his dark glasses on and tucked me under his arm.

"Whatever shall we do until the sun rises?" he murmured as we strolled along the cobblestone streets. The sound of our bootheels rapping on the pavement was barely audible above the growing cacophony of jazz and Zydeco pouring into the streets from the bars and clubs.

"We could dance," I teased, as I knew my own abilities on the dance floor were sad at best, "Or gamble in the casino, maybe get drunk in one of the bars?"

"I don't believe the prophecy will be totally fulfilled," he sighed as he watched a couple of young men go by, talking and laughing loudly.

"What do you mean?" I stopped and looked at him. Though I could touch his mind, I wished I could see his eyes. I was afraid to remove his dark glasses in public. The neon signs threw brightly colored lights everywhere but I couldn't risk someone noticing us, screaming at the sight of Amon's blood red eyes.

"I think I need to feed, Cat," He bowed his head sadly, "If the prophecy were totally fulfilled, I would not feel this hunger ever again."

Considering this revelation, at last I shrugged, "It's a small matter, if everything else comes to pass. And maybe with time, this need will go away too."

I touched his chin and he raised his eyes, peering over the tops of his glasses. His blood red eyes were haunting. At last he smiled at me, though it was a disappointed smile.

"Go," I whispered, "Go feed. But make sure it's only young men."

"Stay here, Beloved," he nodded as he pushed me into the doorway of a closed and darkened antique store. "I'll be back as soon as I can."

The very air seemed to change as soon as Amon was gone. What I had reveled in as joyous and rambunctious suddenly turned sinister and intimidating. I leaned silently back against the carved marble façade of the antique store, barely daring to breathe. In the distance I could hear the sneering, mocking voices of several young men calling to each other and laughing like hyenas. The sound grew louder as the men approached. I held my breath and leaned as far back into the shadows as I could. As the rowdy group moved into my line of sight, I decided that they were too inebriated and far too caught up in their own silliness to even notice me and relaxed a little just watching their antics. As the five of them reached the sidewalk before the antique store one of them, a particularly mean-looking hooligan with red close cropped hair, stumbled on the uneven pavement. As he caught himself, he cursed loudly and wrenched his head in my direction. My heart fell as he smiled broadly and straightened his shoulders to approach me. I wished myself invisible.

"Well, looky, looky, looky," he grinned an evil leer, "What do we have here, boys?" He stepped to the edge of the sidewalk, peering into the shadows. I said nothing.

"What's a sweet lookin' little yaller-haired blind girl doin' out here by herself?" he cooed and my skin crawled at the cruel set of his mouth and the beadiness of his close-set black eyes. I could smell the liquor oozing from his pores from four feet away. Apparently he and his buddies had been drinking or wallowing in booze for several hours.

"You want to have some fun, little blind girl?" he smiled, revealing a mouth full of rotten teeth. I had a sudden memory of the inbred hill people from Deliverance come to mind and I recognized the danger. "Hey look boys, it's Helen Keller."

I was amazed and slightly impressed that he even knew who Helen Keller was.

"I'm just waiting here for my husband," I answered with a voice as steady as I could manage.

"What kind of man would leave a pretty little thing like you out here on the street?" he shook his head, "The streets are a dangerous place for the likes of you."

"I'm fine," I smiled sweetly, "And my husband just went around the corner. He'll be right back."

Reaching the entrance, Evil Boy grabbed my arm as he laughed to his buddies, "Why don't you come on out here where we can get a better look at you? Are you bashful?" His pals laughed as he dragged me away from the doorway and out into the light.

"Yes," I looked down. "I'm shy."

"No need for that," he breathed a foul odor at me and moved toward me. When he leaned forward, presumably to kiss me, I surprised him by moving toward him, lifting my skirt slightly, and driving my knee as hard and as fast as I could up into his groin. He groaned loudly as the air was driven from his lungs. As he started to bend or topple forward, I curled the fingers of my right hand down and drove the heel of my hand up, catching him beneath the chin. His teeth clacked together smartly as the impact caught him off guard and tossed him backwards. He landed with an "Umph" on his backside on the street. His buddies stood frozen in surprise, their inebriated brains unable to understand what had just happened. Finally, one of them started to laugh. Evil Boy glared at his friends then yelled, "Don't just stand there, you idiots, get her!" His

pals first looked at him, then at me, then back at him as if they were uncertain what he meant. As he scrambled to his feet, the air suddenly changed. Power and menace, like static, crackled around me and Evil Boy's buddies dispersed, running as if they were on fire. Amon appeared out of nowhere, his eyes glowing with rage visible through his dark glasses and his hands clinching into fists. He grabbed the drunken fool by his collar and hoisted him into the air.

"Amon, no," I called as I tried to put myself between the drunk and Amon's fury. "Don't kill him."

"He laid his hand on you," Amon roared, "He insulted me by touching you. He has to pay."

"Okay," I tried to calm him by speaking earnestly, "I wasn't especially thrilled that he touched me, but he didn't intentionally insult you because until a moment ago, he didn't know you existed."

"And now he knows and now he'll pay," he exclaimed, still dangling the drunken redhead by the scruff of his neck. I was sure that in his state of inebriation and with the pain in his privates and his jaw, Evil Boy had no idea what was happening.

"Amon," I tried to touch his arm to make him lower the man. He glowered at me. "You're justified in killing someone who is threatening your life or the life or someone you love. You don't kill someone for a social infraction. The punishment should fit the crime."

"I should destroy him," he snarled, "I can see into his black heart. He is mean and ignorant, as well as drunk, a lethal combination."

"If you love me," I dared to play my trump card, "You'll put him down." Crossing my arms on my chest, I tapped my toe on the pavement and waited expectantly for Amon to decide on a course of action.

"You do not play fair, Little One," Amon sighed as he dropped the young man in a heap on the cobblestone street.

"You can punch him in the nose if it makes you feel better," I grinned and reached up to touch Amon's face. He looked down at the mess of a man and lightly kicked him in the ribs with the toe of his boot. "Very nice," I added, "At least that way you didn't have to touch him."

"This was a mistake," Amon took me into his arms, "We should not have come here and I should never have left you alone."

"It's not as bad as all that," I pointed out, "I can take care of myself. You'll notice that this was not magic but self-defense 101. Women across the country know this stuff and we use it successfully every day."

"I do not care about women across the country," he shook his head, "I only care about you and I don't want you coming into contact with ruffians like this ever again."

"Ruffians?" I laughed, "Oh, please. Amon you are so sweet, but so old fashioned. I can see I'm going to have to introduce you to Kill Bill and Kill Bill: Volume II."

"I don't know what you're saying," he grumbled, "but I will not feel comfortable about your safety until you are my mate. I think we should leave here now and watch the sunrise elsewhere."

"Whatever you say, Warrior," I sighed and slipped my arms around his waist.

"We will see the sunrise from my aerie in the mountains," he breathed into my ear.

"Yes," I nodded against his chest "And about this becoming your mate thing?"

"After sunset, Beloved," he cut me off, as he wrapped my cape around my shoulders then surrounded us both in his own cape. "Now we must fly for the sunrise approaches."

As he embraced me firmly, I willed my power to stir and join his in our desire for flight. The two powers together first fought then embraced and we moved swiftly through the night sky. Having no idea where Amon's mountainous destination lay, I simply added my force to his and it seemed only moments until we were planting our feet on the rocky outcrop.

Darkness, deep and absolute, still blanketed the land when we reached Amon's favorite spot, though he assured me that sunrise was imminent. The air was cool with mist and the night birds had gone silent. I moved from his embrace and found a rocky protrusion to sit on, out of the way.

"Amon," I called softly.

"Yes, Beloved," he turned to me and removed his glasses. His blood red eyes glowed in the darkness, like the eyes of a wolf in the moonlight.

"What happens if this doesn't work either?" I asked, remembering the scene from Interview with the Vampire when the sun hits the trapped newly-made woman vampire and Claudia the vampire child, and they turn to ash then crumble.

"We return to the estate, of course." He answered matter of factly.

"I'm sorry," I remarked, "I keep forgetting that the sun only causes a Master Vampire a little discomfort. According to all the movies and the literature, you should either explode or at least have your skin blister and blacken when the sun hits you."

"I will be disappointed if I cannot walk in the sunlight without discomfort but we can make it safely back to the estate, I promise," He nodded in the darkness.

A breeze came up from below us and I felt a chill on my arms. Pulling the cape more tightly around my shoulders, I rocked back and forth on the cool rock ledge, trying to keep myself warm. Amon stood near the edge of the precipice, his face to the wind, hair stirring gently. His shoulders were squared and his stance was both proud and powerful. Just sitting there looking at his incredibly masculine form faintly outlined in the dimming moonlight, I felt a swelling of pride that such a man as this could be interested in the likes of incredibly average me. In my world, men who looked like Amon dated supermodels or heiresses, they were not aware that women like me, normal women, existed.

"Will it be long?" I murmured quietly, wishing to not disturb the silence of the predawn hour.

"Forty, maybe forty-five minutes," he answered as he came and sat beside me. He put his arm around my shoulder and wrapped his cape around me. Heat emanated from his chest and I snuggled next to his body for warmth. "You can see in the east how the sky is beginning to turn purple, soon will come lavender, then pink, then finally sunrise red."

"It's beautiful," I whispered. "Talk to me, Amon. Tell me of your world."

"What do you wish to know?" he lowered his head to speak quietly then kissed the top of my head.

"I don't know," I yawned, his warmth and my weariness catching up with me, "Tell me of this whole vampire civilization, community, hierarchy, whatever. How is it that you are the big cheese?"

"The big what?" he remarked, sounding almost insulted.

"You know the Big Kahuna, the top dog, the leader," I chuckled, "How is it that you are the leader?"

"There are five vampire communities here in the United States, three across the upper tier of the country and two down here in the south." He explained as he stretched his long legs out and crossed them at the ankles. "Sabre, a Master Vampire from Romania is now the leader of the community of the northeastern parts of the country. He thinks himself quite a power, but in truth, he is more a political player than anything else. His territory is ripe for the picking, as his power is tenuous at best. Pim is the leader of the midwestern territories and she is an incredibly powerful Master Vampire. She has a tendency to be cruel first, then kind, but she rules empirically. No one would dare challenge her under any circumstances."

Though I loved the sound of Amon's voice, I found that it was lulling me to sleep and I fought to keep my eyes opened.

"So," I breathed wearily, "Who has LaLa land?"

"Lala Land?" he placed his mouth at my temple.

"L.A., Los Angeles," I yawned again, "You know, California? The West Coast where all the beautiful people live?"

"Oh," he nodded, his black braid brushing gently on my shoulder, "That would be Gryffyn, spelled with only y's. He's moderately

405

powerful, but politically very savvy. Though he's not totally beyond threat, he has a vast population behind him and he knows how to play to a crowd."

"And the south west?" I asked as my eyes began to droop and my head began to drop.

"That would be Jacques," Amon smiled in the waning darkness.

"Jacques?" I chuckled, "That hardly sounds Native American, or even vampire for that matter."

"Jacques is a very old and very powerful Master Vampire who governs largely unseen in the desert. Few have personally dealt with him or can attest to his existence. He is very mysterious and very mercurial. His power base is unknown."

"And where do you rate among the five?" I sighed, oblivious to any possible embarrassment I might cause him.

"I am," he murmured, rubbing the top of my head with his chin, "how do I say this with humility? I am the Master of all five communities. You can imagine how fulfilling this prophecy will only serve to cement my position, and how some would seek to thwart my efforts. Though Jacques is, I believe, older than I am, he has little interest in wielding the power necessary to keep us safe and from warring with one another. He is not a fighter. I sense that you are growing weary, Little One and you should rest. Please, sleep. I will alert you come sunrise."

"No, Amon, I'm fine," I shook my head as much to ward off the drowsiness as disagree, "How many of you are there?"

"In this country?" He looked at me soberly, "Or worldwide?"

"I'll make it easy on you," I smiled rather smugly, "U. S. only."

"In this country there are approximately five thousand vampires," he admitted.

"Are you kidding me?" I gasped now fully awake, "How the hell can there be five thousand vampires and you guys are still under the radar?"

"I do not understand," he looked at me quizzically, "what are you saying?"

"How in the world can there be five thousand of you in this country and yet you remain unknown to the masses, unknown to the media, virtually unknown, period."

"We have laws that are very specifically written and mercilessly enforced," he smiled benevolently. "Why are you asking these things?"

"You yourself admitted that there is much I have to learn to live in your world. So, tell me about it."

"Well," he explained, "the main law is that no mortal may consciously know of our existence. Memories must be erased, he or she must be transformed or destroyed, for the safety of our species."

"So," I suddenly understood, "That's why the council took an instant disliking to me? Because I'm mortal, know of them, and you have neither destroyed me nor made me one of you?"

"Because you are a witch," he nodded, "and touched by the gods the majority of the Council are willing to give you a little lee-way. And because you will be my mate, they have no choice but to abide by my wishes."

"And what of the vampire who breaks this law?"

"The punishment is very specific," Amon admitted, "Destruction to he or she who breaks this law and his or her offspring. Basically the whole line is destroyed."

"Wow," I marveled, "Retroactive abortion! That's pretty severe."

"Our laws are meant to protect our species," he nodded. "Just be grateful that you are my inamorata."

"Your inamorata?" I grinned.

"My beloved," he smiled. "And when you are my mate, the Council and all others will have no choice but to pay you the respect that you deserve."

"Amon," I shook my head, "You can't just expect them to respect me just because I'm your mate. Respect is earned, you can't force someone to respect you."

"In our society," he insisted, "Refusing to pay the proper respect and honor to the mate of a Master Vampire is tantamount to treason. It is in no way tolerated. Torture in perpetuity is the penalty."

"In perpetuity?" I swallowed.

"Or until such a time as the Master Vampire feels satisfied," he touched my furrowed brow, perhaps empathizing with my bewilderment at trying to understand this strange new world.

"So what's next?" I breathed as he took me into his arms.

"Let us see what the dawn brings, Beloved," he whispered into my hair.

The heat of the rising sun shimmering on my face woke me and instantly put me into a foul mood. Even through the dark glasses I felt the sting of bright light and winced at the pain. My eyes started watering and blood began seeping down my face. I stirred beneath Amon's cloak, as well as my own, and saw him standing out on the edge of the precipice. He boldly faced the eastern sky, his cheeks and brow bronzed by the morning light, his black hair shimmering in the sunrise. I watched silently for a moment and could detect no discomfort or pain in Amon's demeanor.

"Amon," I murmured, still struggling to shake off the remnants of sleep, wiping the blood from my face.

"All is well, Little One," he beamed as he turned his face to me. "I feel no discomfort. The sunlight is no longer an enemy to me." Then his expression changed as he realized my discomfort. "You, on the other hand, are obviously in pain. We must get you out of the sunlight." "I think I'll be alright if I can just sit somewhere in the shade," I suggested as I stood unsteadily. "I just need to get out of the direct sunlight."

"Come," he drew me into his arms and moved me around a sharp outcropping. He leaned me back against the rock into the shade and immediately my eyes felt better. They stopped watering and I removed my glasses and rubbed my eyes, sighing in relief.

"Oh," I breathed, "that's so much better. Please, Amon, go enjoy yourself, wallow in the sunlight. I'll be fine here."

"No," he pressed his long lean body against mine as he brushed my hair from my face, "I will take you back to the estate and see to your comfort then I will walk my property. It should be interesting to see in the daylight all that I have come to know in the darkness, the woods and streams, fields and hollows." Sliding the glasses back up my nose, he wrapped the cloaks around us then slid his hands around my ribs and lifted me to his lips. "Are you ready to fly, Little One?"

"Just let me tuck my face into your neck to hide from the light," I smiled ruefully, "Am I the only one to see the irony in this situation? You, the vampire, being unaffected by the sunlight while here I am, a mortal with eyes too sensitive for the sunrise even with dark glasses."

"The irony is not lost on me, Beloved," He murmured and placed his hand on the back of my head, drawing me into the safety of hollow of his neck. Holding me tightly, Amon willed his power to touch mine and we rose into the sunwashed morning. I squinted to open my eyes just a little to see the view that a bird sees. Forests of multiple shades of green stretched out beneath us and streams of crystal water glinted in the bright sunlight. I was disappointed that the pain would not allow me to enjoy the sight and closed my eyes before the blood could return to my eyes.

"I'm sorry to ruin your morning," I sighed into his neck. "I wanted you to enjoy your first sunrise free from pain."

"Do not worry, Cat," He spoke tenderly, "I will enjoy my morning once I know that you are safe and comfortable."

Chapter 43

Iawoke in Amon's bed, surprised to find that I was not in his coffin. Stretching my arms above my head, I yawned and pulled my spine as far as I could, brushing my hands across Dave the dragon on the headboard. Rolling over on top of the covers, I was startled to find Amon sitting with his head in his hands in the chair before the fireplace. He appeared to be dozing, sitting relaxed and unmoving. Lying there quietly on my side with my hand curled beneath my chin, I smiled at the beauty of his profile. His now black glossy hair lay smoothly down his back, his brow was relaxed and lacked its usual worry furrows. The black fringe of his eyelashes lay whisper soft on his cheeks. My heart suddenly ached for him and for want of him. How in the world could something like this be happening to me? I loved my independence, my single-minded determination, and my solitary world and here I was hooking my wagon to, of all things, a vampire. Obviously, I needed my head examined, and for a moment I was given pause remembering that Amon had the capability to return me to my world, and deposit me unconscious back in the hospital, brain damage notwithstanding. Somehow, knowing that he was capable of it made me fearful that someday he might actually do it. What would happen if tomorrow I woke up in the hospital with everyone telling me that any story about this world I might remember was a product of brain damage? My heart would know the truth, I hoped.

As I lay there admiring him, Amon stirred slowly and raised his eyes to me.

"Cat," he smiled weakly, "you are awake. How do you feel?"

"I'm great," I murmured as I struggled to sit up. "How was your day in the sunlight?"

"My day was a blessing," he remarked as he stood and approached the bed. He now wore an emerald green satin shirt, unbuttoned and loose, above his black jeans. The silver dragon's head belt buckle stood out, cold and hard, against the naked skin below his navel "I missed you, though."

I reached my hand out and he took it in his own then sat on the edge of the bed.

"I missed you too," I grinned, "but I had Dave to keep me company." Placing the flat of my hand against the skin of his chest, I felt his heart beating and heat rising. "New look for you?" I touched his open shirt and grinned lasciviously at him.

"Dave?" he raised one eyebrow at me.

I patted the carved dragon on the headboard, "Yeah, Dave the dragon."

"You gave my family crest, the symbol of my heritage and birth-right, the name Dave?" he shook his head and rolled his eyes, smiling.

"Hey," I poked his thigh, "Dave really wanted a name. He was tired of being largely ignored. And he told me all about the bimbos that you used to bring home."

"Bimbos?" He laughed deeply, "I brought no bimbos home. Is this your way of prying into my past exploits?" He leaned over and kissed me on the forehead. "You have nothing to worry about. You are the only woman for me. There has been no one before you and there will be no one after."

"Wow," I breathed, "that's a very serious statement, sir. No one before me and no one after? You once told me that all vampires delight in sex, that it fulfills you. Now you want me to believe that you've been both celibate and emotionally unavailable for eight hundred years?"

He slid his arms around me, "I did not say that. I said that you are my woman, my only woman."

"What about Anna?" I smiled coyly.

"Anna was the love of my youth. You are the love of my life," he pressed his lips to my cheek, then my lips. The set of his jaw made it clear that the topic was closed and that no further discussion would be forthcoming.

I touched his face, "Is the sun down yet?"

"Almost," he nodded, "You must have been more weary than you realized for you did not even stir when I brought you in and put you to bed. You have slept most of the day away."

"I hate it that now you can be out in the sunlight and I'm forced into the shadows because my white eyes are so sensitive to light," I added as I pulled my legs up and slid them off the side of the bed.

Amon put his arm around my shoulder, "I know love, and I think I may have the answer to that dilemma."

"What?" I looked into his disconcertingly blood red eyes, the circle of amber around his pupils glowing softly.

"That is complicated," he stood and took my hand, drawing me up. "Easier, I think to show you than to explain it to you."

"Okay, if you want to be all mysterious guy," I sighed, "but I want to change clothes first. It seems that you've already changed. Is this a fashion statement or is your air conditioner broken?" I ran a finger up the hard muscles of his stomach and chest, then lightly touched his opened shirt.

The oddest look crossed his face and he started to say something then he looked at me and smiled broadly. "Oh, I see," he grinned, "why yes, the air conditioner is broken. That is it."

Now it was my turn to look confused. After a moment, I decided that it was probably an errant attempt at humor and that it would be rude of me to press the issue. I just smiled and shook my head.

"Here, Little One," he smiled as he handed me a neatly folded pile of clothes, "put these on and we will go out to the garden. And I do have a request of you."

"Request?" I murmured as I accepted the clothes, "I would do almost anything for you."

"I love how your mind works," he chuckled, "how you guard your words and qualify your oaths. That is so...you!"

"Hey," I grumbled, "I don't make promises I can't keep and I mean what I say. So, what's the request?"

"Would you play for me tonight?" he asked with uncharacteristic solemnity.

"Sure, I'd love to," I answered lightly, wanting only to brighten his mood. "Why don't I meet you in the garden and I'll play for you out there, if you like."

"That would please me greatly," he nodded.

"Are you all right?" I asked, for his manner was disturbing me, "You seem to be in a strange mood."

"Never mind me, Cat," he breathed as he leaned down to kiss my forehead. "All will be well soon."

I added as I went into the bathroom, "If you don't mind I'll take a quick shower. I got a little chilled last night and I think a hot shower might burn off the cold."

"Please," he answered as he headed out of the bedroom, "take your shower at your leisure. Do you wish me to wait and escort you to the garden when you are ready?"

"No," I called as I turned on the showerhead, "I won't be long. I'll just meet you there in a little bit." Silence answered me, so I stripped off the dress and underthings and stepped beneath the spray of hot water. The steam and prickling heat opened my pores and relaxed my muscles.

Amon, are you sure that you're all right?

Do not worry about me, Little One, I am fine. Perhaps just adjusting to all the new developments, with you and with me. You do not mind playing for me tonight?

Of course not, it's been a little while since I've played so I can't guarantee that I'll be any good, but I'll be happy to try. I'll be down soon, perhaps you could get me a glass of wine?

Yes Beloved, I will be happy to meet you in the garden with a glass of wine and perhaps a light meal. Soon.

I shook my head beneath the water, sluicing the shampoo from my hair. "He's still acting weird," I muttered to myself, "I wonder what's going on now." It suddenly staggered me to realize that Amon was distancing himself from me as he had just before he almost sacrificed me to the demon. This so did not bode well!

Determined to get to the bottom of Amon's strange behavior, I finished showering quickly and dried my body and my hair with mounting anxiety. The clothes he had provided turned out to be a white short-sleeved tee shirt and a pair of blue jeans. He had thoughtfully supplied undergarments and a pair of black suede slippers. I dressed as quickly as I could, brushed my hair, and went out to find my violin. It was lying in its case on top of the dresser, its leather gleaming in the soft light. I slipped the dark glasses up my nose as I headed for the garden.

Stepping into the hallway I was brought up short when I nearly ran headlong into Winter and another young man. Winter smiled at me and stepped back politely.

"My Lady," he grinned, "I would like you to meet Dodge. I was just relieving him for the night shift."

Recognition shone brightly in Dodge's big brown eyes, and he smiled and offered me his hand.

"Holy Cow," he gaped. "Boy, do I know you!" He pumped my hand up and down excitedly.

"Do I know you?" I smiled at his obvious exuberance.

"Ah, no, Ma'am," he grinned, "but I've seen you perform at Club Psyche. You're the lead singer and violin player for, what's the name of that group, Hunter's Moon? Man, you guys were great!"

"Why, thank you, Dodge," I bowed slightly, "I'm glad you enjoyed our work."

He looked at me closely then, and took a couple of steps back. He was a very good-looking young man, though he lacked that certain touch of perfection that I now saw as so obvious in the vampires I had met. He wore a light blue chambray shirt and faded jeans. His shoulder holster looked like it was worn and straining against the considerable muscles of his arms, back, and chest. His long soft-brown hair now lay straight down his back, but I could see that it had a tendency to wave and curl at the slightest change in humidity. His skin was smooth and tanned except for the five o'clock shadow on his cheeks and chin. Intelligence radiated from his big brown eyes, in spite of his good-ole-boy demeanor.

"Wait a minute," his eyes grew wide. "You're dead! You were attacked then abducted from the hospital what, a few months ago?"

"I know," I nodded and took his large powerful hands in mine, "I had a stalker before I was attacked. Mr. Montjean, your boss, is an old friend of my family's. When he found out that I was in danger, he set it up with the authorities to make it look like I had been kidnapped and killed. He brought me here to this sanctuary to protect me. You understand, don't you Dodge, that my safety depends on you not telling anyone that you've seen me? Right now my stalker is probably out terrorizing some other poor soul, but if he were to discover that I'm still alive and my whereabouts, well, you know."

"Of course, I understand," he remarked as he pulled my hands to him and kissed each one in turn. "Your secret is safe with me." He turned to go, then turned back, "And Miss Alexander-Blair?"

"Please, Dodge," I breathed a sigh of relief that he had accepted my story, "the name is Cat."

"Right, then, Cat!" He added, "You are very talented. It's been a great honor to have met you."

"The pleasure is mine, Dodge," I answered as he turned and strode down the hall. I turned to face Winter and smiled weakly. "It bothers me how easily lies just trip off my tongue now."

"It is a necessary evil, this secrecy," Winter sympathized. "You were just protecting Dodge by lying to him, you know." His golden eyes regarded me soberly, seeking me behind my dark glasses.

"Yeah," I breathed more relaxed now, "but that doesn't make me feel that much better."

Winter faced me directly, hands on his jean clad hips, leather jacket open revealing his white linen shirt and the butt of his revolver. His fragrance, that of grass, rain, and leaves, wafted to me and touched my soul. He took two steps closer to me and I backed up, brushing my backside against the doorframe. Suspicion was clearly etched in his expression and he barely breathed as he lifted one hand and gently pulled the dark glasses from my face. I instinctively closed my eyes against the light.

"Cat," he whispered forcefully, "open your eyes for me, My Lady, please."

I took a deep breath and turned my face from him. I wasn't prepared for this, for the startled look, the shying and flinching, not from my beloved Winter, my ally.

"No, please," I murmured, tears of blood welling behind my closed lids. I didn't want him to see me like this, like a freak show performer.

Touching my chin with his finger, he turned my face to his. "Cat please," he breathed, "My Lady."

I slowly opened my eyes and looked up at him. Wonder and surprise stole across his face. He looked deeply into my eyes and I saw total and complete acceptance and devotion in his golden eyes. He did not flinch or startle.

"Goddess save us," he cursed. "Did Nemesis do this to you?"

"Amon thought it might be an indication that I had been gifted with another power," I nodded, "but I think it's because I actually saw her in her true form. Winter, the color of my eyes is the color of her hair, her clothes, her skin, it's her color."

"You can see?" He touched my face again, concern wrinkling his smooth brow.

"My vision is fine, big brother," I shook my head, "if a little light sensitive."

"I like that," He nodded. "You know that I was greatly surprised when His Lordship announced that you had agreed to be his mate. I mean, I saw how he looked at you and how you looked at him, but I really never thought that you would agree to such a thing."

"How could I deny him?" I smiled sadly. "I know that he has this hang up about obedience, which I do not understand, but I figure we can find some way to compromise."

"Cat, you realize that his word is law?" he looked at me seriously. "He is our leader, our Master?"

"So, what?" I grinned, "Compromise is out of the question?"

"Think about it '*tite soeur*, the law does not compromise," he shook his head.

"So you're saying that this obedience issue will be a problem?" I fumed.

"Not once you're his mate," he mumbled as if to himself. "I knew that you were remarkable, Cat, but even I underestimated you. I must admit that I'm a bit jealous of His Lordship."

"Jealous? You?" I laughed. How could this beautiful lion of a man be jealous of anyone?

"To wield enough power to attract and claim a woman such as you," he nodded, "yeah, I'm a little jealous. I'll never have that much power."

"Winter, it was not Amon's power that attracted me to him," I explained. "If I had known you before him, I would have jumped your bones in a heartbeat. Any woman would. You just need to find someone who can see what a sweet, kind, loving man you are. Oh," I added, "you might want to leave out that part about being a vampire, at least until you're sure of her feelings and her commitment to you."

"Very well," he smiled ruefully as he slid my glasses back up my nose, "I'll keep that in mind, but I don't think I'll ever find someone like you."

"If she's the one," I met his smile, "she'll be just like me. Oh, I can't believe I just said that." I laughed at my own treacle.

"My Lady," Winter sighed heavily, "I am loyal to His Lordship, but I am your creature and your happiness and your welfare come before all else. You call me if you need me, yes?" He bowed and nodded as I stepped past him and moved down the hall.

"I will, I promise. For now, I'll be out in the garden, Winter," I called gently over my shoulder.

"Oh, I know just where you'll be," I heard him answer cryptically before I turned the corner and started down the stairs.

Chapter 44

The night sky was dark with a small scattering of stars visible between restlessly moving dark clouds. Twinkling lights glittered in the trees that surrounded the garden and the fragrance of jasmine and wisteria wafted on the breeze. Cool water in the fountain gurgled and chuckled as it sprayed from the urn to the pool below and a soft mist was made airborne in the exchange. I stood on the veranda and took in the whole spectacle that was night here in Amon's garden. Filling my lungs with fragrant air, I stepped into the grass and moved to the bench. Placing my violin case beside me, I opened it and removed the bow. Lovingly stroking the bow across the rosin block I hummed a mindless tune that I had learned in music school. The premise, as I recalled it, was that when the song was finally finished, the bow would be sufficiently rosined if you moved it at the proper rate and on the right beat. After so many years, I did this mindlessly as I observed the garden and wondered where Amon was. When the song was done, I took the violin out of the case and tested it for tuning, discovering that at least to me, it sounded perfect. Tucking my hair behind my ear, I placed the violin beneath my chin and closed my eyes as I drew the bow across the strings. I played an instrumental piece whose name I had long ago forgotten, but it was romantic, poignant, and beautifully melancholy. It felt wholly appropriate here in this dark and lonely garden.

I felt it the moment Amon stepped into the garden and abruptly stopped playing to turn and watch him approach. He carried a tray and a glass of dark liquid I took to be red wine. Moving to sit beside me, he kissed my cheek and removed the dome from the tray, offering me a variety of cheeses, meats, fruits, and breads.

"The music was exquisite, Little One," he nodded as he handed me the glass, "Merlot for My Lady."

"Thank you," I smiled, "For the compliment as well as the wine." I took a grape and popped it into my mouth. "Are you feeling better?"

"Me?" he grinned with amazement, "You need never concern yourself with me, Cat. I am fine."

Strangely, I could see that something had changed, he was no longer holding himself away from me as he had been earlier. Taking a piece of cheese from the tray, I turned to him, nibbling the cheese and washing it down with the wine. "So," I swallowed, "Do you have any requests?"

"Requests?" he looked confused, then smiled, "Oh, you mean music? No, I have no specific requests. Just play anything you feel. I'm sure I will enjoy it."

I munched a while longer, then felt guilty even though I was still hungry. He didn't invite me out to the garden to watch me eat. So, I downed the last of the Merlot and put the violin once more beneath my chin. I played a sprightly Celtic tune and closed my eyes to concentrate on the music. Feeling Amon rise from his seat beside me, I was not surprised when I felt him behind me, gently sliding my hair from my shoulder. The soft night air touched my throat a moment before Amon bent and kissed me tenderly there. I may have moaned softly at the sensation, then shuddered briefly when he drove his sharp teeth into my carotid artery. At first, I squirmed beneath him, delighting in the erotic sensations that accompanied his feeding from me. Putting my violin down on the bench beside me, I laughed and cupped Amon's head in my hand, rubbing my palm along the curve of his neck. Amazement at how easily he could turn my body to liquid stole through me as I realized that he should be stopping any time. By now he should have released me and sealed the wound, yet he showed no signs of stopping.

"Amon," I breathed as if to remind him of his actions.

Instead of releasing me, he leaned forward and, wrapping his arms around me beneath my elbows, he drew me up and over the back of the bench. Holding me firmly in his embrace, he drew deeply from my veins and I began to feel light headed and dizzy.

"Amon," I called again, though I think even then my voice was growing weaker. As my knees buckled beneath me, Amon gently drew me down to the ground, his teeth never leaving my neck. Balloons of strange colors swam before my eyes and my breathing became labored and shallow.

When at last he withdrew his teeth from my throat, he held me in his arms, the length of my body stretched out on the ground.

419

"I know that you have agreed to this," he breathed softly, staring into my eyes, "but I need to hear you say that you accept me and that you will be my mate."

Finally understanding what was happening, I gasped, "And if I refuse?"

A look of dismay, then horror, stole across his face. Though I would not have thought it possible, he actually paled as he realized the situation.

"Cat, Goddess forgive me, you cannot refuse," he exclaimed. "I have taken too much of your blood. I cannot replace it but with my own. You are on the brink of death, Beloved, you must take my blood or die. I cannot lose you!"

"Bishop?" I whispered even as I felt my strength ebbing.

"You would be dead by the time Bishop could be summoned. Oh, forgive me, Little One. I thought you understood that to be my mate you would become Vampire. I have ruined everything. You must surely hate me, and I can't blame you. I beg your forgiveness, but I truly thought you understood."

"Amon," I breathed, struggling to hold on to consciousness.

"Cat, say you forgive me," He murmured, gazing longingly into my eyes.

"Amon," I gently shook my head with the last of my energy, "Yes."

"Yes?" He asked incredulously. Relief and something like happiness touched his face.

"Yes," I closed my eyes and gasped my last breath, "I accept you and will be your mate."

The world was spinning away from me as I felt Amon lift my head and cradle me in his hand. Rich, powerful blood tingled across my lips and my mouth opened in mindless response. Clamping my mouth on the wound in Amon's chest, I drew his blood in and whimpered at the feeling. Whereas before when I had fed from him his blood had been warm and fulfilling, now it was scorching, burning everything it touched as it raced through my system. My heart faltered as his blood reached it, then my lungs seized and my breathing stopped. The pain as my organs shut down was exquisite. Silence and darkness surrounded me as my sense of touch and of smell disappeared. For a moment I hovered in absolute nothingness, then noises of the night so loud I clapped my hands over my ears roared over me. Complicated, intensely layered fragrances touched my nose and I opened my eyes to find colors so vibrant that they blinded me even here in this dark night garden. The fabric of my clothing prickled my skin and my teeth hurt. Assaulted by an overload of sensory input, I curled into a fetal position on the ground and closed my eyes and held my breath.

"This will pass, Little One," Amon's voice sought to calm me, "Your senses will be heightened, but right now your mind is adjusting to the change. You are now a predator and your survival depends on your senses. Your mind will adjust to the additional input in a moment. Try to remain calm."

"Tell me what this means," I gasped as I rocked back and forth in his arms, trying to wrap my mind around all that had happened.

"You are my mate," he said simply. "Your soul is mine and my soul is now yours. I am your mate and your sire."

"What does that mean specifically, my sire?" I rolled over to face him. His red eyes glowed with amber light in the darkness.

"You are of my making," he nodded. "I will teach you how to hunt and how to survive in this world. I will train you in the laws of our society and you will obey me as my word is law."

In the distance I could hear the soft thundering of feet padding quickly over the ground, of breath panting with exertion, and of nostrils sniffing the swiftly passing night air. The sound of the rustling of large wings came to me as I struggled to sit up there on the ground behind the garden bench. My vision was perfectly clear, as if it was daylight, and I watched mesmerized as the Alpha male wolf loped into the garden and lay down before me. Licking my hand, he placed his nose on his outstretched paws and closed his eyes in acknowledgement. I touched his thick warm fur and scratched behind his ear. He sat up and looked at me quizzically, cocked his head, then licked my face with obvious joy and abandon.

"Here now," Amon admonished his wolf, "That's enough. She is your mistress, now, not another female for your pack."

The great beast looked properly rebuffed and lay down once more before me, placing his warm muzzle in my hand. The sound of beating wings broke the stillness of the night and I raised my eyes to see a great white owl approach in the dark night air. Agamemnon landed on my shoulder, gently gripping my collarbone. He did not actually break the skin, but he did use considerable force to steady himself.

"I hope the Gods are okay with this," I breathed as I stroked the smooth white feathers of Agamemnon's chest.

Okay, Little Witch? You have honored us by accepting your destiny. Since we discovered Arathia's deceit, it was our intention that you be Amon's companion, lover, and mate throughout the remainder of his journey. The powers that we bestowed upon you are meant to compliment his, to meet his force and match it. He has been a true and faithful warrior, a valiant knight, and has walked lonely through this world for too long. You are mates, one to the other, and we are pleased at your union. Should you ever have need of our assistance, just call Agamemnon and he will see to it that we know of your desire. You have done well, Cat. We bless you!

As Nemesis' voice faded, Agamemnon leapt into the air, his huge snowy wings spreading in the darkness. He flew up and up, then circled once as he called to me, then disappeared into the darkness. The wolf stood, shook himself briskly, and then sprung away into the trees.

"Amon," I whispered as I took in his image with the keen new sight of a vampire and the tender coloring of a lover, "You told me when I first came here that this was not to be, that I would not be made a vampire. I never even considered this when you said we would be mates. I thought we'd have some ceremony or something. Why did you do this? What changed?"

"When I first brought you here it was to keep you safe so that you could live out the normal length of your human days before I would take your Life's Blood. Truly, Little One," He explained, "At that point I did not see this as a possibility. After so many centuries spent alone, I did not dare to hope that there was anything more than freedom from the constraints of being a vampire for me. The mere thought that I might find someone to share my existence with never occurred to me. I thought myself unworthy. When I was made a vampire I despised myself, what I had become, and how I was forced to exist. It wasn't until you and I made love, when you raised your power to meet mine, that I had any notion that you might be the one for me. Even after that, I would have returned you to your world, with much regret of course, before Nemesis changed your eyes and, yes, before you hit me. After that I knew that you must stay here in this world and be mine."

"But earlier," I insisted, "You were morose, distant, like when you were summoning the demon. You were having second thoughts weren't you?"

"It is a very serious thing, this transforming a human." He admitted as he rose and offered me his hand. "Life is very precious, Little One, and I would not take yours lightly. I am still, however, mortified that I did not realize that you did not understand. I hate to say that perhaps I assumed you understood that to be my mate meant to become Vampire."

"How many people have you transformed, as you so euphemistically put it?" I took his hand and easily stood, my body now feeling powerful and almost unfamiliar.

The look on his face was precious, he truly looked aghast, "Why, none before you, of course."

"You mean to tell me that in all those eight hundred years," I teased lightly, "You never once had a babe that agreed to certain favors for a chance at immortality?"

"I assure you," he insisted emphatically, "I have brought no one but you across, and that was the reason for my mood earlier. We all have the natural ability, instinct if you will, to bring a mortal into our world, but as Master Vampire I had no experience with such actions."

"I'm not tracking," I shook my head. "As Master Vampire you don't do this sort of thing all the time?"

"My power is, how can I say this, highly specialized," he nodded as he drew me into his embrace. "My offspring share my blood and my power. It would be unwise to produce a multitude of beings such as myself."

"Wait a minute," I grasped what he was so gracefully dancing around, "Master Vampires only produce Master Vampires? I thought your sire, what's his name, left you when he realized that you were a Master Vampire. Wasn't he a Master?"

"Cesare was my sire," He brushed the hair from my face then looked thoughtfully into the darkness, "But he was no Master. I do not know how I came to be this way, though perhaps it was the gifts of Apollo that raised my status in this world. I have taken this responsibility very seriously and I assure you that you are the only one I have ever brought into my world."

"And the reason that Cesare named you Sin?" I imagined, "It wasn't because you were sinfully beautiful, which I hate to admit, you are. It was because when he discovered that he had sired a Master Vampire he knew that he had committed a sin, wasn't it? He knew that he had disrupted the plans of the Gods when he made you Vampire." Silence hung heavily between us as we both considered all that had occurred.

I let the possibility that I might be a Master Vampire slide by without comment. Knowing how difficult it was going to be to learn all the rules and laws governing this society, the last thing in the world I needed was the additional complication of Master Vampire.

"So what now?" I smiled up into his glowing eyes as I ran my hands up and down his powerful biceps. "Will this mark on my back disappear now that I'm a vampire?"

"No," he shook his head, "your two chances remain, then the physical pain at my displeasure. You should know however, that in this society disobedience by a vampire to his or her sire is not tolerated. Your continued existence depends on learning our ways and it is my duty to teach you. This mark of obedience is between you and me, though, so no outside judgments can be leveled against you."

"What if I healed the mark myself?" I risked his anger.

"That would be disobedience, now would it not?" he murmured.

"So," I breathed as I tangled my fingers into his black silky hair, and brushed my lips along his neck, "how will I know what's considered disobedience in this strange and unfamiliar world?"

"I will teach you," He took my face in his hands and kissed me, his tongue insinuating its way into my mouth. My body reacted to his touch as if by magic. Not only were my senses heightened, my sexual reactions, as well as my sexual appetites, were also magnified and I envisioned the ages ahead of us spent in this deliciously primal past time.

"I name thee Passion," he whispered into my ear.

I pulled away from his embrace and looked him straight in the eye. "What was that?"

"It is customary," he replied, "in our society that you bear the name that I, as your sire, bestow on you."

"Can't I just be Cat?" I asked simply.

"To those whom you knew before your transformation," he smiled graciously, "of course. However, to those whom you now meet, you will be known as Passion. If it is any consolation, as my mate and as a sign of respect, you will most commonly be addressed as My Lady."

"But Passion?" I complained.

"Passion is a force," he murmured, "a power, an energy. It is everything that you are."

"Couldn't you have come up with something, I don't know, more intimidating?" I grumbled, "Something like Poison or Danger?"

"You are intimidating enough in your own right," he smiled and kissed me gently. "You are Passion."

"But it's so," I complained, if not whined, "girlie, girl."

"What?" He grinned broadly, "You would prefer Butch?"

I look into his blood red eyes, dumbfounded. His deadpan expression was perfect and I had to laugh.

"I do believe I'm rubbing off on you, Master Vampire," I exclaimed. "You just made a funny. Your sense of humor is blooming."

"Yes," he nodded, "you are rubbing off on me, as you put it, but I see no sign of me rubbing off on you."

"Relax," I cooed, "another five or six hundred years I may be as stuffy and egotistical as you are. And imagine how you'll be by then?"

"So what is your desire, Passion?" he whispered into my neck.

"A television, a DVD player, a copy of The Wizard of Oz, and some other DVDs. We'll work on your humor. And I'm determined to drag you, kicking and screaming if necessary, into the twenty-first century. You need a computer and Internet access, also."

"Your wish is my command," he smiled as he kissed me again. "I am willing to learn of these things, but for now you must learn of our ways. Come, Beloved, we must feed"

"Why do I not feel the bloodlust that you felt?" I sought to understand, "Didn't you go on some sort of rampage or binge?"

"I did," he admitted, "and I do not know how it is that you are immune from that torment, though perhaps it has something to do with the fact that we have both been touched by the Gods and that we are mates, eternal. My blood may be rich enough now to shield you from the pains of bloodlust, and your blood was certainly powerful enough to release me from at least some of the constraints of being Vampire. Our future together should be quite remarkable."

"The devil is in the details," I smiled as we linked hands, thinking that I should have that tattooed on my thigh. My power rose from deep within me and met his with equal force. Though before we had flown in each other's arms, we now flew side by side. Part of me reveled in the independence and the sight of the darkened world spreading out below me, but part of me mourned the intimacy of our previous mode of transportation. I rolled in the air to face him, his red eyes glowing in the darkness.

"Do you realize, my Precious," he almost snarled at me, "that the only time you confessed your love for me was when you were literally dying? I admit it, I love you, Cat, my Passion." He pulled me into his arms, "I am yours now, and thank the Goddess, you are mine. I now have hope for the future and a new meaning in my existence, thanks to you."

"I'm sorry, Warrior," I purred, "I did not realize that I had never told you this without my continued existence being in question. You read my thoughts, you know that you have touched my heart, why would you even question such a thing? Of course I love you and I have willingly committed myself to you, whatever in this magical world that may mean."

As we flew into the night, I marveled at the unusual turns my life had taken. No one would ever expect such a dramatic change in both lifestyle and, let's face it, concept of reality, but I would not forsake this newly acquired wisdom for a life of normalcy. Centuries, perhaps an eternity, of love, lust, companionship and learning now stretched out before me and I let go and embraced the possibilities.

"You realize that you forced me to solicit your admission of love," Amon complained as we flew through the darkness toward the sunrise.

"I know, I know," I sighed and made a mental note to tell him of my feelings at some future and unexpected moment. "You are well aware of the fact that I love you, Master Vampire. Making me say it is just another boost for your ego, and let's face it your ego is big enough to be self-sustaining."

"You wound me," he pouted, his lower lip poking out invitingly.

"No," I grumbled, "but there have been moments when I would have liked to. I think I've shown remarkable restraint."

"As have I, Little One," he hissed as he drew me into his embrace, cupping the back of my head in his palm. "As have I!" He lowered his mouth to mine, kissing me forcefully as we flew on through the night. Oh yeah, I could see a very long struggle for dominance in our future. Life among the vampires was, at least, not boring!

Epilogue

It has now been three months since my transformation, and though Amon says that I am doing well in my adjustment, I suspect that I have, from time to time, driven the poor vampire to the limits of his patience. Christmas is soon, as they say, upon us and as Mistress of the Estate, I have made my desires abundantly known. There will be lights and a decorated tree, if not carolers. I think it's safe to say that the big Christmas dinner with pumpkin pie, cranberry dressing and turkey is a thing of the past, and I guess that's okay. We, as vampires, can consume food, which is to say that we can eat, but since we get no nutrition or even satisfaction from eating it seems an exercise in futility. On the few rare occasions that Lily traps me near mealtime, I eat with as much appreciation as I can fake and beat a hasty retreat. Goddess love her, she's a tolerant soul and I think she knows just enough to know that she wants to know no more.

One thing that surprised me, initially, is how little I lamented my death. One would think that you would feel certain sadness, disappointment, and even grief over your own loss of life, but I never really did. It seemed I just moved from one situation to another, so I felt no remorse. Perhaps that's what all the dearly departed go through. Maybe mourning is only for the survivors, the deceased being busy with other things. Hey, the dead have lives too!

As we had hoped, over time, Amon has lost the need to feed on human blood. It was a gradual thing. Though vampires do not usually feed on vampires, (after all, what would be the point?), he does occasionally suffer an urge to feed on me and me alone. I have no issues with this as I find this activity both emotionally and sexually fulfilling. Let's face it, it's kinky fun!

We were hoping that since I was sired from extremely powerful blood, I might enjoy some of the freedoms that Amon is now experiencing. Though he had hoped that his ability to walk in daylight would render me impervious to pain from the sun, my eyes are still impossibly light sensitive, in spite of protective contact lenses and the extremely dark glasses. Only on cloudy, dark days can I walk outside without discomfort. Though my mate no longer needs to feed on human blood, unfortunately I do and find myself forced to feed two to three times a week. At first I had trouble with the mere idea of drinking blood from human beings, but I'm now adjusting to the situation. My first attempt at feeding was, I think, a dismal failure. My prey scooted away with a look of horror on his face and I was reduced to gales of laughter. It was not a rousing success, though Amon, most likely in his attempts to encourage me, downplayed the disgrace. I have since improved my technique and I like to think of myself as, at least, a competent hunter.

I'm still working on my understanding of the laws and rules of living in this world. I'm still here so I guess I'm doing okay. At least I haven't been destroyed for some minor vampire social or societal infraction. Vampires have such a different view of things and they're so rigid in their thinking. What a bunch of stuffed shirts!

I'm trying patiently to bring Amon into this century and it's like pulling teeth, I might add. Besides Nick at Nite, we have watched The Wizard of Oz and Pulp Fiction. Though he does not grasp the dark whimsy of the Wizard of Oz, Amon finds Pulp Fiction particularly delightful, so I think there's probably hope for him. After making the mistake of letting him watch "I Love Lucy" with me, I was treated to a ten-minute diatribe on a woman's place in the home and in her husband's life. The speech ended with his assertion that no court in the land would have ever convicted Ricky Ricardo of murder had he ever snapped and strangled Lucy or just whapped her over the head with his Conga drum.

I had, occasionally, made gentle barbs about Amon's lack of humor until he got wise to my sarcasm and decided my humor was at his expense. Though it was unintentional on my part, I might have been poking some gentle fun, I don't know. Oh, who am I kidding? Of course I was laughing at his expense, it was funny! Yes, as you might imagine, the only thing worse than an angry vampire is being forced to live with a vampire that you yourself have angered. I strongly recommend you avoid this at all costs. (Okay yes, I now have the second arm of the triangle of my Mark of Obedience, and I'm not going into details over how that happened!)

Whenever we feel a touch of the wild Amon and I ride out to the forest on Abraxis and Bella to greet our creatures, his pack and my owls. Remarkably, the first time I shapeshifted I fully expected to either fly as an owl or run as one of Amon's wolves. In magic things are never as you expect them, for when I changed I became, of all things, a snow leopard. Apparently my parents touched magic when they named me, for Cat is indeed what I am. As distasteful as shape-shifting is, it's not just that it hurts, which it does, it's that the sound of cartilage snapping, bones moving, tissue ripping and restructur-ing is enough to send you running screaming into the night. I know it almost did that for me the first time. So, I, like Winter, am a crea-ture not really in its element here in Louisiana, and I won't likely be shapeshifting very often. Amon tells me that in time I will be able to shapeshift into a variety of creatures, dependent on my needs. And though he has not specifically admitted that I too am a Master Vampire, I know it to be true. I just wait for his admission. Men are so insecure.

After the start of the New Year I will be returning to my music. Now that Amon is satisfied with my training and my powers, he has agreed to let me go back to playing bars and small clubs with a folk band in Houston. It won't be the same as Hunter's Moon, I'll wear a disguise and use a false identity just in case, but at least I'll be back to my first love, music. Only the supernatural can see the power in my fingers when I play so, though I'll have to be careful, I should be fine.

In the end my suspicions were correct. Amon did take my life, though he gave me a new one, of sorts. He took my soul though he gave me his own in return and, as I so feared, he took my heart. He's keeping that, I think.

Made in the USA
Middletown, DE
29 April 2019